PIXIE

ALSO BY JILL DAWSON

School Tales: Stories by Young Women (ed.)
The Virago Book of Wicked Verse (ed.)
White Fish with Painted Nails
How Do I Look?
The Virago Book of Love Letters (ed.)
Kisses on Paper
Trick of the Light
Magpie
Wild Ways: New Stories About Women on the Road
(ed. with Margo Daly)
Fred and Edie
Gas and Air: Tales of Pregnancy and Birth
(ed. with Margo Daly)
Wild Boy
Watch Me Disappear
The Great Lover
Lucky Bunny
The Crime Writer
The Language of Birds
The Bewitching

JILL DAWSON
PIXIE

BLOOMSBURY PUBLISHING
LONDON · OXFORD · NEW YORK · NEW DELHI · SYDNEY

BLOOMSBURY PUBLISHING
Bloomsbury Publishing Plc,
50 Bedford Square, London, WC1B 3DP, UK
Bloomsbury Publishing Ireland Limited,
29 Earlsfort Terrace, Dublin 2, D02 AY28, Ireland

BLOOMSBURY, BLOOMSBURY PUBLISHING and the Diana logo are trademarks of Bloomsbury Publishing Plc

First published in Great Britain 2026

Copyright © Jill Dawson, 2026

Jill Dawson is identified as the author of this work in accordance with the Copyright, Designs and Patents Act 1988.

All rights reserved. No part of this publication may be: i) reproduced or transmitted in any form, electronic or mechanical, including photocopying, recording or by means of any information storage or retrieval system without prior permission in writing from the publishers; or ii) used or reproduced in any way for the training, development or operation of artificial intelligence (AI) technologies, including generative AI technologies. The rights holders expressly reserve this publication from the text and data mining exception as per Article 4(3) of the Digital Single Market Directive (EU) 2019/790

A catalogue record for this book is available from the British Library

ISBN: HB: 978-1-5266-7106-6; EBOOK: 978-1-5266-7110-3

2 4 6 8 10 9 7 5 3 1

Typeset by Integra Software Services Pvt. Ltd.
Printed and bound in Great Britain by Clays Ltd, Elcograf S.p.A

To find out more about our authors and books visit www.bloomsbury.com
and sign up for our newsletters
For product-safety-related questions contact productsafety@bloomsbury.com

For Poppy and Grace: a wedding present

Contents

Prologue: The Fool   1

1. The Magician   27
2. The High Priestess   53
3. The Empress   85
4. The Emperor   93
5. The Hierophant   97
6. The Lovers   103
7. The Chariot   133
8. Fortitude, or Strength   139
9. The Hermit   163
10. The Wheel of Fortune   185
11. Justice   221
12. The Hanged Man   233
13. Death   245
14. Temperance   255
15. The Devil   269
16. The Tower   285
17. The Star   301
18. The Moon   317
19. The Sun   335

CONTENTS

20	The Last Judgement	359
21	The World	373

Afterword — 374
Acknowledgements — 377

'I've just finished a big job for very little cash! A set of designs for a pack of Tarot cards 80 designs. I shall send some over – of the original drawings as some people may like them!'
—Pamela Colman Smith in a letter to Alfred Stieglitz, November 1909

'Because there are innumerable things beyond the range of human understanding, we constantly use symbolic terms to represent concepts that we cannot define or fully comprehend.'
—Carl G. Jung, *Man and His Symbols*, 1964

I am one big nothing!!

I will exist in a room on a desk in the fingers in a field in the mind of a woman in a house in a field and here I am

am I idiotic am I really or am I the world inside myself.

St Andrew Parish, Jamaica

1896
My mother wants to tell me a secret before she dies. She says it is a very big secret. I'm wondering what it's going to be. How to be invisible, perhaps? How to read other people's minds? Or how to live forever? I am in the house with her, in her bedroom. We are all here, in the house, at home in Jamaica, but Daddy is staying away from the bedroom.

The huge white pillow under Mama's head is giving off a strange scent of nutmeg and limes, wafted by the fan that Neville – standing beside her – holds: a whirring sound as he pleats the air, keeping the insects away. Of course, we know she is dying. It has been a long sickness. Daddy knows too. The house is under a great veil of sadness, bigger than any mosquito net. The last few days, she has been like a little animal – a fox, perhaps – retreating to its den, pulling the white sheet up to her chin, refusing even her favourite dish of ackee and salt fish, only taking sips of her drink; her voice weaker and weaker.

So she beckons me, 'Come close, Pamela', and begins to whisper the secret in her croaky, soon-to-be-dying voice. She's awful quiet – and though I'm close I don't properly hear. It's just a mumble. *I don't understand!*

'Ma, Ma, what did you say?' I whisper, and she tries again. I put my face as close to hers as I can. I smell her lime-scented breath on my cheek. I feel her breath touch me as I lean in, and it's startling, like an unknown hand brushing me.

I step back to fix her a sip of water, but she doesn't respond to the offer. What, *what* is the secret? I know it is Important because she told me it was a 'big secret', and 'long overdue'. It is so hard for a person to talk clearly when she is lying on her back, the words directed at the ceiling and fanned quickly away. I glance at Neville, wishing him to leave.

There is a pause, where she is expecting my reaction.

Do I dare to say, again, 'Mama, I didn't hear you properly. Please – please can you repeat it?'

The effort has exhausted her. It was so awful mumbly. I look to Neville again, but he really is leaving us alone, going out of the room. A tactful thing, I'm sure, but it means I have no one else to ask. *What did she say? What was the Big Secret?*

I bow my head, tears gathering like a storm. And to my surprise she adds, in a much clearer voice, one that seems unrelated: 'Oh! Charles left me alone . . . for too long. I was old. A couple should not be separated for long, Pamela.'

I stand in mute misery. I am a clumsy girl, small and squawking and foolish, and I *never* say the right thing. Yes, couples should not be separated for too long. What has this to do with anything? Mama's last breath is not the moment to be angry with her, or to run to find Daddy or Neville or Nurse Delphine, or anyone else for that matter. I reach for Mama's dry, pale hand and I'm frightened that it feels so cold, in this heat. My own is clammy. I sink heavily onto the cane stool beside the bed, trying to draw some coolness to my face using the silk fan Neville abandoned on her bedside table.

I lean in again and whisper, finally: 'What? Mama, sorry, I didn't hear properly . . .'

But she is stubborn. She does not wish to repeat it. Instead, she says – and the words come from her with a great effort – 'He loved me . . . so well. Your father . . . and he loves . . . you. We both did.'

Something more is here in the room with us. It steps on light toes. The smell of coconut oil and lamp oil and nutmeg, the sweet and sharp, the limes from Mama's water beside the bed . . . The smells are dizzying me, I'm almost nauseous with the extreme sensations, feelings, in this room. Perhaps it's the secret tiptoeing in, come to speak itself? The sun is at its height and a lazy heat oozing. I close my eyes to steady myself and the colours behind my lids flood green and gold and purple.

Yesterday, when she was stronger, Mama said: 'I dreamed that I saw *my* mother. Your namesake. Pamela. She was wearing your coat. You know, that handsome orange one that you have, with the tassels. And she was beckoning, and the Moon Angel was standing behind her, and I asked her, your grandmother Pamelia – oh, her name was slightly different, we dropped the *I* with you – I asked her, how is it then, in Heaven? And she said it was *great fun*. Great fun. That's nice, isn't it? She said, have you told Pamela – the Secret? She's old enough. She's eighteen. She said to tell you. She said you have such an awful great adventure ahead of you, honey, and not to be afraid. And one day millions of people will know your gifts and what you offer them.'

Now I close my eyes to see if my tears might drum down, but – no. There is only a feeling I have no name for. I hear a lullaby that was once sung to me. Some little hopping steps come closer, almost beside me, almost here. What do I feel right now? I remember Mama's smooth hand combing my awful tough hair. This is the person who made me. This is the life – the star, the spark, the love – that nurtured my tiny heart and helped its beat to begin. 'Mama!' I want to cry in a child's voice.

I put a hand to my breast in my dark-green cotton dress: but my sturdy heart is still ticking away as normal. So infuriating, this calm of mine! This time, green, gold and *silver* swirl behind my lids as I press them with my palms.

Hop, hop, a little flutter – something leaps beside us. When I open my eyes, Mama has gone. Flown away with the hopping bird.

In her place on the pillow is the oddest-looking face. The sheet is pulled up to her throat. In death she is just a strange mask with a speckled look, like a waxy egg. Her mouth is a round open O shape. Her eyes are also open and staring. It is nothing like her. Nothing of the woman I've known for eighteen years. I have never seen a dead face or body before. Perhaps now I should run for Daddy or for Nurse Delphine but I am stuck, staring too, for a moment longer. Neville appears in the doorway, says, 'Oh! Mistress!' and turns on his heel to fetch Daddy.

I do not want to look away. Perhaps this chance to look will never come again. To be brave – as Mama would have wanted – perhaps this is all that's needed to know the secret? To know, to dare, to will, to keep silent. (Was it my grandmother back in America who once chanted those words to me?) To understand our existence here on this earth. That it is short. That it will always feel short, no matter how long it might be. A gift for any artist! To study assiduously the face of death.

I lean closer. 'Oh, goodbye, dear Mama, and thank you!' I mutter a short prayer and a sweet goodbye, trying my best to imagine the journey she is now embarking on. I screw up my eyes and try again. The moon path, lit with silver. A journey all must go on one day: *Mama, what can you show me and teach me?* But. One big fat Nothing.

I hear a loud metallic ting: a bird at the open window. It flits outside, flashing its dazzling green wing and fluttering the long black streamers of its tail as if it were a scarf in the wind. Whirring. A doctor bird – a red-billed streamertail. It disappears in a breath of emerald. The Moon Angel of Mama's story.

Then it comes: the familiar feeling, the one I sometimes have, that I am shrinking. Tiny, my arms and legs, my little feet: the size of a bird and then smaller still, as small as a thumb, as small as one of my miniature drawings, and about to be blown away by a breeze. Today it passes quickly, though, and soon I am solid and my own size again, and back in the room.

I thanked Mama in my prayer, for the secret she told me, though I wish I had heard or understood it, or knew what to do with it. Perhaps I might talk to my cousin Mary in Brooklyn. She has been raised in the Swedenborg Church too; I sent her a copy of *The Garden Behind the Moon*. She knows we can see 'through and beyond' the literal understanding of the Bible. And she would be interested in what Mama revealed to me so late in the day – and perhaps help me fathom what on earth it was!

Daddy arrives then, and there is noise and commotion and weeping, and I do not care to tell the rest.

★★★

Later, I am ready for bed in my nightcap (I like to think of it being made of soft green leaves, with a jaunty red feather, but Nurse Delphine has washed it and the feather has wilted and gone droopy) and feeling not really shocked, not really sad, just – as ever – bitterly *foolish*. Why did I not ask again and admit I hadn't heard? Why at such important moments am I always such a prize *fool*?

Wondering if I dare ask Daddy if he knows the secret. I'm scared to ask him – he will surely say that I'm a young lady now, I should not act the goat. I'm afraid of so many things but I guess it's mostly people. Groups of people. Needing to go and lie down alone in a darkened room to hide the fact that I don't know what to say, how to stand there and act like I have a sensible thought when my head is full of little white dogs and clouds and golden coins and magic lanterns. Then everyone staring at me, marvelling at how strange I am, how fat, my stiff hair, how silly, the silly things I say, the silly thoughts I have . . .

Now I will never be able to ask Mama what she meant. Such a gigantic, godawful, gone-forever moment.

Is everyone else such an idiot over simple matters? How to say the right thing, even hello to people who are your friends? How to do what other people do so easily: find their way around, get themselves to places, go to a certain building and not get lost. Open their mouths and not have bats fly out. Not lie in a room with coats at a party. Put a knife in the right place, set a table for folk, cook food. Say 'Can I help you?' and then do it, once told. How not to hover, waiting outside a room like a ghost, the ground crumbling away, crazy bongo drums going inside your ribcage, wishing to be invisible . . . And then, sometimes, dreading and fearing that you are.

I drape myself in Mama's favourite gown, the green one, breathing in the smell. The oriental silk is lavishly patterned with gold circles, but now that I look closely I think they're sand dollars. It's nice to be dressed like this, the sleeves of my white nightdress poking out underneath, a dog barking yap-yappily somewhere, up on its hind legs, dancing. Trying and trying not to think: why am I such a great big *fool*?

That night I write my cousin naught but a short note:

July 25th 1896

Dear Mary,

I hoped you would write first. I was going to write some time ago. The Moon Angel visited here – I have not had time. I have not very much to say.

Your loving cousin in Jamaica

Pamela

(Later, I worry that I should have closed Mama's eyes or mouth before Daddy flew in and saw her; she looked so much like one of those gargoyles on those medieval church buildings back in England, but I found I *was* a little angry with her, after all, and did not care to touch her face.)

★★★

There is a fuss about a cup. A blue-and-white cup. It is a very pretty cup – fine china – and with two blue chim-chim birds on it. Daddy is pounding from one room to another, sweating dark patches on his white shirt, flinging open cupboards, peering at shelves, shoving his head deeply into cabinets, saying: 'Where is it?'

Nurse Delphine runs from room to room, following him, then throwing her apron over her face and wailing, as if he were accusing her.

It was Mama's favourite cup. It had a fine matching saucer, also with blue chim-chim birds. I remember it, but I can't remember the last time I saw it. I take my mind there: I close my eyes, I try to picture Mama drinking ice-cold tea – American tea – in it. I *can* see that, and her soft white hands pinching the fine handle in that rather delicate way. Did it get broken, perhaps?

I try to calm Daddy. He smokes his clay pipe and twirls in the drawing room. He is as tall as a crane, bent and thin, running a hand through his hair, scratching his head in a vulgar way, the way a dog scratches itself.

'We are returning to New York, after the funeral,' he announces, out of nowhere, to me and Nurse Delphine. 'Jamaica is no place for us. You will return to your studies now, to Pratt. Corinne would have wanted it. We have to get away – someone, something . . . wishes us ill. Start packing, Miss Smith.'

Daddy calling me Miss Smith just then, his queer pet name for me, startles me.

'Daddy! Such silliness! Mama's blue cup must have been broken. It was pretty, yes, but why would anyone but us want it? I am sure there's no sinister reason. Perhaps it disappeared long ago . . .'

I have no need of the cup myself. Daddy told me to go through her things and gave me her wedding ring (wrenched from her finger by the doctor and dumped unceremoniously into Daddy's hand). I put it on my finger, my right hand, and to my surprise it fit perfectly. I would have thought my fingers fatter than her fine ones. It soon felt warm, as if her loving fingers now blended with mine. I looked through her jewellery box – full of long pearl necklaces, brooches, a faded flower garland and carnival-style mask, colourful costume jewellery from her acting days in the drawing rooms of Brooklyn Heights – and helped myself to all of those. I will offer

Cousin Mary the long string of violet-grey Tahitian pearls she has always admired. I have not cried since Mama's death, but then I am not the crying sort. But Daddy's countenance makes me wonder. What does the cup mean to him? Why is he so agitated?

Nurse Delphine has ceased her crying and now watches us warily. We're returning to New York. We interrupted my glorious studies at Pratt to come here to Jamaica, and now we are going back. Mistress is dead and we will leave the house and leave Jamaica on a ship and probably never return. She rushes to embrace me, nearly knocking me off my feet.

'Oh *no*, don't take my baby – my Pamela, my Pamela!'

The reassuring scent of her, the flowers and the baking and the sweat: the smell of these last three years. The plays, the stories, the sweet-bite air, the cry of the owl, the huge moon shining so bright through the blue mahoe trees, rises up.

Hers is such a firm, strong embrace, and it's so long since anyone touched me at all that I feel like a big duckunoo being squeezed.

At last – such a relief – she squashes the tears out from me, and they spill over, flowing freely.

★★★

For the funeral I'm mostly dry-eyed, bewildered. We stand under the Jamaican dogwood trees with Mama lying in that box in the fresh earth and Daddy craning over her grave like a heron searching for a fish.

'God is love, God is love!' wails the vicar in his white dress, flinging his arms dramatically. He then glances at the Bible as if remembering himself, adding in more measured tones: 'John, chapter thirteen: "Love ye one another, as I have loved you."'

These are words we have heard so many times in church. But Daddy appears unmoved. The hem of the vicar's white dress trails crumbs of mud, as angels toot their horns and Mama rises from her box to begin her journey along the silver path to the moon. Spots of blue dazzle my eyes, between the sharp green leaves, as I try to catch a glimpse of her. Anger flickers in me, watching Daddy and wishing he would do the same. I touch his arm. All those years in the Swedenborg Church, listening to readings from his *Divine Love and Wisdom* and so much detail about this – the afterlife and what it is like – and yet here is Daddy (I want to stamp my feet!) morose and sealed up; staring at the trees. He has not one word of God's comfort for me.

Nurse Delphine is here, and it is she who puts her arms around me, dragging my face to her chest. She does not like the smell of these trees, she says when I lift my head. 'Fish fuddle, fish poison,' she says. 'Come away, little Pamela.'

I did not catch one glimpse of Mama soaring with the Moon Angel. And as we leave, Daddy is still there, earthly as a stake of wood in the ground.

★★★

I have been on so many long voyages. More than twenty already (I have counted!), back and forth, England, America, Jamaica, over the eighteen years I've been alive. And most people I talk to have not taken any – such a rum thing! I have not approached *this* voyage with joy. My sadness about Mama has nestled into a little part of me and I am constantly aware of it. It comes to me like this: *Oh, I feel so worried and anxious and full of dread: what can it be?* And then I say to myself, *Oh, that is not it at all, it has already happened.* And other times a voice comes to me in my head, just like my speaking one, and says: *It's you one day. You will die too – isn't that the secret that no one believes, nobody wants to know?*

We embark at 6 p.m. Nurse Delphine and many of the staff from the West India Improvement Company (Daddy's colleagues and friends, formally attired) are assembled to wave us off. Although it's hard to know if it is friendly or not, I feel as if some of them are waving rather frantically and perhaps running and shouting to catch Daddy's attention, which is a strange thought. He does not pause nor wave back, turning and hurrying to the first-floor deck, and so I do the same. I've already endured from Nurse Delphine another blustery hug, with her weeping into my new lace collar, and I do *not* wish to prolong the feeling. I know that once I am able to stand on the deck and gaze out at the sea, I'll feel better: calmed.

But as we sail out, it's a grey sea, drenched in moonlight, almost silver. It is not as calm as one might hope: there's a swelling wave. The more I stare at it, the more it feels as if an animal – the giant heaving form of a humpback whale – is about to rise from beneath it. I gaze for a long time, my hands wet and pink as they hold the rail; twice, some kindly young crew member passes me and enquires if the mistress is all right, does she need anything? They are right to be worried: I am thinking of what it might feel like to slip into the water beside a humpback whale, like an insect on the flank of a cow, watching its great wide eye slide past me, wrinkled and wise like the eye of God himself.

'Oh, I'm fine!' I reply merrily. And, once said, it is closer to being true.

After these thoughts of whales and oceans have grown and grown, they are so big that they push out or pound down all the other drearier ones, and I retire to my cabin at once to draw. (I have recommended many times to my cousin Mary this technique for reducing fears and consoling oneself in times of dire distress.) I have only a poor-quality sketchbook to hand but I manage – in pencil – a whale with a pleasing flow of line, and a woman who looks like she might be mermaid or serpent, with great foamy waves behind her. On a fresh page I draw the face of Mama as herself, *Corinne*, young and beautiful, 'a great drawing-room actress' as she was when the Brooklyn newspapers described her – and beside her another woman, a dark sister, lying in the sea, sleeping atop the waves.

Daddy is still dining with the captain, so I am deliciously alone.

I shall do such things, what they are yet I know not . . .

And one day millions of people will know your gifts and what you have to offer them.

I doodle my signature. I have a new pot of deep-green ink, like sea blood. I am perfecting it: the three initials of my name: *P*, *C* and *S*, but hidden.

★★★

Brooklyn, New York

1897

The first thing I want to do in New York is visit the Green-Wood Cemetery. Mama's parents are there and if we had not ended up in Jamaica it would have been her home too. It feels the right thing to do, to visit the relatives and mark the significance of Mama's leaving us (and we are abandoning her, in Jamaica), but Daddy says I'm being ghoulish or, worse (in his view), sentimental. 'Corinne is not there,' he says, and wandering around graves and carved angels or other 'monstrosities' will not bring comfort, nor any other redeeming virtues. It will only contribute to bad taste.

Since the funeral I have felt a painful doubt about Daddy's real beliefs, the ones they both instilled in me about Heaven and the New Church. I am sure he loved Mama very much but he speaks nothing of his grief. There is nought that he is willing to share with his only daughter.

I go to the cemetery anyway. I persuade Mary to accompany me. It is so good to see Mary again. She is as kind and true as ever, with her large beaming face, her vivid yellow scarf a pretty contrast to her dark curls. Her arched eyebrows in their puzzled expression please me as they always did. And as we greet one another I breathe in her familiar scent, taking me at once to the old art room at Pratt, three years ago. Us in rows together, leaning against our easels in that building with its pumpkin-pie colours. Outside, steam rising from the giant incinerator that gave the Pratt campus such a curious, misty air. The smell of inks and warm paper, of rosewood desks in summer, dust motes floating. Oh, I cannot wait, I cannot *wait* to be back there, bent over my easel with Professor Dow, arms behind his back, sniffing and smiling and walking among us, as I dab that first fresh note to the page, that says: 'I'm back! Your youngest-ever student – the one and only – I'm back!'

Mary has grown a little stout since I saw her last, less girlish, broader in the beam, as if gravity now tugs her closer to the earth and she does not float above it untethered as she used to. It suits her.

We wander, holding hands, in our fur-lined boots. Picking our way between graves and grass and tumbling pots of flowers. It is spring now, and delicate pink primroses are popping up among the weeds. A robin pipes out a merry, relentless tune. Mary, I know, is rather startled by my chatter. She imagined me crushed. We can hear a gardener with his snip-snip-snipping clippers and the crickets nearby chirruping. All noisy and alive in this dead place. We trip along among the graves, our toes nudging the nodding heads of snowdrops. Every way we look, marble angels are outdoing one another in scale and showiness.

'Did you ask your father . . . about the secret your mother began to tell you?' Mary ventures when she can get a word in. Curiously we are passing at that moment a gravestone covered in lichen with a monkey carved on it. A *monkey*! And now that we have stopped, I see that one of the angels to my left, sitting atop another crumbling stone, looks rather saucy, scantily clad as she is. The soft sunlight falls across her breast like a hand and gives her face a seductive look. I reach for my sketchbook and pencil, to try to capture her. Then I realise Mary, dark puzzled eyes wide, is waiting for my answer.

'Oh, I think now is not the time. I will ask him, but . . . you know how buttoned-up he is. I called him by his old nickname the other day and he looked as if he had no idea who he was.'

'It is very soon,' Mary says. And then, delicately: 'Does it feel peculiar — is that why you wanted to come? Your dear mother not being here, with her family?'

'I don't know. I thought so until just a moment ago. But Mama loved Jamaica. Maybe it is right that she's there.'

Mary gives me a knowing look and a little *Aha*. She puts her hand on mine and I have a powerful desire to shake it off. I cannot stand being babied!

To change the subject, I ask her: 'Did you read the book by Howard Pyle — *The Garden Behind the Moon?*'

'Oh, it was a lovely fairy story. For children. Didn't he write it because his own son died and he wanted to imagine him still alive, in the Moon Garden . . .'

'What a rompy spook thing to say! No one ever appreciates Pyle, do they? I hope to meet him again when we return to Pratt this year . . . It's not *at all* intended for children. It is an interesting truth about the world that only a few can possibly know. *Ah!* Here it is!'

At that moment we reach the top of a modest hill. The cemetery is so vast that I take a moment to stare out across the green and the trees, all the way in the distance to the horizon and the tiny statue with her crown, on the grey strip of river, holding aloft her torch. I have been looking for something, without quite knowing that I was. It is a headstone I remember drawing once, sitting here with Mary, when we first started our studies at Pratt.

The robin ceases and relief makes the air sharp, clear.

To live in hearts we leave behind is not to die. A headstone for a dead person called Mary Clasing. Yes. That is more like it.

'Were you awful lonely in Jamaica after all our excitements at Pratt?' Mary asks.

'No, of course not! I – I had a hundred little pirates and dragonflies and Henry Morgan the governor of Jamaica himself to keep me company – well, a floppy paper version with wooden supports, of course.'

Mary laughs. I wonder if she is remembering the performance of *Henry Morgan* I gave in Brooklyn for the Christmas social, and how for weeks afterwards people came up to me to comment on its tremendous success. How charming my little figures were! The sets! The painted scenery! The way the figures moved with their little strings and grooves, so exquisite!

I suddenly remember that Mama was always telling me that 'boasting' is wrong, especially in a girl, so I must stop these thrilling thoughts.

'It is very strange to lose a mother at eighteen,' I say, attempting to change the mood with a grave expression. Mary nods. 'Just when I'm becoming a – woman,' I add.

'Why, you look about eight. No one would ever mistake you for a woman!'

This makes us laugh again. We start running. We run past all the bully things: the saucy wench and the monkey and the fierce watching angels, the primroses and the disapproving gardener and the heads-bowed sad mourners, and spring juice flows in my veins and we are soon whooping and leaping and holding one another, shrieking like banshees.

★★★

Later, Daddy and I eat dinner in a private room at Delmonico's on Beaver Street with Mary. Daddy's older brother Theodore – Uncle Teddy – joins us.

Mary being a cousin on my mother's side (I've forgotten how long ago her parents died, or what of, we were so young), she doesn't know Daddy's side of the family well. She is perhaps a little afraid of Uncle Teddy: he is so *big* and so loud. All talk is about the feature written about me in the *Pratt Institute Monthly*, which Daddy conveniently has in his leather bag, producing it with a flourish so that it knocks his pipe from the table. The waiter appears instantly to retrieve it.

'My daughter is a prodigy!' Daddy shouts, and I rush to silence him. He continues to read out from the article: '*Such wonderful elements of difference . . . harmonised with elements of unity . . . the comprehension of form in line and design . . .*' Daddy lifts his eyes from the page to beam at us, pointing to my 'School-girl Song of Spring', with all the little girls in their white dresses singing and carrying lilies, walking two by two. Mary takes the magazine from Daddy to study it. If she is envious – no other student has already received a commission for *ten dollars*! Nor had the honour of being featured at such length in the college magazine – she is much too sweet to show it.

'I love their different shades of skin colour! The super tall one at the back, with the dark curly hair, who is not singing at all but making sure the little one beside her is keeping up . . .'

'"The super tall one"! That's *you*, dear cousin,' I say, beaming. (I am sure she knew that. Her modesty prevents her from assuming.)

Uncle Teddy – a merchant who Daddy says knows nothing about art – puffs out his big chest. 'What clever girls you both are,' he claims, and that's an end to it; that's as far as his interest in us as artists or students goes.

I see Daddy making that gesture he has these days, scratching vigorously, pushing his glasses onto his nose. He clearly feels he wants to say something more, some kindness in support of me, for which I'm intensely grateful. I put a hand on his sleeve to show him that I know and that there is no need.

A waiter arrives with our steaks, and a lobster Newburg for Uncle Teddy. His eyes gleam. 'Best rib-eye in town, Charles – no fussy sauces here! Just an honest steak and a glaze to make your mouth water . . .'

'Why did you choose lobster if you love it so much, Uncle Teddy?' I pipe up. Mary digs me in the ribs, giggling.

'Well, you know, my dear, I have to watch my waistline . . . Lobster is a slimming food . . .'

The enormous creature fills up the whole of Uncle Teddy's plate, claws springing out like one big explosion. But Uncle Teddy has always had a devotion to slimming, and rather mistaken beliefs in what will help him achieve the fabled waistline. So unfair that Teddy, who loves food, has to restrict it so much, while his brother, who pushes it around his plate, is naturally wiry and could probably gain a few pounds without any ill effect.

Now I'm studying him, Daddy does look dangerously thin and pale. Everything is buried with Daddy but not his pride in me, which he wears like a shining badge. He had his own dreams of being an artist, Mama told me that, but I did not learn it from him.

'A shame. Pamela is such an original talent. A shame she won't be resuming her studies at Pratt after all,' Uncle Teddy remarks.

I am about to open my mouth to a huge piece of steak. I put my fork down. 'What?'

'I'm so sorry, Charles! You mentioned it in a letter . . . What a blundering idiot I am.'

My face must be as red as a beetroot. I open my mouth to say something – 'What? Not going to Pratt? Then why did we come back to New York?' – but all I can feel is my heart clanging against my ribs while rage pours upwards from my belly. The fork I just laid down bounces from the table to the floor, landing with a huge clang. The other diners turn towards us, and a waiter quickly provides a clean one.

Mary is staring at me.

Teddy's eyes flit from me to Daddy, a flush rising over my uncle's cheeks. 'In all the rush of moving back to Brooklyn Heights, I'm sure . . . your father meant to tell you, and has been waiting for the opportunity.'

I turn towards Daddy, fastening a deadly snake's gaze on him.

Daddy lowers his eyes and sips his wine. He does the mad scratching thing again and then swallows and mutters: 'Yes, I'm so sorry . . .'

He does not dare to raise his eyes to me. Coward, *coward!* 'Why could you not have told me, or discussed it with me?' I want to say. The restaurant resumes its chatter and noise. The world of fine dining is unmoved. Daddy was ever – compared to Mama – weak. I always knew he did not have her strength.

I can imagine Mama saying, 'But, darling, his pride in you is such a touching thing, and so unusual for a daughter to find in a father . . .'

It is for Mama, then, and for Mary and for propriety that I manage at last to bring myself under control. It must have been some *financial* consideration. Everything always seems to boil down to that. Nothing that we can discuss in front of cousins and uncles.

I take a few breaths. The turmoil in my stomach seems to quell and my heartbeat settles. I force myself to smile. 'Maybe the principal felt that when I left Pratt for Jamaica my artistic education was complete.'

Mary's eyes are still fixed on me. She no doubt feels Uncle Teddy has been a perfect booby. 'Oh, but that means you won't – graduate. That can't be right?'

Daddy at last gathers himself, coughs and addresses me firmly: 'We will discuss this at home, Pamela. My sincerest apologies. It does not reflect . . . It goes without saying . . .'

His distress is painful to observe. I force myself to put my hand on his trembling one. 'Daddy – Mr Smith. *Piggie-wig!* All is well, you shall see.'

I added in the little nickname to make him smile, and it works. It lightens the mood at the table. Soon the waiter is back, bringing brimming glasses from the cellar. Uncle Teddy resumes eating, and Mary, after a moment, removes her worried gaze from me. We pick up forks and glasses and eat and drink merrily as if nothing at all has happened. My life has just taken a new and perfectly horrible direction. No more Pratt! No resumed studies! No graduation! Why did we come back to New York so quickly, if not for that? No doubt some selfish whim of Daddy's that he did not trouble to share with me. I could scream. Mama gone and everything untethered. I am like a tiny being, sitting on a leaf as it twirls down a stream: here snatched up in an eddy, here picked out by a nincompoop of a heron with its damn stupid beak.

It takes me five deep breaths to get a hold of my temper, the way Nurse Delphine showed me. After a good long time I achieve it, as she promised I would.

***

In the carriage on the way home, after waving goodbye to Mary and Uncle Teddy, Daddy tries to explain or to apologise. At least, I think that is his intention. He makes several false starts, coughs, scratches, crosses his legs. 'The principal at Pratt . . .' he begins.

I tire of his weakness and turn to him angrily. 'Pooh! Who cares about Pratt? I shall write a book. I've been thinking of it. Jamaican stories. Folklore. Illustrate it myself. Do we still have money for . . . inks and suchlike?'

'Yes, yes, of course,' Daddy says, his eyes brightening and everything else too; he is sitting up taller. We jog along. It is a bumpy route, or else the horse is a jumpy one.

'I'll start tomorrow. I want to capture the voice in my head — the voice I hear of the northern part of the island and of Nurse Delphine and Neville — before it's too late.'

Daddy nods. He is examining me, rather too close for comfort. It is a little dark in the carriage and smells of hay and cigar smoke and faded velvet cushions. He puts a hand out and strokes my arm. 'You know, my dear little Miss Smith — the nickname is a warning, he's going to say something sentimental — 'you know, it's perfectly all right to grieve. To show your feelings. To cry, once in a while.'

I stare at him. A fine one to talk!

'It will be a book about Annancy. The trickster. And chim-chim birds. I'll start with my favourite: Annancy and how he fools death. I can see him now, big ears, half spider, half— And I will show it to . . .'

Daddy sighs, and then his sigh turns into a deep cough, and eventually a sort of laugh.

'. . . What is the name of that friend of yours?' I continue determinedly. 'Mr Russell? Fairy stories, folk-lore. I'm perfecting my signature. I'll show you! *Annancy Stories*. Isn't it the sort of thing Mr Russell publishes?' Then: 'Daddy, why are you laughing?'

He pats my hand and the bumpy, strange journey – the night I discover Pratt no longer wants me and that the life I pictured will not be my future – jogs on.

I belt upstairs and set to work on my book the moment we arrive home, flinging my hat on the chair and then forgetting and sitting on it. It will be hard to remember the voice if I don't capture it.

In a long before time dere was a Queen who was bery wicked; an' she was an Obeah woman, an her name was Five . . .

Once, in bery hungry times, Annancy him go out walkin' in de bush, fe fine tings fe eat.

At midnight I hear the grandfather clock chiming outside Daddy's study and finally rescue the squashed hat from under my bottom and push the sheets of drawings and scribblings under a book to keep them nice. Drawing Annancy is harder than I thought. In my mind he is a spider, but he keeps developing ears and a devilish, skinny-goblin kind of look. His personality keeps changing too. Of course, I'm mostly remembering stories Nurse Delphine told me. But the details have already shifted and got muddled with other things I've heard and read: Aesop's Fables. Brer Rabbit. My eyes are sore, my hand cramped, and my head spinning with the little fellow grinning and running about in there.

I get myself undressed and under the sheets to sip at the tea that the housekeeper Elsie has left me, which of course is now tepid and rotten-tasting. In New York no one ever leaves out cakes or sweet things to eat and drink.

Daddy is wrong, I think. Silly man! With his white hair and his blue eyes and his worried mouth and his dog-scratching ways! My heart twists picturing him, how tender he is, how kind – and how guilty, I know, about his various financial shenanigans. Of course I know about them. What kind of fool does he take me for?

But he *is* wrong. Weak people are always wrong about strong ones. I *am* grieving, but in my own way. I have that courage that Mama spoke of, the courage to look at bad things. I spend a great deal of time alone, after all, peering into places where Daddy and Mary and others I know would not care to go. My grief comes like damp splotches of rain on a dry pavement. In these moments I know not just that Mama has gone but also that I will go too one day, and like her be reduced to a few letters, some Tahitian pearls and a blue chim-chim cup. And perhaps some books, and some drawings. That is all. Some means of speaking to the world, after I have left it.

When my eyes close, I know Mama will come to me in a dream. Last night we were dancing together in a way that we never did in real life, our arms raised and swaying, she little and sweet, young, I much bigger, older, more grown-up. The night before, I was cutting flowers with her in the garden, English flowers, not island ones. Lavender and hyacinths – lilac and purple and sweetly scented – and choosing a vase (I think we were in Manchester, then, at the wool factory, one of Daddy's other ventures), and I woke thinking, *I must remember to take that favourite vase from her windowsill*, and then remembering, *Oh, we are here, in Brooklyn Heights, and Jamaica – Jamaica is now just a story to me. 'Annancy, is you comin' down?'* Creatures and characters filling my head – *I must try to write them down exactly as I heard them from Nurse and from many different people in different parts of the island . . .*

The saddest of things in this world is how every single experience, good and bad, comes to an end, never to repeat itself.

Mama is gone. I received a letter from a woman whom I'd never met but oftentimes heard about, her childhood friend.

> *Thank you, Pamela, for your kind note telling me about the funeral service in Jamaica. Such sorrow for me that I was not able to be there. I've read your letter many times, read of the hymns, prayers and the order of service. My life with Corinne was all before me – playing in the streets with her when we were young, the pear trees in blossom. I remember the steps to the houses with their newspapers flung there by the paper boy and how we dared one another to steal one! We were always in trouble, the two of us, most times for talking too much . . . marriages, bridesmaids, parents, the Swedenborg Church . . . a lifetime of happy memories together . . .*

The woman's name is Miriam. She is a friend from Grace Street in Brooklyn Heights. It seems she knows plenty about Mama. It strikes me that the friendship between women is much the closest and most honest of relationships, quite unlike any other. It gives me pause to reread the letter and to think this Miriam knows my mother in ways that I never did (and never will). She knew her before my father did. She knew her before she became a mother. How different this letter is to any other condolences I have received: it is almost alive in my hand, like a bird.

Then I wonder: should I let Daddy know Mama tried to tell me some important secret before she died? A rum thought floats up: *Let us go on as normal.* See how long it might take Daddy to ask me or mention it, if ever he does. His little punishment for not having told me things is that I know something he does not know I know.

My lovely Mama is gone. That part of my life is gone. Now Pratt too and a glorious graduation and the life of an art student that I pictured for myself. And I am certain sure that I will never, in this lifetime, go back to Jamaica again.

My little self on my little green boat just tumbled right over a waterfall into the foamy mysteries below.

And so I begin, raising my nib above a chalice of flames.

A white tunic, a red cloak, red berries and fruit bushes overhead.

I do have everything I need: fire, earth, air and water. (Where is the water? I have forgotten the water!) My plain face is small but determined: made of dashes and dots like a code.

Thoughts sprout from my head, longer, richer, darker. Thoughts become things. The me who manifests things.

At my feet a sea of flowers and berries to walk on: I can do anything, I am magnificent!

Daddy does not look well. He says that I am fussing. We go round in circles. His habit of scratching compulsively is producing red spots in his white hair and on his bald patch; he is giving himself a kind of nervous scurvy. He tells me not to mind, what can he do, he finds scratching satisfying.

He is full of contrition about Pratt and says he will introduce me to a friend with a gallery. An excruciating occasion ensues where he and the gallery owner discuss me as if I weren't present: 'Yes, Pamela was the only student to have work in the *Pratt Institute Monthly* . . . Matter of fact, I'll show you' – and surprise! Daddy produces a giant portfolio and the two of them stride towards an office, forgetting about me entirely. A door finally creaks open and the smoke of a thousand pipes and a thousand male minds billows out from it.

The outcome is this: here we are in Mr William Macbeth's gallery on Fifth Avenue one evening several months later, at a private-view event, and *four of my watercolours are on display. Four!* My work, the gallery owner commented, might be suitable for 'connoisseurs who have fine private collections'. They are not my favourite four watercolours, but my joy at Mr Macbeth choosing them is undimmed.

I would like to sing and dance and jump – and most of all I would like to tell Mama and hear her say, in her croaky American drawl, 'Honey, you're on your way!' To make her proud of me, to let her know how my life is taking all the shapes she wanted for me – that is what I long for, and it cuts like a knife to the heart.

The gallery is jam-packed with rummy creatures, sipping wine and talking in solemn tones. A winter night in New York; their coats and hats snow-spattered and damp. Uncle Teddy is not here – thankfully, as he would embarrass me – and though Cousin Mary is here she is awed, silent indeed. I do not know if that is because of the fine ladies in their silk dresses once their coats have been discarded to the hat-check girl, or else a discomfort of some other sort. Mary did not return to her studies at Pratt either, resuming her life as a dutiful daughter, but unlike me she seems not in the least to mind.

'Have you noticed how much Daddy scratches?' I whisper to her. 'His skin looks like a tortoise's. Could it be worry – money, perhaps – would *worry* make someone fade like that?'

Mary knits her brow, considering, but is interrupted then by the sight of someone staring at one of my paintings: a Jamaican scene. She loses all decorum and nudges me fiercely in the ribs. 'They're buying it, look!' she squeaks. 'They're buying *The Wind*! A red dot!'

My painting of Nurse Delphine hanging out washing on a windy day in Jamaica, her long spotted skirt, the chicken at her feet.

'Oh my! Twenty-five dollars!' I feel like my face is on fire. 'What luck. Shall I go and say hello? Explain that I'm Miss Colman Smith?'

But before I can decide, Daddy is somehow there, talking to the gentleman and Mr Macbeth, who has his back to me, partially blocking me from their view. Some words drift over about the subject, the realism, the character in the coloured woman's face. A strong feeling descends on me. Shyness. Even shame. The shame of being singled out, of being pleased, or the shame of money. I don't know which it is, but it's very powerful.

And as if that weren't bad enough, I suddenly hear a tall woman who looks like a long grey worm saying: 'She's just so charming . . . Is she Japanese?' At first I think she is – stupidly – commenting on the painting, and then I realise: she means *me*. I immediately picture myself exactly thus: in a kimono, legs folded, strange sandals. I'd understand it if they were looking at my woodcuts, at my Japanese-style ukiyo-e work, but these are watercolours, all showing Jamaican scenes. Still, the Worm Lady's companion soon puts her right: 'More

Negro than Japanese, I'd say . . . What an odd-looking creature!'

Mr Macbeth turns around and I see – with horror! – that he and Daddy are heading our way, and mean to introduce the wormy guests to us. Hearing only Daddy's 'Yes, not yet twenty years old!' I grab Mary, spin her around and bolt, to the sounds of their laughter, and their 'My, my!'

We find ourselves outside the gallery, in the street near the textiles building. It's cold and the trees are exhausted and spindly, with a soft fall of damp snow on them. The only comfort from the sludgy pavements is the row of candles in the window of a candy store nearby. I brush the snow from the bottom rungs of a fire escape with my gloves, and indicate to Mary that we should sit there. She snuggles in beside me.

'What a piece of Christmas luck!' I shout. 'I saw someone in a huge fur coat looking at *Fruits and Flowers* too, and that one is *one hundred dollars!*'

I feel like I could drink an awful big glass of champagne. Daddy has never yet let me try one. Earning my own money – huge sums! – is ridiculously pleasing, though I try to block out some of the things I heard. (Perfectly horrible to hear discussed, as if I'm not in the room, my technical ability or lack of it, comparing me unfavourably with Beardsley; one particularly ugly man, a crow in his long black cloak, saying firmly that that my work is pure imagination and that's the trouble with the art of most women, their unfettered, untutored nature; being described one minute as a child prodigy, the next as 'crude, naïve, not much of a draughtswoman', 'too much like the children's illustrator Walter Crane' – I soon grew tired of overhearing and trying to be invisible.) I had not expected to feel quite so . . . exposed and pinned to the wall myself, like an insect in a glass cabinet, wings prised apart. A dragonfly.

The feeling of shrinking, of becoming tiny, comes again to me. I glance down and here I am in my long green dress, my grey hat – which so many have commented on, and not in a complimentary way – and I'm as little as that pinned dragonfly. No, I'm smaller: a beetle, scurrying at the skirts of others. I'm running at Mary's feet. I see her shoes, her boots, the toes capped with snow.

When I once tried to describe this troubling sensation to Nurse Delphine – I think I must have been seven or eight, and I assumed all people felt the same in times of crisis – her eyes widened and she did not, as I'd expected, laugh. She turned her back to me. She was shaking, and muttering. When she looked at me again, she spoke in her own dialect, fast, as if it was a prayer or a spell, and I could not catch the words. Obeah, I thought. Some terrible magic or a curse. I learned never to mention it again, to anyone, but instead to contain the feeling, wait it out. It is a little like migraine: a headache precedes it and it feels – well, how to describe it? I feel as if I am in a dream, and yet awake and under a spell. I feel tiny enough to ride on the back of a swallow, like Thumbelina in my favourite bedtime story – the longed-for little girl who grew from a grain of barley given to her mother by a witch. Nurse Delphine would offer me a drink, a lovely warming nutmeg drink, and tell me to take deep breaths, and again not to mention it to anyone. The curious, dizzying sensation did usually pass quickly.

Remembering this now, I take a few slow breaths. I bend over and touch my teeny-tiny cold wet face with both hands, my icy little nose; I take more breaths.

'Pamela – are you sick?' Mary asks. 'You don't feel happy? Will your daddy not allow you to keep the money?'

I stare down at the footprints we have made in the snow. They are normal-sized. Gentlewomen's footprints, made by black, fur-lined boots with a neat heel. A flake falls on my nose. I suddenly straighten and feel a rush to my head. My Lilliputian hallucinations have disappeared. I am myself again. What do I feel? I would love to dance and twirl, but the ground is sludgy and slippery, and Mary now looks worried at my fast-changing moods.

She says we must calm ourselves and go back inside. We both stand up from our damp seat and brush the snow from our skirts with our wet gloves.

I turn to Mary. 'It's very strange when people talk about you as if you are not there. They must know I am there and it's me! I'm so odd, apparently. I'm so odd-looking. *Am* I odd-looking, Mary?' Mary begins to answer but I continue heatedly: 'I heard myself whispered about and called a "Japanese"! Or a "Negro". I did not realise until this evening quite how much my looks draw attention. Have I changed? Why now? When we were at Pratt I didn't feel it. Mama always told me I was pretty. Now I'm not so sure.'

'Of course you're not odd. Your looks are . . . *well*. These are very silly and rude people, unused to a girl of nineteen being a talented artist. That is what the problem is. You're not a tall man in a black hat and that's the only kind of artist they know.'

Kind Mary. She is not a beauty herself, her gangling height, her frizzy hair, her high forehead, her individual features all rather large and easy to caricature, but because she is sweet in nature, together they do form a pleasing whole, a feminine countenance, more acceptable than mine. She is staring at me worriedly and so I shake off the disturbing feelings and grab her arm.

'Twenty-five dollars! Maybe seventy-five. Can you imagine such a bully sum? I will buy so many paints and canvases, and I will buy you a new fur muffler for your hands! And I need a frame because I'm making a new theatre for my latest show . . .'

Mary settles my arm rather less forcefully on hers, and shepherds me back up the steps and inside the gallery. The warmth and the noise engulf us. Mr Macbeth spies us – he seems to have been looking for me – and rushes through the throng.

'Miss Smith! Another watercolour sold!' he whispers, pointing to the buyers, a couple swathed in grey pelts, the lady I saw earlier looking at *Fruits and Flowers*. They nod politely, their eyes flicking over me. 'We must talk about . . . Would you be interested in selling some prints and suchlike at the gallery? I can see how popular they would be.'

Daddy is soon beside us, beaming with pride, and once again their discussions about money begin. They turn their backs as politely as they can, and I return to my talk with Mary.

Vulgar to talk about money, I'm told. And yet the men talk of nothing else.

★★★

At home I ask Daddy, 'How much did I make?' And the answer comes: 'Pamela! You sold four watercolours, and the total sum is one hundred and seventy-five dollars.' Daddy is almost shouting. A mood I've seen many times. His cheeks are a little pink. His eyes glitter. He pulls out of his top pocket the piece of paper on which Mr Macbeth has scribbled the details, and spreads it out on a side table to show me. Next to each painting sold, a star in blue ink, a scribbled figure and a name.

Daddy pours himself a huge glass of brandy and tries to lower his voice to a normal level. After a moment's consideration – and leaping up with a curious movement as if he is jumping over a hurdle – he reaches for a second glass to pour me one too, and when I pick mine up he clinks his against it.

'My word!' he says. We both stare at the names for a while. *The Wind. Fruits and Flowers.* Then Daddy sees my expression and quickly folds the paper. 'Unseemly, of course, to concern yourself with money, my dear.'

Here we go again. I study him closely. That glitter and excitement. The moods: one minute leaping, the next plunging. He – a good man – wants me to share the glory. He is proud of me. He has already told me on the cab ride across Brooklyn Bridge – dangling in that snow-iced cobweb so high above the river – that that Mr Macbeth was thrilled with the reception, and he is suggesting prints and cards to sell at his gallery. By *me*! My mind immediately fills with the images I want to draw. My miniature theatre with all the extensive characters and pirates from the *Henry Morgan* show, or little figures from *Annancy*, the girls in their white spring dresses, arms around one another, playing at recess; the figures going to the fair, the little toads . . . Oh, my mind is full, full as if a vivid flavourful dream is playing out, full of rummy critters! And as I'm taking this in and smiling, Daddy suddenly grows grave.

He puts a hand on mine, coughs once before announcing: 'We do have some bills, of course. Our rent here. Elsie's wages. We will receive the cheques in the post from Mr Macbeth and — well, I see no problem in my taking you to the bank with me, to teach you how such matters stand.' He considers me. 'If you were a boy, I would do that, without thought.' He looks uncomfortable then. 'No, perhaps not. Perhaps it would be . . . Oh, if only Corinne were here. She would be so proud of you!'

And then a kiss, smack on my cheek, and the squashiest of hugs, and I breathe in Daddy with his brandy breath and the scratchiness of his beard, and his sudden mention of Mama has frightened me; it feels like a warning of some kind.

Moments later, he has forgotten any promise of taking me with him to the bank on Fifth Avenue, and instead has a new plan. 'We can buy our fare with this money! We can go to England now, and there are people there . . . There are other important men you must meet, Pamela. We must *capitalise* on your extraordinary success! Of course, my . . . The money due to me from Jamaica, from the West Indies rail company . . . that will come soon, of course, but before then, what about a *trip*?'

I sip my brandy; the hot strange taste of it prickles in my throat. Another long sail. The sea, with the moon flowing silver on it, then rising pink; the portholes. The sea, the sea, every day the sea. My mind is full of the little figures I want to draw, my miniature theatre. I can't wait to return to my room to work on them again and so I blurt out —

'Perhaps I could bring *Henry Morgan*? Perform it on the ship?'

'A capital plan, my dear.'

'But — Daddy. Some people . . . I heard some awful funny stuff said about me.'

He does not ask me what 'stuff', and this tells me he heard it too.

'You are only nineteen and — you sold four paintings! Your show was a success.' He strokes my black hair, tied in its two red ribbons, and pats me absent-mindedly. 'You're all I have in the world, little Miss Smith,' he says, and his eyes are watery, and then: 'What an extraordinary child you are. What a blessing it was when you . . . came so unexpectedly into our lives.'

When he has gone I will light the candle and return to making more of my theatre creatures. I need another dragonfly. A dragonfly is a needle to sew up your mouth and the eyelids of children. Ink on cardboard. A teeny-tiny one, just like me.

Now is the moment, surely, to ask Daddy about the secret Mama tried to tell me. Her odd comment about him being absent. I know that he was in America for a time when she was in Jamaica, and that she was older than him; I discovered when she died some lies about her age too. How old was she when she had me — wasn't that rather late, was that the 'unexpected' part of me coming into their lives? And Daddy was an astonishingly kind man, she always said, unique among men, with 'modern' ideas and an artistic soul; my upbringing was not the kind usually given to girls. Daddy was 'generous'; there was not a man to touch him. So now is my opportunity to appreciate that, be grateful for his kindness, his love for me. Not the moment to ask for more details – so I don't. I flit around, needle-thin, sweeping around the room with my wings beating, swig down the brandy and feel awful swimmy. I decide I need to lie down after all – no further drawing for me. I need to settle. Soon I am in my room, the candle blown out, all thoughts gone and the glorious day, the day of my first exhibition, my taking Fifth Avenue by storm, is snuffed.

★★★

It is no small thing to plan a visit to England, of course, and Daddy in his usual way has underestimated how much planning and money must go into it. But at last – *at last!* – we are on our way. The crossing to Southampton is a mild one, not too fierce – no sickness for anyone in our party this time. Only boredom. I spend, as ever, a long time on the deck, salt spray on my face, staring out for the fountain on the horizon that means a whale is there under the waves, or the sudden burst of dolphins. The world *under* the sea clamours in my mind: not the grey heaving waves that I gaze at, but the merfolk, green with blue hair and coral beads around their necks. The paintings I intend to do. The next miniature theatre production after *Henry Morgan*. Then I hurry back to my cabin to lie on my bed and draw the characters until suppertime with the captain and the guests on the ship and Daddy's instructions as to whom I should talk with and show my drawings to.

In between drawing, I spend long hours in my cabin reading a book by this man Daddy says we will meet in England. A novel called *Cheap Jack Zita*, awful fun and racy: the Gypsy Zita, I fancy, is a little like me, with her rosy cheeks and her rude abrasive manner, saying whatever she will and using the flail against men who are too fresh with her, with her ripe olive skin, her short-cut chestnut hair and her hazel eyes. Oh, what a heroine! Everyone is in love with her and I soon am too. I am already dreaming up ways to *be* her. How to be a cheap jack, a Gypsy: a scarf, big earrings, lots of wraps and colour and a tent to sit in and offer my words of wisdom. When Daddy strides by on his way to brandy with the captain, I quickly hide the book. I've never read anything like it and I don't quite understand why reading it makes my cheeks burn and the entirety of me feel warm, as if something powerful is drawing me tight, as if my body were a purse. Especially when Zita tells Hezekiah Drownlands that she is not in the least afraid of him, and wonders if he is not afraid of *her*? I love that Zita thinks of the general public as 'General Jackass' and I resolve to do the same.

'What an uncommon good-looking girl you are!' someone tells Zita. She replies with indifference. 'Yes, so most folks say . . .'

'What an uncommon talented artist you are!' I imagine. Gentlemen and beautiful women are leaning towards me, fur-wrapped, to smile and tell me so. (I am thinking back to the night at the Macbeth Gallery, where most of the comments were about my 'short stature' or 'queer look', and 'Is she touched by Negro blood . . . or Japanese, perhaps?' – but I push that to one side.)

'Yes, so most folks say . . .' I reply with a little smirk.

What kind of gentleman writes such spicy books? Daddy says he is a churchman, married a local girl, only fourteen when she met him. 'But we will show no shock when we meet him, will we, Pamela?' Daddy says, because the man is influential, and knows everyone, and might buy some paintings from us, or allow me to illustrate a book. He has great knowledge of folklore, fairy tales and werewolves, and other bully things. He will introduce us to interesting people: writers, artists, actors. He lives in a beautiful part of England called Devon with the fourteen-year-old girl who is now a grown woman and whom he raised up and taught fine manners and who has now given him many children. Devon sounds awful pretty – I've never been before.

I race through his novel, heart in mouth lest Zita be tamed by the wicked Master Drownlands in this strange village called Prickwillow, but, thank the bejabbers, she never is.

★★★

Our last day on the ship, the sea is uncommonly choppy. There is a soft grey drizzle that makes walking on deck awful damp and dreary. The captain sends Daddy a note inviting me to put on my 'little show' – *Henry Morgan* – for the guests, who he says are becoming 'restive'.

I am nervous. Or excited – I cannot tell which. I unpack the trunk carefully. Some of the figures have become bent on the journey: the poor old privateer looks far from dashing and needs a quick touch-up, and several of the thirty-nine additional pirates for the procession scene just before Henry Morgan is knighted look awful droopy. Unpacking the tiny stiff-paper feather headdresses from their wrappings, I see that some are broken.

'What will we do about the music? There should at least be a piccolo!' I wail to Daddy. I feel ill-prepared. How can my little folk lead upright lives when they've been languishing in a damn trunk for so long? Why wasn't I given more notice, not just this whim from the fat pig of a captain? (You are set up for disaster if no one gives you the right time to ready yourself.) Of course I intended to give them an outing, but still, every Great Artist needs warning, and preparation time!

I patch up the theatre as best I can. I forgot to bring any proper glue with me and that's what is needed here. Just lumpy flour-and-water paste. I colour in some cheeks and headdresses. The poor glue gives the curtain rope an awful queer smell.

'It is an opportunity, Pamela!' Daddy says, squeezing himself into the tiny space between my bed and the wall. 'Who knows who might watch and want to commission you – for more shows, or costume design or stage design for a bigger theatre, or . . .' He is here to help me carry the theatre and the knights and ladies of the buskin to the captain's quarters.

Everything is *an opportunity* with Daddy. I have to admire his optimism and be glad of his faith in me, but . . . a proper warning would have been helpful.

We arrive at six thirty for the seven o'clock show. I'm togged up in my stage dress, my Gelukiezanger character, a scarf around my head and a few strings of Mama's beads, and when we pass a couple of guests on our way into the room, struggling with the trunk and all the boxes full of little paper people, I feel a hush descend and a prickle of interest from all.

'Where did the Gypsy girl come from?' one man says, and I smile at how complete my disguise is. We've been on this ship together for over a week. Why is it that people can't actually *see* me properly most of the time?

The captain has arranged things rather nicely. He has dimmed the lights a little and set out refreshments, and leather chairs facing his huge table, where I am to perform. He passes Daddy a brandy and a tiny claret for me. When I pull a face on first sip, he laughs, and squirts in some lemonade from a showy glass dispenser. 'All the Irish poets drink this,' he says.

The group of chattering, noisy people begin to quieten as I take my place, setting up the theatre on the table and myself on a chair beside it. Daddy hovers anxiously. 'Do you need me to operate any of them? What about the extra guardsman or the children? You don't seem to have enough hands for all the pulleys . . .'

'Daddy. Don't be silly. You've seen me do it a million times. You're a nuisance. You can announce me and then sit down. Shoo!'

He plonks on a chair and then instantly stands up, again removing his hat with a sweeping, theatrical gesture which gains the audience's attention. Then he steps out in front of the table, a little to the side of me, and says: 'Ladies and gentlemen! I'm proud to announce – a show unlike any you have ever seen! Do not be fooled by its miniature scale. Come closer if you like . . .'

No one moves; the chairs are about as close as they can be.

Daddy continues: 'This theatre – at less than eighteen inches square – will amaze you. First performed by Gelukiezanger here at the Pratt Institute's Christmas social, reviews of this show were many and glowing! Mr Gardner in *Brush and Pencil* wrote: "I have never seen a more gorgeous presentation!" Prepare to be astonished by this fully developed, gloriously imagined, beautifully executed tiny living world, the size of the fairy folk! Miss Pamela Colman Smith presents: *Henry Morgan*, based on the life of the privateer and later governor of Jamaica!'

The clapping is loud and friendly, warmed a little by the drink that folk are taking. My heart jumps as I begin, my hand trembles and my mouth is dry, but I know that if I simply concentrate on the operating of the tiny ropes and pulleys and on every last pirate, lady and buccaneer being in the right place at the right moment, this preoccupation will soon take over, until I can think of nothing else.

And so it proves to be.

I make only one mistake, when I accidentally operate the turquoise dragonfly instead of one of the pirates (I don't know how it got into the box, I usually have it all so carefully labelled); but everyone just laughs as it appears and the dragonfly misbehaves as it so often does, ducking and diving in all the wrong ways.

There is an interesting man, a Mr Debrett, with a loud beard and rather large face, who is in the front row next to a well-dressed lady in an oyster-pink silk dress. He is laughing hard in all the right places and smiling at me, and when (at the beginning) I asked about the music, he said, 'Oh, if only you'd given me some warning, my child!' and everyone laughed with him. Daddy leaped up and shook his hand, signalling none too subtly that this solid man – with his shiny forehead and the woman smiling prettily beside him in oyster silk – was an important one, and something about his remark was to be noted.

★★★

It is afterwards that the incident happens. I don't know how it starts. I'm clearing up my little folk and my theatre scenery, folding carefully. There is a magician figure whose top hat has torn away and I need to wrap him carefully in cloth so as not to lose his hat. The figures have to go into their boxes in exactly the right order, so that they can appear in that order when I need them to come out and play their part.

I hear shouting and I glance up, but even before I do I know instinctively that Daddy is involved. Many of my audience have already left, or gone to the bar in another part of the room. In one corner there is something – a kerfuffle, noise, commotion, men's sharp voices. I stand up, the trunk safely clasped, and stare over at the small group, the melee. The captain is there in the middle, trying to calm Daddy – yes indeed, it *is* Daddy, his hat off, taller than the rest, his white hair mussed – the captain saying loudly: 'It was only said in jest, my good fellow!' and Daddy, cheeks pink, nose red, eyes glittering . . . Well, it's impossible to tell what is going on, or what I should do. My heart starts a drumbeat, and I stand frozen and simply look around me.

Other men have rushed to join them. Perhaps they are restraining Daddy: I think I can see an arm holding his. In the confusion, a bottle or glass goes over and there is a piercing smash. A bosun rushes over and tries to help peel Daddy away from whoever he is angrily squaring up to. It is all over very quickly. Daddy shakes the arms away from him, straightens his collar. Men dust themselves down, their voices calm again and in control. Daddy, stony-faced, strides over to me and wordlessly bends to lift the theatre trunk. He groans with the weight and signals rudely to the bosun to take the other handle and help carry it back to our cabin. The man shrugs equally rudely, and to my astonishment turns away from Daddy.

I fall into step beside him as he lugs the case alone, enduring its lopsided knocking, too stubborn to allow me to assist. I don't know what to say. Why is it that I feel sure the argument was about *me*? Mama would have said 'Pride comes before a fall', and by that she would have wanted me to learn that taking too much pleasure in my own miniature theatre and storytelling skills, or enjoying the attention of the audience too much, has caused this scene.

As we pass them, a lady, the same one in the oyster silk dress, now with a fur muffler and a concerned expression, steps towards me, saying to her husband, 'Charles – offer them some help!' and I recognise the lively man who made the quip about the music, Mr Debrett. He steps in at once where the bosun didn't and helps Daddy to carry the trunk.

I shuffle along beside them, feeling shamed and foolish. Several people pat me or try to tell me with their eyes that they enjoyed my 'little show', but the incident, whatever it was, has coloured everything. Once at the door of my cabin, Daddy has no desire to be sociable and Mr Debrett leaves us with the trunk, bowing to Daddy and offering a sweet smile for me.

Daddy is swollen with outrage, and choleric with the effects of drink and his fury at being manhandled by so many. I do not dare ask him what was said.

I pass an awful choppy night, climbing from my narrow bunk at one point to write in a letter to Cousin Mary that *I will be bloomin glad when we get to England!* But of course I say nothing about Daddy's nightly drinking sessions, or the row and the reason for it.

In some faint place, I feel I know. Did I imagine it – am I imagining it – or am I really the cause of all this gossip and anger? A deep sense of being wrong, *wrong*. My oddness, the sorts of things people say about me, the comments they make about my looks. Was Daddy defending me?

The only person in my life I might have asked for reassurance, Nurse Delphine, is not here to consult. I would once have thought I could ask Mama. But now she has demonstrated her love of secrets, my trust has gone. She would simply have sewn up her mouth with a needle, like the dragonfly in the story.

★★★

And so we arrive, stepping with wobbly legs onto dry land at Southampton. How long since I was here? 'You remember our landlady, Mrs Redgrove?' Daddy says as we join the throng moving down the steps. I think I was ten years old the last time we were here, so the answer is no, but Daddy has already powered ahead, not hearing my response. Daddy is nursing a sore head.

Mr Debrett spies us as we disembark and, full of warmth and loud friendly shouts, wants to shake my hand. I hide a little behind Daddy, feeling shy. The crowds of passengers pressing against us prevent further conversation and soon we are out of reach of Debrett and his wife, and inside a whirl of touts, boys begging a penny to carry our luggage; straggly English men and women offering us apples or beer or rooms for the night. There is such a powerful smell of braziers and horse dung and rotting vegetables and wild-eyed sweaty types. An assault on the nose. Daddy sweeps all away. We will stay with Mrs Redgrove as usual, he says firmly, and tomorrow make our long journey to Devon.

The weariness of nine days at sea and my wobbly land legs render me silent during dinner. It is a strange English dinner: some kind of pudding with kidneys in it. I'd forgotten about English food. Some of it is good but a lot of it isn't. English people seem not to care. The colours and kick of Jamaican food: the saltfish, the ackee, the fried plantain, the curried goat . . . I miss it. Daddy is quiet too; some of his vigour has left him, a balloon with air escaped. Then he remembers something in the pocket of his jacket – a slim book – and offers me it. An unspoken apology.

'Mr Baring-Gould. The man we are meeting tomorrow. You might enjoy this.'

The Book of Werewolves. Being an Account of a Terrible Superstition.

As I reach for it, his old twinkle flares up and he smiles a tired smile. 'But Pamela. Honey. Try to take such things with more . . . scepticism. A pinch of salt. Learn to be less . . . *literal* about the world these kinds of books describe. The Reverend Baring-Gould is keen to see your illustrations for his *Widdecombe Fair*, which I wrote to him about. But not all men are like him.

People — *some* folk — might take advantage of your nature. Of your . . .'

I glare at him, and he falters.

My what? What was he about to say there?

He bursts out laughing. Now this gets my gander up.

'Pammie! Miss Smith! Don't give me that look!' His laughter turns to coughing, a terrible convulsive coughing. The boarding-house lady he mentioned — Mrs Redgrove — rushes over, saying, 'Mr Smith! Charles!' (She is a flirty sort of woman, with an exaggerated bosom, very over-familiar.) 'Can I get you a drink of water?' But he waves her away, eyes watering.

When he has quietened down, I lean forward to say in a stage whisper, 'You and Mama carried me off to sea so often! So many voyages! People you have introduced me too. And now you are saying — what? I should forget? That it's not true that he who jumps for the moon leaps higher than he who stoops for a penny in the mud . . .?'

'Ha! Yes, well, aye, that's Howard Pyle, is it? Never had to grub in the mud a day in his life, did he, our Mr Pyle, unlike the rest of us . . .'

I have never heard Daddy speak like this. Something, some important skin, is being stripped away, and I find myself panicking. Is this because . . . Does he know that Mama tried to tell me a secret? Perhaps it was just an ordinary secret, the story of his failings and his leaving her alone for too long at an important moment (and more, but what was she implying, because she did not tell me the full story, I know that much), and he's decided there's no need to pretend any longer to be more than he is. What of all our years attending church and reading Swedenborg, *Heaven and Hell* — does he not believe he will meet Mama in Heaven one day, that their marriage will continue there? Nothing could pain me more than the discovery of this . . . cynicism. His falseness and deception. Worse even than his failure to fund my graduation at Pratt. I feel like a watermelon about to burst its skin. But in this English steak-and-kidney-pudding dining room – eyes on us – what can I say?

'I don't understand why you are saying this to me. *Why now?*' I hiss.

'Oh, let us forget it, Pammie, and enjoy our dinner. I meant nothing by it. Just a word of warning for the future. Not to be innocent. Or credulous.'

The anger is still there but must be plugged, so I turn to the book, flicking through it in silence, while my furious heartbeat starts to settle down.

'*What is lycanthropy?*' I read out. '*The change of a man or woman into the form of a wolf, either through magical means so as to enable him or her to gratify the taste for human flesh . . .*'

Daddy laughs again. 'I give you the book out of politeness. Baring-Gould – like any author – will be displeased if we have not troubled to read him. But this book is a strange one. He claims it is a scientific work. We must tread carefully, especially if that man, the manager of the Lyceum, is there. Stoker. Baring-Gould says that in the past humans had a lupine nature and the remnants of this are present today in lunacy and disease . . .'

Despite myself, despite my damn cross feelings towards Daddy at this moment, I am intrigued. I turn to reading again. We finish our meal in silence, Daddy calling for several glasses of wine and finally a carafe, out of which he pours me a small glass. Claret. I am about to pick it up and swig it in the same fast manner he does, when he seems to remember himself and calls Mrs Giant-Chesty Redgrove over for a splash of lemonade. She obliges, hovering over our table, trying to engage him in conversation. 'Opal hush,' she says. Claret and pop.

Daddy smiles at her in a way that I do not like at all. But then he thinks he is being fatherly here: having suddenly remembered that, as a girl, I cannot drink as he can and need mine watered down too. My twenty-first birthday, which I had a few months before we boarded for England, cuts no ice with him.

Later, lying on my lumpy cot with the none-too-fresh-smelling pillow and the room full of the scuttles of mice, I read a few more pages of the book by candle-light and find a strange excitement is growing in me. Perhaps Mr Baring-Gould will expect me to speak to him on the topics of the book? On the werewolves of the Middle Ages or the tales of the Austrian woods, so beautifully described. I begin learning phrases, intending to impress Mr Baring-Gould with my memory for such things – the same memory I use to narrate my theatre plays, which always astonishes folk so. *The sun dives among the trees, and paints their boles with patches of luminous saffron . . . contrasting with the blue-purple shadow on the western rim of unreclaimed forest . . .*

As I'm drifting into sleep, I roll against the edge of a nightmare. A terrible monstrous fear starts up in me, gripping tight. A wolf snarls in my dream and it has the face of Daddy. He is lumbering through a forest, flinging children here and there, and then the next minute wearing a top hat and pressing strange powders into his long snout, powders such as I've seen Daddy take sometimes, and his eyes are widening, his nose lengthening and his large teeth dripping with blood.

I force myself to wake up and lie with the room spinning, looking for the candle and a means to light it again. I do not want to lie here in darkness with that beast here and so close by.

Daddy is not a werewolf! Daddy is kind. Daddy is my champion. Daddy writes to people – Mr Baring-Gould, the gallery owner Mr Macbeth – and secures money for my talent, tells them of my gifts. He takes my miniature *Henry Morgan* show to the captain of the ship. I am an individual very dependent on her father, and, if I'm honest, I've been aware for a long time that what Mama was implying in her last words to me was that I needed to grow up fast. Mr Charles Colman Smith is flawed. He is a failed artist. He has some dubious money deals behind him. He is a drinker and sometime abandoner of his wife. He is also my champion and my guardian and affectionate and silly and wildly enthusiastic and of a modern temperament which means he believes in my drawings and my work and believes that I can do as well as any son might do in the world of art. Which of these things to cleave to? What lesson to take? *Oh Lord, help me and guide me. Is he a person to be relied upon?*

I find a pencil and some paper to sketch for a while. This is soothing. The light is poor so some of it is done with my eyes closed, just making little marks. I fetch my *Widdecombe Fair* sketches from my satchel under the window and, flicking through, find them pleasing, with the grey horse ever more ridiculous and the roses on the dresses looking awful scrummy. I have snuck myself into the picture, and a girl – dancing with a fellow in a wig – turns her head to admire me. This feels bold! (Of course I disguised myself, took away the red ribbons and my black hair in bunches, so that no one would recognise me.) And then I find myself doing little sums – calculations. The four cheques for my watercolours at the Macbeth Gallery, minus the money for this trip. The extra money – I have not seen it yet – that Mr Macbeth has made from my cards. Perhaps I could write to him myself?

That's what I do. A polite note with some Pamela humour in it so that it feels light and doesn't alarm him. I will post it tomorrow from Devon. I tell him that I have illustrated two books already and the whole of England will soon be talking about my art. (Of course I don't believe this, but it's the sort of thing Daddy says and it feels good to write it.) I will be able to show him the books soon.

At last my eyes feel heavy, and I blow out the candle. My signature – I have been practising my signature over and over – is imprinted on my eyelids in a vivid red, as if a flame burns there. *Mama, if only I'd understood or heard properly what you struggled to tell me. It was such a moment to choose! If only you had tried sooner, and I could have asked questions.* 'Oh! Charles left me alone . . . for too long. A couple should not be separated for long. Pamela? I always thought you knew.'

Why could she not have been plainer? What, *what* did this Big Secret mean?

THE HIGH PRIESTESS

I'm Isis, I'm the one with the moon in my hair

I'm the light spots on your eyes when you close them

When you are running on grass picking daisies saying I'm glad to be alive but what is my future

When will my future come what are the secrets I'm waiting for

I have many seeds, full to bursting.

I am the longest note your throat will fetch, I am the things you know not yet.

At last we arrive at this cleric's house. Lew Trenchard. In the way of English people, this is the name of a village, a parish, a country estate and a house, and this Baring-Gould man is the squire and vicar, and probably the king too and more besides. I'm already anxious, and it is a *very* full house indeed, with so many people and such commotion and dogs barking and a smog of smoke from cigars. I try hiding behind Daddy as we enter the long hall, heading for the drawing room, and then, spying my opportunity, I rush off to spend a long time in a nice cloakroom, washing my hands merrily in a jug and basin, until one of the daughters of this man has to come and find me, dressed in riding outfit with a whip — I thought she was going to whip me! — and when I tell her this I discover she has *no* sense of humour at all.

In their grand front room I stand a little behind Daddy, feeling like a child peeping out from her mother's skirts, until someone remembers to invite me to sit. I think it is Lady or Mrs or something Baring-Gould — the wife — but she is so much younger than her husband, and quiet and mouse-like with hair so fiercely parted it shows a pink scalp. She pats a seat beside her by the fireplace, and so I shyly move to sit there. She takes up her knitting and the feeling she gives me is of a person who would like — as I would — to disappear into the tapestries and rugs, or perhaps up the chimney and out into the sky.

Drinks and cakes are brought by servants, and other guests enter the room booming in their male voices. A little man and a great bear one flank Sir Henry Irving as he enters, like two pillars at a doorway, gazing at him adoringly in an awful sickening way. From my seat by the fire, I get shyly to my feet (thinking that, as in a theatre, I ought to stand and applaud).

Miss Terry is a step or two behind the men. Her fame is so great that I had expected to find her more astonishing. At first glance she is just an English lady with greying curls, of around the same age as Mama was, coming into the room and smiling at everyone. But when she spies me and turns her gaze on me, *then* I understand. Her eyes are the thing. Her eyes are an unusual shade of blue — almost turquoise. Like two huge stars, beaming on you. And her posture, the way she holds herself . . . Great warmth radiates from her. She is accustomed to being adored, anyone can see that. A High Priestess surveying her subjects.

'And who is this little – person?' she asks, in one of those actress voices, full of charm, holding out her hand to shake mine as I take a step or two towards her. (I feel sure she was going to say 'creature' there, but thought better of it.) This English habit of handshaking makes me feel (though I don't usually) decidedly American. My cheeks must be as red as my hair ribbons, and I cannot think of a word to say.

Daddy steps in to help. 'This is my daughter, Pamela, the artist. She recently had a sell-out show in New York, at the Macbeth Gallery on Fifth Avenue. Pamela Colman Smith. Perhaps you've heard of her?'

Polite murmurs of 'No . . .' and now the whole of me is ready to burst into flames of embarrassment. I can feel – with some relief – my shrinking feeling coming over me: in my mind's eye I am not here at all but am just a teeny-tiny mouse scurrying among their feet, flipping under that rug and beneath the slipper of the kind-faced wife of Baring-Gould and then hiding in her knitting bag.

'I've brought some of Pamela's illustrations to show the Reverend Baring-Gould . . .' Daddy is wasting no time, and rushes to fetch the portfolio, delighting in his audience.

Soon he has spread my *Widdecombe Fair* drawings across the top of a blanket box and the men and Miss Terry are gathering to look, along with one of the Baring-Gould daughters (thankfully she has put down the riding crop, and a noisy little dog is chewing it in the corner of the room). If I could scream, I would.

Or fly up into the ceiling rose, far away from all of them. The terror and the exposure! Why can my trick of shrinking not come at my bidding? I remain horribly large and vulnerable. I hover behind them and put a hand over my face.

Unfortunately Miss Terry, with her beady dazzling eyes, turns around and notices me at once: 'Come, come, this work is wonderful,' she says kindly, stepping over to put an arm around me. (I try not to burst into tears.) 'Such lively figures and such movement and variety! I love this dark-skinned man here, and the saucy bold looks of the women! Do you illustrate programmes? I'd love you to do our next ones.'

Daddy claps his hands. 'Yes! There's nothing she cannot do. We would be honoured to take a commission, wouldn't we, Pamela?'

'Pamela – you're like a little sprite.' This is Miss Terry again. 'A pixie. Pixie Pamela. How old are you? Is one of these ladies in the fair a picture of your mother?'

The snort from the Baring-Gould daughter is so loud that none could mistake it.

'My dear wife, Corinne, has crossed over,' Daddy says, as if announcing it to an auditorium. (These grand theatre folk have brought out the worst in him.) 'She departed from *this* world three years back, very sadly. A short illness. Pamela is older than she looks – twenty-one. She's not the child you think she is. But she was one of the *youngest-ever* students at Pratt, attended when she was fifteen – though we had to interrupt her studies when my work took me to Jamaica.'

'Jamaica?' Miss Terry murmurs, and seems to be studying me more closely. I am – well, who would not be? – overwhelmed to be held in such a gaze as hers. I realise I have seen her image so many times that I feel I already know her very well, when I do not. Now that I have caught her attention, she seems unwilling to let me go. She bends towards me, trying to coax me out from behind Daddy.

'I'm sorry to hear about your mother, Pixie. You must come and see a show when you're in London. As our guest. Or perhaps in New York?'

Pixie. As she says it for a second time it seems to land on me, like a feather floating down and drifting onto my shoulder, or a butterfly settling. I like it. Pixie Pamela. It's a good name for an artist. Or for me: sometimes tiny and invisible, other times bouncing up to the ceiling to look down on everyone. I smile at her.

Reverend Baring-Gould, pushing his glasses up his nose, taps the *Widdecombe Fair* pictures with his finger, straightens and declares: 'Thank you for showing me, Mr Smith. These are excellent. I will show them to my publisher – I would like them for the book!'

And just like that, I have a new name and another commission.

★★★

In bed that night, in the strange grand house of the cleric and his huge family with its noises that never end and its backdrop of strange Devonshire hills, the smell of the fire and the dog and of vases and vases of white roses, I lay there thinking hard. (According to the maid, Miss Terry must have roses wherever she goes.) The mix of scents is heady and mesmerising. I breathe in deeply, and ponder my new name.

It feels as if Miss Ellen Terry with her eyes the colour of hyacinth flowers has seen a side of me that I have hidden from everyone. This curious sensation of shrinking then growing again, something shifting in my perception or my brain or who knows where, is stronger than ever. I have never mentioned it to Daddy. I don't remember ever saying anything to Mama either. But *Pixie*. It's a little creature! A tiny creature! What is she trying to say to me?

And then, later, after supper, when we were seated far away from the others, she said: 'I'm sorry about your loss. Such a terrible age to lose a mother.'

'Is there a good age to lose a mother?' I parried.

There is a pause, and then she laughed. 'No, I suppose not! I'm so sorry. I only meant that being a young woman, embarking on . . .' She coughed and changed direction. 'My mother and I were estranged for many years. I missed her tremendously. It was because I loved an unsuitable man . . .'

I did not tell her that I'd said the same thing once to my cousin Mary. That eighteen was the worst possible age for it to happen — just as I was becoming a woman. I knew this was what Miss Terry meant, but I did not want to give her the satisfaction of being right.

She tailed off and so I prompted: 'Mr Irving?' — and she looked startled and laughed again. I don't know why she laughed; she seemed amused by me in some way. Perhaps I was being too bold or rude in my questions? I found it awful bewildering. In one way, conversation with her excited me. In another, I felt piqued. Slighted. I didn't know which was the true feeling.

'No, this was before I knew Henry. He was an artist. I had two children with this man . . . You can *imagine*!

It was a scandal. This was long ago. My children are not much older than you. Edy and Ted. You must come and stay with us — I would like my son to meet you because you appear to have . . . *industry*. That would be good for him to see.'

Industry. What a rummy thing to say! Again, the funny mixture of feelings. And yet — I was drawn to her. Her fame must have been part of it. I could hardly believe that this extraordinary person was deigning to speak to me. And I liked that she mentioned Mama and seemed troubled by my loss. Daddy is so determined to avoid mentioning it that I've started to feel like a boiling pot with a lid that's about to erupt.

'Was your mother an artist, Pixie?' she asked then. I was surprised: no one has ever asked this before. Why do people assume any talent a daughter has must come from her father?

'My grandmother illustrated children's books. I am named for her: she was *Pamelia* Colman — a different spelling of my name. She illustrated some poems by Mr William Blake but badly, apparently, and everyone mocked her.'

Then I could not stop, and I told her Mama had been an actress and afterwards covered my mouth with my hand, blushed. 'Not an actress like *you*, of course! Not a real one — not a feted one on stages all over the world. Just in people's drawing rooms. In Brooklyn Heights.'

Miss Terry nodded. She was kind but I had now worn out her interest and attention.

Before she got up to join the men with their cigars, she apologised again. 'I miss my daughter Edy when I travel like this. How old was your mother when she — passed?'

And with this innocent question, a tumult began. Because I didn't know the answer! I knew the age Mama had *said* she was, but Nurse Delphine had scoffed at it and Daddy had made a curious remark too, and both had led me to believe that Mama had not told the truth. That she'd been older than she claimed. I did not understand this lie. I had not been allowed, of course, to attend any registration of her death, and Daddy kept all such certificates and paperwork. But even were I to see it, I'm not sure whether it would be the truth – perhaps the lie is continued there.

So now, tossing and turning with the sweet rose scents haunting my room, I cannot sleep. I kick off the sheets and sit up. I swish back the curtain and tie it with the thick golden rope. The moon at the window is awful bright, tipping a silver stream into the room. There is a queer painting on the wall titled *A Husband Returns from His Labours*. What labours are these? What a strange painting! The moonlight has rendered it blue-grey and sinister and I would like to turn it against the wall.

Staring at it, thinking this, I know I'm thinking of something else. I can feel the most pressing questions weighting my chest – ones I have tried to avoid asking myself but which tonight's embarrassing encounters have made painful. Am I any good as an artist? And if so, in what way? I have no idea how to judge my own ability. When others – Daddy, Mr Macbeth, Miss Terry, Reverend Baring-Gould – praise me, I simply think: To what *degree* is it good? Is it just – colourful, funny, quirky? Or some kind of miracle or gimmick – like a dog dancing on its hind legs – that a girl like me can draw *at all*?

How would it be if I'd been allowed to stay at Pratt, to attend the classes with the life model, to study a naked human figure (I've never seen one yet, except for the children swimming in the river in Jamaica, and none were older than eleven), to learn how to follow the line of a thigh, a buttock, to train as men do with the best? What would I know then, what skills might I have? Mama's promise to me. That my grandmother said that one day millions will know my gifts and what I have to offer. I do not know why she said that when I am so small and strange and unimportant. Just a little pixie. A sprite. A nobody. Like the poem Mary showed me: I'm Nobody, who are you? *Are you Nobody too?*

★★★

In the morning, Miss Terry asks casually: 'Would you like to come on a walk with me?'

She is lacing up walking boots. Brisk light pours tantalisingly from the open door. It seems she means that we shall go alone, she and I, not the men.

I rush to find some socks and tie up my red leather shoes and ribbons to hold my hair in two large bunches at the side and then shove them under a woolly hat. She laughs when she sees me. Her eyes – the pupils are especially black, I realise. Is that why the blue seems so vivid?

'You won't need the hat! It's a lovely day. Let's walk along the path.' She strides out, with me scampering behind her.

Miss Terry knows this house and its grounds, and leads me to a wrought-iron gate, gestures me through it. This is leading us away from the house, from the smoke rising from the chimney and the dovecot with its little inhabitants flitting in and out excitedly like guests at a party. A pair of men working on another part of the house pause to stare at her, ceasing their hammering of stones for a moment, in awe. On either side of the path there are magnificent beeches; a canopy to enclose us. Miss Terry walks fast, as if she is running away from someone. When I catch up with her, I realise this is true.

'Fame is a terrible thing, Pixie. Don't ever court it.'

I'm a little breathless, but she is marching along, muttering something that I think is about Mr Baring-Gould: 'The folly! Like someone imagined a grand estate to be . . .' We walk deeper and deeper among the beeches, as if entering a great church. The hammering is now far behind us, and instead we hear the mewling of a buzzard and a crow shrieking as it flies past.

'Has something happened?' I ask.

'Henry says some newspaperman knows we're here. He is on his way down here to take photographs. Something you take for granted now: privacy, going about your business quietly, being alone, when you walk about, not being looked at – all of that is taken from you before you've even learned to value it.'

'I see . . .' (But of course I'm thinking fame is a wonderful thing, and how much I long for it. If I were a beauty like Miss Ellen Terry, I would take it as my due.)

Her stride is awful fast, and at last, some distance from the house, she pauses to look out through the lace of trees lining our path at the extraordinary shades of green in the Devonshire hills beyond.

'I don't suppose I should ever be famous,' I murmur, shy now that we have stopped. I'm kicking at a nodding head of cow parsley, feeling her gaze on me.

'Well, now . . . Your father is pretty determined that you shall be. And to have such early success is unusual. A show in a Fifth Avenue gallery before the age of twenty! Illustrating two folklore books . . .'

'It wasn't only *my* work. Daddy exaggerates,' I say. But I can't resist adding: 'I shall illustrate another book, though – the one by the Reverend Baring-Gould. And your programmes!'

She laughs. 'Yes. These things are significant.'

I begin to feel they might be.

'Also – if Bram likes the programmes, there will be other things. Posters. Perhaps even stage design. He is very keen for you to do it, you know – he's perfectly genuine. But all I wanted to point out is that if you become famous, or "celebrated" or "admired", no encounter you ever have will feel . . . authentic. You will not know whom to trust. You will know the person is thinking: *Oh, I'm in the presence of someone famous! Is there something – money, a connection – I can ask them for?* Never, *ever* can you experience how things would be if you were just a . . . nobody, like them!'

I'm startled by her use of the very word I was thinking about last night. She might have read my mind. And, worse, when she was speaking about people and how they saw her, I found myself picturing a painting *I've* seen of her: naked, an awful rude one – she must only have been sixteen – by that first husband, the one she talked about. I asked Daddy about him – the painter, Watts. Her with her head flung back and naked breasts, so young, and about to be ravished by a forty-seven-year-old man. Ugh! How disgusting. Heat flares in my cheeks; I know I'm blushing. Her red curls are grey now. But the picture is seared in my mind.

Miss Terry is staring out towards the soft green hills spread before us, and thankfully not looking at me. She does seem awful sad. I nudge some beechnuts on the path, staring down at the toes of my boots.

'Henry will be glad of the newspaperman,' she mutters. 'He will give an interview, and Bram will see him off after that. A few days of peace – I suppose that was too much to ask.'

When we arrive back at the house, she's right: there are several men in dark coats with cameras, looking terribly important, and the Baring-Gould daughters (again dressed in their riding clothes) are talking to them. I watch Miss Terry compose herself as we approach. It is a miraculous thing to observe: the shoulders go back, the chin lifts, the expression in her eyes becomes one of practised charm, and she's there – *'Gentlemen!'* – and as they rush towards her I slip unnoticed into the house like a little pug dog at their feet.

In his room, Daddy is preparing to leave. Amongst the cases opened on the bed is a Moroccan leather case with a syringe in it, and with his long nervous fingers he is rolling back the shirtsleeve of his other arm.

'Daddy! Are you ill?'

His eyes rest thoughtfully on his sinewy forearm, dotted and scarred with innumerable puncture marks. 'No, no, it's just the pain. The back pain. This is only a little solution of cocaine which Miss Terry was kind enough to give me.' He shows me the small bottle. I feel a surge of irritation, or fear, or – I'm not sure what.

'But it always makes you so . . . morbid. And, later, a black reaction. And we have a long day of travelling ahead, back to London . . .'

'A long day in a damned uncomfortable brougham! I *need* this . . .'

He rubs at his lower back and, with his pale skin and dark eyes, he does look ill indeed.

'Yes, Daddy,' I say, rushing to nestle against him. It is an awkward embrace as he is so floppy that I'm almost holding him up. He closes his eyes and lets his head droop forward onto his chest.

'He's rather handsome, your father, isn't he? Was your mother terribly jealous?' Miss Terry said it on our walk. Only an actress could say such a thing! What a rude remark. I only stared at her (thinking for a moment of Mrs Redgrove in the boarding-house) and again she gave that tinkling laugh and composed glance and was suddenly kindness itself: 'Come, come, Pixie, you must have noticed? Don't the ladies swoon over him at every turn? And, after all, he adores you and spends all his time extolling your work, a very unusual vice for the father of a daughter . . .'

Now I discover she has had an earlier conversation with Daddy too, and offered him her medication to help. Her own starry look becomes a little clearer to me now. I do not know what to make of her. One moment I like her very much; the next . . .

I suppose at least it will make him bright and talkative at first, and then later Daddy might sleep through the journey. That's something. Otherwise, he would do as he did travelling down here: scratching and fidgeting, twitching and stretching out his long legs, taking up a blanket to cover and warm them, then throwing it off; complaining about the pain in his back, the pain in his neck, and finally, once in the maudlin stage, the pain in his heart.

★★★

Daddy is still very twitchy and itchy for the first part of the journey. We are to take a carriage to the station, then onwards to Paddington via the steam train *The Cornishman*, two nights in London, then to Southampton to board our ship. It is awful rackety and rough over this moorland, and not much to be heard but the whinny of the horse. Daddy cannot stop chattering excitedly about the people we have just spent time with, chiefly the famous ones: Sir Henry Irving and Miss Terry. He says he has secured us invitations to see them act in *Robespierre*, in New York or perhaps Philadelphia, and various commissions: programme design and set and stage designs.

'Stage designs! I have only ever done those when they were eighteen inches tall – are you sure?' I ask, alarmed, but he brushes this aside.

'Maybe she'll wear the beetle dress, the one that glitters emerald green with a thousand wings of insects . . .'

He is very besotted with her, and she an old lady of fifty?

'They are not just wings,' I correct him. 'They used the carapaces of the beetles. Poor dead things.' He gives me a rather craven look and so I press on with my advantage: 'What was *Mama* like as a child?'

'Huh?' He draws his eyes away from me to the window of our rumbling brougham, then turns back and tries to focus.

'You knew her then, didn't you? How old were you when you met? I had a letter: a friend of hers, someone called Miriam, said that Mama had been naughty, I think, or lively – no, she said "always in trouble, most times for talking too much".'

Daddy's blue eyes darken. For a second I think he is going to refuse to answer — he has told me so little about how they met, and their life in America before I was born — and then he says: 'Miriam? Miriam wrote to you about Corinne? That was kind of her. Yes, they were good friends. Corinne was — pretty. Lively. Always running, leaping, never still. And, yes, I guess it's fair to say she was often — naughty . . .'

'Was she like me? Was she an artist? Miss Terry asked.'

'Like you?' And here he seems struck by mirth. He actually — and perhaps it is the effect of his medication, or the extreme pain in his back, but he is snuffling, and giggling, and — why, he is just like a pig!

'No, Pamela. She was tall, and willowy, and I'm afraid — my dear — you are not going to grow any taller. She had a low beautiful voice; she was always singing . . . Her voice, I might add, is the thing I remember most. I hear it sometimes if I enter a room too quickly. Just a trace. The threads of a song.'

'She said you left her alone too long . . .'

'Huh?'

'In Jamaica, I think she meant. That your travels, your work, your . . .'

Here is the moment to tell him, if ever I am going to. Or ask him. That Mama tried to confide a secret, something important, and I'd like to know what it was. His expression — extremely closed up, foreboding — is not encouraging, and I falter a little.

'*Driver!*' Daddy suddenly bellows, addressing the man on the seat in front. 'Put a clip into it! *The Cornishman* will have left for London!'

His shouting startles me, and the book on my knee clatters to the floor. I feel it is deliberate and directed at me. There is something angry in his manner, and something fearful. A warning, perhaps.

If only I had understood that I would never get the chance again.

★★★

Before leaving for New York, we have a couple of days in London with another landlady, and like Mrs Redgrove she seems to know Daddy well. Her name is Mrs Jones but there is no sign of a Mr Jones. She is thin in her long white apron, with a moon-face and a severe expression. She appears to be in a fit of bad humour with Daddy, and thumps the jug of water down on the dining table. She then sets our bowls down so hard that the soup splashes. It is a very dark oxtail soup, with dubious white things floating in it. Daddy accepts it mildly, softly saying, 'Nancy. Some bread, please?'

I'm surprised that he knows her Christian name and I watch how his saying it like that, in that soft male voice, makes her eyes glitter with tears.

In the morning, he seems sorry for something, or perhaps it's that his medicinally induced mood has passed. But he brightens and takes me to my favourite shop in London, L. Cornelissen & Son on Great Queen Street, to stock up on paints and paper and brushes and gouache and pastels and inks and everything else besides. The shop is like a candy store. The coloured bottles glint in the sunlight as we step inside, and Daddy immediately begins a conversation with Mr Cornelissen while I walk along the drawers and shelves, picking up the paintbrushes and one by one digging my nail into the tightly formed sable in the filberts, which is deeply satisfying.

Of course, because we embark from Southampton tomorrow, Daddy decides we do not want heavy canvases or sketchbooks, but concedes to buy me some rose madder, as that is hard to find, and iron-oak-gall ink, far blacker than and superior to all other kinds, and made right here in the shop. Mr Cornelissen (I think he is actually the son but no one troubles to introduce me; indeed, both he and Daddy act as if I'm some queer servant girl trailing behind a great man, not the Artist Herself!) shows me the oak galls he has gathered, which will be steeped for weeks to get the true deep colour.

I ask if I might have one and Mr Cornelissen stares at me as if a grey pigeon spoke.

After a second's consideration, he hands the gall to me: the size of an acorn but with a knobbly shape, a little like a dried flower or nut. 'It's a sort of benign tumour, or wart, on the tree,' he says as I turn it over in my hand.

'Daddy, I think I might like another bottle of this. It's going to be an age until we get back here to London – and what of the money I made from *the sales of my paintings in Mr Macbeth's gallery?*'

The effect is instant, as if I'd just detonated a bomb in the shop. As if all the tiny little drawers had opened and closed and started drumming out a tune. As if the inks and pigment bottles had started dancing and leaping in the aisles.

Mr Cornelissen is all of a fluster. Who can this queer little person be, this strange-looking *child*, or so he thought (since being in England, I've heard myself described as 'Oriental', 'mulatto' or 'Gypsy'), or perhaps an assistant to Mr Smith (no doubt he assumed Daddy the artist), and now to hear me call myself his daughter and, even more extraordinary, an artist who has *sold her paintings*. Well, I damn near lick my lips with pleasure to see the two of them so confused and blustering and Daddy saying, 'Well now, Pammie, most of the money – you know, it's awful vulgar to talk about money . . .'

He knows I am in a mischievous mood, and he doesn't quite pluck up the nerve to tell me the truth. I've long suspected it. He has spent most of the money I earned us on this trip. He thinks I'll be hopping mad, but I'm only teasing him. I like sometimes – when I'm not feeling too much of a Silly Billy – to surprise everyone by actually being somebody. It is the opposite of my shrinking feeling: I sometimes feel as if I'm six feet tall and growing, a vivid vermillion poppy on a hairy green stalk. I can barely bend my head in this crowded shop, craned over like a hairpin.

I can never stay mad at Daddy for long. After all, he has gotten me a commission at the Lyceum, and another publishing deal with Mr Baring-Gould, and – well, Mama would be impressed: my cup runneth over. Programmes and posters and possible set design for the Lyceum Theatre company! Soon we will be rolling in cash. He has promised to take me to Covent Garden, to the little studio and shop that Miss Terry's daughter has set up there, and I am keen to see how these famous and successful English folk do it, make a life for themselves, a thrilling life, living for making and doing and creating things, which seems to me like the most bully thing in all the world, and all I've ever wanted.

★★★

Miss Terry's daughter is called Edith, but everyone calls her Edy. The noise in Covent Garden disturbs me, the shouts and the flower sellers are everywhere, and the smell of steak and onions cooking, and rotting vegetables, all blending in a stew that is a bit too much. Her business – *Costumes Theatrical and Private, Available to Hire* – is on Henrietta Street between an Italian supper club and a French coffee house. The door is garlanded with white flowers, and a sign swinging above it says *Edith Craig & Co.*, with a picture of a bonnet and some flowers. We ting-a-ling the bell and I stare at this sign, dreaming. Imagine your mother buying you your own business! Imagine spending all day every day drawing and making stuff without a care in the world! A huge stab pierces my chest, a feeling of – what? Envy, I guess. A rummy feeling.

A woman's voice shouts, 'It's open!' and we push the door. We are immediately in a cluttered room, tables full of patterns, swathes of cloth and dressmaker's dummies everywhere, and furry cushions and rugs, and there amidst it all is Edy, brown hair pinned up rather randomly, working at a table, with a cup of tea growing cold beside her. She glances up at us, then back down again.

Daddy hesitates before striding over. He says something, tries to shake her hand, but she is mighty distracted and barely rises to greet him, though she gives me a sly look from under her piled-up hair. Miss Terry said she was 'not much older' than me, but I judge her to be approaching thirty. She has an upturned sort of nose, and dark eyes not at all like her mother's. Her hands are the most interesting thing about her: large, with an almost claw-like appearance. I suddenly remember that Daddy told me she was musical, a performer – a pianist, I think.

All around her are patterns, drawings, scissors, pins, little patches of cloth and ribbon and leather and nubs of dressmaker's chalk. The dust motes in the shop dance in the sunlight coming in from one dirty window: the whole place has such a delicious air of industry (isn't that the very word her mother used when speaking of me?) and yet also, very obviously for Edy as well as for me, of joy. A crackle of it in the air. On the table next to her tea is a jug with peonies shoved in it, a flame-coloured explosion of flowers in a plain white milk jug, so vivid alongside the emerald green of the shoulder of Edy's dress and the velvet blue of mine, and the combination is so glorious, so exactly like the brilliant flash of a kingfisher that it almost hurts to see it.

Shyness holds my tongue. *Her* tongue, I notice, is sticking out as she holds the cloth up to the sunlight for a moment and plucks a few pins from the sleeve of her dress to pin it together, then, suddenly seeming to notice us properly, she says: 'Nora is in the kitchen. She'll make you a cup of tea. You could help me do some cutting, Pixie, if you like.'

So her mother has already written to her about me!

I love her use of my new name. How casually it seems to have settled on me. Today I have two huge red ribbons holding my hair in bunches and the azure velvet dress I'm rather fond of (I'm the exact colours of a red-eyed damselfly), and I hope she sees how much the name suits me. I pull out a chair with a horrid screech and smack my bottom down on it. I tentatively pick up some cloth with a pinned pattern of tracing paper on it, and she hands me the scissors.

Daddy goes in search of Nora and the tea in the kitchen she's indicated.

'Have you read *Dracula*?' Edy asks, without looking up from her pinning. I hand back to her the fabric, and she nods and shoves a piece of leather towards me, and some other cutters, and points out the shape she has drawn on it in pen. 'You know how to use leather cutters?'

I nod, liking that she assumes I do. Then, once I've begun digging into the leather with the cutters – such a satisfying feeling – I ask about this *Dracula*, remembering that Daddy has mentioned it too. 'Is it a novel?'

'There's a copy on the windowsill. The American edition is just being published . . . I can lend it to you if you like. By the manager – didn't you meet him down at Lew Trenchard?'

'I don't know. Mr Stoker?'

'He used to read me bits of it in my cabin on the crossing over. To get an idea of its effect on the general public. I'm a very bad sailor so I couldn't leave my cabin, and – yes, the first part is very thrilling.'

The general public: General Jackass.

Edy nods towards the windowsill, at a book with curling pages that looks like it has been dropped in a bath, and I notice with a start a large ginger cat sleeping on a little coffee stand. It's so fluffy I mistook it for a furry rug or cushion. Its tail is curled around its body, which is the most beautiful tigery golden-red colour, its back striped down the spine like the veins of a leaf. The cat does not stir as I move past it to pick up the stained and curling book, unsure if Edy really means me to take it. I bring it back to our table and put it on top of some boxes of ribbon – there is no other space – and resume my leather cutting.

'But then the bit he gloated about was the part where the lunatic catches flies on the windowpane and eats them. He explained the whole theory of it and it made me sicker and sicker. After that I think he had to give it up – I never got to the last part. Perhaps you could read it and tell me how it ends?'

'Why yes, I –'

The same familiarity as her mother. As if we already know one another. I'm unaccustomed to it, especially in British people, usually so formal. It must be the theatre world. All that dressing and undressing in front of folk and kissing strangers and sleeping in lodgings and using the same tooth-mugs and travelling together. She often understudies for her mother, I know that much. She was a musician, and her hands – I stare at them now – something about her hands . . . What was it that Daddy told me?

Daddy returns with three wobbling cups of tea on a tray, one with a broken saucer. He looks pleased with himself and I know he's been deliberately leaving us alone, to 'get along'.

'You don't *sound* American,' Edy continues. I don't know if she means me or Daddy, so I say nothing. 'Mother says you live in Brooklyn . . . Lucky you! You must walk every day along that beautiful bridge that looks as if it were made of thread, and is so very, very high!'

'You've been, then?' I ask, but she accepts the cup of tea and bows her head again to her work.

Daddy coughs and says, 'We lived *here* for a time. Pamela was born in Pimlico. Matter of fact, I was thinking we should pay a visit to our old house before we leave tomorrow. But she's not much given to sentiment . . .'

Edy hardly seems to be listening. Daddy doesn't interest her much, but I do feel – in a can't-put-my-finger-on-it way – that she is interested in me.

Spread on the table in front of her is a wonderful huge sheet with shoes sketched on it, fascinating, shoes fit for the elves and the shoemaker, and each of them dated: *1300, 1350, 1450*. She has lightly coloured them, mostly pinks and browns and reds, and the effect is very tempting; how I love the colours and the multitudes of styles, like the candy store of Cornelissen's again, or staring into a window of rose-flavoured macaroons.

Daddy sips at his tea, gazing approvingly at Edy's workshop and the table spread with drawings. He reaches to pick one up, but Edy's claw-hand flies out, pressing down hard. 'Oh, don't touch any of them! I'll never find them again. These are for *Robespierre* . . .'

'Oh yes, Mr Irving mentioned it,' Daddy says, recovering his manners. He goes to stand near the window, hands behind his back, looking at the tiger cat sleeping there and then at some of the posters and newspapers stuck on the walls. He is reading them, but I know he is also thinking. 'Strategising', as he calls it. I can tell this just from the back of his neck – pinking – and the bottoms of his ears.

'*Friday, tenth of March 1899,*' he reads out, booming. '*Miss Ellen Terry narrowly escapes death . . . Miss Ellen Terry – Miss E. A. Wardell – while acting the character of Portia in* The Merchant of Venice *at Fulham Theatre had a narrow escape from death when the heavy roller of the curtain suddenly fell, narrowly missing the lady's head –* Hmmm . . . I had no idea your mother's name was Miss Wardell.'

Edy laughs shortly – 'How much newspapers get wrong is always a source of amusement to us' – and continues her pinning, folding and cutting, huffing and sighing and making clear signs that she'd like us to leave. She glances over at the piece of almond-coloured leather I've cut and smiles briefly, taking it from me. I can feel how powerfully she is signalling that she needs to get on and it irks me that Daddy doesn't, but I know the 'strategy' is coming.

'Mr Irving and your mother have asked her, Pixie – we call her Pamela – to work on *Robespierre* too. To go on tour with you and the Lyceum. As you can see, there's not much Pamela *can't* do. She can help you with the costumes. She is going to be doing programmes, posters, set design . . . She has already had an exhibition at a major gallery on Fifth Avenue. She was the youngest student to attend the Pratt Institute. She has her own miniature theatre show and is publishing a book of Jamaican folk stories, and – oh yes! – a commission for Mr Baring-Gould. Have you seen her artwork?'

Now I am blushing horribly. Daddy has a satchel with him and it didn't occur to me when we left the boarding-house that this was his intention, to show Edy my drawings. I put a hand on his arm. 'Miss Craig is busy, Daddy. We should leave her to get on . . .'

But he has her attention now and for a moment she turns to sip her tea, sitting back against her chair and staring at me. I feel as if I'm dancing in a dust mote. She nods and, hardly needing any encouragement, Daddy opens the satchel and begins showing her various sketches, my *Widdecombe Fair* drawings and *Annancy* illustrations. She flicks through the pages. She murmurs, I cannot tell whether with interest or disdain, and I find I am holding my breath.

'I like your dancers . . .' she says, addressing her comment to me, not to Daddy. 'They really do look like they're moving. That's difficult to do. Have you seen my brother's sketches for theatre? Everyone standing stock-still, stiff and shadowy.'

Encouraged, Daddy shows her some illustrations for *The Golden Vanity* and *The Green Bed*, but this only prompts from her: 'Folklore. I don't like your giant. I hate big ears. What did you think about Mr Paine? Did you meet him?'

I nod. Cat's got my tongue.

Daddy shows her some illustrations I did for Seumas MacManus, the Irish folklorist. Edy stares at these carefully, picking up each page to squint at it, then says: 'I like the way you seem to be showing that these . . . Jamaican stories . . . are as important as any Greek myths or Irish folklore. Indeed, so many different kinds of folk stories. Did you like Seumas? He's terribly popular in America, Mother says.'

The words are out before Daddy can stop me: 'Oh yes, we met him. We went to Ireland. Donegal. He's a bloomin schoolmaster and awful stupid.'

And this brings hoots of laughter from Edy, her first warm smile, and more studying of me. 'Do people comment on your – on these different kinds of people?' she asks. 'Their skin colours, their nationalities? The ways some of the men and women look alike. They're unusual, to say the least, in an English country tale.'

'Well, the *Brooklyn Life* reviewer said my work would be more at home in the *Arabian Nights*. I didn't understand . . .'

Daddy is scratching himself and coughing and doing a sort of hand signal that means *Don't mention your negative reviews!* but I confess to being tired of his antics and his business efforts, and exhausted at playing along.

'The thing most often said about me is that I have no technique – my lines are "not the defined sort that characterise Aubrey Beardsley" – but that I have natural gifts. Imagination. I think it's an insult disguised as a compliment –'

'Why, Pamela, my dear!' Daddy interrupts, alarmed at the way this is going. 'Of course it is not an insult. They mean that, as a young woman, and unschooled in the draughtsmanship of men, you have *natural* gifts and feminine talent . . .'

At last, *at last*, Edy is interested. She is staring from me to Daddy and taking in my red face and my fury and my struggle to hide it, which now erupts into: 'Well, and whose fault is *that*? My lack of draughtsmanship? Not permitted to attend the drawing classes for fear of spying a – a buttock!'

Edy laughs again, nodding and uttering a 'Brava!' under her breath. She is watching to see what Daddy will do.

He gathers up my sketches, sliding them back into his satchel. 'We must not detain you, Miss Craig. You are at liberty to call on Pamela for any assistance you need. Mr Irving and Miss Terry were impressed with Pamela's gifts, even if she lacks . . . *confidence*.'

'Confidence! I don't lack *confidence* –' I'm about to say more but suddenly the look Edy is giving us, amused, sitting back, queenly, watching her subjects as if to say 'Oh, this is a spectacle I can enjoy', makes me feel queer, a sudden rush of queasiness.

'Well. It was – awful nice to meet you,' I say, trying to recover. Damn, blast and hell – my stupid temper! The things that burst out of me! Mama warned me so often to 'think before you open your mouth'. I never can.

We head towards the door and the ginger cat – until now so still and deeply sleeping on the table that I'd forgotten it – wakes and leaps in front of us, frisking and winding her huge fluffy tail around our legs. I start. Daddy nearly slips.

'*Sappho!*' Edy cries, jumping to retrieve the cat and bury her face in its fur to kiss it, then carrying it to the chair I just vacated. 'You forgot *Dracula*,' she says to me. So then there is the fuss of slotting the big fat book into Daddy's satchel and at last we are free to go.

But as we are leaving, something astonishing happens. I glance towards the kitchen and the light is spilling in a long slant. I catch a glimpse. A darting glance. Nora. The maid or housekeeper or tea maker or whatever she is. She peeks out of the kitchen at us – a small person with curls of glorious ginger hair straying from a cap. She is wearing a white apron over a vivid blue dress, and must be about my age. What is astonishing is the feeling that suddenly comes over me! She gives me the most extraordinary grin, for what reason I can't imagine. It is a look – as if she knows me. Or is it simply the way the light is tumbling over her, like a Dutch Master painting? I almost say as much, then realise Daddy has already turned, opened the door onto Henrietta Street.

The audience at a puppet show outside chooses this moment to burst into cheering and applause. I am thinking about the feeling of that look from the maid. It reaches right inside me. Like a match struck. I have never felt the effect of such a smile. I do not know why. For a strange moment I wonder: was she *real*? Such a quality of heavenly loveliness – something about her was not quite of this earth. Have we met somewhere? I think again of the flame-coloured peonies in the white jug on Edy's work desk. I would like to draw them, to capture them, set against green velvet. Kingfisher colours again. The blue of Nora's dress. What is this mood that comes to me, the awareness that each and every experience will happen once, just *once* in that particular combination? It will stay in your heart, and sometimes not even there, and when you die, where will it be? It makes me sweepingly sad. How wonderful and terrible this understanding is.

★★★

Daddy spoils it all. He is talking about the cat. Sappho. She was a very lovely cat, a fluffy one, and such pretty tigery colours! But it is not that which has vexed him.

'Pamela, honey, you're so . . . I do not know how much you know about the world?'

We are striding through the market. There are so many flowers and colours it hurts my eyes, so I've fetched my hat out of my bag and pulled it down over my hair and I'm hurrying to keep up with Daddy, rushing us back to our boarding-house to pack.

He stops suddenly, almost knocking a small boy to the ground. The child's mama sweeps him up and gives Daddy a filthy look.

'Do you know what — an *invert* is?' he asks. A woman selling apples turns sharply to look at us and bursts out laughing.

I do not. But I'm certainly not telling him that!

'Oh, Daddy, we have packing to do, and you did say you wanted to — I can't remember what it was, visit someone else before we leave? Another possible – patron? Or was it to go to the Lyceum?'

Yes, that was it. We are heading that way. The grubby cream pillars of the theatre soon loom into view. Daddy pauses for a moment, admiring the posters announcing Miss Terry and Mr Henry Irving in another production, but, taking my arm, steers me over the road to a restaurant on the corner opposite.

'Well, without your mother's guidance or . . . Perhaps I'll find a book you can read, to – hmmm – understand.'

I stare at him in fury, willing him to shut up.

Finally, he laughs. 'We have secured you a place with them, Pamela. I feel proud when I consider what we've achieved on this trip. The illustrations for Mr Baring-Gould. Costume and set design with Mr Stoker's company! I think a glass of champagne is called for.'

The place is heaving, stuffed with the smoke from a hundred cigars. Theatregoers in their finery – it is now late in the afternoon, and they are here for the early supper. I look longingly at a little plate of sausages and dark-green things – they might be wally pickles but I thought the English didn't eat those? Daddy is waving his arms about, taking off his hat. He stands at the bar, ordering in his deepest, most American, booming voice. Several women smile at him, and I long to stamp hard on his toe in its Italian boot, to stop him smiling back.

Soon we are jammed on some too-high yellow-painted chairs before a little iron table with cherubs scrolled over it. I am admiring the many signed pictures of actors and actresses on the walls around us as the barmaid approaches carrying a tray with two tall glasses of champagne. Pictures of Miss Terry, yes, the Empress of them all, but also several of Edy as Emilia in *Othello* and Sophie in *Olivia*. Also Lillie Langtry in a great puff of a dress as Lady Ormonde.

Daddy sees me looking and — in a different mood now — beams at me. 'Your mother would be warning me now,' he says. 'For the fast crowd I'm introducing you to. Inverts. Actresses . . .'

'But Mama was an actress! I saw a review once.'

'Oh, in the drawing rooms of Brooklyn, for friends and family. Privately. Hardly the same thing —'

'Maybe she would have liked to have been on the stage, but hadn't the courage of Miss Terry or Mrs Langtry to go against her family and, you know, respectability . . .'

Daddy frowns, surprised. I guess I have never said anything critical of Mama before. Perhaps this is already the bad influence from the 'fast' crowd that he fears, making me feel differently about what is possible.

'I remember Mama singing to me. She often sang. She had a powerful kind of voice, liquid. Like the notes a blackbird sings. I'm not — making it up, am I? You *said* she sang . . .'

He nods. He looks awful sad suddenly.

The two flutes of champagne sit between us, the palest yellow in colour and with bubbles racing insanely towards the top. Daddy stares at them and then back at me as if, once again, he is deliberating, considering telling me something important. He tugs at his goatee. He scratches his head in the way that I have grown to hate: with both hands, like a demented person. In an instant his mood shifts. He snatches up the nearest glass, indicating that I should take the other.

'To us!' Daddy says, clinking his glass to mine. His manner seems falsely gay. 'To *Robespierre* and the

Lyceum tour! To cleverness and to – money! And to my daughter's brilliant career!'

I take a sip – my first glass of champagne. It's pretty to look at but the taste is awful sour; I prefer the opal hush we had at the boarding-house. I put my glass down and Daddy laughs at my expression. 'Gets up your nose,' I say. I mean the bubbles.

A tiny girl could drown in them.

I am a stately creature. I wear a diadem of twelve stars because everything is my creation.

My feet are hidden in this lake of corn, of plenty.

My voice is tender but commands you to kneel.

I am not a gate but a home. You may reach inside me and allow me to deliver you.

I can do things no man can ever do.

You know who I am: I set you going.

The sea. Here we are. Back again, staring at it. Feeling the sway beneath the ship. I hold the rail and lean over, breathing in comforting salted damp air, and letting my hair be tugged loose from the bunches. One of my ribbons flies out towards the waves like a quick red bird and is lost. I feel a tear slide down my cheek, watching the red swallowed up by the grey. Little me, lost in the deep. The bigness of the wide world, and my tiny place within it. My nothingness.

The waves are the swelling sort that speak of trouble. Dark slits keep appearing in the grey surface, and every time I expect something to pop up. Gulls decorate it: folded linen napkins on a table. How many of these transatlantic trips am I obliged to do? Criss-crossing the world, and each time I feel I change in transit and arrive back someone else. I am not the same person who left New York to go to Jamaica, or who came back to New York three years later, or who, in this case, left Southampton, waved off with the hats of a thousand landlubbers and well-wishers. It's exhausting! Who am I this time? How sick I am of the question from everyone, and their surprise: 'Oh, you're *American*' or 'You're British' or 'Oh, this is your *father*' or 'I thought you were Japanese' . . . 'So clever, how you do that queer *dialect*!'

Japanese, for Bully's sake. I've drawn a self-portrait of how I always imagine these people must see me, in a grey silk kimono and red slippers, with my hair in ribbons; my eyebrows high black arches and my eyes black squiggles. *The Pixie.* A second, smaller me standing in the background, like a doll version of myself. Try as I might, I can't make my expression anything other than cross.

Am I an artist with a brilliant career and so many commissioned works piling up? A prodigy, as Daddy would have it? The youngest-ever artist to have her first exhibition in New York? (Gawd. How I cringed when he told people that.)

I'm a young woman who has found out a few things: what an invert is (I found it in a book that I bought for tuppence at the market in Covent Garden); who Sappho was, and about the island of Lesbos. Good tip from Sappho: *If you're squeamish, my advice to you is: don't touch the rubble on the beach.*

How the famous live. How actors and theatre folk make their own rules about marriage and who to fall in love with. About a strange novel concerning bats – supposedly for adults, not children – by a man very much in love with Mr Irving. (I'm still smarting, I guess, about the *Pittsburgh Daily Post* review that claimed my work 'cannot fail to win the childish heart'. Why does no one say that about Mr Stoker? So much rummy stuff!)

Daddy is in his cabin. He is sick. We have only been at sea for one day so this does not bode well. He has taken morphine for his pain – his back, his throat, his neck; it seems to be a pain that coils around him like a snake and can never be pinpointed. I have stopped nagging him, as it doesn't do the slightest jot of good.

We saw Miss Terry again briefly in London before we left. And the conversation I had with her made me mad. I am trying not to 'ruminate' about it, as Daddy says that does no good and gives you dyspepsia, but . . . She was admiring a gift Daddy had given her – an illustration I'd made from *Macbeth* – and then she looked hard at it and read the caption again. She turned to me as she read: '*The service and the loyalty I owe, In doing it, pays itself.*' She frowned and then asked bluntly: 'Is this change deliberate? You do know that it's my *husband* who says these lines in the play?'

I nodded, furiously. How could she underestimate me! I felt as if steam was exploding from my ears. Did she think she was the only one to understand the role Lady Macbeth's actions play in her husband's demise? Or the only woman in the world who thought of women as independent or active and not just in relation to their husbands? Why do people persist in thinking me an idiot *child*?

Now that I've remembered it, I get awful mad again. Better to return to my room and draw some more. Finish my illustrations for *The Golden Vanity*. That will calm me. And they will benefit from the sea I've been staring at, which is fresh now in my mind's eye. As I turn with this new determination, cheered by it, I hear the band starting up. 'God Save the Queen'. Good! Dinner will soon be served. A cabin boy, a peculiar ginger-haired fellow, has been staring at me, and when I spin around, suddenly letting go of the rail and taking my eyes from the sea to set eyes on him, he scurries off towards the starboard side.

What will I do with this temper of mine, if I can't subdue it? And when will I learn the proper moves to make, the right things to say, in the way that Daddy does so naturally? I'm certain I will never have – or keep – a dear friend. I will never charm the theatrical or literary world. I will be alone and cranky and misunderstood forever.

The cabin boy reappears. He is heading purposefully towards me.

'Miss! Miss – Are you Miss Smith?'

'Yes, I—'

'Please come!' He looks worried and is not waiting for my answer. I try to indicate that I am on my way to my own cabin, but with a gesture he makes it clear he needs me to follow him. 'The first officer – and your father . . .'

'Daddy is unwell, I know; he is in his berth.'

He shakes his head. He is hurrying now and we are almost at the first-class lounge, and I can hear the commotion: a male voice, shouting – Daddy's – and another voice, or perhaps more than one, shouting right back, exasperated, saying, 'Mr Smith! Mr Smith!'

Shame starts to flood through me as I wonder what scene I will find. Two ladies in ermine-collared evening coats scuttle past us, eager to escape.

Daddy is not properly dressed: a shirt and black trousers, but no dinner jacket. His white hair is sticking out and his face is tomato red. My first thought is that he is very drunk; my second, that this is one of his wild moods induced by morphine or cocaine. Following that, or somewhere deep inside me, is a strange glad feeling of relief, that he is not as sick and feeble as he was yesterday and seems to have recovered some fight. But this thought feels like the wrong one, so I rush towards him and to the other man – the first officer, a very large man, Irish, with a huge beard and tiny eyes – who is trying to restrain Daddy.

Daddy is bellowing, shouting at the backs of the departing ladies: 'Whores! Whores! How dare they try to eject me? Whores, all of them!'

The first officer, used to his word being God, roars right back: 'Sir – sir! If you would moderate your damn language . . .'

Daddy replies, 'Damn and blast the ladies! I paid my fare and I'm allowed on any part of the ship I choose . . .'

'I'm afraid those are the rules, sir . . .' This is the second officer. More emollient. A tall fellow, shiny hair, shiny face. He tries to step in, to calm the pair of them. A chair tumbles over as Daddy backs towards the window. The cabin boy looks hopelessly at me, as if to say, 'Do something!'

Rats. I step forward. This is not a moment for cowardice. I try to put my arm on Daddy's, but he shakes it off. 'Daddy,' I say as firmly as I can, 'you're not well.' He glares at me. 'Come back to your berth – you need to rest . . .'

He sways and his colour is high, his eyes rheumy. The fight goes out of him, as if someone has cut the cord on his spine. His legs buckle.

'Pamela, little Pixie. Miss Smith. Light of my life. If only I had been a *true* father to you . . . How I wish that I might have been . . .'

I pull the chair Daddy kicked over upright and pat the cushion as if dealing with a halfwit. He sinks onto it.

I put my arm around him and speak in a lower tone: 'Hush, hush, Daddy, that's better. Let's get you back to your cabin. I think the ladies who objected . . . or the first officer is suggesting that – well – you need a dinner jacket to be in the first-class state room . . .'

'That is not the issue, miss.'

I hear in the first officer's voice a great desire to tell me something. One of those self-important people whose small joy it is to give you bad news. I glance around the room: there are only the beautiful velvet chairs, the chandeliers, the mahogany tables. All other guests have hurried to exit the scene.

'I'm sorry to tell you that your father has a debt to the company for his ticket which he has not honoured. He – and you – will be moved to saloon class for the rest of the voyage. Your father will not be welcome in the first-class lounge nor any of the other first-class areas again, miss.'

He stares at me and at a now crumpled, defeated Daddy.

Daddy says weakly, 'My daughter is a – famous artist! My chequebook is as good as the next man's!'

'Laughably untrue, Daddy,' I say. I try to help him up from the chair, but he resists.

Now that he is subdued, the second officer, Shiny Fellow, steps up, offering a strong arm. Shiny gives me a sympathetic look, the only one I've seen throughout this grim occasion. 'Allow me, miss,' he says, and with a brisk movement manages to drag Daddy to standing. He then takes one arm firmly, and I the other. Between us we guide a grumbling Daddy out of the room, the way you would steer a very old person around a country park. I glance back. The first officer is watching with his arms folded, blowing out his cheeks.

I manage to get Daddy to his cabin, and he collapses like a heap of clothes on his tiny bed. I take off his shoes, wondering what else I can do, and then how on earth to pack all his things to move. The second officer leaves us, muttering that Daddy 'should sleep it off', and that he will send a cabin boy to help us in the morning.

Then I go next door to my own berth, peel back the thin navy blanket, staring at the tight white envelope of the sheets, and start tugging at them, intending to climb in and go to sleep. But the queerest thing is happening to me. My heartbeat has started up a full-blown cacophony. A furnace is blazing in me. I leap up. 'Stupid fat pig!' I shout. 'I'd like to – punch his nose!'

And before I know it I'm scrunching up my face, and throwing pillows on the floor and gritting my teeth so hard my jaw aches, and tossing a tin cup of water at the porthole, where it splashes with a satisfying mess, and shouting, 'Pigs, pigs, all of you! Ellen! The cabin boy! Mrs Redgrove! Mrs Jones!' It's odd whose face pops into my mind, and who enrages me further, and whom I'd most like to smash awful flat with a baseball bat. If Daddy were to wake from his liquor slumber and show his face right now, well – I'd smash that too. He is the most infuriating of them all!

Then I lie back on my cot and sob. Stupid, *stupid* Daddy and all his schemes and all those ladies with their stupid bosoms!

It doesn't matter how loudly I sob. It doesn't matter how unladylike my temper is and what Mama would have to say about it. Mama is not here to scold me, and nor is Nurse Delphine. No one can hear me in here, with all the clanking sounds of the ship and the engine and all. Daddy is flat out next door. I'm on my own. Our dismissal from the world of first-class folk has been well and truly achieved.

I am the Father, I carry a Crux ansata for my sceptre.

(I like to use words understood only by those who revere me.)

Right now, I'm half baked. Later, there will be a bomb in my other hand.

I have ransacked seas, slicked oil, fried the earth, striven to tear the veil of Isis,

and still I rule, everywhere, in the world.

Soon even my soft red slippers will be gone, changed to cuisses, and greaves.

The next morning, Daddy is unabashed. He acts as if he barely remembers the incident. We are moved to saloon class – various crew members either trundling cases or standing watching as we pass curious passengers on deck, wondering where we are heading. (Downwards! To Hell!) We complete our journey there, in Hades, and it is hot and smells of sewage. Daddy drinks whisky – a bottle purloined from 'upstairs' – and laughs periodically but is becalmed, the wind dropped out of his sail.

Stuck and strangely still. I keep my attention fixed on my drawing.

Daddy's extravagant unconcern continues once we arrive home. We are escorted from the ship with the other lower-class passengers. He immediately lifts our bags and shouts for a cabbie. He tips the cabbie generously. We return to the apartment in Brooklyn – fall has descended in our absence, sad, naked trees and streets of wet leaves – and we discover from Elsie, one of the two staff who have remained, that the bailiffs came while we were away and took various items of value: the chaise-longue, an antique dresser, a small elephant-legged table, the silver cigar box. Very rum choices! Thank God none of my drawing materials, paints, my easel or desk have gone, but it seems the horrible fellows opened the door to my bedroom, thought it a storeroom or bedroom to a maniac, and shut it firmly again. My beloved pink velvet chair and cushions, tea-stained as they are, remain.

Daddy tugs at his beard, then goes into a fit of coughing. 'Teddy,' he says between coughs. 'I will write to Theodore.'

'Uncle Teddy? How bad is it . . .?'

He waves away my question and disappears into his study, and I hear him shout in a strangled voice: 'Damn! They took my writing desk!' Then a thump as if he's hit the side table with his fist.

I go to find him envelopes and paper and some of the lovely ink he bought me at Cornelissen's. That day, the candy-store abundance, already feels like a dream. How I long to ask him properly, to sit down with him: 'What money do we have? Is the apartment we're living in even ours?' (I believe we are renting, but of course

Daddy has chosen not to share this with me.) 'What about the sales from my paintings, the sales from Mr Macbeth, the deals with Mr Sabine Baring-Gould and his publisher? What about the arrangements made with Miss Terry and Mr Irving's manager, Mr Stoker – will I be paid for those costume designs, and surely, if so, they might advance some of my fee to help us out?'

After I've found the letter-writing materials (hastily unpacking my trunk) and talked with Elsie a little in the kitchen, I resolve to ask Daddy about all of this, striding into his study with some barley soup that Elsie has made (having quickly taken stock of his weakness and blue-shadowed skin – her dismay on seeing him when we first arrived was clear).

He is bent over his side table – now in the place his beloved writing desk always was – in such a strange collapsed position. He looks like an insect, all legs and arms. I hesitate to approach him, take one step, then a deep breath. There is a curious smell in the room. I feel as if someone else is in here with us.

I put the tray with the bowl of soup and glass of beer on his dresser. I take another step towards Daddy. I feel whoever it was, whatever it was, depart.

'Daddy . . .?' My voice comes out peculiar, not my voice at all. I'm aware of my heart beating fast. I'm holding myself still and can smell my own sweat and fear. I hear the grandfather clock in the hall: *tick, tick, tick.*

I don't know how long I stand there. I know – because of Mama, because my eighteen-year-old self already opened that door – what has happened. I just don't want to know. If I stand here longer, it might not be true.

Finally, I step closer. The second I touch him, his body collapses from the very odd, unnatural arrangement it is in, propped up somehow, and now, like a lamp folding, his head slumps onto the table, knocking a glass paperweight to the floor.

The thud on the carpet brings Elsie running – 'Oh, Miss Smith!' She claps a hand to her mouth and screams.

Elsie rushes forward to touch Daddy, to feel for a pulse. I cannot bear to touch him but in order not to seem queer I do all the right things, following her lead. I put the palm of my hand on his forehead. His eyes are staring, his mouth in the same strange round shape that Mama's formed, suddenly like a dark, unpleasant cavern, not a mouth at all. My shock is very great. I feel his pulse. *Oh, Daddy. Please don't leave me now, all alone. This is too unfair, after Mama! After all the unanswered questions! Please, Daddy. Please don't leave your little Pixie when she is just starting out on her grown-up life!*

His wrist is surprisingly cool and a little stiff. No answer comes from him.

I am older than the Pope, and hey, I existed before him.

Don't mistake me for him just because my hand is raised in a sign.

I am not religion; I am the mode of its expression.

Neither am I the prince of occult doctrine. I'm here to assist the High Priestess.

I am a marvellous rummy recourse to the querent too. That's you.

My priestly ministers wear albs and kneel before me, but I imagine you'd prefer to stand.

In the days that follow, I pray to the Moon Angel to join Daddy. I feel like an insect crushed beneath a great weight: I can hardly move my arms and legs for the pain I'm in.

The hours and days and weeks merge. I feel as if I'm living in some fat grey cloud. Perhaps smoke. Sometimes I think I smell the smoke from Daddy's cigar and the smell is so strong, so real, that I look around me. Perhaps my prayers have been answered and I'm in the Moon Garden with him. Uncle Teddy appears, and Cousin Mary, and some dregs of other Brooklyn relatives I barely remember. Uncle Teddy takes charge of the funeral. (A flurry of winter snow: red berries on a white-spattered coffin. A robin peeping, relentlessly cheerful. Uncle Teddy arranges the hymns. He does not remember that Daddy was in the Swedenborg Church and will now meet Mama in Heaven, and I have no voice to correct him.) I learn that Daddy had a heart attack. A weak heart that *just caved in* after Corinne went. (*What about me*, I want to shout – *I'm still here!*)

Papers, letters arriving. And blow after blow: Daddy's accounts. It seems our brownstone is rented, and a great deal of rent is overdue. Debts, further amounts, impossible sums pile up. I discover from Uncle Teddy that Daddy was bankrupted once (in Manchester, England) and that's why we went to New York and then Jamaica, to get as far away as possible. With both sets of grandparents gone, there is no one left to help me. Uncle Teddy has bailed out his brother many times and now the kitty is empty. Uncle Teddy is loud and ever-present, bumptious and enormous in every space and every room during the arranging of things, the comings and goings in Daddy's study, the dismissal of Elsie, the packing-up of Daddy's things. There is the offer made with a sad shake of the head (as if he knows it is no offer at all) that I might come to live with him in his apartment, a sort of 'help' to him. Or other suggestions: a governess to the children of some Brooklyn folk?

'There is my art,' I manage to mutter. 'Daddy arranged some commissions for me. I will . . . With your help, I will . . . When I feel better I might . . .'

Uncle Teddy nods, supervising another great trunk leaving the house, to end up – where? If only I had more understanding of the way things work, of what Uncle Teddy has had to do to pay off Daddy's debts, to ensure that bailiffs and debtors do not follow me around for the rest of my life, so that I might start, as he promises, with 'one hundred and fifty dollars and a clean slate'. This is what Uncle Teddy is offering me.

'And a *husband*, Pamela! Art is very well, but a young lady, even one as odd-looking as you – or perhaps *especially* such a gal – needs a husband. You can't go among polite folk and hawk your wares! That was why Charles was fixing things *for* you, and now another man must take over.'

'Thank you, Uncle Teddy, I will bear that in mind.'

In among this – the worst moments of my life – a letter comes. It is a letter of condolence from Miss Ellen Terry! She addresses me as *Dearest Pixie Pamela* and she signs off as *Ellen*! I imagine she heard from Daddy's contacts in England – perhaps Mr Sabine Baring-Gould. Or, well – there have been obituaries in the *New York Tribune* and also the *New York Times*. After I'd read the one in the *Brooklyn Daily Eagle* noting that the passing of Charles Edward Smith, aged fifty-three, was 'a severe bereavement for his daughter as the companionship of the two was very close and affectionate', my heart pinched with such a sharp pain and my head boiled with so much inexplicable rage that I could not read the ones in the other newspapers, and asked Uncle Teddy to burn them. I suppose everyone knows he's died, and I'm alone.

The entire Lyceum Theatre company is on its way to America. Ellen writes: *Please don't forget we do want you to join us for the* Robespierre *tour – we need your* industry! *We open at the Knickerbocker Theatre, and*

Laurence – Henry's son – will be with us. Henry will play Mathias in The Bells *in Brooklyn* . . . Ellen has added in a dark blotting ink: *If you don't feel up to the entire tour, do join us in Philadelphia . . . and we will of course give you a payment up front, if that helps, as I know that your father's sudden passing may have meant there was no time for him to make proper arrangements for you.*

I kiss her letter. The grey cloud lifts a little and I feel myself reviving, blood flowing in my veins again. *One hundred and fifty dollars and a clean slate.* I wonder how long that will last. And a husband – ha! I can honestly say that I would rather jump over the side of a ship than take a husband (I somehow feel Daddy knew that about me, without us ever speaking of it), and Uncle Teddy's suggestion has acted as the most extraordinary cattle prod for shifting me out of my mood. Darn stupid man! Marriage surely cannot be the only option for someone of my talents?

And dear, dear, Ellen – dear ET! Even I, as young and idiotic as Uncle Teddy believes, can read in those lines the unexpected modernity, tact and kindness of the great woman's attitude towards money. Perhaps her own boldness in living the life she's created. (I do remember her talking a little about supporting her son, Ted, as he is rather lax about the children he has.) Utterly vulgar to speak of money in polite society, especially for the English, especially for a lady – yet for her to remember that an implicit promise of payment has been made and might matter to me an awful lot at such a time . . . Extraordinary! My flinty heart plims, as Mr Thomas Hardy might say.

I write to Cousin Mary telling her to stop worrying about me. I kneel in prayer and tell Daddy to wait for me – I will meet him in the Moon Garden one day when time permits, with Mama too – and that I have work to do in the world. I will never be happy unless I give this small talent of mine my everything and see where it will lead me. *Art is long, but life is short,* Ellen is fond of saying. I feel sure I have Daddy and Mama's blessing, and though I'm mighty mad at them both for leaving me here all alone to suffer so, I understand.

    I set about making a beautiful gift for Ellen: a little wooden box, perfectly round, decorated with flowers and inscribed with her initials on the lid.

First I'm a young man, struck by Cupid's arrow, making my choice between a fair and a dark woman, one a maid and one a mother.

(But this is the French deck; I can change that? Perhaps I am both women, choosing each other.)

I am closing my eyes, opening arms, pouring down my influences.

This is the card of human love, the way, the truth, the life.

Behind the woman is the tree of knowledge. A knowledge snaking towards me.

A choice I have not made. Yet.

And so my life with the Lyceum begins, and it so chaotic, and busy, and full of people and noises and thumpings and buildings and packings and unpackings and sewing and making and constructing; and baskets and baskets of flowers (everywhere Ellen goes, there are flowers); and the yapping and intrusions of Fussie, Mr Irving's dog; and the ever-present behatted Walter, the dresser, with his cat-like whiskers; and Laurence the lanky son of Mr Irving, eating chocolate and reading Tolstoy with a dark expression; and I'm drawing and drawing every moment that I'm not finding a hat, or some feathers, or pinning a dress, or stapling a cloak, or sewing ties to a curtain or pinning a bodice, or being an extra in the crowd scene of *The Bells* and trying to keep Fussie from running onto the stage, or discussing with the Brammy Joker my illustrations for the souvenir booklet of the tour, and being surrounded by so many people and so much to do means that *all* of me is absorbed, and there is no longer even the tiniest opening in me for melancholy. (Later, *later*, I will mourn, I tell myself.)

Practical considerations such as where to live are forgotten, because I'm living on a train or in lodgings or in a bar room with the rest of the cast, or running an errand for Ellen or sitting at whatever table I can find, drawing or sewing or fixing something. I've packed everything I need into one huge carpet bag and it feels good to live like this: light and free. What is happening to all my 'stuff'? Gone, gone, all of it, along with Daddy and Mama's stuff, and along with them my life in Jamaica too, my childhood, my time as a daughter, all of it *gone*! Like the feathers on a dandelion clock.

It is in the city of Philadelphia, during one of the moments when I'm working on something unrelated to the Lyceum for a change (a watercolour I plan to send to Mr Macbeth for his gallery, in the hope that he might sell it), that I experience for the first time in a while the strange shrinking experience. The feeling of disappearing down to the size of a caterpillar. Thumbelina. The dizzy, out-of-body feeling – but it takes a different shape this time. Laurence is playing the piano. His legs are so long that they fold up in front of him, like a crane fly. He is always smoking, and his are the Jamaican cigars that remind me of Daddy, with their powerful leaf and spice smell. We are in a bar, after a performance, and it is late.

There was a woman reading cards for the cast earlier: the Lenormand deck. I'd never heard of it before; it's something from France. The fortune-teller was an old wrinkled French lady who smelled of aniseed, and from what she said she attaches herself to travelling folk, circuses, theatres and puppet-players and had travelled on a train from Louisiana. I watched her with great interest. (Was she a Gypsy? I don't think so, but she'd wound a scarf round her head and wore many beads, in a way that might make people think she was. Like my Gelukiezanger act. I observed her carefully, resolving to make a few modifications.) Laurence translated for her when she only knew the French word for something. There were sudden bursts of laughter – 'This is rider, messenger, he say you will find love in a form *magnifique*', that kind of thing – and once, at something I didn't hear, there was a horrified shout. (The Brammy Joker, looming large over everyone, with his big Irish voice.)

Now the noisy crowd has mostly gone. They must have gone to bed. I don't know why I didn't go with them, except that I was working on my watercolour in a corner of the bar with a candle for lighting and enjoying it too much to stop.

Laurence is so tall and bendy, with curly dark hair and skinny limbs, as if he is a vine that grows along a wall. (He has a habit of walking close to walls – perhaps this is where my impression comes from.) Anyone can see that he wishes his father would notice him more, and when he plays the piano it is always sad.

He begins playing some music by Bach. He pushes a little pince-nez onto his nose, and closes his eyes. The sweetness in him, how he plays the liquid notes, sweeps into me. It's as if a shutter clicks back and leaves a hole in the air about an inch square, and through it I see something. I smell the cigars again, as if Daddy is beside me. I am in a spell of sound. What I see is vivid and clear, alive in front of my eyes. A blue sea, the colour of English cornflowers, with a boat on the surface, but in the sea several women, sirens. I rub my eyes. Then I close them. Each slow note on the piano soaks into me – so slow, so slow, a trickling pain. Why does Laurence play with such melancholy?

Did I hear from Ellen that something sad happened to Laurence, not very long ago? Each note seems to drip. One of the women I'm seeing is sleeping; she looks like Edy. Another sits atop the foaming waves, with Gypsy earrings and a billowing scarf – Nurse Delphine? And then a passionate woman rises, with great force, from the frothy water. A little like Ellen. I fumble for my sketchbook and my watercolours and turn the page to find a blank one. I sketch with pencil at first but give that up so that I can dip my brush in a glass of water and paint the colours quickly. The blue sea, the little boat, the women, brilliant washes of colour. Exactly as I see them, or rather *hear* them – because it feels as if the notes, the mournful, slow little notes, are making the pictures.

I paint frantically but also dreamily, as if my hand is guided by another's . . . I dot a white star in the sky, and then one after another. I feel tears might be streaming down Laurence's cheeks. Or mine? I taste salt. It might be the sea . . . It might be that one of the women – as the notes blur and wash together – the sleeping one, looks so like Mama, or even *her* Mama (Pamelia, my namesake!); or – well, now I have drawn her she looks more like the maid I saw briefly at Edy's studio . . .

Whoever they are, they are vivid and true. I see them distinctly. As the music swells, my heart aches with love for them, for the women in the picture, the nymphs of my life so far. But who is that central one, who sits with her back to me?

Then Laurence lifts his fingers from the keys and ceases playing, sits sighing and stretching and running his hands through his hair, which has flopped into his eyes. Pushing his pince-nez back up his nose where it has slipped. As he does so, the shutter clicks closed again. The women and the cornflower-blue sea dissolve. We are back in an old wood-panelled bar room in Philadelphia, with an out-of-tune piano and a glass of murky water in front of me and only the bartender for company. Laurence stands up, finds another of his favourite Jamaican cigars in a box on the table, chews off the end and lights it. I wonder if it is the smell – the smell that so conjures Daddy – which brought the spell of women and the vision of the sea to me.

I look down at what I've painted. Something melancholy and queer – probably no good for the Macbeth Gallery at all, with ethereal women and white stars, a billowing wind and suggestion of movement. The vision has gone. I stare at the picture for a while. *What made me do that? Where did that come from?*

Laurence strides over to me, ruffles my hair. I wasn't wrong: in his eyes I see tears.

'Edy's the better player,' he says. 'Get her to play that for you. She could have been – you know – *somebody*, if it weren't for her arthritis. I'm ham-fisted. Useless. You ask my father.' He peers at me, taking a deep draw on his cigar. 'I say – are you all right?'

'Yes,' I stutter. 'Just the Bach. Seemed to wrap me in a—'

'Well, you're grieving, aren't you? I heard about your father from Ellen. I'm terribly sorry for your loss and all that, but – say, mind if I take a look?'

I cannot think how to say no. Reluctantly I return my paintbrush to its glass and open the page in the sketchbook to show him. He squints. I hand him the wine bottle with the candle stuck in it, taking care not to drip wax onto the paper. The room has grown so much darker than when I began. I can hardly see what I did myself.

He pushes the pince-nez further up and then crinkles his nose. Hands the sketchbook back to me. 'I prefer your humorous stuff. Your Stoker as a bat and all that. This is all rather, you know . . . Is it William Blake *mystical* or something?' I don't want to hear his criticism, so I reach for the sketchbook and blow on it, hoping to dry the paint quickly. But Laurence is more sensitive than I've given him credit for and, suddenly awkward, he adds: 'Sorry, I know nothing about art. Nothing about anything at all, as it happens. Don't listen to a word I say.'

His self-deprecation catches me by surprise. Not a quality his father has. Nor many men I've met so far. Most of them are pigs! He puts a nervous hand to his chest, right where his heart is. The gesture brings a picture to me that is disturbing. I shake my head to dislodge it. A sadness for him: a feeling that he has some sorrowful pain.

My expression must give me away, as Laurence suddenly straightens and shuts like a clam, saying, 'Well, I think I should turn in. Early start tomorrow. Philadelphia. Rum old place, isn't it? All the clapboard and the Quakers. Like Salem but without the witches. Unless we count *you*, little Pixie: I think you're half fairy but sister to a witch, aren't you?'

His smile is affectionate again. His mouth is the shape of a segment of orange, a little weak at the edges.

'Goodnight,' I say to him, and then, from nowhere: 'I'm sorry if my painting disturbed you.'

But he seems reluctant to leave. He is a night owl. I've often noticed how he lingers after a show, wanting the dresser Walter or one of the extras to hang around with him. After I've spoken, he pauses. He waves a whisky glass towards me and when – after a hesitation – I nod, he signals to the bartender to pour me one. A woman drinking whisky, at night, in a bar in Philadelphia, alone with a man! I feel racy. I act casual and stifle a yawn.

'How does one know if one is any good?' Laurence asks, carrying the drinks back to the round table I'm sitting at and setting them down on it. 'Do you? Do you feel you're a good – *artist*?' We – and the bartender – are now the only people in here.

I don't know how to reply. This is exactly the question that keeps me awake, and what's more, I feel that I have no one, no teacher or mentor or fellow artists, to advise me.

When I look down at my drink, swig and then pull a face, he bursts out laughing, asking suddenly: 'What do you think of Ellen? Are you in the adoration crowd like everyone else?'

'Oh yes,' I begin. 'She has given me a big chance at the Lyceum – I'm sure it was she who persuaded Mr Stoker to employ me.'

'My mother hates her,' Laurence says, leaning in rather intensely to stare at me in the gloom.

'Well, that's . . . Well, of course . . .' What to say here? The word I'm seeking is 'natural'. Or 'expected'. No matter that in America, on this tour and no doubt on previous ones, Mr Irving and Ellen stay in a separate hotel, I am sure it has been understood in English circles that they were in love for a very long time; but now he has another . . . (I can't quite bring myself to use Daddy's word, which would be 'mistress', I suppose) in Mrs Aria, so Ellen is deposed.

'Ellen's quite old, of course,' I say instead, and this cheers Laurence up.

'I reckon *she* always knew she was good. Long before this ridiculous level of fame. I feel sure that as a small girl – you know she acted as a child, don't you? – she just walked on stage and knew she had it. Whatever *it* is. Some of us work so damn hard and have nothing much to show for it.'

He looks so like a younger version of his father, but without the pep. He runs his hand through his dark curls again and takes a bigger slug of the whisky. Mine is burning my throat and making me swimmy.

'I remember reading that your translation of *Robespierre* is . . . you know, top-notch . . .' I try saying. 'I mean, I don't speak much French so I can't read the original, but—'

'You don't read French? Where are you from, exactly? You don't talk like an American.'

'I guess it's hard to say. I was born in England. But my parents were Americans.'

'Were they white? I've heard said . . .'

'Yes, my parents are both white folk! Why does everyone . . .? My family travelled. We lived in London and Manchester. I was admitted to Pratt – you know, the art institution in New York – when I was quite young, fifteen. And then Daddy had some . . . financial troubles and we moved to . . . Jamaica . . .'

I start to twist and turn in my seat, feeling a sweat breaking out over my face. Why does talking about my origins always bring this discomfort, this prickly heat? But I needn't have worried. Laurence, like so many young men, is unobservant of the moods of others. Especially young women of no discernible beauty. His orange-segment mouth is downturned once more and, speaking into his glass, he murmurs: 'Do you ever wonder . . .' His hand goes to his chest again, and his eyes darken. 'I had a shooting accident. That's how they described it. Did you hear about that?'

'No –' But I realise I must have done, somehow, and that's why the thought crossed my mind earlier. Or why the brown mood Laurence gives off affects me so.

While I'm arranging a reply, he says, 'Do you ever wonder what it's like to die? I mean, what it will be like when we die. When we're not here at all. That long empty unfathomable sleep. Nothingness, darkness, for thousands of years. How can anything – reviews, appraisals, accomplishments, art . . . What will any of that matter?'

I understand in a rush. The shooting wasn't an accident at all. Now my heart is pounding, in a panic, a terror rising, and the wild strange sensation of shrinking and flying and being outside my own body is making me giddy, combined with the whisky, the after-show exhilaration, the lack of sleep, the bizarre situation of being in a candlelit dark bar with a young handsome man at such a late hour, but alone, *alone* with no one to guide me, rudderless, flying, floating . . .

'But what about – Heaven?' I squeak. 'The Heaven we create by our good deeds here on Earth. I will be glad to join – my mother and my father and my grandparents and . . .' I know my voice sounds panicky. I push the whisky from me, unsure of what I dare to say.

He glances at me and then quickly looks away. It is not a kind look. He is fiddling with a gold pocket watch, drawing it from his pocket to stare at it – I happen to know his father gave it to him, and gave one to Ellen's son Ted too – and seeming to gather himself back together.

'Oh, I'd forgotten. Edy did mention it. Weren't you raised in the New Church? Swedenborg and all? And your father. Very recent. Like I said, I'm sorry. You believe in angels, isn't that it, and – what is it again?'

I am not about to discuss the New Church with him and so I rather primly push my glass again, this time towards him, and suggest he might like to finish it for me. He downs it in one gulp and then, to my surprise, places his hand over mine.

'Your face is awfully sweet,' he says.

No one has ever said such a thing. I feel myself blushing.

'I know I'm drunk, but – do you mind if I kiss you?' he slurs.

Nor that. The blush threatens to burst my face into flames. 'Oh, *do* kiss me,' I want to say, but I think that would not be the right answer. I close my eyes and slightly pucker my mouth.

He laughs. 'Not here!' He stands up. He is swaying. His handsomeness is very dark. His pince-nez is now in his top pocket and without it his eyes are the violet colours of a mussel shell, not the blue of a cornflower.

'Shall I walk you to your room, Miss Pixie, or will that be – unseemly?'

'My room is very close and I – well, who is there to judge us?'

I don't know what my face is doing, but Laurence suddenly leans close and says: 'Where are they, then, all these souls of the dead? If they still existed, wouldn't it be awfully crowded here?'

'I – Mr Irving. Laurence. Please don't quiz me about the Church. When I paint, I know the answer. The rest of the time I'm as dumb as everyone else.'

He stares at me for a long while. Then he nods, holds out his arm and, linking mine, chaperones me to the door. If there were eyes in the bar, I know they'd be on us. Every step feels significant, and I watch my little boots making them. I feel I am walking the plank, like a pirate's victim.

The boarding-house I'm staying in is a clapboard building right opposite. Laurence steers me towards it. He is courteous, but also addled with whisky. I cannot wait for the kiss to come; I hope he hasn't forgotten it.

I fumble with my door, praying the landlady has not locked it against me. We glance quickly along the street before I squeak: 'Come in!' His mood has shifted slightly, and I wonder if he is having second thoughts. I dart out a hand and tug at his lapels. 'Quickly! Before anyone sees you!' And so I am pulling him into the corridor and then opening the door to my bedroom, my heart pounding, thinking: *At last, at last, I will be kissed!*

On my bed, all over it, are sketches. And they are mainly cartoon versions of Laurence aboard the SS *Menominee*. The nearest one, recently finished, is Laurence with his dark curls and a sweet expression, playing the lute, while his father squints at the piano. He is wearing crazy tartan socks, and shoes with buckles, and a fancy scarf. And I am lying at his feet, legs akimbo, admiring him.

I go to sweep up the pictures, but Laurence stops me. 'Oh, I say! Look at this!'

He picks up another cartoon of himself, this time in a long red velvet cloak and cummerbund, his expression very self-regarding, wearing his pince-nez, seated, looking into a mirror, surrounded by flowers and notes and gifts, and another of him with a stack of Jamaican cigars and books and carrying a theatrical sword, and next to him Ellen wearing a hat called 'HMS *VANITY*'.

'Oh, these are *marvellous*!' he breathes.

I am astonished. I'm trying not to let him see the drawings in case he is offended, but he acts awful enraptured and in the end I relent. He laughs uproariously. 'Why, I prefer these to your – lugubrious ones. What a natural joker you are! Look at Walter! He looks like a sea lion! And all the cigars I'm carrying. And who is that tiny person sitting on my sword? The one I'm carrying with me?'

'Well, it's your . . . I don't know the word. It's another version of you. A tiny one who appears sometimes. I mean, mostly you are this one' – I show him again the picture of him, sweet-faced, playing with his father. He holds up the bedside lamp to study it. 'But you can also be . . .' Do I tell him about the shrinking I experience, do I dare ask if he ever feels it too?

'Oh, Pixie! These are *glorious*! This, *this* is what you should be doing, surely? Have you shown them to anyone . . . to Ellen? Look at this one! Is that Bram, singing? He does look awfully strained when he sings; you've captured that perfectly. Like a man in the water closet.'

'No! I haven't shown Ellen – or anyone. I mean, she – Look at that one, she's pouring out a teapot marked "Money" . . .! My cousin Mary told me I was rude. I ought to be careful not to hurt people's feelings with my – humour.'

Laurence turns to me then, beaming, and takes my face in both hands to tilt me towards him for a kiss. Full on the mouth, his lips hot and rather whisky-tasting. I close my eyes and think hard about whether I like it or not. It's slightly mushy. Strange. Is there something I should be doing back? I also note how some other parts of me seem to be pulled towards the kiss. Lower parts. As if I'm a big drawstring bag and now all of me is tugging towards my mouth.

He pulls his face away. I thought the kiss was usually the start of something else – it always is in books – but instead he is reaching for his hat, one hand on the door.

'Darling Pixie. You are very, *very* sweet. And very talented. But far too innocent! You know, someone could take awful advantage of you, a girl alone, with so little . . . What is it . . . With no guard up! You're entirely unlike other girls.'

'Is that a bad thing?'

He's opening my door, gingerly looking up and down the corridor.

'I like you far too much to ruin your repper for an evening's fun. But thank you – you have cheered me up immensely!' And with that, and a little peck on my nose (as if I were a *baby*!), he is gone.

★★★

It turns out that the fortune-teller is staying in the same lodgings as me (the lower-priced ones), and I see her at breakfast, looking awful wrinkled and her forehead naked, like an old walnut shell, without her trappings of drapes and scarves and beads. She nods to me but does not want to talk. I recognise her for the performer she is, and this morning the performance is over. She orders a strong black coffee and some biscuits – what Americans call biscuits, of course, not the English ones: she is from Louisiana – and then sits by herself, smoking.

After a while she brings something out of her bag. She unwinds a purple scarf from it: her deck of Lenormand cards. She places them on the table in front of her. Now this catches my eye. She is alone. I feel sure I'm invisible, as I so often am – she considers me unimportant, not one of the Lyceum players or the director or the Terry-Irving clan. More like Walter or Sally the dressers, perhaps. I'm allowed into the hallowed circle, but my status is ambiguous: I might be a servant, or even some kind of mascot.

I have been sketching – some drawings I did on waking, of Laurence as I remembered him, looking willowy and languid and melancholic, playing the piano – and now, in order to watch her carefully, I bring the sketchbook out and some pencils and pretend to continue.

She is very intent on her Lenormand cards. She lines them up, she turns them over, she tuts, she sips her coffee, she stubs and lights another cigarette. Agitated. But what fascinates me, what I realise I'm seeing is: *she's reading them for herself.* This is not a performance. She considers herself alone, after all (me being Nobody). She *believes* in what she is doing. Anyone can see how absorbed she is, muttering and huffing and doing that French thing of pursing the lips and blowing (a bit like Nurse Delphine when she kisses her teeth).

My own breakfast of bacon and pancakes and maple syrup is congealing on my plate. The orange juice is sour and dry in my mouth. How I long to go over and ask the funny little French woman: 'What are you doing? What do you see? What on earth is it that a card can tell you, so random and meaningless and just a chance thing, just some images that someone else has drawn and created?' I half stand up, meaning to approach her, and at that moment the landlady appears at my elbow, shouting (she is a deaf), 'More bacon? Another pancake?'

I shake my head, miming that my stomach is full. But, defeated, I sit back down.

'Shall I fix you another coffee and cream?' the landlady shouts. *Yes,* I nod.

The fortune-teller glances up, alarmed by the loud voice of our hostess. She darts a smile to me and furtively gathers up the cards, sliding them into her bag.

I find myself thinking of them as if they were a bomb about to go off, something dangerous, or perhaps a live thing like a monkey. They shouldn't be lying in her bag!

She sips her coffee and stares into the distance. She is pretending not to see me, but I know now that she does.

Finally, she succumbs and walks over to my table. I think for a moment she's on her way back to her room – this is a very small dining room and she has to squeeze her plump figure to get past me – but she pauses and says, 'Est-ce que vous voudriez que je vous tire les cartes?'

'I'm sorry, my French is awful bad . . .'

'You want une consultation de cartes, non? I can do it. Only a dollar.'

'A dollar!'

'Juste un petit tableau. You can buy me un café, no pay.'

She acts awful smug, as if she's caught me out – caught my desire in watching her. True, I suppose. She pulls out a chair and sits down opposite me, as if we have agreed. Up close, her eyes are a little watery, and her hair, I see, is dyed a flat shade of brown. I close the sketchbook, placing the pencil carefully on top of it. The landlady brings my coffee and I order one for the French lady. Her name is Madame Balle. She reaches in her bag once the huge white cup of coffee is set before her. I find my heart is beating fast. I don't know if I like the idea of having my cards read . . .

Madame Balle hands the deck to me, saying, 'It is good, you will be . . . enjoy?'

Damn woman! What to do? We are now on our own in the breakfast room; Laurence and the others must be either sleeping off the night's performance – that would be Ellen's habit, although she is of course staying elsewhere; she brings her own fold-out daybed with embroidered pillows, and her cat has its wicker basket – or up early to ready the set for the matinee. On tour, Henry Irving always stays in lodgings that will allow Fussie the dog. He and Ellen used to use the excuse of their animals to disguise the fact that they would be staying in the same hotel together, but now it has become a habit.

I don't know if I want to see Laurence or not. And now I do wonder if he will show up in some way, in my hand.

The Lenormand pack the woman has handed me is slim, and seems about half the size of a normal one. The cards are very soft and creased, well used, with a greasy sheen, but despite myself I find the images interesting, and the familiar simple symbols – a cross, a coffin, a bouquet – intriguing. Turning each over in my hand, I'm reminded of a regular deck that Ellen has, which her son Ted designed for her, with roses and her initials on the back. A desire forms at once to design better ones. A better deck of cards – my *own*. I begin shuffling, each card slipping effortlessly with the feel of something handled as often as the sea smooths a pebble on the beach. My heartbeat quietens. After a while, the pictures start to leap out at me. Somewhere, I hear a soft murmur of voices.

Madame Balle coughs. She slurps her coffee noisily. She scratches her nose. Finally she says, with some irritation, 'Now you give back cards to me!'

I hand them over.

'The young man last night, he is your . . .?'

'No, no, just a – I don't know, he's actually a writer, a translator, the son of Mr Irving, he's not –'

I don't know what to say here, and I'm cross. *Obviously* this is how she does it. Just deduces information about you from observation and strings it together. In the middle of this, the deaf landlady interrupts us to take away the plate of half-eaten pancake and the maple syrup and the milk jug. She hovers, but with a quick flick of her hand Madame Balle makes it clear she must leave.

'It is a *petit* deck,' Madame Balle says. 'Madame Lenormand – you have heard of her?' I shake my head. On the back of the cards a blue owl stares at me. 'You are artist, with the Lyceum, yes?'

Easily deduced. My hand falls protectively to my sketchbook, but I nod in agreement.

With sweeping gestures, she spreads the deck across the breakfast table, moving doilies and glasses and a stray napkin out of the way to make a smooth surface.

'The cards are burning to speak to you! They are crying out!' she announces, with one eye on the large clock on the wall. She selects just three cards and flicks them over.

'Bon – this is very good . . .' Unexpectedly, she beams at me. Her teeth are pretty, white and neat.

I stare at the cards.

Anchor. Book. Fish.

'Oh, you will go far! You will . . . Poisson for this last card, that is very good. We read it like a story, see?'

As she is speaking, I find I am decoding the cards myself. A whoosh of delight as I realise how easy it is. Anchor: that must surely mean I'm anchored to something, grounded; that must refer to my life in Jamaica and with Daddy and Mama. Or something to do with the many, many sea journeys I've made. Or – could it mean tied down in some way? At the moment I'm wandering, I'm on tour; is the card suggesting that I need to drop anchor somewhere? (Where? Surely not here in Philadelphia.) Book: well, obviously that makes sense – working on my books, my artworks, drawing illustrations for *The Golden Vanity* and theatrical souvenirs. But where is Laurence in all of this? Why does he not figure in the cards?

'This is a card all about work,' she says. 'I expected, in a jeune fille, I expected – amour. The young man –'

Yes. My thoughts too.

'No, no, he's not – it's just a friendship,' I say. I wonder if my voice is bitter. Am I blushing, the memories of last night, of my confusion and how we parted on such an odd, unexpected note, as if on the wing of a joke, coming back to me?

'Livre,' she says. 'This card mean a . . . contract? Is there something written that is très important?'

'No,' I answer.

Flustered by my refusal to play along, she shakes her head and points her bony finger at the last card, tapping it. 'It is upright and it is a happy card. Très bon – many, many good results . . .' She is talking and I realise that throughout my thoughts have been somewhere else. I struggle to listen. 'Poisson,' she says, rubbing her chin and darting little glances at me. I know she is doing what all good diviners do – trying to read *me* – so I determine to keep my face blank. 'Well, Fish – it usually mean: something to do with work or money or independence, seeking . . . working alone. But that is if I read for a gentleman. For a young lady – boff! What can it mean? To make good marriage. To handsome tall dark young man. Mélancholique. Peut-être one who he plays the piano well . . .'

I laugh. A flash of annoyance darts through me, but I bury my face in my huge coffee cup to hide it, finishing the last dregs before I stand up. Well, *that* is not going to happen. Fish. Plenty more fish in the sea. Or just – the sea, or water, which I often think of when I picture Laurence. In fact, in one of the cartoons I've drawn of him he's pouring water from a wine bottle into a vast sea full of strange mermaids, turtles smoking cigars, and ugly sea creatures.

'Thank you so much, Madame Balle!' I say, and with my legs a little shaky, and a dreadful squeaking sound as the chair pushes back on the wooden floor, I rush to leave.

Later, when I close my eyes, the cards are still there. *Burning to speak to you*, she said. Yes. Not that cornball she told me, but *something*. Something significant has happened: an Anchor, a Book and a Fish have appeared. Phrases from the Bible come to me, the lines in Luke saying: *Suppose one of you fathers is asked by his son for a fish; he will not give him a snake instead of a fish, will he?*

No. One thing is not the same as another. I like my own thoughts about the cards. Not her rummy ones! *That* is what is enjoyable to me. My thoughts, pictures – always my own funny ideas. Each card glows as I slide into sleep. They're outlined in black like stained-glass windows. A rainbow light flows through them, into my dreams.

★★★

Laurence says, 'But Pixie! How will we continue? Are you angry with me?'

It is four days after the kiss. We are walking together (that is, Laurence is walking, with his long stride, and I am hop-skipping to keep up, like an idiot) to the theatre.

'No, I'm not angry. Let us never speak again of it. It was a misunderstanding. I am not – as you discovered – very worldly, and . . .' Embarrassment prevents me from saying more.

Laurence has tried to apologise since that night, a million times. He is mortified. The alcohol. The mood he was in. Of course, he cares about my 'repper' and would never compromise it. The bewildering part for me is that in the end I wanted more from him than the taste of his hot whisky mouth and the currents he stirred in me; I found his respect for me infuriating. But as a girl I must never show that. Curiosity about such matters is the height of vulgarity. But at least, now we have both composed ourselves, we can talk.

'I'm not as innocent as you think,' I protest. 'I have a book . . . Daddy was worried I didn't understand about – Edy, so I bought myself it. It was by a sexologist. Rum stuff!'

'A book is one thing. But life – doesn't always follow.' He smiles at me. His sweet chin, with hardly a hair upon it, I'm memorising as we speak, planning to draw it again.

He is very keen to find out what Madame Balle said to me. He says he saw us sitting together and that's why he didn't come into the breakfast room that morning. I am sure he is worried that I told her about him.

'The *future*,' he says. 'Do you really believe it's something that exists already? I can't believe you do. What would be the point of *anything at all* if it was like that, like a long road ahead of us, and all we need is for it to be revealed and to walk right into it?'

We are late! I'm huffing and puffing. When he says this, I feel as if the teachings from the New Church pop again like a bubble. *Of course* God has a Plan for us, Mama would say. The Future is such a bewildering thought: where is it, right *now*, and what does it look like? Where is next year? Where will I be? The moment this thought occurs, a sea rears up, grey and humpy, like a whale's back. The Fish! The card she turned over, vivid and searing. Makes me think of loaves and fishes, the feeding of the five thousand, something to do with multitudes. Multitudes of fish, or of money (as she said), or of people? The millions that Mama said I'd reach? *Do I contradict myself? Very well then I contradict myself, (I am large, I contain multitudes.)* Do I really believe that it's all out there – the future – just waiting for a card to be turned over to reveal it?

'Well, I don't know! Madame Balle seemed awful sure.'

'Did she say . . . Did she mention anything about . . . *me*?'

I flap my glove against him and laugh. 'How vain all men are! Why do they assume everything a girl asks is about *them*?'

The theatre is on a narrow street; it's called Chestnut Street Opera House. We've reached the stage door. Laurence nods to the man stationed there, who recognises him as Mr Irving's son and sweeps us both through. (I guess he thought I was Laurence Irving's dresser or a stagehand or any number of lesser roles.)

We fall silent as we meander down the long corridor with the ropes and strange damp wooden smells, but Laurence suddenly turns and whispers, very urgently: 'Don't mention this to Ellen – or Father. But you know my shooting *accident*.' His expression is so strange, his eyes so intense, that I know without him saying more what he is telling me. 'I was just examining the gun. That's what I told my mother, when it went off.'

'And she believed you?'

He nods, seemingly relieved that I have understood.

'But if I had drawn a fortune-teller's card that evening, before retiring to my study to practise my part of a Gentleman and a Messenger – ha! What would the card have said? Does it read your mind? Does it know the future better than you yourself do? And *which* future does a card foresee? The one I was choosing at that moment, or the one I've ended up with?'

The shock of what he just said makes me trip and stumble, bashing my calf on some stray bit of abandoned furniture that has no right being there. Astonished, I blurt out: 'I guessed! I – did think that, somehow, when you spoke of it.'

And he pauses and says, 'You must be psychic, then, Pixie, because honestly *everyone* – my father, Ellen – acts as if it was absolutely an accident . . .'

A pain stabs at me again, in my heart, the same place as when I first thought about it, and a terrible image of Laurence comes to me, not holding a gun but simply trying to open a door which has water gushing against it, forcing him back, an image that truly frightens me. There is no occasion to ask him – as if I'd dare! – *why* he wanted to shoot himself, or indeed to say anything at all, because he is now racing ahead, his dark coat swinging, his pink-tipped ears burning. His comments, though, do whip up a thought I've been ignoring: why God might want me to lose both parents in such quick succession when I've been a faithful servant. Does God intend me to be destitute too? What is His Plan for what I should do with the rest of my life?

Laurence pushes at a door that says *Do Not Enter* and we tumble together into Ellen's dressing room.

All is calm and grace there. The room is crammed – Ellen can hardly fit in it – with flowers. Roses. Crimson, cerise, others eyelid-white and tinged with cherry pink. The smell: grassy, sweet and heady. Champagne cooling in a bucket of ice. A basket of gifts: maple syrup, cookies, tied with a pink silk ribbon and a note to *Our Darling Miss Terry*. Ellen is seated at the mirror, her hair in a turban, doing her face. She waves at us and speaks as she always does, as if we had just left off a conversation.

'. . . The cuspidor is so disgusting! Did you see it outside my room? Why do Americans need to spit so much – is it the cigars they smoke that give them chronic catarrh, do you think?'

Laurence steps over to kiss her cheek while I bend to sniff some of the roses with a murmur of greeting. I somehow understand that I must keep up the pretence that she sees me or cares if I am there or not, when much of the time she doesn't. Laurence has found one of Ellen's scarves, a green-and-blue silk chequered number, and drapes it around himself, twirling a little.

'This is a free country and I can spit if I choose!' Ellen says, impersonating a male American voice. 'Well, I guess the joke is true: the talk in New York of a man who lost both sons. One died and one went to Philadelphia.'

Laurence laughs in a dutiful way. We both know Ellen is tired of being on tour and Philadelphia is not her favourite city. (When we first arrived she said she was mad about the houses and the white marble and red brick everywhere. She wanted to travel on a tramcar – but she was mobbed by crowds, of course, and couldn't, so we went to visit her friend Mrs Gillespie, a martinet but warm-hearted, and a descendant of Benjamin Franklin. Edy had already warned me about her, saying that as a child she'd been forced to stay with her and the woman had 'an opinion in all matters'. Since the first night in Philadelphia, Ellen has only talked about one thing: Henry. He is sick. His voice is strange and his performances in *Robespierre* are weary and weak. Critics have noticed.)

Ellen is leaning forward to peer into the dusty mirror, applying witch hazel to her skin, and then rose oil in little cotton wool dabs. The smells, along with the flowers, in the hot little room are overpowering. Laurence moves to open a window, but Ellen shrieks, slapping a manuscript in front of her – her lines – 'Oh, don't! They'll float out of the window. Anyway, what are you two doing here? Is there something you want from me?'

'I have a few tiny adjustments,' Laurence says. 'To *Robespierre*. I have thought better of a couple of words in my translation – is it too late?'

An exasperated sound escapes Ellen, but she nods, and hands him a pencil. 'Show me. Write it down. Don't bother to explain, there isn't time . . . And Pixie? Everything all right? Have you received your letter?'

'My letter?'

'There was a letter for you. In among the letters that the stagehand brought. And a nice one from Edy, who can't wait for us to come home. I think yours might have had a New York postmark. It was addressed to Miss Corinne Colman Smith . . . Is Corinne your first name, then? I'd assumed it was Pamela.'

Corinne, Mama's name, startles me. Of course it is my christened name too, but no one ever uses it. Who . . .?

'I really would like to see that letter,' I say, trying to keep any sense of instruction out of my voice. (No one instructs Miss Ellen Terry.) I glance over at the big basket of cookies, beside which I notice many envelopes, unopened. I do not know if I am allowed to touch these. Ellen is now very intent on applying a thick foundation over her newly washed skin, and rubbing it into her neck with upward sweeping motions, designed – she told me – not to drag the skin any more than one needs to.

Laurence, seeing my hesitation, picks up the stash of envelopes and at once singles one out. 'Here you are, Pixie. Or Corinne! A pretty name – why don't you use it?'

'I – thank you – I don't know.'

The writing is Uncle Teddy's. He has addressed it to the Lyceum Theatre Tour, courtesy of Miss Ellen Terry and Mr Henry Irving, which is enterprising, for Teddy. I fear bad news, but since Daddy is already dead, and Mama too, what bad news can there be? (Why does my stomach lurch like that, and my mind fly back to the fortune-teller and her cards, and my heart start up a skittering beat?)

I need some air. I don't want to open the letter in front of them. I feel in my pocket and remember the little gift I've made for Ellen. A circular wooden box, decorated with green leaves and red and white roses, a box to keep earrings or pills, with her initials on the lid and *Robespierre – Philadelphia – Pixie* beneath.

'I will read it outside,' I say, and then, very shyly, 'I made you this. To say thank you for inviting me on this tour. It has been – a lifesaver.'

Ellen stops, stares into her mirror, and then smiles. I am standing behind her so she turns to smile again, more directly. She holds out her hand to accept the little box with a quiet 'Thank you' and, glancing at it – 'Oh, it's so pretty!' – turns her full beam of a smile on me. As such a great actress, Ellen is very used to receiving gifts. She does so with skill. But as she places it in the basket she turns the box over and sees that on the other side is a much more intricate, difficult painting, of a boat in full sail.

'I love the way you've done the waves, those little splashes,' she says thoughtfully. 'That's very you, Pixie. That's why you're good, you know.'

Her words make hot sparkles in my face, as if fairy dust were landing there. And then Ellen turns her attention back to Laurence.

'I have had news. An old run-down farmhouse in Tenterden, Kent – I often admired it while with Henry in the pony and trap. It has come up for sale. Edy is very excited about it. How nice to have a country bolt-hole, when we – when *I* – need to escape.'

Laurence is scribbling on her manuscript. He wraps the scarf further around himself, engrossed. He wants to show her the changes he's making.

I nod to them both and slip out, down the corridor and out onto the street with its American heat and its magnificent chestnut trees and Puritan folk, and, clutching Uncle Teddy's letter, I wonder why I feel, at this moment, so very far away from any home.

***

My dear Pamela

I hope this finds you well. I will be brief. I have now completed your father's affairs to the best of my ability and paid off as many creditors as I could. Now that I've sold his furniture and effects and written to the company in Jamaica, I do not think there will be further repercussions. It has nearly broken me but I have done it. I have succeeded in keeping it out of the newspapers.

The sad fact is that there is nothing left. I did my best for my brother, more times than you know, and now I am done. I enclose a cheque for a further one hundred dollars and I trust you will now do as I advised and find yourself a man from a good family — perhaps in England — to marry and set you up for a new life.

Yours,

Uncle Teddy

Teddy's blunt hand and firm strokes nearly strike through the thin, low-quality paper. Daddy always said he was mean. But I knew — or guessed — that it was more complicated than that. Uncle Teddy more than once bailed Daddy out of some pickle or other (when we sailed to Jamaica from Manchester, I had a sense that money problems were involved) and some hovering disapproval of something in Daddy's life (perhaps his choice to marry Mama?) has always existed. Now this letter to make sure I know this is the last of his loyalty to his wayward brother. My cheeks burn at the lines *find yourself a man* and *perhaps in England*! He is sending me away. He hasn't written *Don't come back to Brooklyn Heights* but he doesn't need to. He is ashamed. He has always been ashamed of his brother, and now, by extension, of me, and who can blame him?

I extract the cheque, fold it carefully and press it into my purse. Then I crumple the letter and throw it into the nearest cuspidor. It lands, satisfyingly, on top of all the other nasty stuff. Then I hurry back to my digs to pack. I know exactly what to do with the money: buy myself a ticket on the SS *Menominee* to return to England. One hundred dollars – well, two hundred and thirty, to total up all my remaining money – can last a while. The moment I read Uncle Teddy's line about finding a man from a good family to marry me . . . the thought came back to me, the same one that formed while Madame Balle spoke, and now it's firm as a hard ball of old gum.

Find someone to marry me! Somehow Laurence has made it clear that this is not a straightforward thing for me. *Entirely unlike other girls.* Huh! Well, if that's the case, then whatever Uncle Teddy says, and though I'm only twenty-one, I feel bloomin sure I never *ever* will marry.

I hold no reins, see, I am driving this by the force of my will.

But if I came to the pillars of the Temple where the High Priestess sits,

I know I could not enter, nor draw back her veil.

I could not open the scroll marked Tora.

In bondage to logic, I'm mired here.

My horses are gone, my chariot drawn by sphinxes, asking: what creature walks on four legs in the morning, two legs at noon and three legs in the evening?

The answer: it's me!

If you get me upside down, I am a quarrel, litigation,

I can be dispute and defeat.

Here I am again. Sea, sea – like Tennyson's poem, *Break, break, break, At the foot of thy crags, O Sea! But the tender grace of a day that is dead Will never come back to me.*

I feel it strongly: I'm never going back to America to live. I am about to cast in my lot with the English. Is that the right decision? Would it be better to build on my art reputation with the Macbeth Gallery? Who can I ask? I'm alone. Not a single fatherly or parental utterance to guide me. It's a delirious feeling. Like a hanged one, swinging on the gallows! Terrifying, liberating. I don't think many have known it. Most people on this earth have *somebody*: they are daughter, wife, sister, mistress, mother to . . . someone. They have family. I guess I have a cousin, Mary, but she and I have not corresponded for a while and it turns out Mary is brimming with convention and about to marry a fat stiff fellow from Harvard.

I'm dressed for dinner but have paused with my sketchbook, sitting on a deckchair on the windy port side of the ship the day after leaving New York for Southampton. In my rather scant luggage I've brought my first copy of my new book, *The Golden Vanity*, with my drawing of a ship and a sea not unlike this one – choppy, frilly, wobbly blue and green lines – on the cover. I'm thinking of this, and wondering about the Reverend Baring-Gould whom Daddy and I met – is he pleased with my illustrations, shall I look him up when I get to England? To my surprise, it's suddenly words, not pictures, that form in my mind, and I jot some notes (perhaps thinking of Tennyson's poem did it): *Alone, alone, and in the midst of men, Alone mid hills and Alone in the valleys fair, Alone upon a ship at sea; Alone, alone, everywhere* . . .

The paper is a little damp from the sea spray so I fold it carefully into my pocket. (I don't know about Tennyson – wasn't he grieving the loss of his son? – but if you're writing poems you have to admit you can't be truly, *truly* desolate, don't you, because isn't there at least one proud, ambitious part of you thinking: *One day I will publish this*? And that part of you is assuming a reader one day, and a future. In fact, by the time I've thought this, I've even decided: it would be nice to publish the poem myself, be a publisher, have my own little broadsheet!) I've cheered myself up. My dark-green dress is spotted with drops of rain and the night air is chilly.

Oh, and I am not actually alone at all: I'm here with the Lyceum players, my new family.

I'm humming a tune by the time I join them in the first-class lounge. Walking into that cigar-fugged place, a memory comes back, a shameful one of Daddy and the first officer, which I push to one side. No one here knows about that, and I could afford a first-class ticket. My chest swells. I press my shoulders back. Fingers curl around the poem in my pocket, neatly folded, small as a postage stamp. I'm not alone at all, that was just a – what – a silliness, a falseness, an illusion. Nonsense!

Indeed, I'm now an important part of the company. (How I would love to write to Uncle Teddy and tell him! I hope he and Cousin Mary read of it in the *Brooklyn Life*. Jam!) Of the one hundred and four passengers on board this ship, I'm among the eighty members of the Lyceum, and, better still, I'm in the inner circle. I'm the Big Cheese, I'm their Chief Bongo! I'm Mistress Illustrator of Programmes, of souvenir material. I'm their chronicler, Resident Artist, sometime costume designer, a valued member of the team. I'm Pixie Pamela Colman Smith: *single, female artist* – that's what it says in the captain's log. And, best of all, I even made eight shillings for some costume sketches – that's my bus fare to London, if nothing else. When memories of Mama and Daddy or when brown moods form,

I have super self-control and I simply push push *push* my thoughts down to the bottom of the sea.

As I'm offered a small glass of sherry and move to watch Mr Irving with his spectacles pushed far back on his nose, playing the piano, his lugubrious son and pet Laurence bent into a hairpin, playing the violin opposite him, the three cards that Madame Balle turned over for me pop into my mind once more. Here I am at sea, writing poems. Anchor, Book, and endless Fishes.

★★★

Well, here we are in old London again. A merry town! Edy has kindly offered me a room in a large Smith Square apartment building she's moving to with Christabel (I must remember to call her Christopher, the name she has chosen for herself, but it does not come easily and I've stumbled a few times). No rent is mentioned, which is embarrassing because I am sure they expect me to pay some. I pluck up the courage to ask, and Christopher says, 'Oh yes, Edy will let you know how much. We hope you don't mind that the woman we share with is a spiritualist? All those tappings and table rappings, that sort of thing.' I'm very intrigued by this and excited to meet her. Edy says her name is Mrs Lake.

They bring the cat, Sappho, in a special cat basket borrowed from Ellen, and the ginger beauty looks out of the little wicker grid plaintively, making a curious mewing which sounds like a baby crying until the basket is set down. Daddy's comment about 'inverts' comes back to me, and now I am a little older and wiser I feel suitably bohemian and grown-up. I might be young (I'm newly twenty-two!) but knocking around with theatre folk will do that for you.

The new home, with its tall chimneys, is a very grand place to my eyes, and arriving here in a cab we pass heaps of tourists gawking and squawking because it's near the Houses of Parliament. Edy and Christopher have rented four floors. There's a little gas lamp hanging in the porch, and a fancy lion knocker to rap if we forget our key. We're opposite St John's, a huge baroque church, like a great white temple. I say that it's awful nice and so is the huge tree of heaven in front of it, but Edy harumphs and says: 'Wait till you see how many tramps and drunks congregate there. The place stinks in an unholy way in the morning!' And Christopher laughs, as no sooner is this spoken than an old fellow appears with a scaly nose and straggling hair, sidling up to us at the steps to ask if he can help with our cases. Edy ignores him. Christopher shakes her head, turning her back. I hesitate but, not wanting to annoy my two new friends, I smile, saying, 'Oh, we're not helpless, thank you!' as I pick up one of my own leather trunks and haul it over the threshold.

The teachings of the New Church, that our thoughts and judgements create our reality, float into my head. Not to see people as dirt but to understand that dirt is in the way of you seeing them. I know better than to say anything – no one likes a girl who is 'pi', Cousin Mary used to say, meaning pious) but the thought has formed. I decide that when Christopher and Edy aren't here I will take my sketchbook and sit on the steps of the church at a safe distance from the urine smell and the abandoned bottles and draw the old fellows with their filthy bare feet, and the stained-glass windows shining behind them, because . . .

I'm advancing my plan to be a Famous Lady Artist with My Very Own Thoughts on every subject, little by little and step by tiny step.

I am here with my hand on the lion's mouth: am I closing it, or opening it?

Look closely, the lovely orange beast is smiling at me, at my strength, my fortitude.

My courage.

To bow my head, to merge flowers from my belt with that golden mane.

Passion, lust, fear, desire. I tilt my head to hear the roaring inside.

And then a little shock.

'You remember Mrs Lake, Pixie, don't you?'

Edy gives a dismissive wave as the small woman with the auburn hair and a cap, in her green outdoor coat, appears in the hallway, clearly returning from an errand and rather overwhelmed by our arrival and all our boxes and trunks. Each floor has a front room, a back room and a powder room – the spiritualist's room is on the ground floor, and a strange room it is, full of fishing rods and with a faint whiff of incense, and now here she is. After removing her cap, she beams at me, and the full force of her prettiness overwhelms me.

Mrs Lake! She is *Nora*.

The maid or housekeeper from the studio in Covent Garden! Nora. I remember her name — it pops up as if a cartoon balloon has formed above her head and she is smiling at me, the same extraordinary grin, though she is not, I notice, beaming it on the others. I don't know why it's such an awful shock. I'd imagined this 'Mrs Lake' as older and dumpier and just a strange person I could mock — as Edy and Christopher do — and dismiss as unimportant. Not this glorious, small, perfectly formed person.

'I've some visitors this evening — I do hope you won't mind them?' she is saying to Edy.

Edy is already halfway up the stairs to the first floor and barely pauses to say: 'Spiritualists? Will give Pixie the perfect introduction!' And she and Christopher carry on up the stairs, giggling, but without a backward glance.

Mrs Lake and I are left alone.

'It's Nora,' she says. 'Mrs Lake is what I'm called in the Church. Well, I mean, I am married. But you must call me Nora. And I hope *you* won't mind the spiritualists?'

I nod, weirdly dumbstruck. I feel awful clammy. To break the mood, I say, 'I won't mind at all. I was raised on Swedenborg. The New Church. We used to live here in England, in Manchester. Until I was about ten. My mother was devout. Well, Daddy too. Although not *devout*, no one could call him that . . .' I'm gabbling. I've no idea why this charming woman only a few years older than me so intimidates me!

She is taking off her coat and seems only mildly interested.

'Sorry about the incense pong, 'We can't get rid of it. It seems worse at some times than at others. The place used to belong to the monks of Westminster. I'm glad you won't mind the meeting. Seven o'clock here. Come along. And bring your father, if you like.'

'Oh!' My eyes fill with tears and I struggle to find a handkerchief in my pocket. I'm still wearing my coat. I don't know if I shall ever take it off, I'm acting so wooden and stuck.

'He – Oh, I forgot you met Daddy, at Edy's studio! He's not – Oh! He was ill. He . . . passed over.'

Nora looks horrified at her mistake. She takes a step towards me and I take one back.

'I'm sorry, I'm *so* sorry,' she says. Her sincerity disarms me, her eyes fixed on mine. She even reaches out a hand, but I recoil, not expecting to be touched. Inching away slightly, I nod, sniffing, and rubbing at my nose.

'I'm fine now. I'm *fine*! Yes, he's in the – you know – the Moon Garden, with Mother.' She of all people must know what the Moon Garden is.

'Your mother has passed over too? That's so sad,' she says, and after hanging her coat on a peg, she pauses and recalibrates for a moment, then offers to help me with my case. 'I loved that book,' she adds, and I feel a lift, a tiny lift, so reassured that she has indeed read Howard Pyle.

'Do you know which room is yours?' Nora asks.

'Edy said this floor. Here with the tappings and rappings, she said. Christabel – Christopher – can't stand it! She's a writer, and can't work except to –'

'Yes, I know Christopher,' Nora says, unconcerned by the implied criticism of her spiritualist calling. 'We all lived at the flat on Great College Street together.'

She has a light voice. A South London accent. The way she says she knows Christopher feels like a tactful way of telling me that the relationship between Edy and Christopher is not a scandal to her. I start to feel more at ease. Nora herself is full of grace. She is a very comfortable little person. Somehow – and I don't know where this thought comes from – she reminds me of Sappho the cat, already twisting her way around our ankles, mewing and asking for food. The cat that I thought of as a 'ginger beauty' only moments ago. Of course, Nora has ginger hair too. Freckles on her pale arms. Darker hair than Sappho's but similarly vivid and notable.

The cat's eyes are the most astonishing amber colour and her back and tail are patterned like the veins on a leaf. Her tail is this huge whiskery, fluffy, ridiculous thing, like a feather duster. Nora's eyes, now I'm close enough to see, are green: the same rich colour as the coat she has taken off.

She starts busying herself in the small kitchen area, making a pot of tea. She remembers how I take mine from last time – two sugars! – and prepares me the perfect cup, in beautiful blue-and-white china, 'borrowed', she says, from Ellen. 'All of the loveliest things are Miss Terry's,' Nora says. 'She has the best taste. And of course folk are always giving her gifts. She has a lot of admirers. You were on tour with the Lyceum? Were you acting?'

'No, I was drawing the programmes and posters and all sorts of other things . . .'

We drink our tea together.

'You're an artist,' she says. I say I am. 'This evening, seven o'clock,' Nora says. 'Edy and Christopher won't come – it brings them out in a rash. Or perhaps they'll join us at the end. But you've been to a spiritualist church before, in Manchester, then? That explains your accent. You don't sound much like an American.'

'Well, I was just a girl. We moved a lot –'

'I think you'd enjoy it, just the same,' Nora says, and smiles into her cup.

★★★

The place is heaving. Chairs have been put out in rows and people are sitting, mingling, taking off their coats. I'm hovering in the background, helping Nora with the teas – wobbling trays of clattering crockery. Edy and Christopher are nowhere to be seen and I don't recognise any of the other people. There is a powerful smell of incense, and sweaty hot people, and dogs. (There are no dogs here but perhaps one of the vagrants from outside has wandered in.)

It's odd to be helping Nora and to see that in this role she is both maid *and* mistress of the hour. That is, we're pouring golden tea over the strainer. (She does everything with a graceful care that is interesting to observe.) The front room is a hubbub of women's voices. A table with a black velvet drape has been dragged to the front; a jug with wildflowers in it – late-June poppies, cornflowers, straggling oxeye daisies, already limping in the gloom of the candles and early-evening light.

'I had some bit parts at the Lyceum. That's how I know Ellen,' she says, for no reason, and I look at her afresh, wondering what prompted this remark.

Once teas are handed out and people have put them awkwardly on the floor in front of their chairs or on a spare edge of bookshelf beside them, Nora taps a spoon against a glass several times, raising her voice above the chatter, and calls for hush.

'Welcome, all!' she says. (That's it. So theatrical!) 'Let us bow our heads in prayer, and recite with me the Vesper Hymn. *Grant us thy peace, O God of peace and love, who dwelleth in the shining realms above . . .*'

Nora is waving to me and it's hard to read the gesture. Is it 'Go and sit down with the rest' or 'Here, help me with this chair!', so I just stand gawping, listening to the others murmuring: '*Grant us with thee forever to abide, where is no night or falling eventide . . .*'

I know she said they wouldn't be, but I am still surprised that Edy and Christopher aren't here. I feel insulted on Nora's behalf. Looking around the dozen or so people squashed in the room, it is mainly women, with one watchful, suspicious man I now know to be Nora's husband, Alfred, and just one other – an Irishman who seems rather aloof and seats himself a little to the back. The women wear housecoats and aprons and darned wool stockings (in summer!) over their sausage legs, and – I'm struggling to accept this thought because it feels disloyal to Nora – but the simple fact is: they do seem to be of a lower class. Not people from the theatre world, as I imagined. Not book types, poets and artists – the kind of people I've just spent months among – but another group entirely. Nora's world.

'Welcome, friends. You all know me: Mrs Lake. Now, let us all stand and sing the Healing Hymn.'

The small congregation shuffle to their feet and with no preamble break into a ghastly tuneless song (with no musical accompaniment!). Alfred, it turns out, has the only good voice in the room, a baritone, and manages to carry the tune loudly and confidently. Nora's husband is some sort of handyman. Does work in the apartment. I find myself astonished (and not a little annoyed, the same annoyance I felt when I discovered the marriage of Cousin Mary) that Nora is already married, and she only . . . what . . . three years older than me.

Gracious Spirit of thy goodness
Hear our anxious prayer,
Take our loved ones who are suffering
'Neath thy tender care . . .

They sit down again. All except Alfred, who stands with his legs slightly apart like a soldier at ease. (Something about him is very irritating. He's a young man acting like a much older one. Handsome, well built, and he knows it. Possessive of Nora, it seems.) The seated group clearly know what's coming next, and what they are here for. One very small woman in a flowery blue housecoat accidentally kicks her teacup and squeaks quickly to the room: 'Ooh, so sorry! *Sorry!* But never mind, it's empty!'

A nervous giggle bursts out of me. Nora shoots me a fierce look. She walks slowly to the front of the table, and I note that she has draped a silky emerald-green scarf around her neck, covering her bosom the way a much older person would, which to my mind looks silly on a girl her age. Alfred steps forward to move a fishing rod – tumbling out of a box behind her – so that it doesn't stab her. Then he glances all around him and smiles to people at the back melting into the wall.

We are all impressed when Nora speaks. She is fearless. 'So, Gracious Spirit, now please join us and shed a healing ray on those of us suffering here in the room . . .' Nora closes her eyes and lifts her arms. The room falls to a hush. Shuffling and tea-drinking ceases. Alfred has a coughing fit and then bows his head as if praying. The smell of incense is very strong, and from outside the sound of a cabbie shouting at his horse floats through the open window. Nora's face is pink and shiny.

I don't know what I'm expecting here. Yes, I have indeed seen mediums at work before. Nora is such a curious person – perhaps, a little like me, she is hard to place exactly. Edy speaks to her with great familiarity, and I realise now they've known each other forever – well, probably from Nora's acting days at the Lyceum. That's where she met Alfred, doing some carpentry for one of the shows. Edy told me Nora went into service when she was fourteen and the family – quite a grand one – were all in the Spiritualist Church, and the master of the house was impressed when she started feeling spirits and that's how she developed this talent. In particular she could hear the voice of his departed five-year-old son, Edgar. The master trained her up in the Spiritualist Church and little by little she got herself into other kinds of households, where she was housekeeper by day, 'sensitive' by night. Edy told me this with a tone of disdain.

My experiences of spiritualism were all a long time ago, as a child in Manchester with Mama and Daddy. There was always upset – someone in the room was always asking about a lost child, and the medium would assure them that the child was loved in Heaven – and there were table rappings, even automatic writing, and there were always tears, sometimes from the medium too. Mama once cried about a message she got from her own mother on the other side and Daddy had to take her outside and talk quietly to her – leaving me behind! – until she finished sobbing. Daddy sometimes called it the 'sad grievers' club' but would add: 'And why not, if it gives comfort to all?' I remember Daddy in discussions with others – serious, loud discussions of Swedenborg that he allowed me to sit and listen to. I never felt like laughing then. And yet today I feel giggly at once. Is it Nora? She has a lively manner, so bouncy, like a bubbling stream, a tremendous force about to spill over.

Nora closes her eyes. She pauses, and then opens them suddenly, jerking as if she's just been pushed in the back. 'Yes, I'm getting, it's a . . . an old lady. I have a lady here. She is bent over, she's old, she is – I can see a chair, and a fire . . . Oh, she's laughing, she's a joker, always has a joke or a kind word . . . Anyone?'

Well, I'm thinking that could be just about anybody's mother or grandmother, an old lady, a fire, a chair, bent over, but I'm interrupted—

'It's my aunt Doreen!' a fat woman at the back barks. 'She passed over last week!'

A couple of heads turn to look at her. Alfred nods in a satisfied way, pulls a chair and sits down, looking around the room, folding his arms contentedly, as if to say, 'Now we're off.'

Nora nods. 'Well, she's—' Nora stares into the middle distance, affecting a sort of glazed look. 'She has a message for you. She's saying . . . there's a sixpence hidden in the knitting basket, if you care to look. Go home and take a look – that's for you.'

'I could do with it!' laughs the fat woman, and others laugh too. 'Ask her if she has any other news? What about our Bernard and his dicky heart?'

Nora closes her eyes for a second and then opens them quickly and says in a booming voice: 'Oh, she tells you not to worry about that. He'll be bloody right as rain!'

The women in the room laugh again, a little shocked at the swearing.

'She says – ooh, I can't stop her now – she says it's not his heart, it's just wind. That's why he's always farting, and tell him to go easy on the beetroots, that's what's doing it . . .'

The room erupts into more laughter. Alfred's deep tone is the loudest.

'Farting! That's right, that'll be our Bernard,' the woman says, looking around her and nodding to others, enjoying her importance. She folds her arms across her chest.

And so it goes on, with spirits coming through thick and fast to speak to Nora, and pass on messages of the everyday sort. Nora pats at her mouth: did the person have a dry mouth, at the last? Nora's ankles feel pain: did Grandfather have swollen legs, a war wound perhaps? Nora sees a woman cradling a baby: oh, she's met up with the spirit of her dear departed Elizabeth, is it? Or Eliza? A little dog. A bunch of snowdrops that the Loved One wants to give you. At one point, speaking of Fred – or Freddie, or is it Frankie? – there is a knocking from one of the fishing boxes piled up behind Nora and everyone jumps out of their skin and stares at it. In front of our eyes, the box seems to rock.

There is a burst of laughter and then sudden silence, as Nora steps towards it and says gingerly: 'Is anybody there?'

She tentatively lifts the lid (Alfred, I notice, is up and standing again, protective) and then 'Oh!' and Nora collapses into laughter as the cat – Sappho – leaps out.

'Time for a little tea break,' Nora suggests.

She goes to use the powder closet and I've no time to speak to her.

I pull my chair a little closer to the open window, lifting the curtain slightly – a candle gutters out – and hoping for a breath of air in the stifling room. I'm thinking of other things, possibilities for performances, storytelling, shows like my *Henry Morgan*, or *Annancy* tales, because I can see how rapt everyone is. And I could charge a fee. If I could find a loyal group to attend. And a living room to perform in. Nora only takes pennies towards the cost of tea, but I can see other possibilities. Souvenirs, cards, painted boxes.

And then no sooner is she back in the room and everyone seated expectantly, Alfred pulling shut the gap in the curtains, than the door opens and Edy and Christopher return, with another boyish dark woman in tow. They take their place at the back, standing behind the seats. Everyone turns to look and there is a kind of stir among the crowd, directed at the friend they have with them. She smiles; she is a little older than them, with an intelligent, fresh gaze. Curiously, it's as if their arrival is a signal. Nora glances at them. The thought that comes to me is: *Stage prompt.*

Nora closes her eyes, asks for quiet, sways a little in front of us. She opens her eyes again, and her expression is glazed, staring straight ahead. She says: 'And now I have a man. A very handsome one. I see him surrounded by . . . paints. Is he an artist? Or he has a bag with him, yes, let me see, it's a leather bag. An older man. He has white hair. He runs his hands through his hair a lot. He's got a bad habit of scratching, like a dog!'

No one replies. I sip the last of my tea: awful cold.

'There are two birds beside him now. Robins. Hopping on a table in a garden. He's very weak, this gentleman, he's thin and overwrought, you know, but he wants to tell me, he has a message, an important message, and it's *definitely* for someone here . . .'

Don't, I think.

'I'll take him. That's my grandfather,' says a woman. A quiet woman with ears sticking out from a ribbon round her head, a thin body in a droopy black dress.

'Well, he – Are you sure?' Nora says in a disappointed voice.' . . . sure he's for you?'

'Yes, that's our Jimmy, all right. The robins. He loved birds. Kept his kitchen window open so they could hop right in, and never kept a cat so they would feel safe with him. And the scratching! He had bad skin. A skin condition. It's our Jimmy. What's the message?'

'Oh, well . . .' Nora seems to be about to argue but then remembers herself and, with a glance at me, she returns to the glazed expression, saying quietly: 'The message is that joy and great fame and rewards will all be yours in the *next* lifetime. Not to seek nor expect it in this one.'

'Well, I'm working hard, right enough,' the woman says. 'Tell him thanks for nothing! Is our Derek with him?'

'No, I'm getting . . . the smell of cigars and, well, a crick in my neck – did he have a bad neck? Oh, I see a cloud of ineffable brightness . . .'

Ineffable brightness! What a phrase . . .

'And bright lights like stars among us! A woman is with him. Now fading, now our little spirit voices are saying goodnight . . .'

By the end of the evening, I don't know what on earth to think of what I've just witnessed. It felt like Nora began something and then stepped away from it. The pounding in my chest has calmed and I've recovered a light, playful feeling, to face the room. I busy myself moving chairs.

Alfred is smiling proudly. Edy and Christopher are smiling and amiable, and they introduce me to their friend. She is tall, with an unaffected manner, like a healthy shoot of something dark and green; there's a sort of stillness to her.

Christopher says to her, 'Oh, you should take a look at Pixie's work: she's so quick and, by gum, you would love her illustrations and costume designs. She could do you a poster for a show or a souvenir programme in the blink of an eye! She's the most prolific little person I know.'

This is the first time Christopher has made any remark to indicate that she even knows what I do, and not withstanding that 'little person' part, I find myself beaming with pride. The woman – I didn't catch her name – beams right back at me. She has such a refreshing, direct manner, her body such slender grace, as if she might be a deer or other poised creature. When she turns, I see how beautiful she is, with her big eyes and dark curls, and I have an immediate desire to draw her. She must be an actress too, and perhaps another famous one, the way the others in the room are craning to look at her.

'What's going on with the Golden Dawn?' Christopher stage-whispers to her. 'More devilment and skulduggery?' The woman frowns and shakes her head, as if to say, 'Not here!' Something clicks into place in my memory then. *Ah.* The actress Florence Farr. For a 'highly secret' occult society, I have started to hear an awful lot about this Hermetic Order of the Golden Dawn.

After a hesitation, Florence Farr leans in to say, in her lovely, clear voice: 'We don't approve of spiritualists. This shows the dangers of dealing with the spirit world when you're not an Adept. When you don't have – you know – our *training* . . .' And she folds her arms crossly, as if to say, 'No! I *won't* say more about the Order of the Golden Dawn! Stop asking me!'

Of course, I am intensely curious to find out more, but if I bide my time someone will surely soon spill all.

Neither Edy nor Christopher joins in with the Lord's Prayer at the end, but Florence, I notice, bows her head. As soon as it is finished she says to me, 'I don't approve, but Mrs Lake – Nora – is *wonderful*, isn't she?'

I nod, surprised again by this sense that everyone already knows Nora. And rather struck dumb and not wanting to reveal my . . . alarm at where I thought the séance was going. Florence is gazing at me and, in the same way that I've worked out who she is, she seems now to have placed me.

'You're the Pixie? Someone described you as the "Japanese toy" . . . but that's nonsense! Why do people say such things?'

Why indeed, I think, but I do not know how to answer. And who was the someone? Jack Yeats, perhaps, who I've been doing some illustrations for?

'I imagined you older, somehow. Say, what was that all about earlier? Nora seemed to be directing her efforts towards you.'

'Oh . . .' I don't want to talk about it, but this Florence has such a refreshing, plain sort of style, that I find it hard not to give in.

'My father. He passed in December. Nora was play-acting because she knew, and she met him briefly . . .'

'Oh, I'm so sorry,' Florence says. 'I remember now it was Willie who told me about you. His brother knows you.'

This Willie, I gather, is the poet all of London seems to be fawning over. 'He also lost his mother recently,' Florence is saying. 'Willie acts as if it's *nothing* – how can losing a parent ever be insignificant?'

The freedom with which she speaks of this man's most private feelings alarms me. (Just as she repeated without compunction the insulting 'Japanese toy' description of me.) And the way she drops his name into the conversation! As if we must all be so bloomin interested in him and the entire Yeats family! I feel hostile towards her suddenly. I thought her direct at first, but there is such a thing as *too* plain-speaking. What would she say of me to others, if I told her *my* secrets?

'Ellen has told me there's nothing you can't do! Didn't you do their American souvenir booklet? Of *Robespierre*. I thought it terribly good. Perhaps you might come along to our next salon . . . Readings, recitations. We do need some help with souvenirs and whatnot . . . Do come with Christopher and Edy to one of our readings with Willie at his father's house in Bedford Park. I think you'd like it.'

Florence seems awful keen on me, and I'm flattered. They need help with souvenirs and whatnot! Hoorah, hoorah! And people to invite to my own salon too. That will build up the coffers a bit.

Christopher is pulling a face and saying, 'Can anyone smell that damn stinky incense? Where's it coming from?' It is true that there is no incense lit in the room, but a residual smell of it, sticky and heady. Christopher gives a shudder, and someone says, 'It's the old monk paying us a visit!'

Florence laughs and, with a nod to me and a brief nod to the room, sweeps out – Alfred leaping first to open the door for her.

The curtains are tugged open to reveal a bright crescent moon, a slice of vivid yellow lemon. When most of the guests have gone, Edy catches my arm. 'This has to be the last séance,' she says. 'We've had complaints. From some of the guests tonight. The bad language. And the ghastly monk with his incense that seems to visit whenever Nora is doing her thing. She'll have to go! In any case, we have another friend who needs the room. Will you tell Nora?'

I try not to show my disappointment. I think I'm a little afraid of Edy. She has a very commanding style.

I say quickly, 'Of course.' After a moment, I add, 'Florence invited me to Willie's salon. In Bedford Square. I – I've been thinking of doing something similar myself.'

'Not Bedford Square! Bedford Park. Chiswick. It's where the family lives. Willie lives in Bloomsbury. Oh! You had an invitation? Florence seemed quite taken with you.'

Yes, I felt that. Florence's interest. I don't know whether to be troubled by it or whether she is just the sort of intense person who likes looking hard at a situation and thinking about it. It's comforting that she noticed Nora's behaviour during the séance too and it wasn't all in my head. I don't for one moment think it was Daddy paying a visit, but rather Nora wanting to tell me something consoling. And, for that, I suppose I should be grateful rather than cross.

The idea of my own salon floats up again. How much could I charge? I want to go along, to see how it's done.

I busy myself picking up cups and saucers and taking them into the kitchen. Puzzling over the evening as I do so, I belatedly realise: what a horrible responsibility! To ask Nora (and hearty, full-volume Alfred) to leave. Why *me*? Not for the first time, I wonder at my role with Edy and Christopher and — well, all of the Terry-Irving clan. I suppose I'm too clever and from too good a family to be treated like, say, the dressers Walter and Sally — indulged and favoured servants. I'm also in the pay of the Lyceum, whether it's for costume design, set design or programmes, so strictly speaking I'm employed by them. Is that why my status is so confused? One minute I'm invited to family gatherings, to share a home with Edy and Christopher (and I fear that when they do finally ask for rent it will have built up to an enormous sum), to go on tour with them, to meet their actor friends and go to their poetry salons and work at their Covent Garden studio and be part of their world, but the next minute I'm told to do something, as if I hold the same place in their lives as Nora. Perhaps it's my youth, or, once again, my odd looks. Maybe the question puzzles them as much as it does me.

Alfred is whistling to himself as he stacks chairs. He gives Sappho a small kick as she tries to wind herself around his legs. She mews and gazes at me with her big, amber-coloured eyes.

Whatever mysterious and muddled feelings I have about what I've witnessed this evening, my feelings about Nora are awful rummy. They remain unchanged.

★★★

It's a few days before I pluck up the courage to tell her what Edy has asked me to. Almost a week. Nora is furious. Her bubbly nature can quickly fizz into a spluttering fire and fury, I realise.

'Am I not making enough money for them? They want to let the room to their *educated* types, folk who write poems, is that it?'

'No,' I stumble, 'that wasn't it at all. They simply said there were complaints, and Christopher said the bad language –'

'Bad language! Bloody hell! Have you heard Miss Christopher when she gets going? She has a temper on her like an East End navvy!'

I clap a hand over my mouth to hide my laughter. But Nora sees it and her manner softens.

'Who cares?' she says suddenly, sweeping some scarves, dresses and hats from a chair and emptying one of the fishing boxes to the floor so that she can put the clothes in it. 'Alfred and I have an offer from someone else, a housekeeper's job in Chelsea. It's live-in, so we'll be fine.'

I'm astonished. So – she knew Edy would give her notice? Was she already planning to leave?

She is watching my expression. Hers softens a little as she guesses at my thoughts. 'You're forgetting. I've known Edy for a while.' I pause to take this in and she asks: 'Will you go to the farmhouse with them? This place in Kent?'

'I don't know. No one has asked me.'

She presses the lid on the box and then sits on it. 'Why do you put up with them, Pixie? How do you stand it?'

'What do you mean?'

'Well, the way they treat you. It's, you know, somewhere between a pet, a child and a maid-of-all-work. I know you're all alone in the world, but these women aren't your friends, Pixie. They think of you as – Aren't they always saying how *industrious* and *productive* you are? A bloody workhorse. And they're drawing on your obvious psychic gifts, your artistic gifts, your very special spiritual nature, for their own purposes . . . while mocking them at the same time . . .'

'My psychic gifts?' Here I really am lost. 'I did get paid for the souvenirs in America,' I protest. 'Five cents apiece . . .'

She must see that her words have hurt and she tries redirecting them. 'Have they invited you to join their Golden Dawn?'

I shake my head.

'They will. It's like the Freemasons. A secret society, secret meetings. Not for the likes of me. You have to know Latin and Egyptology and dress up. Magic – they think it's all queer squiggles that the servant classes can't possibly understand.'

'Well, it might be an awful useful place to meet people. Who want to buy my – art and suchlike.'

She laughs at this and says, 'You're smarter than they think, eh?'

Then she leans closer, her curls bobbing a little at her cheeks, to say, 'There was a stand-off. The scary one with the big eyes, the one they call the Great Beast, turned up in an Egyptian mask shouting, and, I don't know, he had a sword and a shield or something and had to be marched off the premises by the poet!' She laughs. 'And they think what *I* do is a theatre, a racket . . .'

I'm awful spellbound by the way Nora tells me this, assuming me to be much more of an insider than I am, though I worry that Edy and Christopher are somewhere nearby and might hear her.

'Psychic gifts – you know, seeing and hearing things differently from others, *feeling* stuff more intensely, knowing there's more to this world than just the obvious. You do have it. That's why everyone is so drawn to you. They can feel it.'

Everyone is drawn to me? I am about to argue with her, but instead a strange thought bubbles up. *Yes*. I have felt this, and have in some dim part of me known it and puzzled over it since tiny girlhood, in between feeling like a Nobody. I *did* sometimes believe that wonderful magical things were coming my way. But until Nora said it just now, I had not acknowledged the thought.

'Is that why Florence seemed . . . interested in me?' I ask.

Nora shrugs. 'Florence might be the real thing. Who knows? The men have their version of her – you know she was the mistress of a famous playwright for a long time? It sort of gets in the way. Yes, I saw that she was captivated by you.'

Captivated! When I am such a Barn Yard Duck. And psychic? Maybe the part of me I think of as skinless, permeable. Is that what she's talking about? How often I feel such a nincompoop, different from everyone else, getting things wrong with my idiotic foolishness. I stare at Nora's plump cheekbones, her rosebud mouth and perfect little chin, and remember that she – like me – has had to make her way in the world, and after all being a sensitive would be a better way to make a living than being a maid.

It's true that Edy and Christopher have a curious attitude towards me (wasn't I musing on exactly that earlier?), but I am more in *their* camp than in Nora's, being educated, and indeed I'd be able to learn Latin, Hebrew and Egyptian hieroglyphs, whatever, should I truly care to. Florence Farr's mention of the salons in Bedford Park and Nora's despising of the Golden Dawn have only whetted my appetite. I'd love to meet this Irish poet Willie and see what all the fuss is about.

I help Nora as she continues to pack and I scribble down the address of her new post. She offers to 'read' for me – any time, she says, that I want to connect with the spirit world – and for a second Daddy looms up in my mind's eye, exactly as he did when she spoke of him, a robin on each arm. I shake my head and we part with a small embrace; the lace on her collar tickles my neck.

After she has left, I retire to bed. But no sooner have I put my head on the pillow than I hear strange noises in the room above me – Edy and Christopher's room. At first I simply hear their voices, soft and murmuring, though I can't hear what they are saying. And then a rhythmic movement, knocking and bumping, a sound like a heartbeat, very soft and quiet, but insistent and persistent and unmistakable. I listen and listen. I sit up and stretch up and on top of the knocking sound there are soft cries like the sound a wood pigeon makes.

I find myself feeling hot. An awful peculiar feeling creeps along me. I fling myself back down on the bed, turning and turning. My mind keeps returning to the unmistakable sounds, the little voices. It's something so extraordinary to know the gathering melting feeling but have no name for it, no words, as if I'm launching out like a small boat on a dark wave and will never come back.

I feel every nerve in my body, every spring in the mattress, as if it were a coiled snake ready to strike me. *Poof!* I kick off the sheet and allow my legs – my hot legs – to soak up a cool breeze from the window.

I make a noise. A very loud noise. A fake cough. And, just as I'd hoped, the noises upstairs instantly stop.

I lie there for a while (still listening out for them) and begin to feel somewhat cooler. Then I find myself drifting between sleep and wakefulness and arriving in the oddest dream. Florence Farr is in the bedroom with me and Nora. We are sitting on the floor, in our night-dresses, looking at some cards together, a little like the Lenormand ones the French fortune-teller read for me in Philadelphia, except that they have different pictures on them.

The card the three of us are staring at (it floats in front of us) is World, a vivid cobalt blue and yellow, with a naked woman dancing on it, a robe across one breast like an Amazon, and twirling two batons, or are they sceptres? I don't know if she is Nora or Florence but the woman in the picture is pretty with a boyish figure, and I begin to feel very hot in the dream, particularly my chest, and my hair is growing strangely long and black. Suddenly – I'm very frightened – I'm lifting off the floor and flying up with my hair airborne too (like the sail on a ship catching a wind), and I *know* I am a witch, and in the dream I feel a deep, deep fear of some evil magic I have let into the house: outlandish occult symbols I can't understand, something ancient and powerful and irresistible but so very dark, and I cry out, *What is happening to me?* I holler so loud in my sleep – not proper words but slurring, garbled sounds, like the language of a madwoman – that I wake myself.

A door opens upstairs. Footsteps, hurrying.

Then my bedroom door opens and Edy is there, holding a candle and saying, 'Pixie, Pixie – are you all right?'

I sit up, a hand on my hot, *boiling*-hot, chest in my nightdress, feeling the sweat pooling there, but assuring her in a weak voice that I am.

'This *room!*' she says crossly. 'I thought I heard Nora coming upstairs – I heard her footsteps – then when I went to look, there was no one! All her things are gone, and I can see that she left hours ago. It is so beastly here. The sooner we leave the better.'

'But where will we go?' I say, thinking: *But why would Nora venture up the stairs to their bedroom in any case?*

Edy backs out, taking the candle with her, and I'm left in the dark with my loudly beating heart, which feels to be so hot it might burst out of my body like a baked potato from a fire.

I am travelling, travelling

Across the sea from shore to shore, alone alone for evermore

You'd be wrong to fear me as isolated or occult,

I might be the Capuchin (not the monkey but the monk)

But I'm also the Crone waiting on the gate for you with her wise plaits,

Wrecking her stockings like Joni.

I'm holding a beacon, I have a talent for aloneness.

My message is simple: 'Where I am, you may also be.'

Bedford Park is awful grand. Edy and Christopher and I travel there in a cab and I soon feel we've left London and gone to the country (though it's only that we've gone quite far west, to Chiswick): red-brick and white-painted houses, with little picket fences, and so many of them have beautiful green tiles in the doorways with the same repeated pattern of fruit on a high stand. These tiles begin to fascinate me: why do all the houses have them? It creates a feeling as if they all belong together, belong to something bigger, as Edy says they do: an experiment, a new way of living.

The Yeats house is number 3 (the white-painted centre looking like a sort of tower), with faded pink roses and purple hibiscus and a magnificent cherry tree on the pavement outside adding to the country feel. Someone opens the door to us and I realise from glimpsing inside that the salon is more like a big party. In the hallway there are groups of people, waves of laughter and shouting.

Suddenly I spy her, Florence, Florence Farr, making her way towards us with a commanding movement, and the memory of my dream of her, naked and twirling the batons, makes me blush. She is wearing a long velvet dress of a cobalt-blue colour, the material sheathing her body; I'm shocked to realise that she cannot be wearing any kind of corset or undergarment. And a sort of silver headband, like the moon goddess Selene. She is dressed for a performance. She's certainly dazzling as she turns her full beam towards me, suddenly much younger than her forty years. And she is beaming at *me*: at the Pixie! People in the room are decked out in flowers, with garlands around their heads.

Standing beside me, her hand on my arm, Florence begins steering me round the room. 'Oh, this is Willie, and his brother Jack, who says he knows who you are . . . and these are his sisters . . .' The sisters are both wearing black with severe hairstyles and they seem out of place in the flower-strewn crowd. The older-looking one is wearing a dramatic brooch of amethyst in a six-pointed star that looks as if it might stab someone.

They shake my hand with serious faces and say they are pleased to meet me, more or less in unison. Noticing the black – and Willie and Jack wear black armbands too – I remember what Florence said about the death of their mother and wonder whether I should offer condolences.

'Lily is a beautiful embroiderer,' Florence comments. The younger of the two Yeats sisters peers at me.

'And Lolly—' Florence begins.

Lolly, the one with the terrifying brooch – a rather big woman, like a horse – staggers towards Florence and says, 'Yes, and what am I?' but Florence, full of grace and ease, just takes one tiny step back and says to me: 'Lolly also embroiders, but more importantly she is starting a printing press! She is an extraordinary person.' Lolly seems content with this and her fierce countenance softens a little. 'Yep, I am an *editor*,' she says. 'So no one can complain about me, the way my brother complains about *you*!'

This is news to me. I have been doing some drawings for a broadsheet, for Jack, the younger Yeats brother. Arranged by Edy. But how rude of him to say that and ruder still of his sister to repeat it.

'You know who I am?'

'You're illustrating his broadsheet with him, aren't you? You're the American—'

'I'm only part American. I was born in England.'

'Well, you're the – Pixie, aren't you? Miss Pamela Smith. He wrote to me about you. Between you, me and the wall, he said, "Although she has a fine eye for colour . . ."'

I beam here but Lolly shakes her head as if to ward me off.

'He can't take a high hand with you, being a woman, as he'd like! But he says you're lazy.'

'*Lazy?*'

Well, my gander is up now. I look around for Jack. There he is with his stupidly parted hair and his chewing mouth and his cigar. He is talking to Willie and he acknowledges my glance with a wink – a *wink*! – but Florence, who has been watching me carefully, leans to whisper: 'Pixie! Now is not the time . . .' And she grabs a glass of something that a young maid is holding out on a tray and plonks it into my hand. I take a sip and the taste is very strange – sweet and powerful – but I like it, and take another.

I am led away from the Yeats sisters without a proper goodbye and cannot quite reach Jack to tell him what I think, because at this moment Edy and Christopher approach, greeting Florence warmly with a kiss. Christopher laughs as someone twirls past us and drapes a necklace of flowers around my neck, and I pick up another glass of the wine.

Florence says, 'Careful, little Pixie, that's not opal hush, you know . . . Let me introduce you to someone . . .' And then with firmness she takes my elbow and ushers me into the terrifying throng.

My head is now spinning.

'And you know Laurence Irving?' Florence is saying. 'And his new wife, Mabel?'

His wife Mabel! I take a step back. Here indeed is Laurence, standing as he always does like a lugubrious wallflower, sheepish and shamefaced. And beside him a blobby figure. She comes into focus. Black hair cut in a bob.

It is four weeks. Four weeks since our voyage. And here he is, in that time . . .

He greets me with a kiss on the cheek and a look I can't decipher. My face must show shock. His wife – Mabel, dark silky fringe and rather fat bosom – blob, blob! – scowls at us and makes it clear that she isn't remotely interested in being introduced to me.

'Pixie is the most extraordinarily productive and talented person!' Florence says. 'Didn't she do the souvenir booklet of your father, Laurence? Magnificent, I thought, showing all the ways that Irving merges into his roles . . .'

I am grateful to Florence for praising me and changing the subject. Laurence and I exchange the most pained of looks but there is nothing to be done, nothing to be said. I think of my cartoons of him: kind, sweet, playful Laurence, playing on the lute, and then the other drawings I did. Him carrying a sword, and on it that tiny vain version of him in his red cloak, his stage costume. Angry, and longing for attention.

Florence puts a hand under my elbow and steers me away once more. I can tell she saw something. Florence has such emollience, or is it simply confidence, taking responsibility for everyone's well-being, although by rights shouldn't it be the Yeats family doing that, as this is their house?

I would like to cry, but I know tears will never come. I'm incapable of producing them, it seems. Willie is in a corner, surrounded by women. I can tell just by looking at the configuration – at the women's backs in their silk-and-organza dresses – that they are hanging on his every word. An aura surrounds him – draws my eyes. He is tall, must be over six foot, his hair flopping over his brow. He has a sort of fat bottom lip – a pet lip, my mother would have called it – suggesting something sulky or childish, or nurturing slights. I can hear his

Irish accent, the warm tones of his voice, and then the women's tinkling laughter.

Florence whispers, 'He'll do a reading later. Some of his poems. You'll like him better then, Pixie, you'll see.'

I turn to her in embarrassment. 'You read my mind!'

'You have one of those faces, darling. Now, let's see – who else? Didn't you have an illustration in the *Kensington* magazine? Would you like to meet the editor?'

'Damn publishers! Pigs! I can't believe Jack said that about me to his sisters! I'm tired of them!' I say loudly, twirling around just as the girl appears with the tray and helping myself to another glass of the little drink, which has a powerful brown colour and smells of – well, I'm not sure what it smells of. Coffee and chocolate and liquorice and aniseed. It's delicious now that I'm on my third – or is it fourth – glass. Florence's face looms awful close.

'Would you like a glass of water? Come with me . . .'

'No, no, I don't need any water, thanks,' I murmur, tugging myself loose from her grip.

Her big eyes widen and I know she is afraid I'm going to make a scene, and dimly, excitedly, feeling my gander rise again, I also wonder if I am about to.

'Why don't I – do you a Tarot reading? Willie and I don't usually do them here – it's a Golden Dawn thing – but there's a bedroom where coats are and we could . . . I could show you and give you a reading?'

Ha! What a clever person she is. Perhaps she really can read my mind. I know she is only trying to guide me out of the room but she's right to think I'd be fascinated to see the Tarot cards, and that they would be the thing to make me follow her. She is shimmering in that long dress like a slim blue snake with big, *big* eyes – looming larger and larger. The pictures on the cards – will they be the ones I saw in Philadelphia? I'm hotly curious.

A snap of laughter from the women in silk and organza clustering round Mr W. B. Yeats decides it. Either I'm going to wade up to him and tell him he seems an awful vain pig and a rummy critter, as I would call him to Cousin Mary, or Florence is going to lead me away, up some stairs and into another room. I let myself be guided, hand under my elbow again, my flower necklace snagging on something and scattering white daisies and petals on the stairs. I glance down at my feet, wondering when I took my shoes off and changed into the little red velvet slippers I had in my bag. I don't remember doing it.

The carpet is festooned with fallen blossoms, like a bridal path. Or a trail of breadcrumbs, leading up to the gingerbread house.

★★★

On the upstairs floor, Florence opens a door. She knows her way around. There is a pile of coats and hats on one bed, a white cotton counterpane on the other. Next to it a round table, with a pretty blue-and-white jug and bowl, Chinese style, a brush with blonde hairs on it. Two beds: Lily and Lolly's room, no doubt.

Florence reaches for my glass and, snatching my hand away from her, I tip my head back and finish the drink. Even while doing it, something in my gesture feels childish, as if I'm acting a part. I think about Daddy and his behaviour on the ship, and I'm suddenly defeated.

I flop down on the bed without the coats. My heart is beating very fast and the room keeps shifting: looming and tipping as if I'm on a boat.

Florence laughs. 'It's called Vin Mariani. It's wine laced with coca. Have you seen the ad with Maud Gonne? "*By fortifying my voice . . .*" It's rather strong. I'd say three is the limit for a – little person like you.'

'I do feel awful swimmy.'

'You could have a lie-down?' The sounds of the party downstairs are like waves on a ship, rising and falling.

'Oh, I'm much too excited to lie down! I could run about! I could dance! I could shout at that scoundrel Laurence – or Jack! *Lazy!* He just doesn't like that I might have my own thoughts and want to do things my own way sometimes—'

Florence looks worried.

'But I will lie down,' I say to please her, and giggle.

I lie on my back, heaving my feet onto the bed, and close my eyes, and then the room and everything in it swirls and moves around so much that I have to sit up and open my eyes again.

Florence is doing something weird: walking round the room with a lighted candle, standing in each corner and muttering: 'To the East, with Air, to the South with Fire . . .' She makes a sign with her hand – it looks like a cross, or perhaps more like a star. Then she puts the candle in its holder on the round table, coming towards me and riffling in her bag. She sits down at the end of the bed and produces a deck of cards.

I move towards her. The deck is richly coloured and the people and creatures and vivid symbols flash by so fast, tripping and leaping as she is shuffling, that I feel frustrated, and put a hand on one card to stop her. Florence, surprised, pauses, shows me the card.

'This is the Strength card,' she says. 'La Forza. This is the signifier – that means you, Pixie. You are also the querent. Shall I do you a full Celtic Cross reading? Or . . . just show you the cards?'

Her words are slurring. Liquid, like birdsong. I find myself unable to answer, and then a petulant 'No, I don't want you to read them for me' pops out.

I feel that Daddy would have warned me against the cards. That for all his modern thought, his membership of the New Church, *this*, the occult, the Tarot, this kind of thing, would have been something he disapproved of. Dangerous. My heart is doing a very odd thing: sort of shifting and snuggling as if it wants to lie down and then the next minute clambering to get out of my body.

The Vin Mariani is flooding my veins. I feel somehow messy, chaotic. Is my face covered in smuts? Or perhaps a mask, or a fallen crown? Why do I feel like a naughty girl suddenly? Why are the images in Florence's hands leaping like that, skipping, flipping, as if they are alive? The broken flower necklace straggles from me and a phrase Mama used to use, 'dragged through a hedge backwards', floats into my mind.

Florence hands me the cards. They immediately fall from my grip, scattering on the bed and the floor. 'Ugh! They're alive!' I squeal.

Florence leans to gather them up, holding them out to show me the pictures. 'Have you come across them before?'

I shake my head. I am not sure that the Lenormand cards Madame Balle had in Philadelphia count. Those cards were so rudimentary compared to these florid and luscious ones.

'Pick three cards. *Daleth*: a door will open,' Florence says quietly. She is awful serious now. I'm her pupil, and I can tell at once that I must not giggle.

'To experience the Tarot you need only meditate on them and see what comes. You have such gifts. Don't let the men tell you there are fixed rules or meanings. The cards are more alive than that. They will speak to you directly if you let them. In a state of reverie is best. Tell me what you see. Which one do you like?'

Shyly I reach out a hand for one. Number Three. A woman with a gold head-covering and a shield. A jewelled crown and green gloves. L'Impératrice. The Empress.

'Where do they come from? I mean – who invented them?' I ask, nodding at the cards.

Florence shakes her head. 'No one knows for sure. This deck is Italian. Fifteenth-century. Tarocchi. It was played as a card game. There was a papal decree from the *thirteenth* century banning cards and divinations, so we know that they must have existed then. But my feeling is that Tarot originated with the ancient Egyptians – after all, they had papyrus to make into cards, rather than clay tablets . . .'

She picks up the Empress card and holds it against her breast. A drooping daisy from my necklace clings to it, then drops to the divan.

'I believe it was once a book. A very special book with all the secrets of the universe within, all questions of life and death answered. And then the book was in danger, the wrong people wanted it, so, in order to protect its mysteries, it was torn into seventy-eight pages, and the words taken out, with only the pictures remaining, and these were distributed all around the world to make sure their truth was available to all. A Gypsy told me that.'

'I like pictures,' I mumble. My voice sounds to me like someone is holding a glass globe over my head.

'And the deck we have is now muddled – but if anyone can determine the *original* order then they are automatically transformed and transported to another realm . . .'

We both stare at the Empress card and in my mind I'm drawing her, in my own way. A crown with red roses and red hair down to her collarbone and a brown velvet cushion; a face a little like Nora's . . . A dress with red plums on it, or perhaps they are pomegranates . . .

'I am the mighty Mother Isis, most powerful of all the world . . .' Florence says. It is her acting voice. A different voice, sonorous. A beautiful musical voice, much lower than most female voices. I remember then that I read a review of her stage performance that mentioned her 'sparkling' singing voice, and that her speaking voice was octaves lower.

I must Not Laugh. But the effort is making me feel a bit sick. I close my eyes and they swim in a green-and-gold wave. The card – not the Empress, but the one from my dream – is suddenly in the room with us, vivid cobalt and yellow colours floating just above us, a naked Florence with her garland across her breast, twirling some kind of sticks like a circus performer. A green light flows in through the curtain. Florence's voice is lulling. I begin to wonder if she has trained as a hypnotist – is that why reviewers comment so much on her voice?

Somewhere I can hear music, like a lute being played. Laurence? Is Laurence playing?

'Mother Earth, the Creator of all,' she says. 'I am she that fights not but is always victorious. I am that Sleeping Beauty that all men have sought, for all time . . . I am the world's desire, but few will find me. When my secret is told, it is the secret of the Holy Grail.'

The Secret! *Oh, do tell me the secret, Mama!* A child's voice is in the room with us, the wailing of a lonely girl.

Florence leans in and stares at me oddly. I was not aware I had spoken. Some awful feeling of nausea is rising in me. Oh gawd, no! The fortifying Vin Mariani is on its way back up. With great *Strength*. I cup my hand to my mouth – and somehow in my mind there is a vivid picture of La Forza card, not as I saw it but showing a *woman* with her hand on the mouth of a lion. I feel a great heave in my stomach, and in the nick of time I reach the bowl on the table, to vomit up some ghastly brown muck. And as if this isn't bad enough, my queer shrinking feeling is mounting within me; soon I'll be scuttling around Florence's feet like a mouse and the room will grow bigger and bigger . . .

Florence leaps up from the bed. 'I'll fetch you a glass of water,' she says in her normal voice. She pours from the jug into my glass, swishing it out in the nasty bowl and then pouring me a clean glass of water. I glug it down.

Florence staring at me helps. The shrinking ceases for a moment, as if I can't quite do it – retreat to the fairy world – while someone is so intently watching, keeping me normal-sized in her gaze. She passes me a cotton handkerchief to wipe my mouth. She is putting her cards away, as if I have defiled them, though not one speck of vomit flew towards them, I did see that much.

'Have I disappointed you?' I might be about to cry.

'No, darling. Not at all! That is a very – powerful reaction. I think, perhaps, the Tarot did have some kind of . . . impact?'

The Tarot? Surely it was the coca-laced wine? The news that Laurence is married.

Florence sits close to me on the bed. 'You are . . . young. Everyone is saying how talented you are. They keep trying to make a pet of you, Pixie, but you are genuinely special. Such a good sign that you are drawn to the Empress, the card of *female* power, of a Feminine Divine source, of Venus and Isis. Not a card that shows paternal authority. You know, my father died – like yours – when I was not much older than you. And shortly afterwards I made a foolish, dreadful decision. A stupid marriage. Long gone! He left for America. I was glad to be shot of him.'

She pauses to see if I'm shocked, but I nod and murmur: 'My uncle Teddy told me to marry quickly. But who would have me? Even Laurence, especially Laurence, doesn't think of me as a grown woman.'

'Oh Pixie, darling. The question should be: Who would *I* want? If indeed you think marriage might suit you. It doesn't suit everyone, you know. Thankfully, as I've grown older, I've been less impressed by the – by *men*, and tried to listen more to my own wisdom. Wisdom is a gift given to the wise.'

I screw up my nose in a childish way to show I'm just puzzled by this phrase; she laughs and says, 'It's my motto. In the Golden Dawn.' She seems to be considering something. 'When we met, at Nora's séance, I thought at once . . . I have my intuition. Do you ever wonder why the right people and things seem to fall into your orbit? I suspect, like Laurence, they might at first mistake their attraction to you for something else . . .'

I bristle at her mentioning Laurence again, and flop towards her, almost toppling her off the bed. She gently presses me upright, adjusting the silver headdress she's wearing on her curls, the crescent moon tipping raffishly to one side. It gives her a queer look, a pirate with one eye hidden. I reach to touch it – to feel her curly hair – saying, 'Your hair looks springy, and like *heather*!' and she laughs and then is serious. Coming to a decision.

'You might like the Order of the Golden Dawn, you know. Though it's in disarray. I could arrange for an invitation. You have the right gifts for Magical Practice. I can see that, it's an unerring instinct of mine. And these days the Order has me – a *female* Adept – at its helm . . .'

'Yes. I like secret societies,' I say, and then feel stupid.

Footsteps on the stairs, and a knock on the door then startles us. A woman's voice. An Irish accent. 'Florence! Are you in there? Willie is all for starting the reading now. You're on in five.'

One of the Yeats sisters. Perhaps Lolly, as the voice is deep and schoolmarmish, and I think she was the older, bossier sister. I sniff at the residual vomit smell in the room and flash Florence a shamed look, glancing at the bowl.

She stands up and carries the bowl to the window, 'Here –', and, pushing the curtain aside, opening the window, she flings the contents onto the street below. Then she reaches under the other bed and retrieves an instrument – a large wooden thing that at first glance looks like a washboard. But then I see it has strings and is more like a queer, rectangular-shaped harp.

She grins at me. 'My psaltery. I hid it so no one would step on it in the crush.'

Her hair is dotted with fluff and a few stray flowers. She links her free arm in mine, the instrument under the other, and with her chin lifted, ready for her entrance, guides us back into the fray.

★★★

The crowded room is hushed and has formed a horseshoe shape around Willie, in the middle, looking awful serious, wearing a silk tie at his neck in a show-offy fashion, and a fedora. The silk-and-organza women hover like butterflies, fluttering and unable to settle (in case one gets the advantage). I force myself into the only little space I see and find myself next to Laurence and Mabel. She flashes me a cranky look. I smell Laurence's powerful cigars and the cologne he wears. (Today he has his dark hair slicked down and a little moustache, which is new since the tour. It doesn't suit him.)

'Say, are you all right?' he whispers, poking my arm. 'You look — Say, are you a bit squiffy?'

Stung, I tell him to 'ssh': I want to listen as Willie addresses the group. The psaltery shocks me the first time Florence plucks it. So sharp and squawking, not at all like I expected. More like a screech owl. *Pwang!* This cracks the poem apart and makes it odd, as if it were only sounds with no meaning, the way a baby hears sounds (or songs or lullabies) before it can speak. The hairs are standing up on my arms and I'm listening hard, turned — as is everyone in the room — towards

Florence, with Willie now just behind her, eyes closing occasionally, then smiling at her like a fond father.

This strange sound-performance fetches a curious effect, like bells tolling regularly from a church on a high hill somewhere. A picture comes to me: a crumbling church, a valley, with strings of washing blowing outside balconies, and dogs barking and children calling to one another on their meandering walk from school, and mothers' voices scolding or gossiping with their neighbours.

The picture seems something like one I sold at the Macbeth Gallery, *The Wind*. This one is a blowy day, too. A blowy day. A young mother playing with her small child. The girl in red slippers stretching her hands, trying to stop her mother from falling off a cliff. *Catch me!*

'Come – away – O human – child! To the – waters – and the – wild . . .' intones Florence, and any desire to laugh has left me as once again her voice works its magic, casting a sweeping pall over all of us, the weird screeching of her psaltery like a bird that has joined her to pipe out the ancient poems.

My eyes fall on Willie: he is enchanted, his attention fixed. Smartly dressed, tall, in his bow tie. He has taken off his fedora and every time he run his hands through his thick dark hair several pairs of female eyes are drawn slyly towards him.

He said in his introduction that the way Florence speaks is the closest to how he hears his own words, like ones found in the anima mundi, the world's soul. Like music. Or an animal language. Able to speak to our souls directly. He's handsome, yes, but it's probably his own awareness of this that attracts women to him: his arrogance and the sense that what he says and thinks *matters* so much. How mighty fine it would be to be a man and feel like that about yourself! That what you say and do will have lasting significance. Where oh where do such feelings come from, and why have they been denied to me?

I'm not very impressed with him. Am determined not to be.

'For the – world's – more – full – of weeping – than you can – understand . . .' intones Florence now, with a couple of last, ghastly wails plucked on the instrument.

Willie has removed his glasses, his eyes downcast and his full mouth trembling. He might be about to burst into tears. I force myself to have more sympathy: perhaps he's thinking of his mother? Has someone here lost a child? Because that is what this poem is about. I tear my eyes away.

Then another poem starts. Something about sailors. Laurence has his hand on my arm. He leads me into a hallway at the bottom of the stairs. Mabel has remained in the drawing room with the adoring fans and it's clear he wants to talk.

'So how are you *really*?' he asks, straightening from his position of propping up the wall to scrutinise me. 'I haven't seen you since the tour! Are you going to join the Lyceum again? They're touring England next month: Manchester, Liverpool—'

'Were you going to tell me?' I cut in.

He lowers his eyes. He glances across to Mabel and then back to me.

'I'm sorry if I – I thought we understood one another. As friends. I did not think I'd led you to . . .'

'No. Fine. Well, that's all right then. Silly me! As ever, Pixie gets it all wrong.'

'Please don't be angry,' he says, and his voice is so genuine that I'm startled out of my mood, to gaze at him. His eyes are tired. There are creases around them that I'm sure weren't there before. His skin, always pale, is almost blue-white.

'Well,' I say, changing my tone, 'as for the Lyceum, they haven't asked me.' (This is the first I've heard of it.) 'They only ask when they need work doing, so I guess I'll be hearing from them.'

There is abrupt applause; people are coming out of the drawing room and trying to move between us on their way to the front door.

Laurence's expression is embarrassed. 'Thought you might be glad for me. Given that you – alone – know I had turned my face away from happiness.'

Yes. Except that he doesn't seem any lighter in mood.

'I *am* glad for you,' I say quietly.

Laurence pushes his pince-nez up his nose, a gesture he makes when he wants to change the subject. 'A little bird told me you had joined some highly secret Order. Is that why you're here – in cahoots with Florence?'

'Honestly, this evening is the first time anyone's even suggested I might like to join! I don't think I understand what it is. A secret society that eminent people belong to, which meets to learn magic. But if it's so secret . . . which little bird told you? Edy?'

He taps his nose. Then, laughing, 'I suppose you've heard about their various fallings-out? Do you really want to get involved in something quite so vicious and dramatic? Led by a chap who wears an Egyptian mask and claims he's the Devil? You're still looking for this – what is it – evidence of an occult world, a world beyond ours . . . Isn't it hard enough to live in this one, without the need for another life later?'

'*Occult* means *hidden* – knowledge of the hidden. That's all. It doesn't mean wicked, or evil or in league with the Devil, or *sinister* . . .'

And yet earlier, upstairs with the Tarot cards, thinking of Daddy, that's exactly how I thought of it.

Mabel is now weaving between people to reach us, her small form, her dark shiny fringe and bob, her intense expression – trained on me.

'She is awful protective of you,' I say as she approaches. 'That's good, I suppose. Is she another actress?'

Laurence smiles, relaxing. 'Yes, of course. She was in the company. She can dance too. I've given up the chocolate! Mabel looks after me in every way. Especially money. She's a demon with money – so practical. No one at the Lyceum can touch her!' He beams, suddenly so different that it makes me smile back. Maybe I can be a very little bit happy for him, then. In this mood he has also shaken off his resemblance to his father: serious, craning, straining to be always so – what is it – so *important* again, like Willie, so undeniable. The pain in my chest that I always feel when talking to Laurence melts a little and, as Mabel reaches us, it disappears.

She is staring in an accusing way.

'Pixie was in Philadelphia with us for *Robespierre*,' Laurence quickly says, introducing us. 'She drew the programmes and designed costumes and more besides. She's a bit like you, Mabel – a *powerhouse*.'

'Are you an artist, then?' she asks in her London accent. 'But you prefer poetry events and theatre to all those other things, private views and exhibitions and being with . . . other artists?'

This arrow reaches its target. I have wondered this myself. Why are all my new friends in London – Edy, Christopher, Florence, Laurence, Ellen – from the theatre world rather than the world of artists?

'I expect the theatre world is where the work is,' Mabel says primly, answering her own question before I can. Laurence laughs, clapping her on the back. 'You see, Pixie? Mabel has an unusually practical mind for a woman! She's a tonic!'

And, with that, his attention shifts to someone else in the crowd, another friend from the Lyceum, and Mabel totters after him, clamped to his arm like a limpet. *Come away, O human child.*

That sadness that Laurence brings, the feeling that some hand is grabbing at my heart and twisting it, returns. What is it? Perhaps just the trembling sense that he very nearly was no longer here and could just as easily be gone, had the bullet found its mark. And what was it that prompted his despair? He never told me, but somehow I always understood it to be about his feelings as a playwright, as an actor, his feelings of unworthiness in the eyes of his great father. How flimsy it is. How do any of us get to be here at all? Dangling over those two great yawning abysses – of *before* we were born and afterwards – like a cradle over a deep gorge. (Why me, for instance, what am I doing here, when Daddy and Mama have both already left?)

I am smarting over that remark Mabel made. She's right. I have ended up simply illustrating for the theatre world and for friends' broadsheets. Did I intend it otherwise? Daddy set me up to work for the Lyceum and for Mr Baring-Gould – I mean, I never finished my studies at Pratt – and I have to earn enough to survive, so how on earth am I supposed to be an artist doing grand important work and yet manage to finish all the programmes and cards?

★★★

At home later the same night, back at Smith Square, while Edy and Christopher are sleeping, I light a candle and take out the box under my bed where I keep my money. I count all the banknotes. This is the money that Uncle Teddy gave me, and the money I've earned, and it's everything I have in the world to keep me from destitution. Outside my bedroom window a bottle breaks and I hear the deep voices of a couple of the vagabonds who cling to the steps of St John's Church. I creep to the window and by the light of a streetlamp the white baroque church is lit up like a temple; the figures look like the paper people in my box-theatre. A man and a woman walk past, bent over, the man leaning on two sticks. Looking at them, and folding the banknotes back into my box, I feel sure that this is a lesson for me to stop feeling sorry for myself. I'm not poor! I have a home, many friends, resources, my own talents. Mama would remind me of the teaching of Swedenborg. Why fear death – why have those ugly thoughts that Laurence prompted earlier today – when in our Father's House the angels will make sure that all glories await me?

As it is in our mind, so it is in the world. I must control my thoughts, or else who knows where they'll lead me?

Controlling thoughts is jolly difficult! Climbing back into bed, new ones pop up. The occult world that

Florence belongs to. The glimpse of the cards: Strength and the Empress. Her talk of a 'Feminine Divine source'. Daddy would not approve. And yet, how tempting it is! And then I remember my other idea, of running a salon myself (better than *theirs*!), with invited guests, where I could put on my own performances of *Annancy* and other folk tales, and my miniature-theatre *Henry Morgan*. Where would I do it? Smith Square is not the right atmosphere. And I'd need more space. This bedroom is too close to the water closet and its various unpleasant smells (probably why the ghostly monk always turns up, waving his incense around). That noisy scrum at Bedford Park was not quite the mood I want either: something cosier and more secret and more midnight-feeling and *special*. What Florence said when she wondered about me joining the Order did sink in. People *are* charmed by me. There is a dim part of me that feels the sizzle.

I wonder how much I could charge at the salon . . . Charging for attendance, though, is perhaps crass. Maybe I should just casually sell some of my work there. Decorated wooden boxes, postcard-sized drawings, cartoons.

'You have the right gifts for Magical Practice,' Florence said. And when she said it, yes, I felt . . . a shift. Like water trickling down my spine. And the sense of growing bigger and bigger and, yes, wanting to join her secret society and, yes, wanting to find these gifts she says I have and fully explore them. I am soaring to the ceiling, leaping, flying like a star, shooting, cartwheeling like a crazy child, all around the room. The lovely orange beast is smiling at me. At my strength, my fortitude, my courage. I tilt my head to hear the roaring inside.

I am Hermanubis, the jackal with a human body,

wheeling you to the spirit world while my pals, the four Living Creatures of Ezekiel, are intent on their books.

Success! Fortune! Destiny! (Those three look like Ellen, Edy and Christopher.)

I am Karma, I am the Goddess Fortuna, and a secret name that none can speak.

I'm rolling rolling rolling . . .

Until you make the unconscious conscious,

I will direct your life and you will call me Fate.

The address Nora gave me just before leaving Smith Square – where did I put it? It takes me a while to find the scrunched-up piece of paper in the pocket of a dress and I struggle to read what I wrote down: *Chelsea. 14 Milborne Road.* I heard it wrong – it's Milborne Grove. The cabbie is cross and keeps shaking the reins and saying, 'Nah, not round here . . .' – so it is dusk and has cost me a shilling and sixpence by the time I arrive. He drops me off as the streetlamps are being lit; a waxing moon appears in a yellow sky. I wander around, rehearsing: 'I just thought I'd say hello'; 'I wondered how you were.'

It's a fancy place with silent streets, few horses or cabs, and row upon row of pretty, white terraced houses. I pass two ladies walking their dogs, one, rather hunched, giving me a curious look, and I feel at once that I might seem odd here. Is it too bloomin posh for me?

I'm gazing into a garden, trying to look nonchalant and as if I might have some purpose here, to throw the hunchback-lady's glances off. This would be the moment to take up cigarette smoking – Christopher has an awful bad habit and is always offering me one from her American stash, and it would be the perfect excuse to stand here. Damn!

I stare at the low white wall and a pink rose-flower bush in front of me, a small front garden, next to a smaller building on the corner (a sort of studio), before I realise that this is the house I wrote down: number 14. A yellow ribbon floats from the branch of a London plane tree on the road right behind me; a linen bonnet rests on the rosebush, fallen from the window above, as if somebody had a disaster with the laundry and dropped it everywhere. Is this a good sign? As I'm biting my nails and deliberating, the door opens and a young maid in an apron comes out carrying a bin of vegetable scrapings for the compost. She turns in surprise. She squints a little and steps towards me, where the streetlamp illuminates me better.

'Pixie!'
'Nora!'
'Were you looking for me?'
'No! Well, *yes* . . .'

She smiles and, having emptied the bin, wipes her hands on her apron.

We pause, awkward for a moment. Nora's eyes go to the bonnet and she picks it up, folding it and putting it in her pocket.

'The birds. They try to make nests with my laundry!'

I nod, staring at her rather dumbstruck.

'I'm so glad you came!' she says.

'I just wanted to say hello,' I stumble. Then, very quietly: 'I wondered how you were.'

Nora beams at me. 'Come in!' she says. 'I'll introduce you to my mistress. She will be impressed that you're a friend of Edy and Christopher. You know, she has a studio next door and she's hoping to rent it out. It would be the perfect place for you – you could live and work there . . . Oh, I'm *so* glad you came!' she repeats with warmth.

And, just like that, my new home appears, and my new life with Nora and Alfred, and the first studio of my own.

★★★

March 5th 1901

Dearest Cousin Mary

Thank you for your letter. I am glad to hear of your happy life with your 'dear Gerald' (is he really a dear? I do hope so!) and I am glad – I suppose I ought to be – that Uncle Teddy is in good health. My life in London is Very Exciting and Ripping Fun and Full of Exciting Twists and Turns, and no! you can bet your boots I am not Sad at all.

I have moved to a new home, please note the new address: 14 Milborne Grove in Chelsea. I have my own little self-contained studio, and it's perfect. I can hardly believe how I chanced upon it. Sometimes my life is just JAM. I mean it has a little oil stove on a soap box in a corner, and all my things in one place, and I'm busy decorating it as I have Big Plans for it.

I am working very hard, at some poems and illustrations – Pixie's Book of Poetry. I met a poet, I think you will guess who – I went to a tea with friends and WBY was there and he is a rummy critter! Seemed most stupid and had on a tea-party air and posed about and looked bored. And when all the ladies with ermine collars had gone, who all told him how very much they liked his bloomin poetry, which probably they had never read or heard of . . . then WB began to talk! Folklore – songs, plays, Irish language and lots more – reciting a sort of folk song which was splendid.

Then I liked him a little more. Willie belongs to a Secret Society, which of course is so secret I cannot tell you about it!!!! Instead, here is a drawing of the lady who tells me a little, the little she is allowed, about it and makes it seem intriguing: Florence Farr.

Florence is a famous actress here. Well not as famous as Ellen of course. (I call Ellen The Peg. I can't now remember why.) Florence is about forty and has the most darling tight curls and big eyes and always a wistful look. She is awful slim and sporty and not at all fainting and ladylike. Also, that golden voice which makes her seem so serene and gracious, even when she's not! Florence is teaching me to read divination cards, a special set called the Tarot, which only she and Willie know anything about in all the world. I love Secret Things. It has twenty-two trump cards and then a lot of pips and court cards, so a little like a regular deck, if you don't know what a Tarot deck is, but with powers to do all sorts of fortune-telling and soul-peering (that is the bit I like) and suchlike. Florence is truly an expert.

And of course, since last I wrote you, the Queen has died and all of England is in mourning. Last month from a balcony in St James's I saw the most wonderful sight, watching with Edy and Ellen. The tiny coffin on the gun-carriage was drawn by cream-coloured ponies and it was all silent in a way that London never is. The grandest carriages out for the occasion. Hordes of people. When we got to the street level Ellen was completely mobbed — she is more famous than ever, you know, as I said — and we had to fight through the crowds and return to the balcony.

We saw the Duchess of Albany's son, looking like Sir Galahad. Or like a figure from a Tarot card. I cannot stop thinking about the cards since that first glimpse, and they seem to people my mind now. I see things to remind me of them everywhere!

Florence tried to teach me, and I kept saying Awful Stupid things because there is such a lot to remember: each card has an astrological sign and an element, you know, Earth or Air or Water or Fire and whatnot.

You know what I'm like, Mary. Not a Good Scholar! Indeed I am unteachable because I just want to do everything my own way and I Won't Listen. I am like The Fool (one of the Tarot cards). It was ever thus, you say. Oh how

I do miss you teasing me! No one here quite understands how I like to say serious things in jest and jesting things in seriousness, never wishing to be understood plainly.

(In the end, although I always thought it was Daddy's fault that I didn't go back to Pratt, I sometimes wonder if they wouldn't have me, through my damned cussedness?)

Is Brooklyn snow-bound or is spring bursting through? Will we ever meet there again? I hope your life with your dearest Gerald is as happy as you say it is, and I hope that his drinking will soon return to more accommodating levels.

Your little Pixie cousin Corinne Pamela

As I post the letter near my new home, I see at the last minute, as the pillar box's mouth devours it, that the stamp has the Queen's likeness on it, and wonder if it – if the Queen – still has the power and authority to sail a letter across the pond to America in that extraordinary way.

I feel very far from Cousin Mary and my life there with Daddy. I long to tell her more about the Golden Dawn and my friendship with Florence. I received an invitation to become an initiate of the Golden Dawn, as promised, a few days ago, and it was not attached to a spear or an arrow or brought to me in the talons of an eagle either, but just a regular letter, on strangely regular paper. I accepted.

★★★

I have just been informed that you have been accepted as a suitable candidate for our Order. Before joining, it is as well to know a little more about us. At first all instruction given to you will be purely intellectual so as to make a firm foundation for spiritual knowledge – that will not be given to you until you have proved yourself fit to receive it. No worldly or social considerations can be brought into the Order; we leave all rank and position outside. We must be prepared to make sacrifices or else we are not fit for the enormous responsibility of occult knowledge and the extra temptations it brings with it . . .

★★★

It is early evening. I'm wearing my red shoes and carrying a bag with black robes and a red sash that I have been sent in a parcel. There is a fumble with the door of the building I'm trying to enter. Some rooms above a tearoom. I glance up at the two ugly stucco carvings above the window and see a figure move there, and some flickering lamplight. I hear steps, and the door is opened.

'Hello –' I begin, but the figure puts up a finger to indicate silence and turns away, gesturing with one hand to show that I should follow him upstairs. Somewhere on the street there is a clap of laughter.

The room has the usual strong smells: incense, frankincense, benzoin. Several figures are waiting there, wearing robes and masks. They stand in a formal way and the one who met me at the door now joins them.

'I'm the Hierophant, the revealer of mysteries,' he says to me. His accent has a country burr, perhaps Irish.

'I'm Pixie. Pamela,' I murmur.

The Hierophant's hand flies up to his mouth and a finger to his lips. 'Welcome, Neophyte. Remain silent until asked to speak.'

I have my usual naughty desire to giggle.

I gather the robe from the bag I'm carrying and put it on. The Hierophant steps forward, tying a blindfold round my eyes, tying it behind my head, and then pulling the hood down to cover my face. *Hoodwinked.* The word floats into my head. Now I see nothing, and only smell the dusty cloth, but I feel him putting something round my waist and tying that too. It's strange to be touched by hands I can't see in such an intimate place. I feel a little rise of something: a catch in my throat. I am aware of all the others in the room and of my heartbeat quickening like running footsteps.

'Child of earth, arise and enter the Path of Darkness,' murmurs a voice. Not the Hierophant, someone else. An older voice, posh, Oxford-type, male. I feel myself – my hands and shoulders – being sprinkled with water and the potent smell of the incense wafting over me. I long to lift the blindfold and hood but I daren't.

I feel babyish, like an animal being herded to the slaughterhouse. When a voice booms, 'Why do you seek admission?' I start to speak but nothing intelligent comes out.

'Kneel!' says the voice. It sounds angry.

My hand is picked up by another's. A female hand! Florence said that the Hermetic Order of the Golden Dawn makes no distinction, allowing women to reach the same rank as men; I still assumed that the figures I saw before being blindfolded were male. This hand lifts mine and makes me touch a door. The door is dusty and cold.

The woman is still very close to me. My hand is placed on something wooden that takes the shape of a triangle, and someone – the Hierophant or perhaps another of the temple chiefs – begins intoning at me, a lengthy speech about my obligation to the Order.

'Do you promise to keep secret all that you learn here today? Do you, Neophyte, take a solemn oath to all your Fraters and Sorors here not to permit yourself to be hypnotised or mesmerised or placed in any kind of trance state; never to use occult powers for evil purposes?'

I swallow. A hand is on my shoulder, directing me. I hear my own voice, as if accepting marriage vows, saying loudly: 'I do.'

'And if you violate any of these oaths, you will submit to a deadly and hostile current set in motion by the chiefs of the Order . . .'

Something quivers against the skin of my neck. Cold steel. A sword? My hand wants to fly up and touch it but I resist, though I am quaking.

Now a hand under my throat. Now I smell the oil from a lantern which must be wobbling in front of me and the Hierophant indicates with a touch at my elbow that I must follow this smell, moving me around like a piece on a chessboard.

All the voices, rising together in a rumbling wave, are saying: 'Inheritor of a dying world, we call thee to the living beauty. Wanderer in the wild darkness, we call thee to the gentle light . . .'

I'm asked to give my motto next, which I am scared to botch. 'Quod Tibi id Aliis, to yourself as to others . . .' I say. (When learning it I mixed up 'Aliis' with 'Allium' and Florence said that means *To Yourself as to Onions*, so I jump when I hear a snigger from somewhere – the Hierophant? – worrying that I mispronounced it or got the Latin wrong.) Daddy would be proud of me for choosing as my motto the Golden Rule: *Do unto others as you would have done to yourself.* Maybe – I hope – he would not disapprove or would even soften his judgement of the Order if he understood how far from being wicked it is.

Finally, my hood is lifted, and fingers are in my hair undoing the blindfold. Air on my face. I inhale the powerful scent of tree sap and violins. Benzoin. Clapping breaks out among the robed figures in front of me.

'We receive thee into the Order of the Golden Dawn!'

Here I am! I can do anything: I am magnificent!

'Now we will eat the Mystic Repast,' says the chief, pushing back his hood slightly. I recognise that beautiful voice! The boyish shape deceived me. *Florence.* She's beaming at me. She holds out a rose in one hand and bread dipped in salt in the other.

'Welcome, Pixie,' she leans in to whisper. And then, for the first time, she mutters my secret Golden Dawn name in my ear. I feel it tickle my eardrum, as a deaf person might feel the word 'water' tickling her palm.

★★★

I shan't tell Edy and Christopher anything of the Order of the Golden Dawn, no matter how they might plague me about it. After all, I'm sworn to secrecy. The mysteries are about to begin! Edy and Christopher are sneery and dismissive of it. Mary – being in America – is the only one I can tell even a tiny bit to. I know she will be shocked but also incurious; she won't ask for lurid details. Florence has confirmed what Laurence told me about how much discord there is in the Order, and that she has been in some sticky rows with Willie about it.

Florence has a new venture, branching out on her own to do magical work in her own way — the Sphere Group. It is a shame that I've joined at a time of such mayhem and shenanigans, with my loyalties being so bloomin tested. Florence is the Chief Bongo — that is, not a Bongo, but I can't remember the word — of the Sphere Group. Willie remains in the original group (I think), the one with this weird friend of Florence's, Arthur Waite, with a long face (*like a fiddle*, as Mama would say!) and a scholarly manner — he is the manager of a Horlicks factory and gave me a jar, all nice and powdery and malted; you make it with milk and it's *delicious*.

This Mr Waite the Horlicks Man does act as if he *alone* knows all the Secrets of the World and he's an awful rival to the Great Beast, the Crowley fellow (who has the same belief about himself), but Florence is quite fond of both of them, seemingly taking their warblings seriously, though I suspect that's not the *whole* of her feelings. When Willie and she were reading a second poem that night at Bedford Park, I had to put my hankie over my face a few times to hide my laughter — which really isn't the done thing, Florence told me gently, later. Men expect women to be a looking glass, reflecting them back in all their glory. Like the butterfly women in their silks and ermine do. She has learned this trick, and it has served her well, she says, though she fears *I* never will! Laughing at men is really a Big Mistake if you want to get on, according to Florence, unless you are very beautiful and loved like Ellen, and then they seem not to mind.

Most exciting of all, once Willie was shown my sketches (by Florence), he said that my drawings remind him of 'an innocent Aubrey Beardsley' and that he loves 'the simple Zen-like qualities of my lines'. Not sure what he means by that (he must have been drunk! Or maybe looking at earlier drawings when he said it, maybe my self-portrait as a Japanese girl), but I'm delighted to be praised by him, and pleased that he has admired my illustrations in Jack's broadsheet too, even if, like everyone, he does insist on seeing me as a Japanese toy.

★★★

Nora and I are walking in the Chelsea Physic Garden, discussing my salon. Nora thinks it an excellent plan and has many ideas for how to decorate the studio and light it and invite everyone we know, and says we must serve opal hush for most of the guests (cheaper) and whisky for the men.

'I'm tired of being a Japanese toy. I'm going to be a Gypsy girl,' I say as we plonk down upon a bench in front of the ornamental pond.

Nora laughs. 'Play them at their own game!' she says.

'And I think a shilling each for the postcards, or is that too much? If I sold twenty, that's a pound . . .'

It is so blissfully easy to talk about money with Nora; after all, she has to earn her own living and runs her own séances so has a practical mind. It's an early-summer day, hot and still. No birds anywhere in London. The pond has a great hump-shaped rock in the centre, which, now that I'm staring at it, might be a giant tortoise, as it appears – ever so slightly – to be moving, as if the rock is alive.

Nora is talking about tablecloths – green velvet – and whether we have enough glasses. We are both gazing towards the pond, eyes fixed on the tortoise or rock or whatever it is. I glance at Nora. Is she seeing what I'm seeing? Something moving there. As if the rock is breathing. I stop mid-sentence to stare at it. I glance at Nora, following her eyes. Yes, she is staring too.

And now I feel a powerful desire to close my eyes. I feel drowsy, the warm sun licking my face. The soft beat of a distant band approaching: a march. Drumming. Reed pipes, cymbals, singing. A small troupe of players and performers arriving from somewhere. Hot air wafts through me as if from a fan. As if I am back in Jamaica, with the red-billed streamertail bird and the fish and ackee and coconut rice . . .

I feel Nora's hand reaching for mine. Her callused, hard-working fingers. Her warm palm, folding around mine. I open my eyes to gaze, surprised, into hers.

There is no band of pipers and drummers. Only us two women sitting on the bench in languorous sunshine. Nora's hand is firmly clasping mine. She has a strong grip. She smiles, as if I had said something.

Then we both turn to stare again at the tortoise-shaped rock in the ornamental pond, the breathing rock, as if nothing out of the ordinary has happened.

★★★

I'm full of terror the night of *my* first salon. My studio is small, and stuffy.

'Is there enough opal hush?' I wail, going into the kitchen for the hundredth time to annoy Nora, who is wiping glasses with a dishcloth and putting them on trays to take upstairs to the table, next to bottles of claret and siphons of lemonade.

'Of course!' Nora says, whirling around and shooing Alfred, who is supposed to be carrying chairs to the area we've carved out for my performance. 'Any case,' she adds, 'turning into a fine evening – folk might prefer a stroll along the Fulham Road!' She winks at Alfred, and they both laugh at my face. I don't know which is worse: people coming or no one coming! Once Alfred has gone, she turns to me. 'Come on, I thought you were going to be *Gypsy* tonight? You know you're good at this . . .'

In my bedroom, I pull on a green skirt – I'm all for green these days but the waist is awful tight – and a black blouse with my long coral necklace, and over it an orange silk coat with black tassels that Mama always liked, though it's rather hot for a summer evening.

Nora has set up my performance room: a silver lamp, shawls draped about the windows, and in the middle my big round table with its green velvet cloth. Nora says that to reassure and 'centre' yourself, you must fill the space with your favourite things: so I have put out bottles of painting inks from Cornelissen's with beautiful, coloured stoppers, drinking up the light; cigarette boxes, and a papier-mâché cast of my head that Edy made once, when trying out hats on me; so many books, an old grand piano (which was here already), a small mirror, a heap of crimson silks, another low table with a candle flickering among boxes and bottles and glasses, and a blue velvet sofa (carted from an antique shop on the Fulham Road by Alfred, with much huffing and puffing), and—

The doorbell goes. I let out a little scream.

Nora: 'Go on, then! Let them in. I'll take their hats and bring them drinks.'

I open the door to Laurence, standing with a man I've never met, who he says has newly moved to Chelsea. Laurence seems a little intoxicated (no Mabel with him! *Jam!*) and, leaning in, says, 'Pixie, this is a clever young man who has read philosophy.' The clever young man looks as though he would like to kick him.

'Come in!' I say, and then, over my shoulder, leading them to the room with the blue velvet sofa, 'I'm Gypsy for this evening, you know . . .'

Nora serves drinks to Laurence and the clever young man, who has never heard of opal hush and is indeed young – fresh-faced with a pink nose. He watches the foam rise to the brim, saying, 'What a beautiful amethystine rose colour . . .' I somehow feel he is mocking me and so I add, 'All the Irish poets drink it' – knowing that evoking Willie will always impress.

Two women follow them shortly afterwards, and some further friends of Laurence's. He has done a good job of drumming up a crowd for me. I hesitated over inviting him but Nora insisted, saying he was a 'social butterfly'. She met him at the Lyceum, of course, and I guess she meant him being the son of Henry Irving and all.

There is a sudden tap at the window of my drawing room and this time, when I shriek, the others laugh. Two more women are coming around the front of the house: Edy and Christopher. The bell rings and Nora ushers them in and towards me.

Christopher seems in a rare funk. She is blazing about something. 'I bet your boots,' she snarls towards Edy, and then: 'Didn't he play mouldy sort of stuff anyway, and how *dare* he?' Distractedly she seems to remember where she is and leans in to kiss my cheek, murmuring, 'Mighty impressive, Pixie! What a turnout, huh?' and helps herself to a large whisky and seltzer, shunning the opal hush. She downs the glass in one and helps herself to a second. Her hand is shaking. 'Just come from a club. Some fellow was rather shocked by us! We saw a play, *Love of Women*, which I understand has been banned because some fool thought it entered the homosexual zone . . .' She stares around the room, challengingly. I glance nervously at the people packed like herrings in a box and wonder if I dare tell her to 'shh'.

A powerful sense of fear, of shame, of something dark and ugly and serpentine, is here with us. I want to open windows or make Christopher leave or ask her to be quiet, but I know she won't, and the awful feelings in me are growing and growing.

Laurence, arms folded, his usual stance of hugging the wall, says with a slightly mocking tone, 'And did it? Enter the *homosexual* zone . . .?'

Such a sizzle in the atmosphere! Laurence has wrapped some green silk thing around himself and for the first time, seeing how challenging his look is at Christopher, for the first time I wonder something.

'It merely reconnoitred timidly on the edge,' Christopher says with great bitterness.

The room (or is it me?) is bathed in embarrassment. Laurence is busying himself with a cigar, refusing to look up at us or at anyone at all. No one seems at ease.

Christopher glances around to see where Edy is. Seeing that she has her back to us – perhaps rather pointedly – and is choosing not to involve herself in this awful moment, Christopher takes a dive off the high wire: 'It kept well out of danger. The ladies concerned flew into a frightful pet at the very idea of anyone being a *Lesbian* . . .'

And so the word is out, and licks at everyone's face like a long tongue of fire. We all turn red.

'I will have one of those, if I may?' Christopher says with shaking boldness. She means a cigar. She leans in and there is nothing Laurence can do: he has to light it for her.

I rush to the kitchen to place a cold glass against my face.

'Beastly, beastly Christopher, embarrassing everyone, ruining *my* event . . . Why must she – dress like that! Such a rummy creature. Why must she – speak so loudly – of *such beastly things!*' I'm furious. I'm ready to cry. Nora is there. She looks up from drying *more* glasses and gives me an odd look. Then, a motherly hand on my shoulder, she directs me back towards the room, whispering, 'You'll be fine, once you start . . .' I resist her firm hand, hot on my shoulder, and am surprised by the strength of her. 'But what about my postcards?' I wail. 'Have we displayed them? The painted boxes? Will anyone *buy* anything?'

Upstairs, on a small side table near the sofa, spread on a green silk scarf, are my drawings, hand-coloured, postcard-sized, and three painted boxes like the one I made for Ellen, which took me forever. Next to them is a Chinese box, one drawer opened, with a sign, *Your donations here*, propped against it. I suddenly feel embarrassed and want to rush into the room and snatch the sign away.

Nora presses me down onto a kitchen chair and busies herself, taking the glass of opal hush I've picked up from somewhere and putting a big slosh of whisky in it before handing it back. 'Don't worry – go back in!' And she shoos me away.

So, I do. I step into the room. It's a dense fog of smells: the candles, the perfume, the cigars. I cough. I ping a spoon against my glass a few times – so hard it almost breaks – and try to get people's attention.

'Give us a song, Gypsy!' calls the clever young man, drunk already.

'Got very little voice for singing tonight,' I say, coughing again and taking a huge swig of my drink. 'But sit yourself down, I'll tell you a story . . .'

They fall into chairs and onto cushions on the floor – the room feels awful jam-packed – and Laurence lights up another cigar (is it my imagination or is he rattled in some way?) and a woman I don't know lights a silver incense urn which pours smoke upwards in a fine column. The woman leans in – edging her podgy self between Laurence and me – to blow out two candles, to make the room spooky, smiling at everyone in a mother-hen sort of way. The light from one remaining lamp falls on my orange coat, making it the most alive thing in the room.

I take a deep breath. I remember the moment on the ship with Daddy, and my performance of *Henry Morgan* for the captain. I have my little figures, and the miniature theatre set up on a table in front of me, and all are in much better shape for not having been squashed in a trunk at sea. *I can do this*, I say to myself, but the wobbly feeling, the horrible sense that I am swirling into a teeny miniature form, has already begun stealing up my body from deep in my belly. Soon I'll be the size of a beetle. Again, silently, I talk firmly to myself; I imagine all the preparation we have done and Nora saying, 'Go on with you', and I remember Florence saying to Laurence and Mabel, 'Pixie is the most extraordinarily productive and talented person!' and I stare round the room, cough a few more times, and try to *still* the wobbling in me, the feeling of all the blood draining from me. The shrinking stops. I'm about the size of a rabbit at least, not a mouse or a teeny beetle. I stretch up. Now I've elongated further, as if I were a long piece of dough, to the size of a hare.

I begin. '*Once, in a long before time, before Queen Victoria came to reign over we . . .*' I'm starting with the story of the chim-chim bird and the Obeah woman 'with wrinkles deep as ditches on her face'.

I scan the room for people's expressions, glancing at the clever young man, who is staring at me with naked curiosity; at a fat man, his dark eyes black currants in a cake; at Laurence, stroking his chin, a laconic stance. (Yes, Laurence is definitely trying to look as if he doesn't care one jot.) My heartbeat settles a little.

And then I begin one of Willie's poems that I've learned by heart and can recite perfectly, in a deep, slow voice that doesn't sound like me.

'*I went out to the hazel wood,*
Because a fire was in my head,
And cut and peeled a hazel wand,
And hooked a berry to a thread . . .'

This poem and the way I read it: I feel the audience's rapture. I have them. I feel the room calming and their breathing slowing. My voice a net, all the hearts lifting and trapped within it.

> '*But something rustled on the floor,*
> *And someone called me by my name:*
> *It had become a glimmering girl* . . .'

As I say this, I have the same drowsy feeling I had in the Physic Garden with Nora. The girl is in the room with us. First a silver fish and then – *whoosh* – casting off glittering scales and here she is; she looks like someone I know, like . . . Mary, my cousin Mary, no, not Mary but Florence, and then just as I'm sure – I can smell the apple blossom, fresh, tart, and the big eyes and the hair that feels like heather and I'm amazed at my own ability, my own magic, how I've conjured her here with me, and then a laugh – a loud laugh breaks the spell and she's someone else, a girl I don't know at all, more lovely than all the others put together . . . and even as I'm chanting, some true magic has happened and Willie himself has entered the room. Nora went to the front door to answer it and here he is: extraordinary, miraculous in his fedora, a cream suit, so commanding, handsome, like a painting – and just behind him, a striking woman, now towering beside him, golden hair swept up, handing a green velvet cloak to Nora, like a queen or a lioness, and I pause, just for a moment, for them to settle . . .

Willie stares straight at me, removes his glasses. Challenging, as if to say, 'Go on, then. You think you can read my poetry? Better than me – better than Florence?'

I stare back. My voice comes out warm, and old, like tree bark.

It's dark but I swear Willie's eyes are glittering, filling with tears. The lioness – she wears a red dress with a silver belt – has her hand on his arm. I've no doubt she is the inspiration for this poem, though I don't know how I know that. It feels as if she entered the room just as the fish turned into a beautiful woman, the silver belt her only relic.

> '*And kiss her lips and take her hands;*
> *And walk among long dappled grass,*
> *And pluck till time and times are done*
> *The silver apples of the moon,*
> *The golden apples of the sun.*'

A long, *long* pause, and only Nora is smiling at me, encouraging. The other faces in the candlelit room fade into grey petals on a wet bough. I long to shrink, but alas even the shrinking feeling won't come to save me. What have I *done*? How could I have recited Willie's own verse, without his permission, and – oh my Lord – him arriving in the room to hear it?

Then: 'Brava, little Pixie!'

He has taken off his fedora. He is clapping. The magnificent creature beside him – pushing some golden curls from her face and drawing every eye in the room to her – is clapping too, and others smile and gaze at them. I am all but swooning as I recognise her: Maud Gonne at my very first salon! The clapping grows louder, with others joining and smiling appreciatively. The other guests move towards Willie and Maud. I know they are asking him to recite, and I see him shake his head, laugh, turn to Laurence, to Edy and Christopher. All talk is suddenly of Maud's recent lecture tour and the police being called to Liverpool to stop her speaking of 'Irishmen in the English Army' – her fearlessness, her resolute voice for the Irish – and my performance is forgotten. I make a move to sneak past them, to go to the kitchen, but Willie stretches out an arm to catch hold of mine as I scuttle past.

'Your musical speech . . . The way you spoke, delicately where the emotion was most ecstatic – definitely not singing, but speaking. Thank you, Pixie. You and Florence are the only ones who understand what I intend – you are as abnormally psychic as she is . . .'

'I hope you weren't angry?'

'Why should I be angry?'

I bite my lip, hopping a little from foot to foot because I need to visit the water closet.

He whispers something then. My secret name in the Golden Dawn. But I barely hear it, and I feel as I did when Mama tried to tell me a secret, that things are just out of reach.

My expression must show my bewilderment.

From the corner of my eye I see Nora, watching us and nodding, smiling, gathering empty glasses and ashtrays; and Laurence leaving, and the clever young man being wakened from a tipsy slumber. I'm longing to make my escape to the water closet but, as I rush past, my eyes fall on the side table with my picture-cards on it and painted boxes and the sign propped up in a Chinese lacquer box. My painted boxes and my drawings – one was a sketch of Willie, reading, one of his brother Jack – they've all gone! Joy leaps in my heart. My mind runs to all the bully things I can do now. I will be able to pay the studio rent, cover the cost of the opal hush, maybe pay my train fare to join the others on a trip to Kent, or run another salon, without dipping further into my dwindling money from Uncle Teddy.

Then I see it. The little sign, *Your donations here*, on the floor, forlorn. I move closer, eagerly . . . but there is not a single note or coin in the open Chinese box: it's resolutely empty.

★★★

'Surely my friends didn't steal from me?'

In the kitchen, I sit on a stool while Nora makes me some Horlicks, spooning the malty crystals from the jar that the Horlicks Man gave us. She bustles around me, washing up, clearing up and yawning.

'Perhaps they didn't see your note? They thought they were – you know, gifts? *Souvenirs* . . .' she says, rubbing her back.

'Oh, it's so embarrassing, so embarrassing, because the cards took so long and the boxes even longer and now I can't give Mrs Fortescue any money to thank her for letting me host it here and I can't – pay you either!'

'Don't worry about me – it was a success! A grand success, and the Oirish Poet himself and his queen graced us with their presence.'

Alfred blunders into the kitchen carrying a tray of dirty glasses, and we fall silent. It's curious how we talk so easily, like equals, like sisters, but when Alfred or anyone else arrives we are stiff, with a consciousness that our conversation is wrong, too familiar.

Once Alfred has gone out again, I mutter: 'If only publishers weren't such pigs! That bloomin Grant Richards kept *Little Charles* six weeks and then *returned* him!'

'Who is Little Charles?' Nora asks, fetching a dry dish towel from a drawer and putting the damp one above the stove to dry.

'Oh, it's the *Lessons for Children* book. Heinemann and Lane and Duckworth have also returned *Little Charles*. An older and sadder Charles lingers. Damn publishers, anyway! I'm tired of them.'

'You're *tired*, yes, that's all. Your event was a triumph. Drink your Horlicks and' – she flicks the clean dish towel at me – 'away to bed.'

This motherly remark, so kind, and her hand holding mine in the Physic Garden, the sweetness of the malty drink, bring warmth into my cheeks and a memory of something I wanted to ask her.

'You said I was "psychic". Willie said the same thing. Why do people keep saying that about me?'

'I don't know what *he* means. He's part of your Golden Dawn lot, isn't he? Why don't you ask him?'

I spin around, shocked. 'How do you know I've joined *that*?'

She breaks into a grin. 'Pixie! You're so funny. You joined? Of course you did.'

'It's meant to be *secret*,' I protest. 'I'd like to know who told you about it . . .'

'I imagine it's a good place to meet fellows to invite to your salons,' she says provocatively.

I act as if I haven't thought of this, and then grumble, 'Well, they're all masked. You can't see one another for incense. There's no occasion for chit-chat about such things.'

Nora laughs, and after a moment I join in. I laugh more than I feel I ought to, but it *is* funny, and laughing is opening up a space in my chest, and *oh*, I feel relieved, now the evening is over.

Nora straightens up. 'Off to bed with you,' she says with a smile as Alfred enters the kitchen, sipping from one of the abandoned whisky glasses. He pauses and, seeing it's just me still here, tips his head back and drains it.

Later, in bed, I think about my salon and I know with absolute bully certainty what a *huge* success it was, and how *clever* and magical I am – yes, *psychic*, if that's the word they want, though I would call it *magnetic* or *charismatic*. Inspired by God, not the Devil. That day with Nora, staring at the pond, or when I was reading Willie's poem, I conjured things. Another world briefly revealed itself to me, and then sealed shut again.

How much bolder I will need to be when I ask my guests for money.

★★★

I wake with a thick head. Out of sorts for my trip to Winchelsea, to Ellen's house there by the sea. The train journey is sixteen shillings because Ellen insists on travelling first class, and I will have to take the money from my savings – that's my waking thought. Savings which are not being replenished. The triumph of my salon is forgotten when I remember how many drawings (including the clever sketch of Willie, glasses teetering on his nose) have gone, and not a single penny to show for them!

I arrive at the station in a disgruntled mood. Ellen is on the platform surrounded by a cluster of excited people. She tries to wave, her lilac hat almost knocked off her head by an over-eager gentleman pushing his autograph book at her, and I see that her dresser Sally is with her, arms piled with the roses that Ellen is given wherever she goes.

I join them and the three of us huff and puff and bundle into the first-class carriage, Sally and I almost pushing people aside in our attempt to protect Ellen from the fray. 'Miss Terry, Miss Terry! We love you!' accompanies us as the carriage door closes. Sally immediately tugs the curtain to cover the window a little, waving distractedly at a gawper standing there; she helps Ellen off with her coat, and places it on the rack above our seat.

Ellen takes off her hat, pats her hair, and breathes out loudly. 'Oh my goodness,' she sighs, closing her eyes for a moment. Her cheeks are shiny with sweat and she fans herself with an envelope, then opens her eyes, remembering something, and offers the envelope to me. 'Your ticket, Pixie. I meant to have it delivered to your home, but with all of this dreadful kerfuffle to leave London, I forgot.'

'Oh, thank you! I – Oh darn! I've already bought my ticket . . .' My cheeks burn. How kind Ellen is, and how thoughtful, especially about that gruesome subject, *money*, and how mean of me to doubt her. But I jolly well hope I get a refund from South Eastern Railway! Doubts about that immediately start up like a chugging beat, steam coming out of my ears, as I wonder which ticket master to ask about this (London or Winchelsea?) and how urgently I should do it to get the full sixteen shillings back.

Sally leaves us to go and sit in second class, asking 'ma'am' if she has everything she needs, and when Ellen nods she gathers up the volumes of roses and unceremoniously carts them off.

A guard has followed us onto the train with Ellen's luggage and cat basket, and now stands goggling at her until Ellen bestows one of her most gracious smiles and 'Thank you's upon him, and he can leave, step back onto the platform and blow his whistle hard enough for his eyes to pop out, signalling for the train to – *Hallelujah!* – leave all those admirers and well-wishers behind. With another great whistle, the train starts moving; the faces at the window in the gap of the curtain clamouring to get a glimpse of Ellen are suddenly forced to race alongside us, until the platform runs out and Ellen can stop her genteel waving.

She sits back, the cat basket on the table in front of her, and peers in at the big green eyes through the wicker.

'Poor little Sappho. Edy insisted we bring her. Do you think she minds being carted from pillar to post? I'm sure I'm heartily sick of it myself.'

The two gentlemen in our carriage smile at us from behind their newspapers, not wanting to seem as crass and adoring as those folk on the platform but fascinated just the same.

Ellen leans towards me to whisper, 'Henry is more seriously ill than anyone realises.'

'Oh!' I say. For a moment I can't think who on earth Henry is and then, realising she means Sir Henry – Mr Irving – I am surprised all over again to be the recipient of such an important disclosure, out of the blue.

'I'm terribly worried about him. But of course there's Mrs Aria . . .'

Her voice drifts off. Henry's new lady-friend has taken her place and now rides around the country lanes of Rye and Hastings with him in the same pony and trap in which Ellen once reigned.

Her eyes are glittering with tears, and she turns to stare out of the window, mindful of the two gentlemen.

'When my mother died,' she says, 'I came back to my dressing room to find someone had filled it with daffodils. Everywhere! They smelled strange, like cats on grass, as daffodils do . . . Henry did it, of course. He said it would make it look like sunshine.'

I cast about for something to say, something to relieve her mood. 'When my mother died, I just remember how strange her mouth looked, like a big dark hole.'

Ellen's eyes widen, and I see shock there and think: *Damn! That wasn't the right thing at all* . . . But then she smiles, almost laughs, and says, 'Yes, hark at me. You lost your mother so young. And it sounds as though you were whisked from your home without a daffodil in sight. How spoiled I am.'

She seems vulnerable without her hat. A snail without its shell. A short, stout grey woman, still beautiful and smartly turned out, with fierce kingfisher-blue eyes.

'Oh, I didn't mean – I only meant . . .' I try to apologise, but she is composed now. Dabs a handkerchief on her cheeks, with a sigh, then turns back to me, hands on her knee, steadied and proud.

'He used to get that pony going at a spanking rate sometimes! I hope Mrs Aria has the presence of mind to catch hold of the reins – or it might be a sudden death for both of them!' And then, leaning forward to whisper, 'Or better still: just *her*!'

I splutter into laughter.

Soon we move to the dining carriage, where we are served tiny glasses of champagne and plates of smoked salmon on soft bread with butter, with slices of lemon squished in a silver squeezer; and we give all our attention to handling this on the jiggety train for a while, and the mood lifts, and fields in every colour from

Brunswick to apple green appear in the windows – then a deer launches itself over a ditch – and Ellen says, 'How lovely! We've left London' and starts to relax.

'You remember when we first met, at the Reverend Baring-Gould's house?' she asks presently.

I do remember, and a picture of Daddy floats into my mind, and the shady walk among the beech trees: my first encounter with Ellen.

'I said to you that fame is a terrible thing. I sensed you did not agree. That you would like to be – famous.'

I finger the lace collar on my dress, wishing I'd worn something lighter in fabric, feeling hot under Ellen's gaze.

'Well . . .' I venture finally, 'I had my first salon last night. It was great fun. But – for me, I need to . . . Yes, fame would allow me to . . . My paintings would have a better chance of selling. And I guess, just the feeling, for a Nobody like me, you know, of *mattering* . . .'

I'm truly stumbling. Ellen's question is like a sword touching the tip of my heart. Why do I long so much for this thing, after all? But she's right, I do, and perhaps when Mama promised me it – *millions of people will know your gifts and what you have to offer them* – she put the seed in my mind, where it has grown and grown and grown and grown like a storm of starlings, or better still a cloud of bluebells.

Ellen listens, and nods slowly. 'People admiring your work. That's different. That's what you're wanting, isn't it?'

'Well, something that stops me from feeling this terrible . . . *invisible* feeling sometimes. Like I'm Nobody and no one anywhere cares about me.'

What a booby! I wish I could take it back. But Ellen continues to stare, her gaze very probing and thoughtful.

'You know, Pixie, invisibility is not *nothing*. Sometimes I've longed to just slip a cloak over my head.'

This brings a flash to my mind of our Golden Dawn Neophyte ritual. And she's right: becoming invisible is a desirable thing in the magic world. There is a joke about the Great Beast, that he walks about tearooms in London in his full Egyptian regalia and has waiters say of him, 'Oh, that's just Mr Crowley, being *invisible!*'

'I have felt so *looked-at* . . . since childhood,' Ellen continues. She makes it sound like a molestation. That famous painting of her, naked, by her first husband, Watts. The picture in my mind when I first met her. Her head thrown back, her breasts displayed, and in her face such a private expression, one which only a lover should see . . . I squeeze more lemon onto my sandwich and wonder if my cheeks are pink. Ellen is dabbing at her mouth with a napkin but I have the feeling she is being tactful, that something in my expression is visible to her. She changes the subject. 'That's why it's so wonderful to get away, though the farmhouse is possibly a mistake.'

How you could spend sixteen hundred pounds on a property and land and not work out that it isn't near the sea, as her beloved house is, that it's 'a mistake' . . . I'm just about to say so when some unemployed part of me remembers how often my cousin Mary remarked upon my lack of tact, and my earlier blunt remark about the dark hole of Mama's mouth; I suddenly wonder if Florence's comment about men not liking to be laughed at extends to women like Ellen, prideful as she is. She has already suffered quite a lot of teasing over the buying of the farmhouse at Smallhythe. Her money is her own, and nobody's business but hers. So, for once,

I sew up my mouth and congratulate myself on how grown-up I now am, with my new-found continence.

'Edy says Smallhythe is in awful repair,' Ellen continues. 'Great holes in the walls where the wool sacks had been leaning, and the Martins – the farmers I bought it from – still living there! We'll stay at my house in Winchelsea. Until the girls have got the farm ready. You will *love* Tower Cottage. Wait to see my view! The view is the best, most English in the world!'

And she's right. On arriving, after a bumpy ride in a cab from Winchelsea station and a very hilly ascent to Tower Cottage (next to a tower! And a lookout point! And opposite a strange stone cottage where the cellar is open to the street! And with palm trees!), we are finally standing at the bay window in her bedroom, the cat freed from her wicker basket and crooning around our feet.

Ellen murmurs, 'It's just a dream of a dream, this view, isn't it . . . but *you* could paint it and really see it.'

And we stare in awe over the curving lines of Romney Marsh: bobbles of trees, all the way to the milky-blue line of the sea. Sally brings in the flowers in several china vases and jugs and the bedroom is soon a rose garden of every colour and scent. I bury my face in them, and Ellen declares her favourite to be a white with delicate red edging around the petals. I fetch my paints and sit on the window seat and begin sketching there and then – she seems to have requested it, and I'd like to give her a watercolour of the view as a gift – and feeling such a welling-up of emotion that I might leap into dancing and shrieking, but I'm calmed, all is calmed, the moment I dip my paintbrush in the jar of water Sally has brought, turning it sea green, swirling my brush around.

Ellen leaves me. She is smiling, and not her actress's smile either, because above all else she has so wanted to share this with me, I can feel that she has – her love for her home and her view of the sea and her joy at being able to provide for herself hums in the room like the engine of a great, newfangled train.

★★★

In the morning, Sally returns to London and a local woman, Nancy, takes her place at the cottage. We walk down the stone steps of Ellen's garden, gingerly, with Ellen holding my arm and tutting at the cat, telling her to stay at home. We open the gate carefully, not wanting to let Sappho out onto the road where a passing pony and trap might knock her down. Ellen checks to the left and the right for prying townsfolk, and when none are seen we hurry to the lookout where we can hide a little, behind a stone wall, under a shelter, and sit on a bench looking out to sea, as the Duke of Wellington once did, according to Ellen (he even stayed in her house, though obviously this was Long Ago). I stand up to see again the sweeping hills, the green of Romney Marsh, with the sea sitting atop it like a blue cream on a layer cake. I love the scale – how far we can see – but then how domestic and English too, coming right up to the tiny pink-and-white daisies of the fleabane peeping out from the cracks in the stone wall. I can't resist another sketch, unpacking my satchel in haste – this time a new sketchbook, and charcoals.

'I knew you'd love it,' Ellen says happily.

'This is what *I'd* like,' I say, unguarded, wiping smudgy hands on my dark-navy dress. 'To buy my own house, by the sea, with my own money, and paint all day, and live there with a cat!'

'Yes, it was *Nance Oldfield* money that allowed me to buy Tower Cottage. One mustn't crow, of course . . .' She beams, and the wind catches a curl of her hair and unravels it from her bonnet, whipping it all around her face. I know she *would* like to crow and is glad that I allow her that joy in her own success. There is a pause in which the only sounds are my charcoals on the page, and a seagull somewhere faintly crying, and the wind flapping the pages of the sketchbook a little, making it impossible to continue. Ellen seems to remember something, and says, 'But live *alone*? Is that right, Pixie? Edy says . . .' She coughs. 'Edy might be a little worried about you. That you're getting in with that strange crowd, Florence Farr's lot, the Golden Dawn?'

'Oh, for Bully's sake!' I shriek.

I clap a hand over my mouth and feel my face redden.

'Oh, I'm so sorry, Ellen!' (This makes her smile and she pats my hand.) 'But . . . why does *everyone* keep discussing the Golden Dawn? I'm really not supposed to . . .'

'The theatre is a terrible place for gossip. But it's all the in-fighting that has brought it to everyone's attention, the resignations and the . . . well, that rather scandalous story of, you know, that couple, in court — it was in all the papers . . .' When I blink, trying to look ignorant, she taps my knee with her glove and laughs. 'Oh Pixie, you *do* know about it! The couple arrested in London six months ago for the rape of that poor girl, "Madame" aiding and abetting . . . Don't pretend. I have the news article somewhere; Edy sent it to me—'

'They're a travesty. She – the woman – was pretending to be Madame Blavatsky! Just two degenerates bringing the name of the Golden Dawn into disrepute. Florence says—'

'Well, that is how the general public will think of it.'

'The general public is a General Jackass!'

'That's as may be, but I feel some sort of – Since your mother and father aren't here, I feel—'

'I'm a full-grown woman!' I'm almost crying. I don't know why this attempt to *advise* me fills me with such rage, but it does. Perhaps it's just that, having no parents, I'm not accustomed to it. But even when I did have them, Cousin Mary used to say it about me – that I was uneducable, unwilling to listen to anyone else.

Ellen rests her eyes on me for a moment and then, the wind lifting her bonnet almost from her head, she notices that a man is hovering near the steps to her garden, and that he is using some opera glasses to stare at us, not very subtly.

'Let us go back. Nancy will make us tea. We can ride over to Smallhythe later and see how Edy and Christopher are getting on. I've asked Ted to join us. He is still in a brown mood about his work: it might do him good to meet you.'

Back at Tower Cottage, wordlessly, Ellen gives me the cut-out pages from *The Times*. I did know of the case – Florence mentioned it a lot and Alfred too – but as I haven't gone to many meetings of the Order, I . . . conspired somehow not to know the details. My stomach starts to churn as I read. The fraudsters were arrested in Birkenhead, Mr Horos sentenced to fifteen years of penal servitude and Madame Horos to seven years in prison. All of us in the Order – Florence said at the time – know that they were never *real* members of the Golden Dawn, that the idiot Mathers (our founder!) gave them secrets in Paris that they should never have seen, but of course General Jackass doesn't know that.

According to the article, young women were enticed into the home of this couple, and one victim, sixteen-year-old Daisy Adams, described Madame Horos holding her head while the husband, Theo, raped her. He said he was making her into his 'little wife' with the Spirit of Christ. The descriptions of the rest of their rituals *are* horribly like the Neophyte one that I went through, and a very hot and strange fluttering begins in my chest as I continue to read. Rituals that only a real member of the Order could know about: Daisy blindfolded, the language the same, even a touch of cold steel and a Mystic Repast! Oh, what must Ellen and the others – Laurence, Chris, Edy, all of them – what must they now think of the Order, of *me*? Is this what they think we all get up to?

I know that, for Florence, the most upsetting thing is not this shame, but how many of the Order's important secrets have been exposed. For everyone else, Willie and the Horlicks Man, it's surely the same feeling I'm having now: it's bad enough for the Great Beast to create such embarrassment with his 'goings-on', but this is far worse. Now I understand why they all rushed to distance themselves from it, starting up and joining new groups, and, if asked, clamping up.

I fold the newspaper as small as possible, sighing. Ellen's new housekeeper, Nancy, has brought me a cup of tea, which is on a tray on the window seat in my bedroom, turning grey. I sip it and stare out of the window, watching the sun slipping into an ugly red mouth, wondering what to say to Ellen. 'Thank you for your concern for me', perhaps. 'Thank you, I'm awful grateful, but that's not what goes on at all: these two are fraudsters and degenerates, old mountebanks, as Uncle Teddy would call them, bringing the Order into disrepute'? I have only been to a few meetings, after all. I like secret knowledge but am not really a meeting kind of person, it turns out.

Whatever I plan to say, I can't get rid of the pictures. Madame Horos is so fat, claiming this is because she has imbibed the spirit of the great Helena Blavatsky! And Theo, thirty years younger than her, is a slithering, ugly man. Madame Horos said he couldn't possibly be guilty of the rapes because he was a castrato and incapable of sex. *Doctors were called and although found to have only one testicle, the other was 'small and perfectly formed'.*

Such pigs! I can't shake it. And the newspaper reproduced – badly – a portrait Madame Horos proudly unrolled in court, to much amusement, it being a portrait of her enormous self reclining against a live tiger, in a temple in India. Somehow the Strength Tarot card that I saw in my mind's eye, the woman holding the mouth of a lion, will not budge from my mind.

I am Astraea, Lady of Justice, but also the Lord.

I wear no blindfold. I have foresuffered all

I judge thee worthy to attain thy freedom:

'tis thou alone canst show that thou art worthy to retain it.

Go forth to achieve with tears; and bear within thy heart this word of mine: thy soul alone is free.

Go forth: the world is thine... Oh, use it well! Thou hast an equal, not a master.

So we travel over to Tenterden in the horse and trap and it rattles our bones and children run beside it when it slows through villages, holding out their autograph books and shouting. The trap gives Ellen the perfect excuse to smile and say, 'Oh, I'm *sorry*!' but to move on, faster than they can follow.

At Smallhythe the others are gathered in the garden, and laughing about some mishaps, and the sun is out under a blue sky with clouds rolling like balls of uncombed wool. The mood is gay. The farmhouse certainly is a mess, with wool sacks everywhere, tumble-down walls and a cheesy smell of sheep, mixed in with a profusion of plants and flowers, lavender, mint, parsley, rosemary, gone crazy. Edy and Christopher have been staying next door, a cottage called the Priest's House. They want to show me the summerhouse; Christopher says it will be her study when it's cleared, and she's brought a chair and a typewriter and she's awful pleased.

Ted arrives – Ellen's son – tall and (to me) rather frightening, with his sweetheart Elena hanging on his arm, a doting beauty who eloped with him despite being a Catholic and thereby caused a scandal. They have two young boys with them, who belong to Ted and his first wife, May. I gather there was an older girl, named after Ellen, who died in infancy. Ellen swoops on the two blond cherubs, John and Peter, smothering her grandchildren in kisses.

I'm so afraid of Ted. He swaggers about, feeling himself to have the natural rights of belonging to a famous theatre family. It's strange, because Laurence Irving does the same and yet I've never felt *he* despised me. Nor Edy, come to that! I guess you can always tell when someone thinks little of you. Ted and Edy are talking about the new production they're working on: sixty costumes for a nativity play where he says he will 'borrow images from Rembrandt'. His elevated talk – the sense he has that what *he* is doing matters – makes me feel smaller and smaller. Soon I will turn into a harvest mouse, running at their feet.

I surreptitiously hide my sketchbook. All the artists that this crowd have known! Watts. Burne-Jones. Singer Sargent painted Ellen, after all, in her beetle dress. Suddenly ashamed of my lowly status, I take my picnic blanket to a further spot in the garden, near the orchard. But Ted's son – chasing a butterfly – runs close to me and soon the others come, sitting beside me, smoking and lolling on the blanket. The younger boy, Peter, has a cheeky manner and pushes his face close to me, his mouth open. I stare back at him. Elena pays no attention to me: why should she? I'm neither pretty nor famous.

Christopher – thank goodness for Christopher – has a gift for me. A smock. Heavy linen, embroidered sleeves. She smiles as I unwrap the brown paper, feeling all eyes on me. 'Come on, Pixie, everyone's wearing 'em down here, gotta look the part – keep up!' she says somewhat gruffly, taking a drag on her cigarette. I unfold the garment, admiring the fine ruching at the cuffs, and under their watchful gaze feel obliged to stand up and put it on. It smells of the farm, and the sheep – a comforting smell.

'Thank you,' I whisper. I see Ted's eyes on me then, and his thoughts are very clear. He thinks I'm *one of them*. An *invert*. That expression of Daddy's comes back to me. How shocking I found it but since knowing Christopher and Edy it has taken on a different feel. The word itself I looked up in a book by sexologist Havelock Ellis: 'Sexual Inversion'. Christopher is so open about such things, so clear about her love for Edy, that it's impossible not to feel admiration for her. Still, am I one of them? I have no idea. I have no desire to take a man's name, nor dress like one, as Christopher does. But I think that, in Ted's eyes, being a woman not worth bedding makes me nothing at all. He is so very cranky in his manner, and I find myself thinking he would make a great study for a mad person in a book.

Peter wants to play ring-a-roses. 'Come on, Daddy!' he shouts at Ted. Ted – dragged from a declaration, or perhaps an argument with Christopher – is still saying crossly, 'But of course it is the *director* who is the real genius of the theatre – the actors might just as well be marionettes!' and out of the corner of my eye I see Ellen approaching, stopping dead, and turning away from us towards the summerhouse.

We form a circle to dance with the children. The boy whirls for a moment and then, grabbing his father's free hand, puts his other hand in mine. I am between him and Christopher as we dance in circles around the garden and 'all fall down'. It's impossible not to laugh and feel the energy of the little boy and his sister, laughing with us.

I seek out Ellen at the summerhouse. She is sitting on the chair Christopher brought, a faded orange velvet cushion on her knee, staring.

'Are you all right?' I ask her.

I suddenly feel I should have knocked. Ellen is crying. Her face is wet and her eyes red; the tears simply slip down, and she makes no attempt to cover them. She raises her eyes to me and nods, allowing her tongue to peep out and catch a tear.

'I'm being silly, Pixie. Pay me no mind.'

I cannot prevent myself from kneeling at her feet and putting my head on the cushion. It smells faintly of Christopher's cigarette smoking but it is a soft, comforting fabric, warmed by the sun, and she rests her hand in my hair. With my face buried in her lap (like a supplicant), she begins speaking.

'It's Ted. So painful. The children! And he won't see May, and May is still angry, and he won't give her money for them either. Oh! I'm paying that. It's fine, but what a mess, what a mess.'

I lift my head and offer her a handkerchief. I sit back on my heels on the dusty summerhouse floor while she blows her nose, murmuring her thanks.

'And here he is in love with another, and I believe she might be expecting too . . . and how can that help?' she says. Her eyes drift to the window, to the orchard, the well, as if the answer is there. 'It must break May's heart. I feel so sorry for her: she still loves him. Do you see how grown-up John acts at only six, and Peter hopes for just a tiny jot of attention? "*To you, your father should be as a god . . .*" Ted longed for *his* father too, and Laurence for Henry. Oh, and there is nothing one can do, nothing at all.'

'You mustn't blame yourself. You are a wonderful mother. How I wish you were . . . *my* mother . . .' This part I say so quietly, I wonder if she even hears it.

But she looks up at once, those piercing eyes suddenly dry. 'Ah, dear Pixie. Here I am, crying over . . . goodness knows what, and you, you are alone in the world and yet I've never seen you anything other than cheerful and – *industrious.*'

She straightens her spine, and throws the faded cushion onto an upturned pail as if to say, 'No need for that! What weakness and poppycock!' She sniffs loudly, pulling in her sadness: tightening the ribbon on a drawstring bag, all sorrows safely inside it.

'Thank you,' she says. 'You are very kind, aren't you? And you seem to spend no time at all blaming *your* parents, or your father—'

'Why should I blame my parents?'

'Well, I did rather think your father left you – forgive me if this is not true – but he did not seem to make the proper provision for you.'

Indeed. She has known all along, and, indeed, her kindness to me has been, as I suspected, a subtle attempt to help me. The confirmation of this – my heart swells, and for a moment I'm speechless. And then she adds, with a bitter tone: 'Ted makes no secret of his blaming *me*.'

'Ted is his own person – I can't see what he has to blame you for . . .'

'Oh, but a mother should never be young, or in love, or so caught up in the romance of her elopement that she forgets what an impact it might have on her children . . .'

This seems the time. The moment to confide something so weighty that I realise it has been sitting on me, on my shoulders, for a long, *long* time.

'Before she died, my mother told me – that is, she *tried* to tell me – some kind of secret . . .'

Ellen's eyebrows draw together and I feel her interest quicken. Suddenly footsteps and loud breathing: the summerhouse door is pushed open and Peter rushes in.

'Nanna! Where have you been? I bumpf my head and Daddy says I can't have honey on it!'

'Honey on your head? I should think not! What a terrible mess it would make of your lovely hair,' Ellen says, sweeping him into her arms. He is carrying his sailor hat in his hand and his bottom lip juts out stubbornly.

'But my mama lets me at home,' he says. And then: 'Look at that big spider! And can I have the feather?'

Ellen gives him the feather from a jar on Christopher's desk. She stands up. 'Let's go back. I will ask Nancy if you can have some honey on toast. Will that do? And some for you too, Pixie,' she says, pausing to point out the roses curling around the door frame to Peter, inviting him to sniff them.

Watching her make her way across the grass with Peter's hand in hers, I feel a strange sense well up: as if I've always known her, or knew her in another part of my life, another garden, another summer. And in that summer she leaned against her orange velvet cushion like an empress, wearing a crown of flowers and a dress smothered with roses and pomegranates, and knowing and understanding all the unspilled secrets in the world.

★★★

The others stay longer at Tenterden, but after a few weeks I eventually feel I need to leave for London as I have another salon booked and (I don't mention this part) another Order of the Golden Dawn meeting.

Ellen stays because she has lines to learn and Ted's stage designs to approve, also Mr Irving and Mrs Aria to avoid, so no great urgency to be back in London. Winchelsea agrees with her. Yes, she is a curiosity here, but the townspeople are respectful and in awe, and they never shove autograph books under her nose, only the straggly little posies from children, plucked from nearby sea pinks. One is presenting her with flowers at the door as I leave, Ellen, in her gown, bending to pretend to sniff them.

The train journey is smooth and the ticket master friendly. I travel with the first-class seat and the refunded money safely in my purse.

Arriving in Chelsea, I'm marching at a lick, carrying my case, when I feel and then see a man fall into step beside me. A shadow at my shoulder. He tips his hat: a man of about forty-five, with a moustache drenching his top lip like an overgrown cliff.

'It's Pixie, isn't it? It's me – Mr Waite. From the Golden Dawn?' The Horlicks Man. He mouths the last bit, with a finger to his lip in case anyone might be watching. What a queer fellow! I quicken my step. 'You're the draughtswoman, aren't you? Florence Farr's friend?' he asks, quickening his own. I slow down a little then, lest we look ridiculous. *Draughtswoman* is nice.

I nod and, glancing sideways, take him in. The dome forehead, the dreamy, sad-looking eyes. 'You're the manager of the Horlicks factory? Thank you so much – we've been enjoying it!'

'That is my employment, why yes, but I – I'm a poet. A scholar. An Adept in the magic arts. *Songs and Poems of Fairyland*. I could – If you'd like a copy, I'd be exceedingly happy to give one to you.'

Another poet. I put my case down; the leather handle is starting to bite into my hand. Mistaking the gesture, he picks it up at once. 'Oh yes, do allow me . . .'

Annoyance sets up a drumbeat inside me. Surely this awkward critter is not going to walk all the way to Milborne Grove with me?

Chelsea at this time of the morning is empty except for the workmen, cheerfully whistling, the sounds of tools being slammed and dropped. We pass The Boltons, glittery and white like a giant sugar cake. I imagine Mr Waite lives somewhere like this.

'Why do they give you that sobriquet?' he asks.

'Hmm?'

'Pixie. Are you one?'

The man is an idiot, then, as well as a prowler. 'My name is Corinne Pamela Colman Smith. It's a nickname – bestowed on me by Miss Ellen Terry.'

'Oh, you know the Lyceum crowd? Mr Irving too?'

Yes, yes. Get to the point, man! Why were you waiting for me? What do you want from me? Why are you walking so fast beside me that I'm practically running? I'm forced to skip to avoid stepping on a workman sleeping on his folded bag of tools. How to shake this pretentious Horlicks Man?

'You know Nora. Mrs Lake. A very gifted psychic,' he says in his mumbly, faintly American kind of drawl.

Ah. *Nora*. She is a beauty, for sure. Men are often curious about Nora. Is this why he's walking with me?

'Would you like an invitation to one of her spiritualist occasions?' I try. 'I believe there's one this evening?'

He stops. 'Oh. Well, in fact, I'm already coming along.'

'Oh!'

This is surprising, and further irritates me. People who beat all around the bush! Why can't the damn man come to the point?

'Scientific interest only,' Mr Waite says. 'A study, an examination, you know.'

Naturally. He huffs a little with the effort of carrying my case, and puts it down on the pavement, distracted. I'm tapping my toes.

He says in a low voice: 'The Order is falling apart. I've founded something else. Can't say. And sadly, ladies are not permitted. The scandal lately . . . That dreadful couple. I blame Crowley. We should have cut him out earlier, like a fungus . . .'

Talking about the Order, he becomes a schoolboy. My anger bubbles over. For Bully's sake – 'ladies are not permitted'! As if I care about his silly nonsense! What an over-educated, puffed-up, Latin-speaking booby he is . . .

We are standing near the Japanese cherry tree at the front of my studio.

'You know what, Mr Waite—' I begin, and the trembling in my voice is a warning that he doesn't heed.

'*Arthur!* Do call me Arthur!'

'Arthur. If you want to say something to me — I'd much rather you were brave enough to come out and say it.'

'I beg your pardon?'

'You have followed me from the station. You know who I am, because you called me the draughtswoman. Is there something you would like to ask me? I don't bite, you know. I realise you've probably never spoken to a small person like me, without your airs and graces . . .'

'Airs and graces? I'm so sorry if I have offended—'

'You haven't! But now, if you're not going to tell me—'

Oh my goodness. I know my face is very red. I know that addressing him so directly, demanding he speak to me and accusing him of following me, is rude — *rude* — and much too straightforward. What would Cousin Mary say? Or Daddy, come to that? But something in Mr Waite's manner I find irksome. *I'm a poet. I am a scholar.* What a silly way he has of speaking to a clever but not very pretty young woman who can't be flirted with or patronised.

'Was it Nora you wanted to see?' I snap.

'Nora bears a great resemblance to my — sister, my sister Frederica. That dear sister has since embraced another aspect than that of earthly life . . .'

I've already turned my back to him and moved towards the door. 'My sincere condolences,' I say without sincerity.

He blurts: 'Oh, Frederica — that was almost thirty years ago!'

And yet he spoke of it as if it were a raw, new thing. Oh, what a wearisome man! Does he have some fixation on Nora because she looks like his long-dead sister?

'Well, if you don't mind, Mr — Arthur, as you mentioned, I'm a draughtswoman and I have some — work to do.'

I almost said 'some very important work' but I stopped myself. I notice the ghost of a smile under his moustache as he tips his hat and backs politely away. I have at least amused him. Or is it that he finds me . . . admirable? I cannot shake the idea that he had something to ask me and didn't quite dare. Oh well. Good job I got a hold of myself before I said more, plainer and ruder things. Perhaps I will find out what he wanted to ask me this evening.

For now, here I am, with the sun through the cherry tree branches dazzling like silver stars, spots dancing in front of my eyes. Home. *My* home, and Nora.

Fear death by water, the poet said. And he was right. But although I'm suspended here

From my Tau cross and my feet forming another Fylfot cross, I'm no martyr.

Look closely and my face is suffused with enchantment, my head a nimbus.

Who am I and what do I signify for you? I'm the hardest to decipher

That's why the poets and artists love me so. Even your friend here has summoned me before.

The electric bolts of my hair! My dainty feet!

Make them the green of that juicy grass and all that lives and breathes

Hey Pixie! Make me live forever.

Nora looks bonnier than ever. In fact she has become rather plump, and when I tease her about it, saying how well she looks, she blushes and says, 'Oh Pixie! What an innocent you are. You know I'm expecting, don't you?'

I didn't know, and now I feel foolish. And something else. If I think of Nora with a baby, or picture her crooning over it, I feel a twisting kind of anguish. But yes, now I look at her, the plumpness is rather in her middle, disguised though it might be by her dress. As if she has a big plum pudding under her apron.

Plans for the evening's spiritualist meeting are already in place, chairs being drawn up, incense lit, the room swept and tidied, because, Nora says (with a grin, as if it pleases her), some men are coming from the Society of Psychical Research to 'test' her and she is ready for them. A thought strikes me: *Mr Waite?* I mention that I met him and Nora rolls her eyes.

'Oh, him! What a drip he is, don't you think? Always mooning over me. I didn't know *he* was with the Society for Psychical Research. I thought your other friend was coming, the poet?'

'*Willie?*'

'Hmmm,' she murmurs. She's distracted, looking for Alfred to bring more bottles up from the cellar and anxious about the curtain that needs fixing in the front; it doesn't close properly.

Willie is the first to arrive, before the clock strikes seven, with a serious air, not quite himself, as if he has some other purpose. He has a man with him I've never seen before. This man wants to sit right at the front, and before he does so he checks the curtains, the wine glasses, lifts the cloth from the table where Nora will sit. I see her watching, her face unreadable.

Most definitely, this man is looking for something. Others start to trickle in. Mr Waite arrives with Laurence's friend the clever young man, whom I think he calls Arthur Ransome. Around ten people, mostly men, many of them smoking cigars and pipes and Willie in his fedora looking very self-important: nothing like the usual crowd of sausage-legged ladies. Alfred takes their coats and hats and stands around in his menacing way. He seems particularly aggressive tonight, perhaps aggrieved by the news that Nora is being tested. Nora, though, is glittery and excited: I guess she loves a challenge.

In the kitchen, she stands alone by the pantry, swigging a quick finger of whisky.

'Nora!' I whisper. 'Shouldn't you drink stout, for the baby?'

She gives me a strange look then, one that I can't fathom.

'How many are out there?' she says.

'Are you nervous?'

'No more than usual. It's just . . .'

'Well, about ten, I'd say. Not the usual crowd. Of course, you don't like to be doubted – to be called a liar or a fraud . . .' I suggest, though this is met with a hard stare.

'I don't think folk are calling me a fraud, Pixie. They're just – They want something to measure, you know, something to "prove". Can you measure feelings? If a woman said to someone "I love you", could anyone possibly know how true that is or how strong her feelings are?'

It is queer, the way she says this, staring at me with such fierce intent. Tonight she's wearing a plum-coloured velvet dress and her eyes are shining (the whisky!) and her voice is soft. Her little chin upturns defiantly. Then she bursts into a giggle.

'Oh Pixie! Silly men, eh? How they want to pin everything down . . . Even your man Willie can't just let things *be*! Well, if they want science, I won't disappoint. If they want fun and games . . . *well* . . .!'

'Now you're making *me* nervous! What do you have up your sleeve?'

She shakes her head. Smooths down her dress. Braces herself, shoulders squared, and heads back to the room.

I'd imagined it would be like the last spiritualist meeting I attended at Smith Square, but the atmosphere is starkly different. These are not guests, not an audience, but examiners. The room is dark and smells powerfully of incense, coffee, cigars and some strange chemical smell that I can't name. Other men are lifting curtains, lifting the cloth on the table, crawling on the floor to look under it, opening cabinets, writing things down in notebooks. The chairs are not in rows like last time, but positioned around the table, and Nora sits down without any preamble. She doesn't smile and welcome us as before, and there's no prayer, no message for the congregation. This all feels sobering, without light or joy.

Alfred stands by the door, arms folded, legs wide. I hesitate, not sure if I am welcome at the table.

'Come and sit here, Pixie!' Willie whispers, indicating a chair he has saved for me. The man he's brought with him introduces himself as Professor Courtier in a strong French accent. 'I am the director of the laboratory of physiology and sensations at the Sorbonne,' he says. For a moment I cannot understand the word 'laboratory', thinking he is saying 'lavatory'.

I sit down, feeling a dangerous trembling within me. I hope I'm not going to burst out laughing . . .

Willie has a notebook in front of him and is sharpening a pencil. He moves the candle a little closer towards him, a quiet intensity in his manner. The men are impressed with each other and further introductions are made. Willie addresses us in his deep Irish voice: 'As you know, I believe in the practice and philosophy of what we have agreed to call magic, in what I call the "evocation of spirits", though I do not know what they are . . .'

The men murmur their agreement.

'I have noted in the past that the strain of the watching makes taking notes difficult. Might I suggest that I write things down, and you make sure all eyes are fixed on the medium?'

Nora, sitting very straight, puts out both hands and closes her eyes. She breathes deeply and then quietly, seeming to soften and relax. I think of her hand, touching mine, and the upturned palm looks small just now, and pale, a petal fallen from a large white flower. Her shoulders in her plum velvet dress with its low neckline sink lower. On her right, Willie takes one hand; on her left, Arthur Waite takes the other.

'You may begin, Mrs Lake. We are ready,' Willie says.

Alfred snuffs out a few candles, leaving only a couple burning at the table, and returns to his standing position. Everyone else is still and silent. This is very odd. I mean, if Nora can't stand and command the room, speak, summon any angels or spirits or do her thing . . . what on earth is everyone waiting for? (And why are these men breathing so very loudly? That alone makes it feel as if there are extra folk in the room with us.) Willie has his pencil poised, like a dart he is about to throw.

Suddenly Nora stretches, moans a little and stands up, shoving her chair behind her. Seeing her, my heart knocks in my chest. All eyes follow Nora. The black lace at the neckline of her dress. She takes a few steps, walking as if in a trance, until she is at the window, and then she begins fiddling with the curtains. She is clutching at them as if she means to open them and shine some light on things. (It wouldn't work, as it's dark outside without a moon.) She has a glassy look and is nothing like the lively Nora we all know, nor even the confident Nora of the spiritualist meeting, with her jokes and her saucy messages about farting. This performance is *not* great fun; instead it's what her examiners expect: serious and somewhat sinister.

After adjusting the curtains, Nora comes to sit back down with us. I find I have been holding my breath, watching her, and as she sits I breathe out. And then a rather horrible thing occurs: she has her eyes closed, her face intense, and she starts retching, as if something is trying to escape from her. She grasps both of Willie's hands and shrieks: 'Oh, here it comes, it's *coming*!' – which makes me jump about a mile in my seat. She makes ghastly twisting movements like spasms, and more retching sounds, though nothing comes out of her. And then, the strangest thing of all: a weird green light appears on the breast of her dress. Willie gasps. Monsieur le directeur of whatever at the Sorbonne squeals (in a rather let-loose kind of voice): 'Mon Dieu, look at her hands!'

She shakes them loose from Willie's and we all stare. There is a bizarre green light in her palms, flitting about like a small dragonfly.

'Spirit is here with us,' Nora says in a very deep voice. 'And now it is – there!' She points to the curtain and the green light is indeed there – a luminous mass about the size of a coin – and then this curious dancing light shifts and appears on Nora's breast, where she quickly covers it with her hand. My gaze goes to the candles on the table, wondering if a trick of shadows or light is being created by them. The candles are behaving oddly. One has gone out. There is no draught, but the remaining candle is bending, leaping, almost gone.

I did not expect to feel fear this evening. But, watching the candle, I tremble and feel a sliver of ice at the bottom of my spine. Who am I to doubt this? Who or what is here in the room with us, hovering close to Nora? Does it mean us harm? Are spirits here? Are they always here, as Swedenborg teaches, as so many poets and visionaries the world over have suggested? My hands feel sticky. There is a quiet music somewhere, far away, perhaps from the street, just a few piano notes, drifting, and the sound of them fills me with a chill, a great clanging somehow, telling me what is coming, what I have not understood about the world. I would like to leap up, run from the room, but a sudden snatching of my hand by a large hot hand makes me jump.

The Horlicks Man has leaped up from the table and is now beside me, clutching my hand. I feel his breath on my face as he hisses: 'Oh, ask her! Do ask her what she sees! Is it – *is it* my sister Frederica?!' He stares at Nora's breasts, and murmurs, in the saddest of voices, 'I see her face, I *do*, I see it in the green light . . .'

Nora's head suddenly drops forward, with more retching sounds. My heart flies up to my mouth. 'Nora!' I whisper.

The others seem to be holding their breath, spellbound and watching to see where the luminous green shape might appear again. A spot leaps up on Nora's dress. And then, with a groan, she falls forward onto the table, banging her head.

'Nora! Are you all right?' I shout this time, jumping from my seat. I can't help myself. My fear for Nora has got the better of me, and of course my shouting breaks the tension. Other voices begin to mumble. 'Give her some air!' a man who was introduced as 'the Baron' says firmly. The Horlicks Man's voice is almost a wail: 'Did she see her? Did she? Oh, *what* did she see?'

Professor Courtier is determined to keep things in order. 'Do you have your camera, Mr Waite? We must record this green – spot . . .'

To me, the spot looked something like a green leaf – maybe better described as shoots of green? It did seem to flit about, changing in size and intensity. But it is obvious that it has gone now. Though the Horlicks Man rushes to fetch the camera, there is a commotion at the table, with Alfred bringing Nora a glass of water, and Nora opening her eyes and looking around at us all.

Alfred lights all the candles again and the men speak excitedly. 'I most definitely saw it,' the Horlicks Man says to Willie.

'But *what* did you see?' Willie asks.

'Some green luminous threads passing between her hands . . .'

'I saw a vivid green leaf!' I say, unable to stop myself. The men turn towards me, seeming to register me for the first time. Nora, sipping the water and smiling, looks around her as if she's waking from a long sleep. Alfred stands behind her chair, glowering; being of a different class means the gentlemen only address him to fetch their coats and hats or a glass of whisky, but his striking bulky figure and the strength of his feeling for Nora make me smile: how hard it must be for them to treat him as they might wish to, as if invisible!

Willie is writing things down in his notebook and announces to the others: 'So, I saw a green light object, like a slowly falling drop, on her dress. The materialisation also appeared in a rounder and I think somewhat larger shape minutes later. The medium did not put her hands below the table: they were visible at all times. She made some convulsive sounds, but there was no crisis . . .'

'Well,' Nora says, in her bright, awake voice, 'anyone like a nice cup of tea before they go home?'

Her eyes flick over mine as if she dare not let our glances meet. When I look over at the Horlicks Man, I see to my astonishment that his eyes are full of tears.

★★★

'But what did you *do* there?' I ask her later in the kitchen, drinking our Horlicks.

Nora, now wrapped in an apron, is unmistakably perky, lit up. Being with child certainly is making her glow. Her little turned-up nose, the shiny auburn curls framing her face, her big eyes: I have my sketchbook in front of me at the table and am making a quick charcoal likeness of her while she watches me, only mildly interested in the drawing, her gaze turned inwards.

'Spirit chose the form of a – little light . . .' she says.

'I guess you're not going to tell me,' I say, adding some little devil horns to the drawing, and a forked tail.

Nora laughs. 'Why, Pixie, what are you suggesting? All I did was allow Spirit to come through me and show itself, just as they were hoping.'

After a pause, I put the charcoal aside and with a coloured crayon add a green fairy, appearing just above Nora's head.

'I'm only sorry your friend Florence Farr wasn't here to see it,' Nora says, and her voice is awful smug.

'Why, Nora, are you – *jealous* of Florence?' The minute I've said it, I regret it. A hand flies up to my mouth and I feel the colour flooding to my cheeks.

Nora's expression darkens and she stands up. 'That Willie with his bow tie and his fedora, hovering over me and writing notes. Who does he think he is? "*She made some convulsive sounds, but there was no crisis.*" Does it never occur to men that, if we wanted to, we might be able to *fake* such things as a . . . *crisis?*'

This makes me splutter; her meaning is very clear.

'But what does it matter?' I say. 'You ran rings around them! They were amazed by you – the Horlicks Man was even weeping! The evening was a triumph!'

Running rings around them: I picture a hare, the golden auburn colour of Nora, belting across a field, outrunning all the hounds.

'Pixie. I survived their silly tests. I gave them the show they wanted. But they did not change their opinion or credit me with intelligence or skills or any ability that they don't have themselves. Can't you feel – their *belittling* of me? They did not believe Spirit was in the room with us.'

'I don't – I'm not sure that's true. Willie believes. He has told me he knows that spirits after death keep the shape of their earthly bodies . . .'

'He says that to *you*. Or Florence, or his other Golden Dawn friends. But when in the company of other men from his . . . bookish world . . . he quickly denies it, lest his *literary* friends mock him.'

She is right about that. And now I see how angry she is. I'm fascinated. The same temper as when Edy and Christopher asked her to leave Smith Square. The kind of anger that everyone suggests women should never show: Nora is fearless.

'And the Horlicks Man! What the devil is wrong with *him*? Can he never spit out what he means? He has some bad conscience – some guilt or something about his young sister – and hopes to find her in *me*. But he dresses it up to impress everyone.'

Ha! I've thought the same thing about all the flim-flam and bunkum.

Nora puts her hands on her hips, sniffing and sighing; she's not quite done with her rage. 'That Willie! I heard him, Pixie, talking about "fat old women who speak with the dead in a Cockney language"! Oh yes, I know his opinion of me. Bloody men! To be respected by *other men* is all they ever want.'

Nora's pride strikes me as similar to Florence's, when she spoke to me of the Tarot, and that phrase she said in her actress voice flows back to me: 'I am she that fights not but is always victorious . . .' My admiration for Nora grows and grows. I look at the drawing I've done and it's true, she's a goddess. The feeling as I look at it . . . A warm feeling, creeping from my toes upwards.

Nora sees me looking down at my picture and puts her hand out. 'May I see it?' she says distractedly.

I hand it over. 'You can keep it,' I say. 'I'm sorry it's so smudgy. Charcoal makes an awful mess.'

She holds it for a moment, staring. Her rage seems to leach away.

'Thank you: that's so sweet,' she says, and kisses the top of my head.

I feel as if a glittering, sizzling thing just landed on my crown. The green spot! All I can think of, on my way to my bedroom, is how much the Horlicks Man, or indeed Willie, or all of them, would like to be kissed by Nora, and I have no idea why this idea makes me blush and laugh in equal measure.

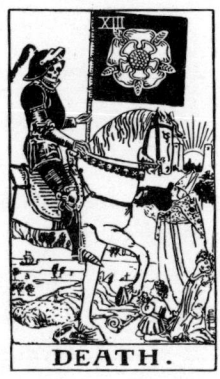

I have been inside you from the beginning, a seed.

Each day growing like a tree. Of course you are afraid of me.

Is it today? Shall I come today with my terrible grin?

No one escapes, neither pontiff nor king.

Shall I carry you off to your den, tiny fox, leave you there alone?

My flag shall be – not these old bones, cliché! – but a blazing white rose,

the better to show you all that you lose:

Your bright world, tossed to a button.

In the morning, something floats into my head on waking: a picture of a sheaf of green corn, bundled together and tied with a red ribbon. It is the lost straggle of a dream; I had a shifty, scratchy, restless night, thinking about the flitting green light and Nora, and the baby, and Spirit, and then flipping onto my back, seeking out the shape of the ceiling rose in the darkness and pondering my usual problem: *money.*

Now, I think: *A magazine.* My own little magazine. Not illustrating broadsheets for other people who think me lazy and unable to take instruction (though that part is true). A magazine. My own one! Once roused like this, I jump out of bed.

I scribble a letter to Florence and Willie and send it express delivery, asking them to meet me in a pub later today on the Fulham Road. I don't say why; I imagine they both think it's about the Order of the Golden Dawn, which will mean, their curiosity piqued, they will definitely come.

I arrive, a little breathless, at four o'clock. They are both there. Willie is drinking Ram's beer, dark hair flopping into his eyes, his hat, pince-nez and a notebook on the round table in front of him. His slumped posture – head close to Florence, elbows on the table – suggests he is a little worse for wear. Two lamps are lit and the barmaid and her friend in their white aprons and long black dresses flit busily about the place, bringing Florence a glass of red wine. I sit down and ask for coffee.

There is a powerful smell of lilies, and I look around at the huge bunch in a vase at the bar. Lilies in a pub: is there a funeral planned? The waxy smell mingles oddly with the smell of beer.

'Were you at this – séance – last night, Pixie?' Florence's tone is a little accusing.

'Yes, and—'

'Goodness knows what might happen – so disorderly! That Nora – well, I know how fond you are of her . . .'

Now I know I'm blushing, which is rather infuriating.

The girl brings me a large black coffee, asking, 'Are you here for the funeral tea, miss? It's in the back room.'

'No . . .'

The girl nods and goes back to the bar. Women in public houses can only be there for funerals, it seems.

'Nora was magnificent,' Willie says. 'She conjured Spirit in the form of a luminous green light, sometimes small, sometimes looking a little like a lace pattern . . .'

'She thinks you a coward, and duplicitous,' I think, but manage not to say it. Instead: 'I thought it looked like luminous green shoots. Green fingers, or sheaves of corn?'

'Baron Schrenk was there. And Professor Courtier from the Sorbonne! Sometimes the light spot grew bigger — almost a foot in diameter,' Willie tells Florence.

'I don't remember *that*,' I say. Then: 'I've decided to start my own magazine. And I thought you two might like to help me with it.'

Florence and Willie both stare at me. Willie is the first to start laughing.

My chin juts out. 'You know I'm perfectly capable of it. I could . . . hand-colour the drawings. Sell it myself at my salons.'

'You'd no doubt make good use of Jack's broadsheet mailing list!'

'Jack! Pooh! And what if I *do*?'

Florence is smiling, a look of clear admiration in her eyes.

'There will be thirteen numbers in the year,' I go on, 'printed on handmade paper and hand-coloured, and the subscription will be thirteen shillings annually, post free. Single copies I shall sell at my salon for thirteen pence each.'

Willie smiles. 'Slow down! I think your becoming an editor a capital idea. And what will you call it? *Hour Glass*? An excellent name . . .'

'*Hour Glass*? Isn't that your new play? No. This morning it came to me: *The Green Sheaf*.'

There is a pause. Florence and Willie glance at one another.

Florence: 'Like *money*, you mean? Green dollars . . .?'

'No! Not *money*. Just a bundle of things tied up together, you know, fresh and green things, that last forever . . .'

'An hour glass is easy to draw,' Willie says. 'You know, dreams of an ideal state, beautiful or charming. Perhaps a dedication on the opening page to "the art of happy desire" . . .' He is tapping his empty pipe on the table, making an awful mess while he searches for his tobacco pouch.

'It shall be dedicated to "pleasure",' I reply. I'm surprised how certain all these decisions are; I had no idea I even knew the name of my new magazine.

'How will you pay for it?' Florence asks.

I'm so proud – *so* proud – to say, 'Well, I have some savings, from my work for the Lyceum, so, you know – *my own money*.'

'How will you print it?' asks Willie.

'Well, doesn't your sister Lolly have a new press? I'm sure she would help me.'

'You've thought it all through!' Willie says, pressing tobacco into his pipe. And then: 'But what's wrong with *Hour Glass* as a title? What has this green sheaf got to do with anything?'

'Ripe ears are good for bread, but green ears are good for *pleasure*.'

'Pleasure!' Willie says grumpily. And then, as if a thought has flitted through his mind, 'We had quite the night of it last night, didn't we, with your – Mrs Lake. My, what a stunner that woman is!'

I am outraged that Willie should speak so of Nora, yet at the same time another feeling, like a great hot flame, flickers inside me.

'You two have done nothing but laugh and tease since I sat down! What is wrong with you both?' My outburst surprises them. It comes out more forcefully than I intended. Even the young woman at the bar looks over our way as if I might be a madwoman.

Willie and Florence give each other sheepish looks, as if sobering up.

'Did you know Nora is expecting?' I announce. My temper has cooled but not my hot strange Nora feeling, and I am gratified to see that this startles Willie; he did not know.

'That husband of hers. Alfred. There's something threatening in him, to be sure.'

I don't like to think about Alfred's part in the making of Nora's baby, so I add, a little sadly, 'Well, she is awful pleased nonetheless.'

'I can't imagine Nora with a baby.' Willie sounds as if he doesn't want to.

'Oh, I can, easily!' I blurt out. Nora with a child on her knee, a little boy in a white knitted bonnet. Green eyes like hers. How to see things that don't yet exist on the earthly plane? It's the easiest thing in the world, of course, natural and ordinary: available to everyone.

'*The world of imagination is the world of eternity*,' I say, quoting Blake. 'I shall have that in *The Green Sheaf*. '*This world of imagination is infinite and eternal, whereas the world of* – What's the rest?'

'*The world of generation or vegetation is finite and temporal,*' Willie says.

'Yes, I'll have William Blake in my *Green Sheaf* too. I can't wait!'

Florence smiles. 'So, poems? Great poets? Translations from the Irish and illustrations by you, is that it?'

'Yes, and dreams!'

'Tell a dream, lose a reader . . .' Florence murmurs.

I've turned an envelope over and have been drawing all the while in coloured pencils on the other side, without being aware of it. Drawings of couples caressing and standing tall and entwined on grey clouds . . . Willie takes it now, turns it the right way round and removes the pipe from his mouth to burst out laughing.

'We shall face the wrath of the censor over this, Pixie!'

I snatch it back from him and then shriek with laughter myself. It's true that the little drawings of tall couples standing on clouds look – from a distance – like sketches of something very rude indeed, a naughty shape that boys back in Brooklyn drew on pavements with chalk. What curious things the mind produces while happily occupied with something else!

Willie calls to the barmaid for another Ram beer and the girl hurries over. (She has been watching him, resting her bosom on the bar, slightly hidden by the lilies.) When she arrives, beaming, he orders coffee for me and wine for Florence, and we pull in the chairs and set to work on a list of contributors to ask. Willie, as stubborn as me, mumbles just the once, 'I still think that *Hour Glass* would be a better title, but not if you illustrated it like that!' – pointing at the rude drawings. We all crumple into laughter again.

Then we address more practical details: whether I will be able to use Lolly's new press, how to request permission to use certain drawings that I might want to include. Florence suggests that hand-colouring every issue will be awful hard going and has the bully idea of my starting a hand-colouring school to get students to do it for me. I show them shyly the poem I wrote, 'Alone', and a new illustration. They murmur, 'Oh . . .' It shows a woman with her back to us, under two trees, unmistakably pregnant.

Alone and in the midst of men,
Alone 'mid hills and valleys fair;
Alone upon a ship at sea;
Alone – alone, and everywhere . . .

No one mentions that the poem is a bad one, nor comments that the woman looks like Nora. For this I am glad and feel that my friends have forgiven my outburst and my ornery ways, and that we are back to the excitement of the new venture: the magazine.

'You are so clever,' Florence says affectionately, and I do feel that I am and that ideas just seem to come to me while I sleep and then – *poof!* – burst into being before I know it.

Florence leaves us to find a water closet. As the public house does not have one for ladies, she is forced to ask the barmaids to use their back room, but she does this boldly, in a way that I cannot imagine any other lady would.

Willie says to me, 'Have you been to any Golden Dawn meetings since your induction?'

'Just one,' I say. 'I haven't progressed beyond Zelator level.'

'You know that Florence and I have both formed other organisations? I hope you're not tempted to join *her* new group?'

I *am* tempted, of course, by the Sphere Group, which seems more fun; at least I'd get to try new things like astral flying and whatnot. I assure Willie that I will make up my own mind, when I am ready, and he seems to accept this.

When Florence returns, we part ways: me to my studio, Florence home, and Willie to Bloomsbury. Their goodbye is lingering – he kisses her gently on the cheek, touching her hair – and I become aware, for the first time, of something that has been just beneath my consciousness throughout this meeting: they are so *intimate* with each other. They are not merely friends! Florence is older than him – by about five years – and so independent, so boyish with her little curls and her big eyes and her slight and healthy beauty, like a green shoot, something good and strong and growing. She has never appeared in public as his mistress – but how naïve of me to only just figure it out. That feeling, of them giggling and teasing, that sense of something bubbling under the conversation – at last I have deciphered it! I plan to talk to Nora. For once, I believe I have understood a secret, the kind that seems the hardest of all to understand. These things – sex things – never escape Nora.

But on my return Nora is taking a nap and Alfred – telling me she's resting – makes it clear she's not well, something to do with her condition, and is not to be disturbed. I go to my bedroom to dig out my box of money. I need to do some sums and find the list of subscriptions Jack left with me and tell all the

subscribers about the new magazine. *The Green Sheaf.*
I'm so excited I'm practically skipping.

Counting the notes is sobering. Not nearly as many as I thought. The cards I sell at my salon, some money for costume designs. I sit back on my heels, sighing. Where does everyone else get their money from? Why am I the only one who has to even *think* of it? Ellen is always talking about her son Ted and how much 'worry' he causes her because she has to pay for his children, but the truth is: Ted isn't going to fret about earning money the way I do, is he, because he has Ellen to bail him out. *Pooh!* 'Tis that simple. Where does Lolly get the money to buy a letterpress and all the rest of it? Family money. Florence once mentioned casually that Willie gets money from his patron, Lady Gregory. Lucky critter!

For a quarter of an hour I rock back and forth on my heels, getting angrier and more outraged by the minute. Then I shove the remaining pounds and coins back in my tin and stand up.

Oh well, what's to be done? Maybe this new publishing venture will make my fortune. In any case (and my heart swells a little here), there can barely be – apart from Lolly – another editor in all of London who is a woman! I am a *phenomenon!*

I might be an angel, with this sun upon my forehead,

Or maybe I am Iris, goddess of the rainbow, pouring blue from my cups. Mixing it up.

(You say I am the Lady of the Lake? You know what she's like, that will never wash.)

This music crept by me upon the waters

And all the little fishes in their multitudes swim past.

Remember them? From another wicked card reader, another time.

I embrace all, for I am Temperance, I harmonise.

If you draw me you will know in your rational part from whence you came

And whither you are going.

Envy of Willie and Lady Gregory reminds me a letter is long overdue to *my* old patron, the gallery owner William Macbeth, to thank him for subscribing to *The Green Sheaf*. We have been out of touch for so long that he only now mentions his condolences at Daddy's death, and I reply that the magazine does look well and

I'm proud of it, but it's very expensive and tiring to run, and how nice it would be to have another exhibition of my work as I now have quite a lot of my music pictures, the kind I did that time with Laurence when he was playing the piano, which come to me in a dreamy way, fully formed. Macbeth writes back with enthusiasm and admiration but no mention of any possibility of an exhibition.

Nora and I sit in the kitchen, putting *Green Sheaf* editions into envelopes and stamping them. Nora is awful huge and looks like a watermelon about to burst. We are in the kitchen alone, Alfred out on some errand. Sitting down gives Nora heartburn so she stands up, rubbing the top of her belly, to allow the baby a bit more room.

'It's such a lot of work, Pixie. Why don't any of your other friends help you?'

But whom can I ask? As if Edy or Ellen or Florence or Willie would lower themselves to put little magazines into envelopes and chase people for thirteen pence, or thirteen shillings to subscribe for the year; none of them appreciate the cost of stamps and paper and printing, and how I am having to pay for all of it!

I am also smarting from a review that mentioned 'the strange little periodical' produced by that 'strange personality whom we call Pamela Colman Smith'. Strange! Why am I always so *strange*? What pigs people are!

I leave Nora with the envelopes and return to a watercolour I was painting, an illustration for a poem by Willie – well, more a description of a curious dream he had – to go in *The Green Sheaf*. I'm quite pleased with how the painting is coming along, and I murmur quietly to Nora, 'Oh well, perhaps this will be the last issue. It is too much work, it's true, but the part I love best is the illustrating. It's so magical how you don't know you know something, or can do something, or think something, and then you put a paintbrush in your hand and – hey presto! – here it is . . .'

'Well, that's what talking with Spirit is like,' Nora says. I pause, paintbrush poised above the jar of water. Nora doesn't often talk in this way: she's always joking or smiling or otherwise playing, like it's a trick or a theatre show. She has gone to the cupboard to fetch more stamps, and I stare at her back, the shape of her, the bow of her apron, the tendrils of hair beneath her bonnet, the colour of the glowing copper at the fire. Her sleeves are rolled up: her elbows pink like crinkled rosebuds.

'Do the spirits tell you . . . secrets?' I ask.

Nora turns around. 'Anyone's in particular?'

'No. But I was thinking – about Florence. Florence and Willie. And how I always seem to be the last to know things.'

Nora laughs. 'Yes, that one. That's a very open secret. Didn't you guess?'

'I thought he was in love with Maud.'

'He is! I heard he asked her to marry him – *again*. But Florence is – you must have noticed? – Florence is so much warmer and more human towards him. Maud Gonne is in love with Ireland, and not much room for anyone else.'

'Oh. I find myself not wanting Florence to marry anyone—'

'*Marry* him? Who says she'd marry him? I'm sure she's no intention. She's already escaped one marriage.

Wish she could give me some tips!' This hangs in the air between us and then Nora hastily carries on, as if sweeping up the remark. 'I've heard Florence give a talk about street women and the diseases they suffer from and how they might be prevented. She is bold, all right. Very modern views.'

'*Oh* . . .'

'Why does it upset you? Thinking of Florence as a New Woman?'

'I am always the last to know! I feel awful silly.'

Nora comes to peer at me. 'Is there another . . . secret you're wanting to know about?'

Nora's skin is so pretty, with a light sheen and a glow of pink. I wish I could put out my hand and touch her cheek.

'I keep wondering about – Mama,' I answer. 'Just before she died, she said I'd be famous – millions of people would know my drawings – well, I don't see any sign of *that*. And she had a Big Secret to tell me but I didn't hear properly and I didn't like to ask again!'

Nora laughs, a short laugh, but then, seeing my face, the smile vanishes, and she sits down at the table with me.

'My mother died too, you know. I was six. My grandmother raised me. I often feel my true mother near, as familiar as any earthly mother. I don't remember much what she looked like, so in my mind she looks like me. Small, auburn curls like mine. I talk to her in my head. Ask her things. She's my Spirit guide.'

A sadness settles on Nora and I realise that I didn't know this. That we share this great loss.

'I think as a child I was sad and thought about death more than other people,' she goes on. 'That was the truth of my "great powers" that so impressed my old employer. His little boy – Edgar, a sweetheart – died in a terrible accident, fallen into the fire. He was blond and chubby. No one wanted to think of him; they tried to block it out. But I could feel him all around, hear his footsteps running in the hallway, or the sound of a ball being bounced, or see a shape behind the curtain when he hid behind it. The pity was that they couldn't.'

As Nora speaks, two things happen at the same time. Part of me feels a great prickling fear creeping up my spine. I look at the window, as if expecting something – someone – to be there. Four o'clock. Rain spattering the glass and the lights from a streetlamp making a yellow blur. The other part of me cocks my ear, as if to a shell, and leans in.

'You make it sound so ordinary, and so simple. Is it just imagination? And *wanting*?' I ask.

'Shouldn't we all listen to our dead? Don't you think that's important? I feel like my mother had much to tell me, and as if – well, my purpose was to complete her life for her. Have opportunities she didn't.'

I muse on this. The idea of dead mothers talking to us. When Mama died, I told Cousin Mary that she'd gone to the Moon Garden. That simple belief seems like decades ago, rather than just – what is it – seven years? It was Daddy's death that changed me, that made it hard to believe the things I'd been raised on. It was so much more of a wrench, so much more brutal and unexpected, and such bad timing.

'We could try and – contact my mother,' I say very quietly.

'Do you have anything of hers to help me? A handkerchief, that kind of thing?'

'Oh no, I—'

'You're scared. That's natural. But you know it might be possible.'

'I have her wedding ring. It's very thin now, the gold – very worn.' I show Nora my hand. She reaches for the ring and I struggle to take it off. My fingers seem to have grown fat. Nora goes to get some soap and rubs it on the ring, and then, as we wrestle, it suddenly flies off, disappearing down the front of Nora's apron.

We burst out laughing while she retrieves it. I try not to think too much about her hand, delving into the bib of her apron and deep into her bosom.

'Pretty,' she says.

'I have other things,' I say, feeling sure I'm blushing. 'Mama had a carnival-style mask. She was an actress. Costume jewellery.'

'You never told me she was an *actress*!'

'I'm ready. Let's try,' I say.

Nora stands up and draws the curtain, then closes the kitchen door. The room is awful snug and smells oniony, of the stew she made at lunchtime. 'We don't want Alfred coming back in the middle,' she says.

She places the ring on the table in front of us and then takes hold of both my hands.

'Don't be scared,' she says. 'What was your mother's name?'

'Corinne,' I whisper.

Nora lets go of one of my hands to pick up the ring and turns it a little between finger and thumb. 'Was she pretty?'

'Oh yes,' I say, 'and she had a beautiful singing voice and—'

Nora is looking at the hallmark on the inside of the ring, using the candle to light it up. She stares very hard, and then slips the ring on her own finger. I gasp – a little shocked – but then she clasps my hands in her warm ones and I like this feeling so much . . . Nora drops her head forward, closing her eyes. She is still for a long time. I just hear her breathing. I watch the rise and fall of her chest inside the starched white pinny.

I recognise from the séance we had with Willie and the Horlicks Man that she is going into a trance, so I try to quieten my breathing too. But my heart is jumping like a frog and won't be stilled.

'I have her,' Nora says. 'She was near. She's been waiting.'

A shadow dances on the wall, where the candle dips and flickers.

There is a loud clock in the hall and I fancy I hear its tick through the closed kitchen door. But perhaps it is my own heartbeat. The smell of meat and onions seems to have been replaced with a sharp smell, not a nice one, like fruit gone high. *Mama, I miss you. I wish I could cuddle you, ask you things. Where are you?*

'What does she have to tell me? Could you say to her, I'm sorry that I didn't understand . . .'

'It's fine,' Nora says in a low voice. 'You did not need to understand. It wasn't important; it was a family secret, that's all. An open secret, she says, and everyone understood it. It was something to do with her and your father travelling so much . . .'

'Yes!' (She did say that. I think I told Nora that detail, once? Nora would know that. This might just be Nora talking.) 'She said he had left her alone for too long,' I reply, 'and I thought to myself, she loves Jamaica best, and her freedom, and she doesn't want to come back to New York.'

'Was your father called something . . . I'm getting a name beginning with N—'

'No, he was *Charles*. You met him, you remember . . .?'

'Oh yes, Charles. Well, she doesn't seem willing to talk about that. She says you've always known in your heart, and no need to rake it up now. She wants to talk about your paintings, your art. She simply says to keep on, keep drawing, keep listening and doing what you do. That's it. That's all. There is – I can see – a lighted, book-lined study in the middle of a field. A candle burning and a strange sound like a whooshing fan, and a person, a woman, who is talking to you, across a great divide, an abyss that is a sea . . . and this person is staring at your drawings, she is holding them . . .'

None of this makes sense. The secret. A family one. Not important? That is what I want: I want an answer! Not this rummy twaddle! I long to stamp my foot. A book-lined study in the middle of a field with a woman in it? Who cares about that?

A banging door somewhere in the house makes us both jump. Nora opens her eyes at once. There is nothing in her face to suggest that she was ever *anywhere else* but in the room with me. Alfred. She slips the wedding ring off her finger and is about to give it to me but stops as the door is flung open.

'Blimey! Warm in here,' Alfred says, in his outdoor coat and hat. He looks from one to the other of us, suspiciously. Nora takes the ring from her palm and hands it to me.

'We were trying to find the sex of the baby . . . You know, with a wedding ring. Pixie was looking for a string to tie it to . . . but anyways, it's definitely a boy! I can feel his little fists today.'

I close my fingers around the ring, a bright circle of warmth.

Alfred beams, unwinding the scarf from his neck. 'Got ourselves a prize boxer,' he says.

Nora stands up, one hand at the small of her back, to put the kettle on the stove. I try to push Mama's ring back on my finger, but nothing I can do will achieve that, so I slip it in my dress pocket and scuttle out, nodding my goodbye and mouthing to her, over Alfred's head, *Thank you.*

★★★

Lying in bed, I *know* the secret. I have always known it, the way a poet knows a poem before it appears on the page, or the way my drawings come to me fully formed. Mama did not have to pretend to return from the dead to tell me it.

I remember. I am four years old. Inside a house. Manchester or London? I cannot be sure of that part. I am playing with my doll's house, and a governess or nanny or someone is in the room with me. (I can't remember who . . . A shadowy sense of Nurse Delphine, but that can't be right . . .) Mama and Daddy are in another room, close by, and I can hear them arguing. They don't often argue, so when they do it makes me tremble. The house shakes. Their voices are loud, and scary. Walls quake. My hands jiggle as I try to put the teeny wooden doll with little foldable limbs onto a teeny wooden chair in the upper bedroom of the doll's house.

I decide the little dolly should not bother with the chair but go to straight to bed. She has painted black hair. I have drawn a face on her with blank ink, and her expression is vexed. Mama is crying – even through walls I can hear this – and I hear Daddy shout: 'Why is he still *sending you things*? Corinne, the Lord knows I have been tolerant. He has no right to contact you here!'

I do not hear what Mama replies.

I guess what he means, young though I am. He is talking of a man, an outsider, someone who has no right to send Mama gifts, but loves her. And does that not mean that Mama had a secret lover? And that Mama's terrible secret is that this man is my father and Daddy has known this from the beginning but has come back from wherever he was to be with her and make her life respectable, which means that Daddy, the man I've loved all my life, is not my father?

My father is an unknown man. No. I do not care for that man, and I do not care to know who he is.

Love is the thing. Love for a daughter is what makes a man a father, not some quirk of nature. But listening, then, to their argument, I felt as if my world might crack apart. Crumble into rubble.

I peer inside my doll's house. The walls close around me. I shut my eyes and sing a little song to myself. The shouting ends with a slammed door and someone – Daddy – leaving the house. Might he leave forever? And then Mama, who didn't even love him enough to be faithful to him – might she leave too? And where will I be? Tumbling, tumbling . . .

I climb onto the teeny wooden bed, small as small, and shut my eyes.

There is a cup of milk bigger than I am, a blue chim-chim cup, on a tray next to the doll's house. The blue cup — two of them — arrived this morning. Daddy unwrapped them and it was this that made his mood turn sour. I understood they were some sort of gift. Something significant to Mama, because she didn't want him to smash them, as he threatened to do.

I admired the pretty cup. I wanted a drink of milk in mine, and the nurse brought it to me.

I am inside the doll's house and I tiptoe with tiny steps down the ribbon of carpet on the staircase and push the little door and step outside, and there on the tray is the chim-chim cup. I climb into it, using the handle to pull myself up and then to stand on the rim, and of course, it being slippery — wet china with blue birds on it — I fall in with a milky splash. I keep my head above the surface and look around in amazement at the creamy liquid. I manage to climb out just in time for the shrinking to end: there is an aching in every limb, and my body starts to stretch and grow; my clothes, the hairs on my arms are shining with white; and I feel myself returning to my true size. My nightdress is mysteriously dry but my hair is damp. Milky drops plop to my lap. When the nurse sees me she rushes to get a towel and *that is all* I remember of the secret, the Big Secret that has dominated and shaped my life.

That was the very first time I shrank to a teeny doll size. But, after all, Daddy didn't leave. He stayed, and the secret remained, but closed inside a clam shell. It is painful and too late to prise it open. Better, after today, to keep Mama's ring safely in my pocket, along with the secret, and never try to examine it again.

★★★

Christmas, New Year, then spring with daffodils appearing in the window boxes of houses in Milborne Grove and blackbirds chirping in the Chelsea streets as I step over a workman, his head resting on his chest, a bucket of bright-yellow paint beside him. The bells of St Mary The Boltons ringing out.

Nora's baby has come: a tiny bundle called Freddy, who lies with eyelids fluttering, luxuriating at Nora's breast. I have to keep backing out of the room when I see her dress unbuttoned like that, my face aflame.

Nora's employer, and my landlady, Mrs Fortescue, is even more embarrassed than I am, and one day, arriving in my studio, she bursts out with: 'She'll have to go!'

Something shoots inside me: a fear, a wail, a real terror. But I calm it and continue sitting at the little desk with my colouring of another *Green Sheaf* issue, pretending nonchalance.

'She doesn't behave like – like a servant, does she?' Mrs Fortescue goes on. 'I mean, she welcomes guests as if she is the lady of the house. And the – the séances! The rappings and tappings! I can see now why her previous landlords turned her out.'

'Well, they *said* it was the swearing . . .' I reply.

Mrs Fortescue is a loud person, very huffy and puffy, with a little sweat always forming on her brow and her chin. 'Yes, and her rows! The rows with Alfred – have you heard them?'

I have, and they give me a gleeful feeling, alongside the tremor of anxiety for Nora.

Mrs Fortescue comes to look at what I'm doing, standing over me, breathing heavily as if she has just come in from a nippy-aired walk. Her sniffing and the feeling of her breath on me is suddenly intolerable. I try to shift away without her noticing.

She gazes at my drawing for a long time, moving her head around as if to understand better. Her next remark, lowering her voice conspiratorially, catches me unawares. 'Also. *Nora*. Have you wondered how she – tolerated living with the Sapphists? You got out of Smith Square pretty fast but she was with that Edy and Christopher for – oh, years.'

'What do you mean?' I find I'm jangling – whether in anger, or defence of Nora, or of my friends, I'm not sure. I didn't even realise that Mrs Fortescue knew Edy and Christopher, and a fearful resentment fires up the moment she mentions their names.

'It's such an . . . *unnatural* life, isn't it! Wearing trousers and taking a man's name and – well, the mind boggles – goodness knows what else!'

She sniffs loudly enough to draw in every particle in the room, and I do feel it, I feel as if I'm suffocating, furious, in a full rage that descends like a cloud in which I can see nothing and do nothing except want to – leap up and hit her!

I keep my head down. I watch my fingers around the pencil trembling and I almost crush the thing to splinters. Then I watch as the quivering stops and my breathing steadies. I did not know that I felt such red-hot loyalty to Edy and Christopher. I did not know that others – this woman – harboured such great repugnance for them.

Mrs Fortescue sits down beside me on a small stool, very heavily. Her eyes are hazel, watery. I settle my thoughts on how much I dislike her.

'I will give Nora notice. She is popular: someone will employ her.'

This is a blow I did not expect. Are we arguing now? Is she sensing my anger and punishing me for it?

'You can't!' I cry. 'Turfing her out with the baby and all, that would be – heartless!'

Mrs Fortescue bridles. I have struck at the heart of her. She considers herself a modern woman. Her ideas about Sapphists she feels certain are shared by all decent people.

'Well, perhaps you might suggest she find someone to mind the baby while she does her duties?' she concedes. 'I can't have the Monday's laundry pushed to Tuesday and the hearth not properly cleaned . . .'

'Yes, let me speak to her. Don't say anything, please. A new baby is a – delicate time.' I hate that my tone is so plaintive. I'm begging her. But to give Nora notice makes a fear scurry down my spine.

'Hmmph' is all she says.

The mewling sounds of the baby's cry draw our attention. Mrs Fortescue heads for the door, muttering, 'It's like living in a kindergarten!' and I – icily cold – return to my colouring.

I have begun, and now I give my sensual race the rein.

He says I am the Horned God of Mendes

but you can make me the Brammy Joker

with wings of a bat if you deign.

Maybe I'm not wicked at all

But simply the one you love to dance with

I'm the five o'clock shadow, that first dark sip.

Make those enslaved figures perky, their chains loose, so they can come meet me at night in the wood.

Oh darling! Keep their lovely tails alive, the needle in a compass, showing the route.

But before the week is out, the deed is done, and Mrs Fortescue – after all, it is her home – has given Nora notice. Nora is (as usual) outraged, and my feelings on the matter are shocking to me. I cannot stop crying. I sit in the kitchen watching Nora carry in her few things in a large doctor's bag, the baby in one arm. Tears stream down my face, for the first time in my life. I did not cry like this when Mama died. I did not cry like this at Daddy's funeral. Why now, why has the dam broken?

In between her comings and goings, packing, wrapping, jiggling Freddy, Nora keeps anxiously peering at me, offering me her handkerchief or a whisky and patting my hair.

'We'll stay in touch! I'll write to you. You can visit. It's only the Yeatses, for goodness' sake – you can easily find an excuse to visit.'

'But *Devon*! So far! It's – five hours on the train. And yes, I know it's only Jack and Cottie, but how would you and I spend any time together? Oh, why has she done it? I feel so furious with her, and I can't forgive her; it's so unfair. You know she was – a week ago – saying awful things about Edy and Christopher . . .'

'What kind of things?'

'Oh, you know. About how they *live*.' My face is red, and I find I cannot repeat it.

Nora looks thoughtful. Her little determined chin juts out just a fraction more and she gives a look I can't understand. 'I thought she had joined the suffragists? A pity she's so easily shocked.'

'Yes. She just pretends to be unconventional.'

Nora pauses to put her arm around me. I smell the fire in her hair and the baking smells, ginger for the cookies she makes, which she calls, in the English way, 'biscuits'. The flood of tears pouring from me astonishes me, as if a great waterfall has decided to cascade down my face. I have no control of the tears, they flow and flow, but they startle Nora, and suddenly she kisses me, a very hard, fast kiss, on my wet mouth. Her strong, hot, salty mouth. My heart tilts like a planet. The room contracts, and the fire – I see it out of the corner of my eye in the hearth – the fire blazes, flames leaping.

'Don't cry, darling,' she says. I can only sit wordless, wondering what Nora knows that I don't. My body now feels to be melting. I feel swimmy and queer, as if I've been drinking whisky. I think about the kiss with Laurence long ago, and the way that the lower parts of my body seemed to tighten, drawing towards my mouth. This time those feelings are stronger. My tears cease as I stare at Nora, now sitting at the table with me, in astonishment.

'Oh Pixie, why are you so – innocent? Did your father tell you nothing? What about – I mean, for goodness' sake, you've lived with Edy and Christopher, you know that I was friends with them from the theatre, that I helped Edy at the studio in Covent Garden . . . Didn't it occur to you?'

Freddy, despite her leaning across him to kiss me, squashing him in her arms, has fallen asleep, so she goes to put him in the wooden cradle by the kitchen door and then returns to me, mopping my face with her handkerchief.

'Didn't you think a suspicion that I might have some of the same . . . *tendencies* was behind Mrs Fortescue's wish to be rid of me?'

'No,' I begin. But then . . . Mrs Fortescue *did* begin her talk last week with a complaint about Sapphists. Such a strange realisation, to know that, somewhere, I was dimly conscious of a connection. That we have understanding and knowledge beneath our thoughts, and only the tip of the iceberg is available for examination. The other thoughts lodge in the depths, float up by and by.

Now another wave of tears washes over me and: 'You're *married*,' I say, miserably, needlessly.

'What can I do? Alfred got me in the family way. That time turned out to be a false alarm, but, unfortunately for me, the husband stuck.'

Shock after shock. She is right: I *am* innocent. Florence once spoke of husbands as inconveniences, and remarked how sensible it would be to live together first without a lifelong commitment to someone you might be incompatible with. I thought it was useful advice for *me*, for someone who did not want to marry. But I've never thought to apply it to Nora. What to do if you've already made that pledge, and now regret it? Florence says there is much debate in Parliament about divorce laws and most of the men who discuss them have no intention of changing them. What could Nora do? With a child as well? She does not have money of her own to fall back on.

A mean thought occurs to me then. 'Didn't your spirit guides tell you not to marry him? Or predict about the – false alarm?'

She studies me carefully. I see that she is assessing the challenge. I remember Nora then as she was when I first saw her in Edy's studio. Looking like the subject of a painting by a Dutch Master, the light cascading over her. Her full mouth. Her glowing skin, a dusting of freckles across her nose. That firm jawline, the uptilt of her chin. The vivid intelligence in her eyes, a little frown often between them. How stunned I was at seeing her, as if she was from another world. And now I think: is that what happens when you fall in love? The person looks different to you as light bathes them? Kingfisher colours. The heavenly streak of blue, and gold.

'Whenever I pictured my future, there was a baby,' Nora says. 'Remember my mother passed over? I wanted so much to be a mother. I was picturing *him*: Freddy. I didn't love Alfred, nor any man. But how else to be a mother?'

She has been watching my face. She leans forward and puts her arms around my neck. I think she is about to kiss me again and close my eyes in swooning joy, but at that moment I hear the door open and instead I leap up as if scalded. I turn towards a kitchen cupboard to fetch the Horlicks jar: a way to shield my face from Mrs Fortescue, who has just entered.

The kiss is here in the room with us, like a vivid flower floating in the air above our heads. Mrs F, the world's biggest sniffer: surely she can see it, smell it? Lordy, how to hide my thoughts, squash them down?

She hands Nora an envelope. 'This is a reference for Jack and Cottie. Also, a fortnight's wages. I am sorry, Nora, truly. You can work out your notice. But you know when you and Alfred first came, I did say the spiritual meetings had to be kept in check.'

Nora nods, in her proud way. Her eyes blaze but she is polite and almost bobs a curtsy as she accepts the envelope without opening it. She glances over at Freddy in his crib and murmurs, 'I know it must be painful for you, to hear a baby crying . . .'

Yet another thing I didn't know, but Nora did: Mrs Fortescue, a widow, must have suffered the loss of a child. The woman's expression – startled, vulnerable, as if someone just jabbed her hard in the ribs – and the way she crumples onto a chair, winded, tells me that Nora is right, and this is another true reason for her dismissal.

★★★

In my little bed, the tears begin again. My pillow is soon soaked. They are the same silent tears, flowing like a waterfall down a mountain. I feel odd, and clean, and relieved. As if the grief and loneliness of the last years, the crying I never really did for Mama or Daddy, has found release at last, in the discovery of my feelings for Nora. I'm not sad, exactly. I am not sure what I am.

It is snug here under the heavy eiderdown. All the candles and lamps are blown out. The curtain is open slightly and I can see a small crescent moon, comforting, like a slice of lemon. In here, the darkness loiters, breathing, brushing my cheek.

The door to my bedroom opens with a creak. Desire leaps in me like a fish.

Here is Nora, in a white nightcap. The nightcap is the only thing I can see in the darkness. She removes it and it floats to the bedside table, lying there as white as a sand dollar. The bed moans as she climbs in. Her warm self, quivering a little. I feel her fingers undoing the tie at the throat of my nightdress. She kisses my neck, my cheek, my hair.

She pauses, discovering my wet face, the damp pillow.

'Oh darling,' she whispers. She kisses my mouth and I feel her little tongue, hard and strong and wet, pushing my lips apart. Her kisses rain on me and the wetness is everywhere: my whole body has become one long stream. I am a silver river, travelling far, far out of this little room, this little life, a journey awful far, one I know I will never come back from.

On the street I hear a dog bark. But now I'm somewhere — something — else. Not a dog, but a wolf stretching its throat to the night. The room is lit with silver, my silver path to the moon.

★★★

So *this* is the secret. This sweetness in the dark that I have no name for. The climbing, climbing, gathering feeling. The convulsions. The curious sensation that I am not shrinking but instead *expanding*: bigger and bigger, some kind of giant crown on my head, right up to the sky, the moon, and whatever is beyond. Florence says one day human people will step on the moon. It is ordinary, she says; she has seen it in a dream. The surface is not like cheese at all. I cannot quite believe her, but I want to.

I hug my secret to me, and every time I remember I blush. I cannot look at Nora. I avoid her all morning. But Florence calls by and she has some excitement she wants to talk about – would I like to show my art to a photographer friend of hers (my answer: which art, I have only the cartoon pictures, the costume designs, the illustrations for *The Green Sheaf*, which ones would he like?) – but as Florence is speaking I am looking at her curls and her dark lifted eyebrows and thinking: does she know? Is this it, then? This is what she experiences with Willie or with . . . whomsoever she loves? – and the thought is delicious and curious and makes me dissolve like some sort of sherbet ice.

I find myself childishly re-thinking so many occasions. Daddy and Mrs Redgrove. Is it possible a woman like that could have elevated feelings like these? Or only night-time, sizzling feelings? Most women seem so feeble! Whom can I ask? The answer is no one. Only

Nora can know this madness, which only makes it more delicious. I feel – at last – part of something else. I am living; I am alive. At last I know for sure that I exist, and that I did exist long ago, and one day will no longer exist, and someone will read of me or look at one of my drawings and – Laurence is right after all – I will only have existed like a small flower that grew and then died with great chasms of history on either side of me, dark bookmarks of unfathomable size. Why does my night of passion make me feel this?

Do women experience these feelings with men too, or is it only the love of a woman that produces them? Nora certainly understood my body in a way I cannot imagine a man ever would. I want to relive it and relive it, and I love to make myself blush and feel the kick in my stomach when I remember a detail: her face, in the candlelight, just *there*.

How I long to talk to someone, and Florence, Florence with her modern ideas, is the most sympathetic of companions. We now trundle out to a bookshop in London, her favourite on Museum Street, a small place with a golden lamp over the door and a glass cabinet full of strange objects, books full of dusty promise, art materials, candles. I lean in and whisper: 'I have a secret. Can I tell you?'

Florence smiles at me, pushes the book she is flicking through back into the shelf. 'I know it! I can see it in your face! You are in love.'

'I wonder if there is a book here about . . . the sex union,' I say proudly, wanting Florence to know that I am no longer a virgin, but a woman of experience.

She pauses and then steps to another shelf. 'Have you heard of Ida Craddock? A theosophist?'

I shake my head.

'Nobody else seems to have heard of her. I tried mentioning her to Crowley. She claimed to be the wife of an angel but a paper she wrote called "Heavenly Bridegrooms" is very good.'

'Will I find it here?' I ask, meaning the bookshop we're in.

'Oh no! She lived in New York. It came my way via . . . Perhaps it was Moina at the Golden Dawn.'

'Well, could we get a copy from her? Perhaps I could publish it – or an extract from it – in *The Green Sheaf*?'

'Oh gosh, I'm not sure that would be wise. She killed herself. I think it was last year. The work was so shocking that she lost a case in New York for circulating obscene literature and could not face a prison sentence.'

Florence says this with some passion, and I fear one of her feminist lessons (these can be very long) about the ways in which women's freedoms and education are suppressed, so I quickly interrupt with: 'I'd love to read *your* copy, then? But shall we have a cup of tea, right now? It's so cold in this draughty place!'

The shop owner, a witch with hair that looks like brambles, glances up from her book as we let the door swing behind us.

We go next door to a camera shop, where the proprietor – a tall fellow with a mouldy-looking hat – produces a small tea urn and cups and a jug of milk and there are rickety chairs we can sit on, next to a lit fire. The fire is a feeble one but the logs crackle and scent the air, and we are left alone. We are near what I assumed was a cellar but now realise is a basement floor: the proprietor's photography studio and equipment. Florence has been photographed by him recently, to accompany a book she is writing. Glancing at him when he brings us the tea, I see (with my new worldliness!) that he would like to do more than photograph her. Florence pours our tea and he disappears: we start to hear piano music floating up the stairs.

'That's him,' she says. 'Danny. I didn't see him go downstairs, did you? He's terribly good. He could have been a concert pianist if it weren't for his arthritis. Like dear Edy.'

'Edy?'

'Yes, haven't you ever heard her play? She's so gifted. But her poor hands.'

I picture Edy's hands. It is true she has a habit of clutching them together and I have, now I come to think of it, noticed them being claw-like sometimes, when she's been sewing for a while. But my ignorance astonishes me. Why does everyone else know so much more about everything than I do? Where am I when this knowledge is dished out? (In my own head thinking my own thoughts, I guess, which always seem to me the most vivid living things.)

The music starts to swell over us: Schumann. A piece I know well. I think perhaps Daddy used to play it. The tears of yesterday; the shivery exalted state I am in . . . Each note plucks and tugs at my heart.

Florence puts her head to one side, removing her hat and nodding lightly to the music. I take my sketchbook out of my bag and place it on the table. While she is preoccupied, listening, I begin to draw with a soft pencil, just whatever comes into my head, my thoughts loosened and set free by the spell of sound.

After a while, I sip the tea she poured me. It is cold. Florence is staring at me.

'Where have you been?' she asks dreamily.

We look down at my sketch. I rotate it slightly to face her. A woman in a soft dress, stretching out her arms, her hair flying; a little girl reaching for her to stop her falling? To stop her leaving?

'Is it the music?' Florence asks. 'The music seemed to work some magic on you.'

The pianist has stopped. Pockets of silence hover over us.

'I don't know. I was only thinking about—' (Here I simply blush.)

'You were thinking about your new love. Are you going to tell me who he is?'

'It's impossible,' I murmur.

'Is he married?' Florence asks kindly.

I nod.

Florence, seeing I'm not venturing anything further, says, 'It is a very good sketch. We should try it again. Perhaps it's like automatic writing . . . Your hand guided by Spirit?'

'It happened once before. With Laurence. He was playing Bach and I saw colours. And pictures. And then the sea and maidens . . .'

I find myself tongue-tied.

'Do you feel yourself? You look very pale. As if you've been on an astral journey,' Florence says.

'I unlocked a door to something. I feel as if I've been breathing the crisp fresh air of a mountain top.'

We smile at this. The little camera shop we are in has a fug to it, and rain outside adds to the steamy feeling. There is no freshness in the air.

'Is it only Bach and Schumann who produce the pictures?'

'I don't know. But if I listen to Wagner my scalp tingles and my hair pricks: I feel so full of rage that I want to crack people's heads together like nuts.'

Florence whoops with laughter and reaches across the table for me. I move, startled, not understanding. She tries a clumsy hug and, when I fail to respond, sits back down, laughing again, then saying, 'You're so *lovely* – there's no one like you! Oh, *do* let me show my friend your work, Pixie. Alfred Stieglitz. He has a gallery in New York, and I plan to go there next year. You should come with me! Would you like to?'

'Oh!' I reply. I am flattered, but the question comes out of the blue and, seeing my confusion, Florence rushes on: 'I'm giving some talks and travelling and there's another gentleman I'll be visiting –'

Something in the way she says this. *Another gentleman.* 'Not Willie?'

'No. His name is John Quinn. He is an art collector, a philanthropist. Willie will not be joining us.' After a pause, she says, 'It's better for me to remember that I might play the old mother, Herodias, but not Salome. Gentlemen prefer young actresses, not seasoned old bats like me.'

I stare at her for a moment. She is so composed that it is hard to read her, but her voice, her modulated voice, is the true instrument of her feelings. In that I hear hurt. My mind clangs on, though, tactlessly asking, 'Could we sell any to this Stieglitz? Of my music pictures. I have others. I've done nothing but lately.'

'Darling! Of course. Can you package some up and I'll send them to him? You seem melancholy. Is there no hope for you to be together with him?'

I shake my head and I know she is convinced it is Laurence.

'Bring some round to my house in Warwick Chambers. Bring this one. Honestly, I feel there will be great interest.'

'I am not convinced.'

'You know, half-baked people like Willie have tremendous influence, but they only tell half-truths.'

'Men, you mean? Are *men* the half-baked people?'

She laughs. 'Shaw is the same. They take for granted something we never assume. That they speak for the whole of humanity, rather than just the half that *they* know. Oh, Shaw thinks he understands women . . . but we know *men* – our lives depend upon understanding them, otherwise how could we survive in their world? *I stood naked in a dark and bleak eternity and filled it with my exultation.*'

When I stare back at her, puzzled, she says quietly, 'A line I wrote. My play: *The Mystery of Time*. Don't worry, no one has heard of it!'

Now tears threaten again. I'm grateful for Florence's kindness, and for all her gifts – in writing, in acting, in speaking poetry – and I'm touched by what she has just shared: a wish to be seen, a longing to be taken seriously, a wish to exist in the dark phase of non-existence, the time of dark eternity.

★★★

Later, Florence gives me some pages by this Ida Craddock to read. It is so shocking I can see why the poor soul took her own life rather than face the world.

I find myself blushing and flinging it down and then growing hot and flustered and picking it up again.

Sometimes it makes me laugh: *For a man to exhibit, to even an experienced wife, his organ ready for action when she is not amorously aroused is, as a rule, not sexually attractive to her: on the contrary it is often sexually repulsive, and at times, out and out disgusting to her. Every woman of experience knows that when she is ready, she can cause the man to become sexually aroused soon enough.*

Every woman or girl must know the truth of that 'repulsive'! There was an occasion in Central Park, strolling there with Cousin Mary, when a man appeared in a long fur coat and poked something out of it and waggled it as if it were a beak emerging from an egg and we should be thrilled to see it. Our shock rooted us in the snow. Then we simply turned around, put our hands in one another's and walked in the other direction. We never spoke of it again. The wonder is that some women change their minds! Has Mary, now that she is married, learned to find it an appealing organ, after that initial disgusting sight?

I have learned so much from Ida Craddock: about a mysterious and wonderful organ called the clitoris; that a man should excite with the tip of the male organ, never his finger; and that, if the bride is very small of orifice, then, on their wedding night, *it can be quite stimulating for the woman to proffer herself to her husband by kneeling on the bed on all fours lowering her head to a pillow and thrusting her hips high in the air so that he can see her genitalia and stimulate her from behind with his lips* . . .

I read that section over and over. I imagine showing it to Nora, for her opinion. I feel every shade of heat and cold when I read it, a delicious wave purling up and down my body. My legs turn to silk and flow away from me. I think about Ida Craddock with sadness, because she was shamed into taking her own life, but there are many who should be grateful for her words and her astonishing wide knowledge.

Though she never once mentions love with a woman, her mind is so open that I feel no judgement is intended towards us. When I read the words 'heavenly bridegroom', I simply picture Nora. After all, Edy and Christopher have shown me that love between women is commoner than people think. I feel sure that Ida's comment that *her partner's body is a sacred vessel and love-making need not become monotonous* is intended just for us!

At every opportunity, in the fortnight up until she leaves, Nora comes to my bed and demonstrates to me the full range of my own feelings and all the joys of this new world. And Ida Craddock insists that God or the Divine is included in the union, the third partner during the sexual embrace. I whisper this to Nora and she only lifts her head from beneath my nightdress to giggle and murmur, 'If you say so!' It is because God has given us – Ida says – a box of sexual bonbons and it's our sacred duty to share them with the Divine.

One evening, dressed and in the kitchen, laying a fire in the hearth, Nora, with her back to me, says quietly: 'Pixie, you don't have to take everything to heart. This Ida might have the odd helpful thing, but must you immerse yourself *quite* so in every new discovery . . .?'

This wounds me, and we have our first sulky argument, which lasts until the next evening, when Nora can only escape for twenty minutes after putting down the baby and tiptoeing from her marital bed.

The following day, at breakfast, Alfred safely outside, cleaning windows up a ladder, she admits she is jealous, she says, of me going to New York with Florence to meet this man Stieglitz.

'But Florence is ancient! She's over forty!'

'But she's very beautiful,' says Nora. 'Those big eyes! And so clever and, after all, famous for being a New Woman, so anyone can tell – *interested* in exploring all things.'

I ponder this. Florence is indeed striking in looks; her perfectly formed head, garlanded with curls, like Demeter in the British Museum . . . Have I found myself a little in love with her? Such feelings are a new discovery, but, seeking them, I run up against something else. A sharp stabbing feeling. Seeing Nora with Alfred, or when Willie spoke of Nora's looks. Jealousy. I did not have a name for it before.

'But you're moving to Devon!' I wail. 'With your husband and baby!'

We sit gazing at one another. I wonder if this is it, if this is my lot? A brief season with Eros, and then . . . what? Darkness like the grave.

'I hope you will visit us,' she says quietly, and the little crib on the floor at our feet comes alive and starts rocking, as Freddy wakes and begins to clamour.

My world is crumbling.

The House of Life, the Castle of Plutus, lies in ruins.

I have news for you: I am a tower you built yourself.

Now lightning strikes, lava and fire rain down like tears,

But where is the falling man?

Where are the twin figures, crying and tumbling,

Where have you hidden them?

Nora leaves. The house is cold and cavernous without her, and without a new servant the fire is never lit, the floor dusty with balls of fluff everywhere, while Mrs Fortescue lives on Horlicks and toast and marmalade, the only things she can prepare.

In my bed, I wake, and fear steals up my body. I fear for my survival. I look at the pounds folded carefully in my box and wonder, what if it is the only twenty pounds I ever have: can I live on it for the rest of my life? I am behind with two months' rent to Mrs Fortescue. My savings are perilously low and I owe the printer four pounds for *The Green Sheaf* – which I must surely abandon because Lolly did not allow me the loan of her printer after all, I have ended up paying students to hand-colour for me, and subscriptions are almost non-existent. My salons are currently stalled because I am in no mood to be entertaining. I am living on boiled eggs and toast because I have no money for suppers and Nora no longer shares whatever she was cooking for Mrs F, and it's made me awful constipated.

I picture those homeless men outside St John's Church as if they were a stained-glass window: one man bent on a stick, the companion, a woman, holding his arm. This image has never left me. I am surely one of them: poor, destitute, on the streets. Where would I live? Who would take me in? Do I even dare break into these twenty pounds – shouldn't I save them? Fear, fear!

It seems to me that fear has got hold of all this land. Who dares to do anything without fear of what some other will think and say?

I start a feverish new drawing phase, my music drawings, done whenever someone – Mrs F or a neighbour – is playing the piano and sadness and dreaminess and the sweet grief of Nora's absence wash over me. The drawings please me. They are different. I use a black ink, sometimes a sepia tint; other times brilliant washes of colour. Women, nymphs, goddesses with dark or red curly hair. While I paint like this, time rushes on and I am not here. Making my music pictures, I can achieve the impossible: an escape from my longings for Nora while at the same time conjuring her before me, vivid and true. More and more of them materialise: not pictures of the flying notes, but just what I see when I hear the music. Different music brings me different pictures. For a long time when I heard Beethoven the scenes were unpeopled, but one day a community of far-off spearmen appear, in a clanging sea strong with the salt of lashing spray.

I show them to Florence.

I ask her about joining her Sphere Group. If she can organise astral travel, does she have some magic for conjuring money?

'Don't you think all would do it, if they could?' she laughs. 'Mr Aleister Crowley – surely he would have perfected that by now?'

'Well, has he?'

For an answer she produces her Tarot pack again. 'You have a natural gift for understanding symbols,' she says to me, and begins turning the cards over, showing me their images. 'There are twenty-two trumps, corresponding to the twenty-two letters of the Hebrew alphabet.' She shows me a card of the Magician. He has a strange big hat, red and yellow, very bent. 'Let's go and look at him in the British Museum? There is a different kind of Tarot deck there.'

This does not appease me.

After trying to put her hand on mine (and me subtly shrugging it off), Florence says, 'Yesterday I was flicking through a book of five hundred pages for some half-remembered passage, with no luck. I gave up the struggle and named out loud the passage I hoped to find. The next minute, my fingers landed on the exact page in my book.'

'Huh. Are you going to tell me Spirit was guiding you?' I try not to sound as disgruntled as I feel, but Florence laughs anyway.

'No, not at all. I was going to say that when you express a desire clearly and without agitation it is efficacious and has a better result. A sort of flow is achieved, gathered in from somewhere. In prayer or otherwise. That is the truth that the Magician knows.'

'He looks like a street magician. Uncle Teddy would call him a mountebank, a conman . . .'

Florence gathers up some of my drawings, putting them carefully into a leather folder. 'You don't mind, though, if I show these to Stieglitz too? He loved the others. He has a gallery for photography but is keen to show other art too.'

I have produced so many of the music pictures. I have shown Florence, but I fear allowing others to see them. I love creating them, but afterwards I'm awash with shame. They're nothing! They're silly! Silly nymphs and seas and towers and drifty people and whatever else. (They remind me of sitting in the dark stalls, watching Ellen and the women sweeping around the stage until dust flies up in motes into the light and the magic occurs: my mind allowing me to be there, experiencing all unfolding in front of me.) Memories of that very first exhibition in the Macbeth Gallery flood back to me and I shrink in embarrassment, remembering how I heard people speaking of me, and that early review of the *Green Sheaf* and how 'strange' the reviewer found me.

'I'm tired of other people's opinions of me,' I say crossly. 'Charming. Odd-looking. Strange. Part Negro. Japanese. Psychic. A Gypsy . . . Why do they need to pin me down? Why can't I just be me?'

Florence gives me a great smile that disarms me. 'But, darling, you're so talented, and these last few months I've noticed a great change in you. And, in time, you'll find out who you truly are and do it on purpose!' She pulls me towards her in an easy embrace.

I want to resist but her words ring with a loud clang of truth. Yes. At my salon, didn't I understand that I had some sort of power, that the right people seem to be drawn to me, and in the end accept it as my due? I am a Very Appealing and Talented and Special Person. I feel a little stir of gratitude to her.

When one day she comes by and announces that the tickets to New York are her gift to me, my eyes spring with tears. The tickets are for January next year, 1907. 'You needn't thank me,' she says. 'It is entirely selfish. I want you to accompany me, as I am a little afraid to make the journey on my own.'

I know that this is not true, Florence being the most independent woman I have ever met, but I do appreciate her tact in not making me feel indebted to her. Meanwhile, she says, might she send Stieglitz some more pictures in the post? Her enthusiasm reminds me of Daddy.

I begin to fixate on how much I could charge for a music picture. Five pounds and five shillings, or even six pounds, perhaps – is that too much? What is that in dollars – around twenty-five. The sums absorb me for a while, as does the possibility of being able to pay some bills. I would love to move to a different home: my anger at Mrs F for turfing Nora out has not abated but instead grown harder like a big ugly gall. I can barely look at her over the constipating boiled egg in the morning. She really is awful conventional. No one could ever imagine *her* with her bum in the air and her face in a pillow.

I send two of my music pictures to Nora and write to her every day. I keep the letters light and meaningless in case Alfred should read one. I sign them *Affectionately, Pixie Pamela,* and after a while I run out of things to say.

Nora tells me in her letters that she has been making tea for many heated suffragist discussions held by the Yeats sisters, Lily and Lolly, frequent visitors in Devon, and that I ought to look into it because there are so many things that a man can be – a drunkard, a convict, a lunatic – and still have a vote, and yet a woman might be a nurse or a teacher, a mother, a doctor or a mayor, and yet *not* have it. *Succinctly put!* I write, trembling like a pan of simmering milk about to boil over.

> *Oh dear, dear Nora, I feel now that I have waited all my life for you. What marvellous Angel or Sprite brought you to me? How I miss you . . .*

A ghostly swift shape slips through a door with a glimpse of red curls and my heart leaps like a deer flinging itself recklessly over a ditch.

January 1907 feels an awful long way off. New York will be cold and snowy at that time. I write to Mary, telling her of my visit: *And a few of my new paintings, watercolours mainly, might perhaps be on display in a gallery in Manhattan. If it happens, I do hope you might come!*

Mary says that she lives out of state now, with two little ones, but will try her hardest to see me.

Nora writes back with a passion that astonishes me. Coded letters, but bold, brave and loving, and with the clear voice of Nora in them, with all her good sense, honesty and natural intelligence. They hint at things, impossible futures, courage, recklessness. I almost want to burn them, fearing that such hopes will destroy me.

★★★

On the crossing to New York, the SS *Minnehaha*, there is a curious moment when a man approaches me and says: 'Miss Smith? I think I knew your father . . .'

Fear ignites in me, as if a match has been struck. The memory of that last trip with Daddy. The shame and kerfuffle of being evicted from the first-class lounge, that fat pig of a first officer. It feels so long ago, and yet the pain flaring is *now*. Is he here to tell me that my ticket – bought with the money from Florence – is in some way not good enough?

'Daddy? My father's name was Charles. He passed away,' I answer, my voice a little shaky.

'Oh! You're not Colonel Smith's daughter? You have a look of him. I thought I heard the captain mention . . .'

'Perhaps you heard *Colman* Smith? That is my name, sir. Miss Pamela Colman Smith.'

'I see. Are you perhaps the wife of Gerald Smith?'

The interrogator is a tall, bendy man, who leans over the rail to look at the night sea with an alarming frailty, as if a gust of sea wind might topple him into the well of ink.

'No, sir. Not the wife of – Gerald Smith, either.'

He takes a swig from a flask in his top pocket and stares at me for rather too long. 'You do look rather like Colonel Smith. *Definitely* no relation?'

And for a moment, I wonder. About my father, my *actual* father, and whether it is possible he shares my family name, since Smith is a common one? But that way madness lies. Such thoughts can never be answered, so I shake my head. I see that he is trying to place me, and that I cannot simply be a young (twenty-eight! Am I still young?) woman, travelling.

'I'm here with my friend Florence Farr, the actress,' I volunteer.

'And you are chaperoned by . . .?'

'We are travelling alone. That is, together.'

His surprise is palpable. Not some fellow's wife, or daughter. Who on earth am I if neither of those? He takes another quick sip from the flask and does not trouble to offer it to me. We both lean over the railings, staring at the black sea, crested with flashes of brilliant white, caught by the moon, then turn back towards the ship. I taste an almond biscuit on my tongue that I ate earlier, and long for another. I had intended to sit on a damp dark deckchair and draw the scene from the deck, but it is too drizzly to bring out my sketchbook, though the sea is pleasingly still, as if poised, holding me for a moment, waiting.

'Are you sisters?'

I laugh. 'You can't have seen Florence! She is beautiful. Tall and slim. Big dark eyes. A crown of dark curls. We are not alike.'

He is being so rude, and so probing, that my answer is direct.

Across the sea from shore to shore, alone alone for evermore . . . My poem. How men expect you to be in relation to another man. Daughter, wife, mistress, sister: which are you? It seems to bother men that they can't place me. I am a man's *niece*, I guess, if Uncle Teddy is still alive. It is many years since he wrote to me. Should I volunteer that?

'I am an artist,' I say, out of the dark pause. A seagull squeals excitedly. 'I am on my way to a gallery in New York where my work will be exhibited.' The seagull squawks again.

The birds are awful chatty tonight. The drizzly air snatches my words. I don't even know if the stranger has heard me. He has not troubled to introduce himself and yet it seems he must discover *exactly* who I am. I feel like a magician, waving a flaming wand, creating a circle of incense around him, smoking the night sky into a yellow fog: *I am Pamela Colman Smith. I am me. I am an artist. (Offer me some whisky, why don't you, obnoxious fellow?)* One day, one day . . . I shall not have to stand here explaining myself to a man who might have no discernible gifts at all but still feels himself naturally superior. One who believes he has the right to interrogate me.

The gull falls silent but the moon picks out a huge white egret sweeping past, long slow wings, beak and neck extended like a pen against the black page. A perfect quill or a plume for a hat. Or a message from an ancestor: Nurse Delphine used to say that, whenever an egret or heron flew over. A message in another language, I always thought, since I could never decipher it.

Maybe just: *Take that, you drunkard, you lunatic, you bloomin rummy critter!*

★★★

All night the sea sloshes me like egg white in a basin. I am turning into stiff white peaks: I'd make a marvellous meringue.

A siren pierces my dreams. I leap from my bed but the room is in darkness. There is a frightened figure in a nightdress beside me. I'm sharing a cabin with Florence but this is not her. This woman is younger; she looks – as far as I can make out – like Mabel, the wife of Laurence. And she is crying, 'I can't *swim!*'

We hear water, terrible water, sloshing somewhere. The ship is listing to one side. A great powerful smell of sewage and oil and seawater fills our noses, and the panic is so great that for a moment I feel my heart has stopped, and I'm surely already dead? I reach for the lifebelts, on the rack above our bed, to help Mabel – or Florence – put hers on, over her nightdress. We hold hands and push the door open, to find ourselves already ankle-deep in water in the corridor outside. Hordes of people, voices shouting, a man's voice, over and over saying: 'The portholes. Close the portholes!'

The black sea is spun with a white fog. And then the shock. The tumbling fall, my hair flying out behind me. It seems to last forever, my skin scraping as I slide along something, before a savage smack and then I hit icy water. The cold is unlike anything I've ever felt. My breath is seized from my lungs, my ribcage clamps in pain, I open my mouth to scream. I *hear* myself screaming but it is a weird sound, underwater, and clotted. My mouth is full of salt. I am drifting and twirling at first, but as the great liner sinks I feel a powerful suction dragging me down and I kick frantically to try to escape the pull. The ship's cat – Emily – is in the water with us, but she is miraculously dry, upon a sort of tray, eddying in white waves, and surrounded by little tabby kittens.

A big man, wounded in the head, approaches and tries to cling to me. He has white hair, blackened with blood. I am trying to shake him off; he is weighing me down. He looks like Daddy! Is it Daddy, asking me to save him? When I see his head fall forward, I know he is dead. He drifts away. I am floating away myself. The slivers of ice slice my face.

I involuntarily begin to paddle with my feet. I'm kicking and kicking and I come to the surface and something wraps around my legs. 'What have I done!' I scream. I have opened a portal and allowed all the horrors of the world inside.

I feel strong arms around me, and I mutter to myself: *I am saved.*

'Darling, darling! It's all right! You're having a dream.'

It's Florence. Her face is close to mine, and she is stroking my cheek. The bed is rocking and listing and water splashes up to it. As Florence continues to stroke me, the water stops. The fog stops whirling. The sea ebbs away. I put my hand out, gingerly. The bed is dry. The air is dry. I make out the dark porthole in our cabin: it is safely closed. I pat myself. I'm dry, and sleeping, with only my racing heart and the sweat on my back to let me know the icy cold sea I've been drowning in.

'Oh God . . .' I moan. 'That was so real. I dreamed the ship was hit by another and strangely Mabel and Laurence were drowning . . .'

'Did it feel like a premonition?'

Horrible thought. I sit up, taking a moment to stare at Florence, her face orange in the lamplight, and I pat the bed, and my legs under the sheets. All is dry.

'I hope not! Laurence . . . I hope he is happy now, with Mabel, but I always feel sad for him,' I venture.

'Well. Maybe just your sensitive self, responding to Laurence's fragility. Is he the one, dear? When I asked about the music pictures, you said it had happened before, when *Laurence* was playing. Is he the one you're in love with?'

I long to unburden myself to Florence. How much of a New Woman is she, really? What are the limits of her modern ideas? She is a suffragist. She knows Edy and Christopher, and the theatre world. She has spoken of her approval of Ellen for sending flowers to Mr Wilde. She is, of all the people I've ever met, the most refreshing, direct, clear-sighted. And yet, and yet. I don't want her to disappoint me.

'No,' I murmur. 'It's not a man at all, it's . . .'

'Oh,' she says, after a long pause. And then, with the loveliest big-eyed stare at me, she says: 'Nora?'

'You knew.'

She nods.

A surge of joy flows through me. I realise how much I've wanted someone else to know. Love feels real with a witness.

We are both sitting up, wide awake, becalmed on this sea. The squall has passed. Florence pulls a lilac wool cardigan over her nightdress, opens the little cabinet next to her bed and brings out a small bottle of Scotch and two glasses. Dawn is starting to flood the room through the portholes, suffusing it with pink.

'But Nora has a child and I can't expect her to – to give up respectable life and live like a pariah!'

Florence frowns a little. 'Nora is an uncommon person . . .'

'Uncommonly beautiful?' I blurt. Exactly the thought I had myself.

Florence laughs. 'Yes, she is charming! But she is also uncommonly brave, living differently from others of her – forgive me, darling – others of her class. She squares up to Christopher and Edy, doesn't she? She speaks to Willie as an equal. I believe she was orphaned young, is alone in this world, as you are, and she has made her own way, with her séances and her resourcefulness . . .'

I had not thought of that. A glint of hope.

Florence returns to the little cabinet next to her berth and brings out her Tarot deck. 'Would it help? Shall we see what the Tarot says about your love?'

I finish my glass of whisky and hold it out for a top-up. Florence obliges, muttering, 'Ice would be nice, wouldn't it.'

The white slivers of my dream float past my eyes and I shudder.

Florence starts shuffling her deck. To my surprise, it's not the Italian one with the intense colours that she's shown me before. These figures are different: clumsy and blockish and the writing is in French. I ask to look at them. I hear, somewhere on the ship, a band start up. A drum, the blast of a trumpet. My excitement, my thrill at all the figures and images, immediately takes hold of me, shifting my mood entirely.

'Yes, it *is* a different deck. Don't ask where I got it from,' she says mysteriously. 'I will shuffle and you can pull three cards. One is you: the querent. One represents the beloved, and one for your understanding of what is between you. It will perhaps suggest an action.'

'A card to show my future?'

'You should have attended more Golden Dawn meetings. You are leaving out the presence of the Divine.' When I start sulking, she smiles, offering me the deck. 'Reducing the cards to tricks to tell the future is . . . rather trivialising. Consider *all* that is implied by the cards. All that they might want to say to you. The letters, the numbers, the symbols. I'll use only the

Major Arcana.' She begins separating out the trump cards. 'Swords, of course, they are the element of air. *Deniers* are earth. *Coupes* are water. And *batons* are fire.'

Why is asking about my future trivial? If this Tarot thing is to be taken up by General Jackass, and not just languish in the secret Golden Dawn world, won't that be *exactly* what people want to know?

The cards in her hands glow and flit and dance in the pink morning light, exactly like the little figures from my miniature theatre. I put my hands in my lap so I'm not tempted to reach for them while she shuffles and then dart a hand out to select the three cards when she tells me to.

Me: Justice. Nora: The Fool. Outcome: L'Amoureux. The Lovers.

We are both laughing as I hand the cards back.

'That's a positive card, right?' I point to the Lovers.

Florence glances at the cards. 'Mathers says it means "trials surmounted". Waite would say "natural love, harmony, union". De Mellet – his was an eighteenth-century view – "hesitating, making a choice between vice and virtue".'

Nora flashes into my mind: her strong firm chin, her cheeky smile, her clever, mischievous eyes . . .

I shake my head. 'All these different meanings, given by different men. How do we know what to make of it, then?'

'Meditate on the card. Tell me what *you* see.'

I see sunshine. I see a Cupid figure with an arrow, and a man making a choice between two women. And I see Nora and my heart contracts because it can't be. She's married. She has a child. She's moved to Devon. I think she might love me – and I think of what Florence said about her uncommon bravery. Could we ever live as Edy and Christopher do, flagrant, flouting all convention? I hand the card back with a sigh.

'It's just wishful thinking. Putting your hope in silly signs. When my mother died, I believed she had gone to a beautiful garden behind the moon because I read a book by Howard Pyle and that's what *he* said happened, after death.'

'And now?'

'I can't understand how a deck of cards might be able to give me an answer – one card out of twenty-two – to my life questions. It's chance. I picked a card, that's all. But who is directing the cards? Is it God? If the Tarot is wise, where is the wisdom coming from?'

Florence – infuriatingly – repeats her Golden Dawn motto, which she has told me many times: 'Wisdom is a gift given to the wise.'

I let out an exasperated sound and then modify my tone. (These days I am in much Better Charge of Myself.) 'But why *that* one? The Lovers: of course that's the one I hoped for most, that is to say I would have done if I'd known of its existence. Why *that*, rather than any other card?'

'Oh Pixie.' Florence smiles. 'How sceptical you've become! A person has two minds: a subjective one and an objective one, and the subjective mind – outside of our everyday awareness – can direct things, powerfully.'

I feel I have disappointed her, failed a test. Florence's enthusiasm for the Tarot, for all things Golden Dawn, her endless conversations with Willie about it all . . . I know she wants to include me and educate me, but in my stubborn disgruntled way I can't accept things because . . . Why would God or any gods or ancient 'wisdom' from Egyptian times want to speak to me, Pamela Colman Smith? I just don't get it.

Florence pushes the stopper into the bottle of whisky and, loosening the tie at the neck of her nightdress, yawns and says, 'Oh, it's so early! I need more sleep . . .' and takes her cardigan off, nestling back under her blankets. The band I heard starting up seems to have come to an abrupt end. Now there are only the usual gruntings and groanings, mechanical sounds of the ship. I lie on my bed, on my back, on top of my blankets, and stare at the ceiling.

'You forgot the Fool,' Florence murmurs sleepily. 'The card you picked for Nora. A sacred clown who breaks convention, opens hearts and stands closest to Spirit. The Goddess's special and favourite child. A pure energy to act and create, no matter what anyone says.'

Could it be? The Fool used to be me. I always thought of myself that way. Now it is Nora. Nora with her naughtiness, her boldness and vivacity. I fall back to sleep picturing her, and feeling the warmth creep through my body like the flushing of the dawn, making our cabin flame red.

I am a star! A fairy tern hovering over your head;

the fluting notes you hear beside the river.

I'm here in darkness, always here, with my streamer tail, whether you see me or not.

I might be Sirius or Starhawk,

I'm the poet, the Star Goddess. I might be privation, or hope.

I have one foot in the pond, my knee on the ground.

Tea on the lawn at the summerhouse.

Mine are the voices of the birds, singing:

If that which you seek you find not within yourself,

You will never find it without.

For behold, I have been with you from the beginning . . .

The gallery is empty. I have come alone and I'm early – it's only half past six and the invitations are for seven – but still, it is empty. A young man in a smart white shirt and a suit is standing behind a table presenting rows of champagne in flutes. I grab one. And there are my music pictures, in vast spaces, and here, rushing towards me, is Stieglitz, his great shock of grey hair falling over his eyes as he towers over me, seizing my hand, kissing my cheek and overwhelming me with his powerful scent of – what? – white spirit or rabbit-glue, I decide; Daddy used to use it when he was mending violin bridges. Or perhaps it is some other chemical Stieglitz uses in his photography?

'Pixie! May I call you that, or do you prefer Pamela? Florence is not with you?'

I see them now. All the little white signs, under my paintings: *Pamela Colman Smith*. I realise I am trembling and my stomach dissolving like sherbet. Oh, why did Florence not come with me? She said she had someone to meet and would arrive a little later with him. I suspect it must be this John Quinn she has come to see. I force down the flute of champagne in one or two huge fizzy gulps and feel it soften and warm me, and at last I'm able to look Stieglitz in the eyes.

'She said you were shy!' He smiles. 'And it is terrifying, is it not, a private view? Not many would find it otherwise.' I catch him staring at my empty glass, but he does not offer me another. Now he goes to the window and stares down at the street. 'I sent notices to all the press . . .' He glances at his watch, pulled from his pocket. 'I can't understand it.' He runs his hands through his hair, agitated, the way Daddy used to. He fetches himself a glass of champagne and another for me. The waiter stands with six glasses on a tray, pretending not to notice the emptiness of the gallery.

We are standing beside my painting *The Fugitive*, which feels apt. Next to it is *Castle of Pain*. With its grim and solitary tower. Underneath, Stieglitz – or someone – has printed a card: *Concerto in A Minor*. Next to it is a painting of figures ringing bells in the sky: *Chromatic Fantasy, Bach* . . . All the paintings have these explanations, the ones I provided in my letters to Stieglitz – what will people make of them? The fizz in my stomach leaps again, a shot of fear.

At last we hear footsteps on the stairs – one person, not a horde – and a man appears. An older stout man with a cane, tapping his way across the wooden floor towards us. I am frightened: why is he striding like that, so purposefully, as if he would like to attack me?

'Pamela! My Pamela!' he cries in a hoarse voice.

'Uncle *Teddy*!'

He swamps me in a stiff embrace. Stieglitz steps politely to one side. When Teddy releases me, there are tears in his eyes.

'I had to force my way past that great crowd of journalists out there. The door was locked and the bell does not work! *Finally* someone unlocked it. What on earth is going on? But look at you, my Pamela, so grown-up and a whole gallery full of your work, and announced in *Brooklyn Life*, so that your poor old uncle had to find out that way!'

'The bell doesn't work? The door had to be un*locked*?' Stieglitz shoots away from us.

Uncle Teddy makes his way to a gallery chair and falls creakily onto it. He is breathing noisily. He points his cane at my drawings. 'You have some special mystical gift that produces them when you close your eyes and listen to music? Is that it?'

We are closest to a painting with a note saying *Beethoven, Sonata No. 11*. Teddy waves his cane dismissively towards it and I see it through his eyes: muddy shades, a pale sea and the rocks and waves forming two figures, one of them enormous, garlanded with red hair (in my mind it is a man, but I imagine those looking at it might not be certain), and the other, smaller figure staring up at him.

'And this one? The same thing? *A Pilgrim Followed by Its Own Doubtful Thoughts*? Why "it", not "she" – isn't the figure a woman?' He is standing now, staring at the painting, then turning back to me, bewildered. I had forgotten just how loud Uncle Teddy is. In the empty gallery his voice booms.

Before I can answer (and what will I say – Daddy always assured me his brother knew nought but the price when it came to art, and Teddy's eyes are goggling now, holding the list of paintings on a sheet he has picked up or perhaps been sent), there's a great bother and fuss on the stairs and something of a stampede interrupts us, as number of men in suits and women in furs arrive and I realise Stieglitz has fixed the problem with the door.

'So are you married, my dear?' Uncle Teddy is trying to lower his voice, but it still comes out in a huge boom. I murmur something and move to avoid him, spying – in the crowd – Florence in a new hat of green velvet and grey silk gloves, accompanied by a man with the biggest dome of a forehead I've ever seen: exactly like a bulbous moon! Florence hurries to my side and introduces me to John Quinn, and Uncle Teddy introduces *himself* proudly to John Quinn, and I see at once that this man is an art collector and somewhat important in Uncle Teddy's eyes.

Florence takes my arm, drawing me aside. 'Are you all right? You never told me you had an uncle still living!'

'He usually – doesn't want to know me. I'm as surprised as you are to see him.'

'But what a turn-out! Aren't you delighted?'

The place is heaving now, skirts sweeping across the floors, women's voices clattering like crockery, laughter tinkling and male voices rolling under it all like waves. All of it is a garble to me – I somehow can't manage to hear any of it – but before I can answer Florence, Stieglitz is trying to introduce someone else to me (a very beautiful older woman, swathed in furs, but inside them as frail as a bird, with a little nose like a beak) and I feel so . . . very fizzy and bubbly and yet with a pit of terror in my stomach and I cannot I just cannot seem to make out what anyone is saying to me . . .

'I need to – go outside!' I tell Stieglitz. I fear he will find me rude, but he is busy talking to another journalist and in my terror I feel my shrinking feeling descending: I fear that tiny me might just slip over the edge and into my champagne flute and drown there. I plonk the glass down onto a tray, rush down the stairs and push past new people arriving, to reach the street, breathing in the cold New York air, the comforting smell of meat cooking somewhere and a warm brazier roasting chestnuts. I sit on the bottom step of a fire escape and burst into tears. I am hungry.

I could just leave. Whether good or bad, success or failure, the number of people, the excitement and the clamour: it's always too much. I just feel plucked and strung up by the legs. Alone is easier. Or with a dear, loving person, who makes me feel coddled and safe. *Nora*.

I remember my great success that night with Daddy when I was nineteen and had to run outside to escape into the snow with Mary. If only it had been Mary, not Uncle Teddy, who had surprised me tonight, but I know that she has moved away and has two young children to occupy her. I remember the evening when Uncle Teddy let slip that my fees for Pratt had not been paid, and I was not going to graduate. I forgave him then – blundering, oafish man that he is – but I was only nineteen. Am I to forgive him again, ten years later, for this evening? On the night of the greatest triumph of my life as an artist – for I am starting to understand that the evening is *indeed* a success: Stieglitz's list of paintings has many red dots on it already, and John Quinn the great collector is here and murmuring to Stieglitz about my painting *The Blue Cat* – and amidst all of that, Uncle Teddy's first remark to me is: 'So are you married?'

And here he is now, coming slowly down the steps, out onto the street, adjusting his hat, a little wobbly-looking, lifting his cane to hail a cab. He seems bewildered to find me here. At first I thought he had come outside to find me, but now I realise he was about to leave without saying goodbye.

'What are you doing out here?' he bellows upon seeing me. I stand up. He takes my face in his hands, and I think he might be about to plant a kiss on my nose, but instead he says, a little quieter than usual, 'How like Charles you are.'

That's a rum thing! What to say? After my séance with Nora, and knowing that his brother is not my father. That, in fact, Uncle Teddy is no relation of mine.

'It was a terrible thing he did. Your mother was a very good person to forgive him.' He seems to have drunk a great deal of champagne. (It being on the house, he would be sure to make the most of it.)

He searches my face to see if I understand. I know he sees my blankness.

Teddy gives a very loud sigh and then feels in his pocket for his pipe and begins filling it from a tobacco pouch.

'Your family life was bathed in secrets,' he says.

'Yes.'

'I imagine you longed to know – who your real mother was.'

'My real – *mother*?'

Uncle Teddy looks confused then. Frightened even. The tangled white hairs of his eyebrows knit together: he seems to be wondering whether to go on.

'I assumed that somebody – perhaps Corinne herself – had told you? In Jamaica? I think – you must have wondered, about your looks? Your dark skin? Your round face and stout figure, when Corinne was so pale and such a beauty?'

Uncle Teddy, as tactless as ever. But my mind – my heart – is in tumult. Here I am on Fifth Avenue, with a horse and carriage drawing up, and this is where Uncle Teddy chooses to enlighten me about my parentage.

'Mama did say, on her deathbed, that she had a very Big Secret to tell me. But then, she did not impart it.'

Uncle Teddy draws deep on his pipe, a red bloom starting to creep over his face.

'So. You didn't know. About your father's mistress in Manchester?'

'What?'

'Oh my Lord. Child, I have blundered in and there is no way to say this so I will be plain. Your father had a mistress. She fell pregnant. When you were barely a week old, she died. Sepsis, I believe.'

I give a short gasp and, knees buckling, sit down heavily again on the step of the fire escape.

Uncle Teddy glances around and then squares his shoulders, continues: 'Your mother found out and – I guess because she was an old gal by then, forty-seven, and never likely to have any of her own – they agreed to adopt you. In London. I believe your birth was registered twice and no one was the wiser. Eventually, you went to Jamaica and your father hoped to leave it all behind. But – you know Charles. He was really just not able to –' (Here Uncle Teddy coughs.) 'He was a man of appetites. Don't misunderstand: he loved your mother. Oh, how damned awkward that it should be I who is forced to tell you! What an unholy mess those two made of it.'

I feel as if two strong hands are squeezing my ribcage.

'I can't breathe –' I say. Uncle Teddy looks alarmed and, changing his mind about the horse and cab, lifts me from the fire escape and takes me by the elbow towards a coffee shop.

'Brandy,' he says as we enter. The dark wooden interior feels as if I'm stepping into a smoky cigar box. I barely look up, but even without checking I know I am the only female person here.

And when we are seated, and the brandy has been brought and is scalding my tongue, I think: *this* was the secret she tried to tell me. Not about *her* love affair, but Daddy's. Nothing beautiful or mystical, but just sordid. I was not hers. My mother died; was someone I did not know.

'All my life people have commented on my strangeness. Am I a Gypsy? Am I Japanese? Am I part Negro?

My queer face. My short stature. I *have* wondered . . . I thought perhaps a great-grandfather . . . I *have* felt . . .'

'Are you sorry I told you? Should I have taken the secret to my grave?'

'What about a cup? A blue chim-chim cup? There was a fuss . . . It seemed to be a present from someone significant?'

'I'm afraid I know nothing about that.'

'And how certain are you?'

This could be a story Mama and Daddy told him. A story for Theodore, to – to make sure he continued to support Daddy financially, and me. It might not be the truth. (But what does it matter? Would I prefer my father not to be my father or my mother not to be my mother? One way or another, I am not who I thought I was and I'm destined never to know for certain my true parents, or who I am.)

'Thank you for telling me,' I say, not sure if I mean it. 'There has always been something – complicated – about our family life, hasn't there? I could feel that. I have struggled to – find my place among friends or discover quite who I am. I feel sometimes as if I am – *whoosh* – shrinking or growing, always turning into someone else. Or rather that others are always trying to pin me down with their definitions while I try to resist it.'

'I take it you are *not* married, then?'

This again! I want to protest. I want to tell him about Nora, and Edy and Christopher and Ellen, about friends who are suffragists or New Women like Florence, but all the strength has puffed out of me, like a flattened bladder. I have no anger left, towards him or my parents. Only confusion and a tiny flicker of pride. I am an artist. My show upstairs is a huge success. Surely *now* money and fame will flow my way and my life will change forever.

'Did you know my mother's name? Anything else about her? How old was she when she died?'

He shakes his head and then, after a cough, he seems to think better of this and says: 'I do once remember your father mentioning her. Her name was Sophia. I'm sorry, but that's the only small detail I have.'

★★★

That night, a rage consumes me, of the sort I haven't felt in a long while. I astonish myself, tearing things up in my hotel room, flinging pillows, biting them, screaming into them, exhausting myself. I kick a drawer so hard that a maid knocks on the door, anxiously asking if Madam is all right? I reply with great dignity that I found a mouse in my room and, after listening for a moment, I hear her footsteps leave, presumably to get someone else to come and deal with it. I fling myself on the bed, and sigh.

I want to go home. I want to tell Nora my discovery. I want to leave: I can no longer stand to stay in New York.

Daddy. Once again, white-hot fury flares. Loser! Cheat! A picture from the Tarot flashes in front of me, of the Devil in chains, a stupid beast to his own selfish needs. But immediately this image appears, love for Daddy overwhelms it. I am exhausted and a great sadness pools in me. Why, *why* did no one tell me the truth?

The day of our passage home cannot come fast enough. Stieglitz brings a copy of *Brooklyn Life* the morning Florence and I are leaving. We are at breakfast, our trunks and bags beside us, and look up to see his striking figure striding towards us. All eyes in the breakfast room turn to him.

He drops the newspaper on the table among the eggs and coffee. 'Every painting sold!' he announces. A queer sort of shiver runs through me as I unfold it to the page he is jabbing at and begin reading.

Pamela Colman Smith is exhibiting, at the Little Galleries of the Photo-Secession, 291 Fifth Avenue, a collection of twenty-two drawings, colored and black and white. She is a young woman with that rare quality in either sex – imagination . . . Many of them seem to show a spiritual exultation. Death in the House is absolutely nerve-shuddering . . . Munch himself, a master magician of the terrible, could not have succeeded better in arousing a profound disquiet . . .

I fling the paper back towards Stieglitz with a loud 'Ugh!'

He is dressed like a dandy in a smart suit with a black bow tie, and I realise he has come here to celebrate, or perhaps to do so directly somewhere else. He is wearing evening clothes. His hair is ruffled and extraordinarily thick, like a shaggy dog's. He puts his glasses in his pocket, leaning in to stare at me from under that great cloud of fringe, astonished. 'But Pamela – it's all mighty fine! It's better than fine – it's dandy!'

'But I hate reading about myself! I feel – I feel like a mollusc without her shell.'

Florence laughs. 'Ha – poor Pixie. At least success keeps the wolf from the door.' Florence is sitting with her Italian Tarot deck this time, and wants to show me the card she just pulled, the Lovers. 'Look, darling, see how this card follows you around?'

I am indeed thinking of Nora and she is the only person I want to talk to right now. This morning I tried to write to her, but, aware that Alfred might read the letter, I found myself stymied and unable to even start, beyond *My Dearest Darling Nora*.

Stieglitz is intrigued, putting his glasses on again to peer more closely at the card. 'Do you know the work of Marcus Ward? An illustrator who made illuminated works in a sort of medieval style. Where did you get these?' he asks Florence. She shows him the deck, saying, without looking up, 'You know I'm descended from Gypsies? My grandmother used to read the cards. This is a deck that Willie gave me, from Italy. Beautiful, aren't they?'

This is the first I've heard of any Gypsy connection for Florence. I glance at her, wondering, is she flirting with Stieglitz?

'May I?' he asks, and she hands the deck over to him.

'I know Marcus Ward's work,' I say, feeling that Stieglitz and Florence have instantly forgotten me. 'His family home was next to mine, when I was a child, in Chislehurst.'

'Is that Manchester?' Stieglitz asks, shuffling through the deck.

'Outskirts of London.'

'I thought you grew up in Jamaica and Manchester?' Florence remarks. 'My, your early years are an adventure, aren't they?' I do not think she means to be hurtful, but my mind flies back to the conversation with Uncle Teddy. A feeling of shame flows through me. What do I really know about my own early years? And why was I so sure, after Nora and our séance, that it was Mama who had strayed and taken a lover and Daddy who was the pretender?

Is that why the Lovers card follows me around? A lesson I need to learn. I try hard to remember that occasion with Nora, and I wonder, did Nora actually *say* that that was the Big Secret? All I can recall is her comment: 'Your mother says you've always known in your heart, and no need to rake it up now.' And then I went to my memories about a row Mama had with Daddy when I was little, and a blue cup that is vivid in my mind, and a story I didn't understand, and I put two and two together and seem to have made one hundred! Oh, how painful and confusing it is not to understand your own story, your own past. Why is everyone obsessed about knowing the future when the past is mysterious enough!

Stieglitz has sat down heavily and is trying to find places to put the breakfast things, summoning a waitress to take them away. He wants Florence to give him a reading: the full works, he says.

'Not here,' Florence says, glancing around at the curious guests of our hotel, all trying to pretend they are not staring at the three of us. Florence and Stieglitz are tall, arresting. The reasons they stare at me might be guessed at. Standing up, she waves towards our trunks and hatboxes. 'We leave quite soon,' she tells Stieglitz. 'We should go. Another time,' she adds politely.

Stieglitz pats the pocket of his fine wool jacket. 'I almost forgot! This is for you, Pamela. And there is more – send me more pictures when you return. This is just the start!'

With a small flourish, and a playful bow, he hands me a cheque.

My heart plims and I feel like dancing, like smiling and twirling or riding on a horse, legs akimbo, shouting: *Hallelujah!*

Of course, I merely thank him and pretend not to look at the sum, and my eyes fill with tears, while Florence pats my back and murmurs 'Well done' as she signals the bellboy to help us carry our cases.

★★★

With the money from Stieglitz, I can move out of my Milborne Grove studio. I can pay Mrs F what I owe her. And I can pay the printers of *The Green Sheaf* too, and leave all my debts for that abandoned enterprise behind. In the end it was just damn onerous chasing people, no one ever submitted their work on time, nor in the right format, no one else seemed to care that lateness meant our subscribers fell out of love with us and that in the end it was me, and *my* time and *my* money, that was always being compromised.

Florence has a friend (another gentleman friend: I'm discovering she has many of these) who rents out a place right opposite Battersea Park with a balcony full of hanging baskets and a bird table where blue tits and coal tits and bullfinches gather. The birds entertain me while I'm shown around by the gentleman friend (Mr Avery, which I hear as 'Aviary'), drinking the coffee he offers me and nodding, *yes, yes,* to the newness, the new start, the new space, the new view of the trees with their great puffs of pink blossom and the powdery white sky overhead.

Handing Mrs F her envelope with all of my late rent in it, I try to be casual when I say, 'If any letters come for me, my address is 84 York Mansions. You will forward them? Especially any from N— from Devon?'

She says she will. But: 'You won't forget your old friends?' she asks, pointedly.

I am thinking: *I will forget you, strange huffy-puffy Mrs Fortescue; you are not my friend.*

'Do please pass on any correspondence *at all* that comes for me,' I repeat firmly.

I'm awful popular with Mr Stieglitz right now. There might be more cheques arriving, I think with the happiness of a person who now feels herself to be a well-paid artist, no longer a grubbing one, and who is enjoying every moment.

You saw me last night, didn't you?
You looked up and saw my pearl eye on you.
Here is a long silver trail you might follow
To meet the owl who wears my face.
The same silver path Mama and Papa walked.
I never shine there. Howl all you will.
I'm five fathoms deep. So dark.

The first forwarded letter I receive is not from Nora, but Arthur Edward Waite, the Horlicks Man. The invitation is uncharacteristically clear: would I like to meet in an Italian restaurant in Park Close. He obviously thinks I still live in Chelsea as it is near there, an insider alley hidden in Knightsbridge. He does not trouble to mention work or money, just that he has a 'suggestion', which he 'feels sure' will interest me.

And, curiously, on my way to meet Arthur, I bump into his rival, Mr Crowley, in Battersea Park. I am sitting on a bench under a tree, eating a piece of bread and watching a squirrel. Its tail whisks back and forth, frisky and disturbed; it is spring, and perhaps it's looking for a mate. Two crows stare at my sandwich from a branch. Sparrows pick up the crumbs. I'm dreaming, thinking, reliving my success in New York, and the man is almost upon me before I realise he is expecting me to greet him. Or perhaps he even said something? I jump up.

(Christopher says Mr Crowley described one of her friends as 'the ancient Sapphic Crack, unlikely to be filled', and somehow this rather rude thought is now in my head as I brush crumbs from my lap and tremble in front of him. He is smoking a big thick pipe and wearing some kind of fur tippet.)

'You are . . . Soror . . .?' he says, clearly not really able to remember me at all.

'I'm Pixie. Most people call me Pixie. But yes, I am – I was – in the Order.'

Without any niceties, he sits down on the bench and leans his head in his hands. His hair is all over his face, and his eyes are friendly. He is something like an unruly collie dog.

'You know me, I'm sure? Perdurabo. This morning I was badly obsessed and five times have lost my temper, utterly without reason or justification. The horses have bolted at the sight of me. I come here for a rest and – here you are, and there are crows, mischievous devils, already with their eyes on me!'

He does not seem to expect a reply and as I now dare to inspect him a little, I see that the fur tippet is stained, his hair and his jacket dishevelled, eyes red. I imagine he has not slept at all. He sucks on the pipe as if it is a baby's bottle; it is unlit.

'You are probably in a different temple now? With the silly Mr Waite and Soror Farr? Or – I try not to listen to gossip, but I know she founded her own Sphere Group . . . Well, servant girls must be advised to keep an eye on their half-crowns as I know Mr Waite is writing a book on fortune-telling!' He gives a sharp bark of a laugh here, and for the first time I notice how vivid his eyes are, how black the pupils, and suddenly a sort of handsomeness appears. 'Nobody but Mr Waite knows *all* about the Tarot, it seems, and he won't tell us what the mysteries are! He seems to think that the vaguer his style and the more obscure his pomposities are, the greater an initiate he will seem . . .'

He is staring very hard at me. My bread swallowed (with a big gulp and an effort), I can't help but smile.

'I see you agree, Pixie!' he growls. 'Reminds one of a story about the student who slept, and woke when the professor thundered, "And what is electricity?" And the student panics and says, "I know, sir, but I have forgotten." "Just my luck," moans the professor. "There was only one man in the world who knew, and he has forgotten!"'

Despite myself, I laugh out loud. Mr Crowley – the Great Beast, as everyone refers to him (and the picture of the Devil in the Tarot deck always pops into my head when his name is mentioned) – is a Great Swell and damn entertaining compared to the Horlicks Man. He takes himself far less seriously, but you can't help feeling he might be onto something with this magic lark; he might actually know something.

He is pleased to have amused me, but in an instant his mood plummets and he puts both hands to his head and sways. 'Oh! I'm dizzy and sick, too much of – various things . . . Do you live near here? Might I beg a cup of coffee from you?' He looks like he might slump to the ground. The birds fly off, crowing. A sound just like you'd expect: mocking laughter. I wonder whether to touch Mr Crowley, but he leans heavily on me and there is no avoiding it: I help him to walk the short distance from the park to my front door, navigating the busy road with its horses and cabs and perilous dog walkers.

'It's here, Mr Crowley,' I say, stopping in front of 84 York Mansions, extricating his arm from mine. I'm extraordinarily pleased at the grandeur of my new address but trembling at my own daring to invite a man into it, unchaperoned, in daylight. We pause and he murmurs, 'It's pronounced *Crow*-ley. Like the bird' as he props himself against the boxy privet hedge (almost falling into it) while I search for my key.

The place smells like paints as we trundle up the dark stairs to the first-floor flat. Many of my boxes are still not unpacked. The smell of turpentine mingles with the hyacinths I picked from the park yesterday, now bent over in a jar of water. I pull out a chair for him to sit on, find us two cups and, after a great deal of fiddling around, proudly set a little pan on the stove. I open the window, widening the wooden shutters a little; he winces and shades his eyes. Outside in the street we can hear a lady singing a warbling song. Some of my music pictures are propped against the wall, one on an easel.

'Yes, you're the – draughtswoman,' he says.

'I'm an artist – just back from New York. I had a – a sell-out show.' I know women are not supposed to boast, but that only makes boasting irresistible to me.

Mr Crowley raises his head a little, gives me an appraising look. 'Do you have anything stronger than coffee?'

I fetch the brandy and offer him it, along with the coffee. He lays his pipe to one side to accept the cup. For some reason, I do not like seeing him holding my mother's chim-chim cup, and wish I had chosen another, less delicate one.

'You are very brave, Soror Pixie!' he says out of nowhere. 'What dog dares to be a friend of that dirty fellow Crowley? I beat you with my shoe! Go away! Get intellect! Get English!'

I don't know if I'm supposed to be horrified by this but instead I burst out laughing again and pour brandy into my coffee too.

'I share your misgivings about Mr Waite – about Arthur. I call him the Horlicks Man.'

'He is perfectly competent to produce indefinite quantities of malted milk—'

Again, I laugh, astonished at how passionate his hatred is. 'But I have heard he has a job for me and I'm going to meet him and find out what it is.'

'A job? I am infinitely sorry for any artist who tries to draw after dipping her hands in the insufferable dogma of such a dolt and a prig.'

As we are sparring like this, a thought occurs. I feel as if Mr Crowley knows it in the same instant too. Why it is that I have felt Mr Waite pursuing me, as if he has been trying to assess me, come to a decision. What it is that Mr Waite wants of me. What he would like me to draw.

The woman outside has stopped singing. The crows are gone. The room feels awful quiet and poised, as if we are in a church. My eyes fall on a little figure I bought for myself in New York, only half-unwrapped: a small wooden statue of the Virgin Mary, eyes closed, baby at her breast.

Up close, Mr Crowley has a powerful smell. I don't know if I like it. One moment it makes me think of earth, of plants, the next of something dirty and rotten. He reaches for his pipe and then, patting his pocket, looking for tobacco, he finds something else. His Tarot deck. He brings it out as if surprised to find it. On first glance, it looks like the same Italian deck that Florence has. Opening the box and taking out some cards, he says, 'You've seen these, I imagine? Florence is quite the Adept. I've written Waites's obituary already. I shall send you a copy. *Dead Waite.* The poor man suffers from chronic crapititis in his writing – like our other crapulous contemporaries: Frater Yeats—'

I'm starting to suffocate under this bile and the strong smell of sweet earthiness, and I make a second attempt to get up and open the window blind. On my way back, I pick up the statue of the Virgin, feeling the need of it somehow. Mr Crowley goes to shield his eyes again – a gesture of affectation – and spills the deck of cards all over my floor. I kneel to pick them up, conscious of the cup of coffee close by. I move the cup to one side.

My cartoon drawing of Mr Bram Stoker comes to me then. The drawing of him as a bat, with wings. The Brammy Joker. Crowley is the Devil. Fat legs, horns, a pentacle on his forehead, a goat's beard and wings.

'Why *do* they call you the Great Beast?' How long I have wondered this!

He shrugs. 'Why do they call you a pixie?' He nods towards the statue. 'Are you a Catholic, like Waite?' He is glancing at the statue of Our Lady.

'No,' I murmur, 'but I find her – comforting.'

'He is a dead weight, though, isn't he?' And this time he's giggling.

I gather up the cards and hand them back to him, but one springs from the pack to the floor again, as if escaping. The Justice card. The same card that came up for me when Florence asked me about my secret love. I must remember to ask her what this card means. Why does it keep coming up? Justice . . . Weighing up the rights and wrongs: is Mr Crowley right about Mr Waite? I also find him . . . pompous and irritating, but is he a fraud?

Mr Crowley gets up, bowing stiffly, to replace his cards in his pocket and thank me for the coffee. 'The trouble is, he does know something, despite all.'

'Who? Mr Waite?'

He refuses to answer this time, perhaps regretting his concession. 'The life we live is the only law,' he announces, then burps. I do not know what to make of this. But I will find out, I suppose, at our meeting. And I shall be very tempted to accept whatever Mr Waite proposes, because this new-found success with my music pictures might not last forever. And, sadly, neither will the money.

★★★

I arrive early for my meeting with Mr Waite. It is difficult to be a lady and walk alone into a restaurant, so I'm pacing outside, beneath a mackerel sky, wishing I had a little dog in a coat to fuss over, like the other women I see. I'm trying to get my hair pinned right inside my hat, pretending not to be waiting for someone. A thickset man with a sweaty forehead, smoking just outside the door to the restaurant, is welcoming people inside. He spies me and with exaggerated graciousness invites me in. There's nothing to do but scuttle inside, with him following.

Mr Waite is already there. He stands up as I enter. The table is so small it looks like a school desk, and he looks like a wolf, with his tangle of iron-grey beard, and his saturnine face. The place smells of Italian cheese and for a second I feel as if I've walked into a boys' locker room. The restaurant is lit with little lamps, despite it being daytime, so that it's like stepping into a dark cave. Mr Waite already has a carafe of wine next to him and an empty glass for me. Although this restaurant is trying to suggest Italian rustic with the red-and-white tablecloths and pots of basil on each small table, I have the immediate impression from the intimacy and the cosy feel that it is *very* expensive.

The waiter takes my coat, standing patiently with it over his arm while I struggle to unpin the hat I was pinning so firmly a moment ago, all elbows and fearing that in such a confined space I might knock something over: a carafe from another table, God forbid! I am awful glad to sit down and give him my hat too.

'Hello – Mr Waite.'

'Oh, *please*. I've asked you to call me Arthur. I trust I may call you Pamela?'

'Pamela is fine,' I say, sipping the wine and feeling its effects at once. I think of Mr Crowley calling him Dead Waite and saying he has already written his obituary! I smile broadly at Mr Waite – Arthur – and take another slug. All such thoughts – publishers as pigs and poets as rummy creatures – comfort me. Maybe I *am* more like Crowley than I allow?

'I was very impressed with your little magazine,' he says. '*The Green Papers.*'

'*The Green Sheaf.*'

'Yes. Do you have a current issue? I haven't seen it for a while.'

'Did you subscribe? No? Well, I don't have any free copies to hand out. Lately I've been finding it tiresome. I have no time for it. I had a big exhibition on Fifth Avenue and the music paintings have taken up all my time.'

The waiter brings us some warm bread and oil in a little skillet. There is scarcely room for it on the table. Arthur begins dipping his bread at once, but although I am hungry I content myself with sipping the wine (after the waiter has topped it up), enjoying the softening feeling, my edges blurring; I'm flowing more freely now.

'Oh yes, I heard about those too,' Arthur says, 'and the extraordinarily magical way you create them . . . You see music as images, is that it?'

'Something like that.'

'I've heard that one composer – was it Debussy? – claims it is exactly what is in his mind too as he composes. You have some direct – You have an astonishing facility.'

I beam, and finish my wine, reaching now for a large piece of bread and dripping oil over the tablecloth as I bring it to my mouth, salty and delicious. The waiter has spread my napkin over my knees.

Arthur manoeuvres a book around the bread and oil, across the table towards me.

'I thought, in light of the proposition I'm about to make, you might like to read some of *my* work,' he says. I glance at the title and thank him. *The Book of Black Magic and of Pacts.* I'm instantly worried about the olive oil staining it, so I slip it into my bag, under the table, forgetting even to pretend to look at it. I will donate it to Florence: she will find it interesting. When I face him again, he is watching me. His expression is amused.

'The proposition I have for you is to draw a Tarot deck. It will contain all of my vast knowledge of the Secret Tradition . . . of the correspondences and the Kabbalah. I have great knowledge afforded to very few. I will describe to you all the meanings and symbols of the cards and you will – draw my designs. There are seventy-eight cards in total, so that will be approximately eighty drawings I'd need, including one for the back of the deck and a cover illustration. Then I will publish it with a book. I wonder if you are familiar with the Tarot? There is a Sola Busca deck on display – well, black-and-white photographs of it – at the British Museum. Several members of the original Golden Dawn have been using a secret version for some time . . .'

At last!

'Is that what you wanted to ask me? That day when you followed me?'

'I was not following you!'

'You were. I passed your test, I take it?'

He seems surprised. And then – unexpectedly – begins to smile. 'You're plain-speaking. There is something very – refreshing. You have confidence, and I have since seen many excellent examples of your work. You are familiar with the Tarot?'

'Florence Farr has shown me. I mean Soror—' I try to remember Florence's name in the Order, but I can't. Their silly names and Latin mottos never come easily to me.

'Florence is not an expert in the Secret Tradition,' he says sniffily.

'Oh, but she has her own deck! A beautiful Italian one. Willie gave it to her. She showed me the Tarot de Marseilles too. She is always at the British Museum. She knows about Egypt and hieroglyphics and goddesses and—'

'You will take instruction from *me*,' Arthur interrupts. 'I do not share Florence's confidence in her own understanding of Egyptology. There has been deception regarding the cards originating in Egypt, India or China — lies which we will not continue. There is in fact no history prior to the fourteenth century . . .'

And he is off, a very long speech in which every other word is 'Albigensian' (some kind of sect, I gather), and as he doesn't pause to give me the opportunity to ask him anything I can't follow most of it. Thankfully a glowering waiter appears to take our order and stands for a long time, sighing loudly, before Arthur sees him and pauses. I glance at the Italian words written in chalk on the board the waiter points to.

'We'll both have the house special, Luca,' Arthur says, and continues: 'I should call it a Eucharistic emblem after the manner of the ciborium, but this does not signify at the moment—'

I sip my wine, my stomach grumbling. I'm thinking of the Tarot cards of Mr Crowley, and the same deck which Florence showed me. The court cards, the figures. The swords, the cups, the pentacles, the wands. Here they all are, the little cards, sprouting beside me like this pot of basil, like a big tree sprouting cards. Here is the gift that Mama predicted for me, here it is, surely, a long time coming, but at last, at last! The longed-for fame and fortune. *One day millions of people will know your gifts.* Is it here, has it come, at last?

'Don't worry that you can't follow all I'm saying,' Arthur says, finally breaking off from his monologue. 'I will spoon-feed you everything you need. Colours, symbols, figures, designs, all the references. The Kabbalah correspondences. Can you start on Monday?'

I dash my wine glass down, almost spilling it in my eagerness to say yes. And it's only later, at home, that I realise no sum of money was ever mentioned.

★★★

The first person I tell is Florence. I even tell her the bit when he said he did not share her confidence in her own knowledge of Egyptology, which I realise – too late – is a mistake.

'He said *what*?' she asks as we pass between the two huge sleeping lions ominously flanking us on Montague Place, under a powdery white sky, and enter the marble halls of the British Museum on our way to look at the Tarot deck. I offer her Waites's book, but she shakes her head. 'I have it. He obviously knows nothing of *my* work, while I know plenty of his.' She tosses her head. 'Isn't it always the way with men? We read *their* books and subscribe to *their* magazines. We see their art shows and keep abreast of their great successes in New York. We speak the language of men, but they never speak *ours*!'

I concede: 'He knew something of my music pictures . . . I imagine that is only because Mr Stieglitz, a *man*, told him.'

Florence is striding ahead. She pauses to say, 'I shall think twice about putting his aphorisms in my *Calendar of Philosophy* now I know what he thinks of me!' When I pause too and make no reply, she adds, '*It is easy to conceal the nakedness of the body: it is not easy to hide that of the mind* – A. E. Waite indeed!' Her voice is so loud that a group of foreign students stare at us and giggle.

'Will it have illustrations? Your *Calendar of Philosophy*?' I ask.

'Oh Pixie! You surely have enough on your plate? When does he want these cards by?'

And we're off again, her black heels clicking against the marble floors as if we are entering a huge seashell (albeit one where lions appear everywhere, throats outstretched towards us). This part of the museum always makes me shudder: the columns and grandeur, the feeling of power and plunder. All the marble from all the world, all the hard surfaces – the feeling that if you slip on this grey mosaic floor you would crack your skull.

I'm glad when we arrive in the Egyptian rooms; the mood there changes instantly. Leaving the icy-grey marble behind, we step into a living place, a warm, breathing vault, coloured and dusty and strange, with the little bound cats in baskets, the entombed figures with their amulets; the smells are so different, and the feeling of being in a bric-a-brac shop, where any minute one of the cats might sneeze and prove to be a living one.

Florence pauses, clearly not done with her irritation at Arthur's comments. 'And to pretend – did he pretend? – to hardly know me? When I was the Praemonstratrix of the Order at the height of its troubles . . .'

I have never seen Florence so vexed. For the millionth time in my life, I wish I had learned to button my mouth.

I try to distract her by pointing out a beautiful statue of Isis. She stops to consider her and, after gazing at the enormous figure, turns and says, 'She should be the High Priestess. Waite will want you to use medieval costumes and settings because he does not believe in the origins of the deck being in Egypt, but he does understand that the deck contains true mysteries, older than time, older than him or me or any of us . . . I know he does get that. You can subvert his ideas. Use your *own* understanding of Tarot wisdom.'

Or yours, I'm thinking.

Florence seems to catch this thought and adds, very seriously, using her most sonorous and persuasive tones: 'This is just the beginning. There will be many such books and decks, I'm sure. But what an honour! Because in your images, your drawings, your decisions about symbols, you can share such important secrets with the world for years to come. You're the chosen one, Pixie! I hope you feel it.'

A terrible shudder runs through me then, and the room starts to darken and close. I'm in danger of experiencing my weird shrinking feeling, slipping to the size of the little figures in the cards. I hold my breath. I count to ten. I try to concentrate on conjuring something wonderful and cheering in my mind's eye, but all that conspires to arrive is a vision of Nora's buttocks, white and moonlit. Still, the buttocks are enough. They make me smile. I feel a bit swimmy but I return to the room.

'He's given me six months,' I say. 'And he didn't mention money. But yes, I guess, I *am* honoured.'

I fetch my sketchbook and make a quick pencil doodle, leaning my pad on my knee, drawing chiefly the shape of Isis's headdress. Because Florence's ire is up, she is walking at a clip and I can barely keep up.

'And how funny: you met Crowley too,' she adds once we are seated in the reading room, going through the Major Arcana of the Sola Busca Tarot and trying to speak in hushed tones. 'What did you make of him?'

I point to the Justice card. 'This card came up. I liked him more than I intended! He says he is knowledgeable about the Tarot; he wanted to do a reading for me. But he was drunk – or, I don't know, had taken something. He smelled funny and his eyes were weird. Why that card?'

'Justice can mean a bracing honesty – an absence of the protocols and veils that society expects. You and he share that.'

'It's the card I got for me when we spoke of my love for – well, you know.'

'Yes,' Florence whispers, before catching the eye of the librarian, forming his mouth into an O and about to stride towards our booth. Florence raises her hand to say, 'I know, I'm sorry!' and we put our heads down, begin our work in earnest. Me with my sketchbook, Florence cross-referencing with the deck she has brought with her.

I do love the cards. These ones are different. I'm startled to see that the pips are not abstract, they have characters and stories depicted, and the trumps are numbered. They are rummy and strange and they make me feel things I have no name for. I breathe in deeply, thinking of my music pictures, but the sounds in the library, of scratching pens and old men coughing, prevent that door from opening. I close my eyes and open them again and content myself with a very rough sketch of each of the Major Arcana and the court cards. The pips can wait for another day.

★★★

But starting does not prove easy. The gas light is all wrong at 84 York Mansions and in the morning it's too noisy. I do not feel inspired. It's *so* noisy! The postman rings the bell to the main front door, the porter lets him in, and I hear them talking in the lobby. Outside, a rag-and-bone man yells his incomprehensible *Yaggiyo* call. The milkman's horse clatters up the street. Hansom cabs pass beneath my window.

Then Mr Waite himself calls in, saying he forgot something Very Important. I wait expectantly while he fiddles with his moustache and his rheumy eyes travel around my room, taking in the shabby paint-stained armchair, the brushes and pots and fabrics and beads and cloths used in my salons, and then he says, inexplicably, 'What order did you reach in the Golden Dawn?'

I tell him what I told Willie, that I never progressed beyond Zelator.

'Well, the problem is – Have you started the drawings?'

I shake my head.

'Yes, well, now I'm speaking in my other capacity. As Grand Orient.'

I try to keep my face composed, betray nothing.

'We cannot reveal . . . certain . . . knowledge to you. We cannot show you the Golden Dawn versions of the cards. You will have to – intuit them. You have seen the Italian one, you said, and the Marseilles deck, so I suggest you begin with the Fool. The long sequence of lesser cards... Telling you certain things would involve facts in occult divination that have never been made public.'

'How am I to draw the cards if – I'm not allowed to know things?'

'Well, it is only – I can show you them without revealing their meaning, perhaps.' And he writes down a series of symbols on a piece of paper and hands it to me. 'This is for the Fool. Put it on your – easel – or whatever it is you work on. The Opening of the Key must not be divulged,' he mutters. 'Use your intuition and discernment and talents and then – post the drafts of the sketches to me. I will suggest revisions. You can suggest colours or send in black and white, as you wish. Here –'

He has brought me a great heap of good-quality large envelopes, already stamped and addressed to himself. I should put my drafts in these. He looks for somewhere to lay these down and, sighing unmistakably, puts them on top of a pile of books.

When he leaves, I slump in my pink velvet chair with my face in my hands. He wants me to use my intuition... but there is a strict and secret knowledge that must be followed. He will spoon-feed me the cards but he won't tell me the meaning of any symbol. Some mysterious 'key' – the Golden Dawn way of reading the cards – will not be divulged, and I must use my 'discernment and talents'. Ugh! What on earth have I got myself into?

I pick up the envelopes he's left me. His writing is as obscure as he is. Twenty-two envelopes. He obviously means me to start with the Major Arcana. And beneath them, another envelope, which he said the porter handed him when he asked for Miss Colman Smith. A letter. I tear it open. Smallhythe. A note from Christopher.

Dear Pixie,

The weather here is lovely. The farm is in much better order. Edy and I rode down from London on bicycles (Edy had a skirt on with braid, and a bolero). Edy and I are putting on plays and exhibitions for the Women's Social and Political Union. We have joined the Freedom League and we need you to do some programmes for us for a new play we are devising to help win the Vote. Do come and visit us! Ellen is staying at the nearby Priest's House because we cannot stand her husband. There is plenty of room and the frogs are positively orgiastic.

Your friend,

Christopher

Look at me, look at me!

Wheeeee!

I tried me wearing a crown of thorns

But the sun's rays soon had me warmed

I am success I am joy

I am a girl not a boy

I know more than you think I might

The horse I straddle should be brown not white!

Smallhythe

August 1909

I arrive, and Smallhythe is so much more homely and inhabited and tidy than it was last time I was here. As I put my hand on the rickety garden gate, I smile to see the roses exploding around the door in a profusion of every shade of pink. The sheep are still in the garden, nibbling Ellen's herbs. But at least the sheep and their smell are no longer in the house.

Inside, there is such a sense of industry. Nancy, the housekeeper, greets me with a slice of blackberry tart she's been baking, dolloped with a lump of cream, on a beautiful rose-garlanded yellow plate, as Christopher strides into the hallway to say hello. Somewhere I hear a voice reciting: Edy, learning lines. And a child's voice. And a dog.

'Oh Pixie, you're not wearing your smock!' Christopher says, releasing me from a fierce hug as I try to eat my tart.

'I have it in my bag . . .'

'Oh, do put it on! And – I've very generously decided you can work in the summerhouse while you're here. Isn't that peachy of me? I'm not writing at the moment. I'm working with Edy: we're rehearsing a pageant – well, a play I've written with Cicely . . . to raise funds for the cause. I have to keep an eye on Edy.'

I blink innocently, pretending not to have heard the gossip about Edy.

She adds darkly: 'As if it isn't bad enough Ellen marrying! Edy – You know she was proposed to by some godawful *man?*'

I did know this. I nod, my mouth full of blackberries. The strange expression in Christopher's eyes, and then the arrival of Edy, singing a silly song and with a child in tow – perhaps Peter, perhaps a different one – prevents me from asking more. Edy hugs me too, and the colour in her cheeks makes me wonder if she overheard. Christopher's manner betrays some very real pain, I feel sure of that – the sort of pain I feel towards Nora. The fear that, in the end, convention, a 'normal' life as a wife, will always win out against the only charms we might possess.

But today I am not in the mood for wallowing in feelings for Nora. The sense of being back in the bosom of my old friends envelops me. I let myself succumb to the happy, chaotic feeling. Nancy skuttles beside me and takes the plate away, balancing it on a basket of washing. I close my eyes and breathe in the voices, the squeaky bark of a dog outside, the bleating of sheep. The opposite of my aloneness at York Mansions. Will I be able to work in this environment?

'How kind you are,' I say.

Christopher claps me on the back, so hard I start coughing. 'Good old Pixie! You've stayed away too long. Come and see my gramophone!' And, enveloped in her warmth, the last blackberry on my tongue, I follow her out to the summerhouse.

The garden is just as overwhelming, with its cacophony of smells and noises. A dog – Ben – chases its tail. The dog is Ted's, though he is sleeping on Ellen's daybed upstairs, Christopher says, rolling her eyes. The day is breezy and choppy: leaves bouncing on the ash tree, laundry flapping on a line and a blackbird peeping dementedly.

'So, what is this marvellous commission?' Christopher asks, pushing open the stiff door to the summerhouse. The room is hot, with its large glass windows, and smells of Christopher's smoking overlaid with a small posy of lavender in a glass jar on the table. She beams at me, as if to say: 'For you!'

'Well, it's to design a Tarot deck. For sale with a book of divination. So that people can – Oh my goodness, the gramophone!'

And Christopher shows me how to use it, carefully placing her favourite record down, lifting the needle and stepping back. In the warm room a wasp buzzes and the terrifying opening of Beethoven's Fifth Symphony leaps out like a tongue and lashes us.

Christopher closes her eyes, and the dramatic sounds lick over us. I am transported instantly. I feel like a tiny creature in the mouth of a dog. I instantly picture the music painting I did to this piece of music (sold by Stieglitz! For fifty dollars! Which has paid my rent and allowed me to come here!), showing shadowy women in front of towers with their arms raised – in exaltation or supplication. I have such a strong desire to leap up and assume the same pose! But I don't. That would be strange. I concentrate on not shrinking, and on getting out of the mouth of the dog.

We just listen for a while, and let the sound wash over us, building as it does to such a tremendous crescendo, and then the record crackles to an end.

The wasp buzzes softly. The day pauses, sun pouring in to caress my back, my hair.

'Well, you'd better start, then, hadn't you?' Christopher says creakily. I sit down suddenly so that she can't see the tears in my eyes. The desk is laid out for me: next to the lavender are sheets of fresh paper, inks, pencils, a sharpener, brushes, a jar of clean water. Christopher nods, and with more grace than usual, hands deep in the pockets of her trousers under her smock, backs out of the summerhouse, closing the door behind her, leaving me alone with only the sparrows and chiffchaffs wittering.

★★★

At first I try drawing the Fool like Pan. Then a boy, like one of Ellen's grandchildren. Then a Green Man.

Greens: a sea green, a grass green, verdigris, eau-de-nil, shamrock green, spring green. I try a deep Brunswick green, a mid-Brunswick green, a Kelly green, a celadon . . . I tear it up.

Ted appears in the garden. He waves to me but makes clear with a gesture towards his son, steering him away, that he knows I'm not to be disturbed. He is flouncing around wearing a silly silk kimono in shades of green and gold. It probably belongs to Ellen. He is prancing, and again a vision of Pan and his pipes comes to me. Peter Pan. Youth. Hope. A Fool. *A fool and his money are soon parted. Fools rush in. 'Tis a naughty night to swim in, nuncle.*

Then I see Nora's sweet face, chin uplifted, defiant. Why do I sometimes doubt her? What courage it must take to kiss someone the way she kissed me. And in her last letter to me she wrote of Freddy growing a little older and less dependent on her, and about being patient, for she is earning money for herself, and oh, again, the hope of it is painful, too painful.

Green, green, I am green. Ignorant. Ellen's green dress, the green of her beetle wings glittering, broken occasionally, dropping to the ground. *I who am the beauty of the green earth, I call upon your soul to arise and come to me.* Sargent's painting of Ellen, and the feeling that Ellen, of all of us, her otherworldly beauty and her loving nature, her boldness will live forever. The beetles shimmering: like the tiny faces of an audience lit by theatre lamps, millions and millions of them.

Next I try remembering a Green Man face carved over the walkway at the front of York Mansions. *For if that which you seek you find not within yourself, you will never find it without.* No, *no* – that won't do at all.

I throw those sketches in the waste-paper basket, feeling ready to give up and go into the house in search of a cup of tea. But I hit upon the idea of tearing pages out of the sketchbook, just a little bigger than playing cards, and drawing a border, and writing in black ink *FOOL*, and then I close my eyes and try to imagine this existing, being printed as a Tarot card. I open my eyes and draw some boots on my person – is it a girl or a young man? – and draw the figure about to step off a cliff. In the background I add a tower, like the tower Ellen lives near at Winchelsea. As I draw, I can see Ellen coming and going at the next-door Priest's House, wearing a wide hat with a rose tucked into the brim, a man occasionally appearing beside her in the garden. The way she leans on him. Touches his arm occasionally. Even from here I can see it, those feelings I have discovered, which women are not supposed to feel. Her new husband. He trundles a squeaky wheelbarrow. I draw Pan again, playing his pipe, his beautiful hair flowing, and a woman (Ellen?) admiring him.

In front of me, eight drawings, all versions of the Fool, and one rummy sketch of the World card. Most of them are pretty crude. Towers. Waves, dogs, roses, sand dollars scattering the short robe the Fool is wearing (it looks exactly like Ted's kimono). I added a dog too, which looks like Ted's dog Ben. Some drawings have dabs, washes of suggested colours; the first four are just pencil and then inked in. I've added the sun. And Mama's wedding ring. Hopefully Arthur will think that is a zero. Without even looking at them I shove the Fools into the first envelope Arthur gave me, scribbling my return address on the back, and after a moment writing on the back of one of them: *Green Man series. Nature ideas, the Gods as green. Smallhythe.*

I hold back the World for now.

The envelope comes back by return post with one word only: *Rejected.*

★★★

I am exhausted. The gramophone needle sticks, repeating the last phrase. I stand up, rubbing my lower back to fix it. Ted has gone inside. Soft rain prickles the glass of the summerhouse. The garden is quiet. How long have I been here?

I hear voices. It is Christopher and Edy and their friends rehearsing the pageant. The play seems to consist only of women – great women, forgotten by history – stepping up and speaking. I feel as if in some queer way I have heard their voices before. As if, in my life, some people have been stepping up and introducing themselves like that. My eyes are heavy, and a delicious drowsiness steals over me.

★★★

'Men are such pigs!' Christopher says when I show her my returned drawings from Arthur. She is standing in the summerhouse, smoking, staring at them and the letter she's just brought me from Dead Waite, as she calls him. (I made the mistake of telling her what Crowley said and she hooted with laughter.) Through the dusty window we can see Edy with a spade, busily planting a hedge between the Priest's House and the cottage, so that – as she has told us – she need not look at that 'dreadful man' (Ellen's husband). Ted is still here with the youngest of his many children.

'My exact words!' I laugh. 'Pigs, publishers – all of them!'

I put the drawings of the Green Man version of the Fool face down, and tear out some fresh sheets of paper from my sketchbook. Christopher offers me a cigarette; in my mind's eye I see the rejected sketches going up in smoke.

'Do you know I was arrested?' Christopher asks proudly. I didn't know. 'Yes, I spent one night in prison. I'd set fire to a postbox – threw in a cigarette. They are never going to just hand us the vote on a plate, you know. Edy had to pay a fine and come and rescue me. By gum, it was terribly exciting.'

Arthur has sent me instructions. The Magician is the next card. The 'countenance of divine Apollo, with smile of confidence and shining eyes'. More Hebrew letters and some limited Kabbalah information, such that he believes I can handle. The cards, he insist, must follow a strict order. I'm not feeling inspired.

Since the cock crowed this morning, all I have heard is sheep bleating, children laughing, and the voices of various women rehearsing *The Pageant of Great Women*. Ted's children Edward and Nell have appeared and are taking turns to ride a hobby-horse, shouting, 'Giddy-up, giddy-up!' as Nellie prances around the garden.

Earlier I heard the women in a ripping good argument: should they stick with the original name, *A Tableaux of Famous Women*? No, *Great Women* is far better. It's not that they are simply *famous*; it is that they achieved things! (This discussion alone lasted twenty-six minutes.) Edy is the pageant master, so she does the announcing in her lovely fruity voice, and then they take the parts of the famous women from history parading onto the stage, from Sappho to Florence Nightingale and everyone in between.

Notes for the pageant are in piles everywhere in the summerhouse. Even Ellen, despite the current coldness between her and Edy, is taking part, reprising her role of fictional Nance Oldfield, which she is very fond of. I understand now her remark about *Nance Oldfield* paying for her house in Winchelsea: it has been a huge success for her and the public associate her with Nance.

Christopher pushes some of the pages towards me, saying gruffly, 'Oh Pixie, you should have a part! Why was I so slow to think of it?'

'But I'm mighty busy! I have seventy-eight drawings to do and at this rate, if he can't even accept the first, there's going to be a lot of toing and froing . . .'

'Oh, you must be the Artist. The idea is that she – well, all of our great women – approach Justice—'

'Justice? You know that is one of the Tarot cards,' I say, though I do not mention that it is the card I most associate with.

Christopher turns towards me, stubs out her cigarette and takes up her 'acting' voice, reciting: '*Oh, think you well, what you have done to make it hard for her, To dream, to write, to paint, to build, to learn . . .!*' She flaps the pages, addresses the room: '*Oh! Think you well! And wonder at the line of those who knew that life was more than love, And fought their way to achievement and fame!*'

She is not an actress, but she would make a great station announcer. I laugh, but despite her delivery I'm moved. Somewhere I see that a cloud has occluded the sun and that it's almost midday. Christopher's impassioned championing of forgotten women is not helping.

'*Working with man as eagerly and hard, And oft denied a man's reward—*'

'Christopher, I need to—'

'*And though you barred us from the realms of art, Decreeing love should be our all in all, Denying us free thought, free act, free word—*'

'Christopher, I'm sorry—'

'Oh yes, yes, I will leave you. I jolly well hope he's paying you well, this wretched man!'

Christopher pushes open the door to the garden and we both see Ellen now, lying on her back in her little boat, on the Smallhythe pond. She seems to be in a position of complete repose, dangling one hand in the water, a big hat with roses garlanded round it hiding her face. And yet, somehow, I have the strong impression that under that hat she has been listening to us. And that she is well aware of her grandchildren playing, and of Edy sweating and cursing a few yards away from us as she plants the hedge. I believe Ellen is only affecting calm and grace. How clever she is. She knows very well the tension her handsome new husband has caused.

Nancy appears, bringing us tea. She weaves between the apple trees, her tray wobbling, followed by the two skipping children. Christopher changes her mind about leaving, finds a blanket folded on a chair and spreads it on the lawn, her back – pointedly – to Ellen and her pond. 'Come on, Pixie, you are allowed a break, surely . . .?'

Nell barrels by with the hobby-horse between her legs, and stares at me for a good long while though the windows of the summerhouse. Finally, I go outside to give her some feathers to play with and she hobbles off.

When I return to work, I ball up Arthur's instructions for the Magician and throw them in the waste-paper basket. I make a preliminary pencil sketch for the Star card, writing out the references he gave me at the top of the card. Then I draw a naked woman, with long yellow hair, one foot resting on water. She can walk on water, like Ellen! She holds jugs in each hand and pours water onto the grass, and into the pond. Oil on troubled waters? I add fruit trees – the craning apple trees from the Smallhythe garden, which always remind me of old people. A moon balanced over her head, which I colour in. I erase the moon, replace it with a large yellow star. *The Great Mother in the Kabbalistic Sephira Binah*, Arthur has written.

Then I tear out another page from the sketchbook and draw it afresh, changing the background. Hours pass. Next, I try number nineteen, the Sun card. 'Grand Orient' writes that he cannot divulge the Golden Dawn version of this card. But he hints that it is something to do with Christ. My pencil wanders as I read his notes, sketching, trying out a crown of thorns. *The card signifies transit from the manifest light of the world . . . typified by the heart of a child*, he writes, and suddenly here she is: little Nellie appears on the page, her sturdy limbs, her intense gaze on mine before I gave her the feathers, naked on a brown horse. Behind her is a garden wall, behind that are the dark faces of sunflowers. The sun is setting.

My eyes are salty and my back aching from my day's labour. I light a candle to better see my work, but while looking for matches I find some notes of Christopher's. I know that alongside her co-authorship of *The Pageant* she has been writing a novel so, seeing the pile of papers bound with a thin piece of string, and the title on the first page, *Hungerheart*, with the name I've never known her by, Christabel Marshall, curiosity gets the better of me. I untie the string, carefully putting it to one side, ready to retie in exactly the same way. I push the candle out of reach, lest any wax drip onto the manuscript as I read, and open a page at random to find this: *For years I could not see a wedding without a pang, a pang not of jealousy, but of terror.*

I think of Christopher's remark, delivered in jest but with a sharp glitter in her eyes, about Edy being proposed to. And of the pair of them, and how they are towards Ellen's new husband.

> *The idea that there may be women, neither wives nor mothers, nor mistresses, who are yet fulfilling themselves completely, who are not poor or starved or in their singleness, but rich and fed with angels' food, is one which the natural man rejects as incredible, and the natural woman entertains perhaps for a moment in a lifetime and dismisses forever as the folly of dreams . . .*

How my admiration for Christopher soars, reading this. And somewhere, like a shoot that has not shown itself yet in dark soil, something else is growing.

The candle flickers and the light is no longer sufficient. I hear Ellen singing to herself as she trundles a barrow of apples towards the Priest's House. Nancy brought out an oat-and-date cake earlier with the tea, and I eat the last few crumbs of it before putting the light into a bottle to guide my way across the grass, to head inside.

★★★

Back at the cottage, there is a knock at the garden door. We are sitting in candlelight, with windows still open, peacefully occupied: Edy with her sewing, Christopher writing in a notebook on her knee, and me with my drawings.

Ellen says, 'He's gone. My good man. To London', bending half of herself around the door as if it were a screen and she a siren. She means her new husband. She curls one leg provocatively round the door, chiefly to make us laugh.

'Good riddance!' says Edy aggressively. 'I hope it's for good.'

'May I come in?' Ellen says, lowering her leg and brushing down her skirts. She brings in the smells of the garden: apples, cut grass, the persistent sheep smell. She bustles in to sit at her favourite chair in front of the unlit fire in the hearth.

'Peace offering,' Ellen says: a bunch of roses. Yellow, with a strong, sweet smell. Since neither Edy nor Christopher moves to accept them, I put my sketches aside and fetch a jug of water to put them in, breathing in the intoxicating freshness, seeing how pretty the cobalt-blue jug looks next to the delicate yellow petals. A memory of picking up rose petals as a child in a garden somewhere floats back to me. Making pretend perfume with them. How dark they grew, and soggy, and what a disappointment that the smell could never be caught.

'You know, Mother, you've grown awfully fat. You won't fit in the dress I'm making for you if you carry on like this,' Edy says, putting her sewing aside, stabbing several pins into a pincushion so hard that one of them breaks.

Ellen looks crestfallen. 'Have I, dear? It happens to us all, I suppose, once we reach this age. And to think that Sally used to wish it on me every time, just before I went on stage. I was so thin in those days. "Beautiful and fat tonight," she would say . . .'

'You look fine to me.' Christopher can't help herself: ever loyal. She glances fiercely at Edy.

I have been moving my gaze from one to another, wondering if anyone might actually mention *James*, the cause of all this anger. The mood seems to be relaxing now that Edy has had her chance to be mean.

'We disgruntled devils don't please anybody,' I announce to no one in particular, thinking of my own increasing plumpness. Mine caused, Florence says, by my habit of enjoying red wine and too much butter on my bread.

Ellen smiles at me, seemingly seeing me for the first time. 'Oh Pixie!' she says softly. 'It has happened at last for you, then?' At first, thinking she means becoming stout, I struggle for how to reply, but seeing this, Ellen laughs. 'The fame! Your music pictures. Three exhibitions, I heard! And each of them an enormous success. Last time I was in New York you were the talk of every party and restaurant in Brooklyn. Mr Stieglitz is a very good friend to have.' Ellen spies the tea and the date cake on the table. 'Has Nancy gone?' she says, helping herself to some lukewarm tea. She pulls a face. 'Shall I make us another pot?'

As she goes to fill the kettle, Christopher stares at me. 'You never said!' she exclaims. 'Are you famous now, then?'

'Oh, hardly!' I say. I feel their eyes on me and splutter a little. 'It was swell to see my show at the Photo-Secession, but I could do with some of the money, that's for sure. Transatlantic crossings are costly. And paints and new brushes...'

'Yes, hmm,' Ellen agrees. 'Money seems to pour from me like water. And my ungrateful children are very cross lest I spend any of it on myself or God forbid on my—'

'Don't mention his name!' Edy shouts. She puts her hands over her ears. But she is laughing now. The mood has relaxed.

'That's the trouble with fame. We don't want it, but when it comes it never feels to be enough. A teeny taste of it, and we want more at once!' Ellen teases, kneeling, with creaky knees, to light a fire for the kettle. Christopher rushes to do it for her.

'Well, I hardly feel — any different,' I answer, rather astonished at the direction this conversation has taken. I fix my gaze on the yellow roses in their blue jug, aware that my face is reddening.

'We never know what amount might *be* enough,' Ellen goes on. 'We feel hungry and crazed. We dread it being taken from us and despise ourselves for craving it. We long to experience life again without it, just for a week. I told you once — when we first met — to be careful to appreciate the joys of privacy, in case fame ever did come your way...'

'Oh well. It's nice to sell paintings. It's rather... strangely embarrassing and humiliating to read about oneself in Brooklyn newspapers.'

'Yes,' Ellen says quietly.

'I suspect it will be over soon! That's how it feels. And everyone has a different... version of me. I can no longer be myself. Do you know in America I found out that – Well, one of the secrets of my parents was revealed to me. By my uncle. And fame – I hardly dare call it that – feels like a bubble ready to pop. Whoever knows if their fame will be lasting? I mean, *yours* will be, of course,' I add hastily, gesturing towards Ellen and the room full of portraits and paintings of her, her desk with so many of the gifts she's been given, the basket of letters from admirers.

'What did your uncle reveal?' Ellen asks gently. But she is tactful and, seeing that Edy and Christopher are waiting for my reply, she leans over to put a hand on mine. 'Tell me another time, my dear. Let us have our tea. Or no, it should be something stronger for you, Pixie, in celebration! I'm sure Nancy has hidden a bottle of champagne somewhere; do go and look for it, Christopher . . .'

That first time I tasted champagne: with Daddy, near the Lyceum. Remembering brings back the strange sensation that I might slip right inside the glass, like a tiny creature, and drown in the bubbles.

★★★

Later, I draw Ellen, in the garden picking flowers, and behind her the romantic husband: James. And then, before I know it, I've drawn Ellen as one of the Tarot cards: the way I saw her once, several summers ago. The Empress. The Divine Mother. Kind, regal, wearing a crown of flowers. It is late, and I am in my bedroom at Smallhythe, but I cannot stop drawing. Sketches pour out of me. Now Ellen with a sword, as I saw her playing Hjordis in *The Vikings*, in the beautiful cloak Edy made her, and this seems to be right for a Minor Arcana card, the Queen of Swords. And roses: red, white, pink and yellow – flowers everywhere. I go to bed dreaming of Ellen and Edy and Christopher, and dreaming of the Tarot, and a little voice inside me says: *Damn Arthur Edward Waite – what does he know?* Drawings pour out of me. I've never felt like this, or if I did it was long ago in childhood, before the mania for earning money and achieving things began to consume me.

I must learn from everything, see everything, but above all *feel* everything, and make sure that others looking at my work are able to feel it too.

I fall asleep with the drawings scattered over the eiderdown, the pillows and the floor. The Tarot figures, the roses, the little dog, the pomegranates, the birds and stars and wands and children are sprouting from me, growing out of my pores, spooling out from the long tendrils of my hair. All night long they parade in my dreams, in Edy's pageant, carrying their swords and wands and announcing themselves, explaining themselves, a hundred different voices, telling me their secrets.

★★★

In the morning there is another letter from Arthur, with more obscure instructions. It seems the Fool card, now that I have abandoned the Green Man theme, is halfway acceptable to him, with some modifications. I turn my attention to other cards.

The happy mood at Smallhythe now that Ellen's husband has left for London is distracting. More friends arrive: Cicely Hamilton, the co-author of *The Pageant*, with a glorious head of hair intricately pinned on her head and a terrifying hard stare; a woman called Reggie, an actress; a famous woman writer called John. All dressed like Christopher, in long smocks, black cravats and ties, or masculine suits. Their laughter, their smoking, their drinking of wine and their messy picnics on the grass loudly debating whether *The Pageant* will, as they intend, *educate* the public on the enormous and overlooked achievements of women. Will it persuade the general public (General Jackass) and those who despise all the throwing of stones and smashing of windows that women are accomplished creatures and deserving of the vote? Cicely pats the giant edifice of her hair. She is not convinced. But when Ellen wafts about, a basket of yellow jasmine over her arm, reciting '*By your leave, Nance Oldfield does her talking for herself. If you, Sir Prejudice, had your way* –' Christopher leaps up, and nods at her, playing the part of Sir Prejudice.

The other women fall into an awed trance around Ellen, like bewitched flowers wilting on the grass. Ellen addresses them now: '*Why, there would be never an actress on the boards. Some lanky, squeaky boy would play my parts: And, though I say it, there'd have been a loss! The stage would be as dull as now 'tis merry – No Oldfield, Woffington, or Ellen Terry!*'

The women burst into laughter. Christopher pumps the air with her fist, shouting, 'By gum! I can't wait! I can't wait to see it! Oh Cicely, of course it will be *terribly* affecting . . .!'

Edy continues her sewing and making of costumes, always with cloth across her knee and saying the least, but a contentment radiates from her. How lucky she has been with Ellen. To have a mother who accepts you, as you are, feels rare indeed.

The garden is full of buzzing bees and laughing women, debating and shouting and tumbling their wine glasses over on the picnic blanket. Work on my Tarot deck is impossible. I take myself off up the lane, and then wander into the church next door to admire the stained-glass windows, knowing that some of these images will find their way onto my cards. Arthur has not made many suggestions about the pip cards; those will – thankfully – be left to me.

Some pages of Christopher's novel are carefully stashed in the pockets of my skirt, hidden beneath my smock, and I unfold and read them here on a pew, a section in which – fittingly – Christopher has written about the ancient ceremony that nuns go through to commit themselves in the consecration of the Virgin, where 'souls of nobler stamp' (the nuns) proudly decline the marriage bond. I had not been aware of Christopher's deep Catholic leanings. She and one of her friends have a little statue of Our Lady in the Smallhythe garden and have garlanded her with white flowers from a nearby clematis.

Christopher's writing about women and how they are commonly perceived is fierce: *She exists for certain episodes in a man's life. Her glory is to bring him into the world. It is maternity that crowns her existence, and the life of barren women is always represented as miserable and incomplete.*

I think of Nora, saying simply: 'I wanted so much to be a mother.'

Then I think, dangerously, *And so you are one now, Nora. So you need look no further. As for me, I have no such desire* . . .

Christopher writes that she is touched with pity for those who are wholly ignorant of the existence of a mystical union – of nuns with the Virgin – but I know Christopher means something else. I bow my head. Am I a believer? Who am I, how did I come to be here? What is it I have struggled to understand my entire life about my own existence, who is it that brought me into the world, and if there *is* a director, why will he – or she – not show themselves to me?

Oh, my heart staggers under the weight of these feelings about love and life and meaning, alone in the little church.

I love the stained-glass windows with their black edges; they give me ideas for my own drawings. And that picture of the Virgin there – baby at her breast – she looks a little like Nora. And then, like the vision that visited my salon the night I read Willie's poem, haunting lines come back to me:

I will find out where she has gone,
And kiss her lips and take her hands,
And walk among long dappled grass . . .

For a moment, I kneel at a pew. I feel the dusty floor against my dress. I bring my hands together and put them up to my face. I close my eyes. I begin, as I've been taught, 'Dear Heavenly Father . . .'

And then I stop. I change it: 'Dear Whoever', and then I change it again: 'Dear Holy Mother', and then: 'Dear God of Art and All Things', and then I bury my face in my hands and cry. And Christopher's words, merging with nuns and the Holy Mother and the women next door in the Smallhythe garden, exert a power over me, flowing through my veins and softening my vision, and the cards that poured out of me last night are dancing along, tiny figures in their own pageant along the nave in front of me. Justice, the card I puzzled over: that's the name of the character in *The Pageant* who squares up to fight Sir Prejudice. The Tarot might know something after all.

When I return to Smallhythe, there is a letter for me. My own letter, written to Nora two days ago and posted to my last known address for her in Devon: Snails Castle, the home of Jack and Cottie Yeats. There is a scribble across the unopened envelope: *No longer at this address*. I have left it too late. The life of a housekeeper is not given much importance: no one seems concerned to tell me where she might be living now.

★★★

I decide I should go back to London for a week and try to work there. The clamour and chaos and rehearsals at Smallhythe are too much. This desire comes to me strongly as I wake in my bed, the light slipping in across the sheets, the floors creaking as Nancy goes about her work, the cockerel crowing outside my window. London. I must go back *today*! It is an intense feeling. I gather up my drawings: the Lovers card, clumsily rendered, the figures with their legs too fat, slips to the floor, reminding me of the reading Florence did for me on the SS *Minnehaha*. Maybe Florence can help me? Arthur may say she's wrong about the origins of the Tarot being Egyptian or even Gypsy, but Florence strikes me as knowing plenty. And having listened for days to the women assembled here discussing which great women to include in *The Pageant* (Florence Nightingale: my Florence was named after her) and fighting over which of them will play Joan of Arc . . . After hearing so much about how women's intelligence, women's contributions to the arts, sciences, history, and every aspect of the culture have been overlooked, I feel buoyed up. (And I'm reminded of Florence describing men – grand men like Willie and George Bernard Shaw! – as half-baked.)

I will have to tackle Arthur about some of his more incomprehensible instructions concerning the Kabbalah and suchlike. In his last letter he suggested a fee of twelve pounds for the whole job, which doesn't seem enough to me. It's easily going to take me five months at least, if not six. If he wants these cards done before Christmas so that he can publish the deck and its book of instructions next year, he will need to pay me at least a little more. 'Grand Orient' can appear behind a bloomin screen or wear an Egyptian mask if he must, but I – the artist – need some payment and a bit more clarity.

I take the afternoon train from Tenterden. Ellen has piled presents on me: bundles of flowers wrapped in brown paper, jars of honey and blackberry jam, a dark-red silk kimono, a proof of Cicely's book *Marriage as a Trade*. Christopher and Edy make me promise to stay just a week in London: 'Don't be tempted to stay longer.' I feel laden – filled to the brim – with love and gifts.

Arriving back at my apartment, walking through Battersea Park in the evening and reaching home, my heart full and my mind occupied with the scenes from the Tarot, a heron swoops past me in the dark, on its way to the boating lake, making me jump. How sharp its shape is, like a pen nib scratching across a page. *A message from an ancestor.* I see a shadow in front of the building. A woman. A woman in a long dark dress, her back to me. In the lamplight outside the flats, it is hard to see more. She seems shifty, as if she is hiding. Or waiting for someone, perhaps. Her head is covered with a scarf, like the Hermit in my Tarot drawings.

And then, stepping out from the shadows, she says quickly: 'Pixie! It's me. Do let me in, for pity's sake, I'm bursting – I might have to go behind that tree!'

As she speaks, a cloud shifts away from the moon. It's a full moon, fat and weighty like a big silver apple. Her eyes glitter and her lovely little face, pointed chin, upturned nose, lights up. How could I not have recognised the familiar, beloved shape?

Nora.

Rise up, little figures, dead folk, rise out of your tombs
And lift up your arms. I'm a world of fire and ice
Searing you with my bannered light.
(Those dark souls floating at sea . . .
They will have to go, in future drafts.)
What is it within us that calls
And rises in response?

The porter, Bradley, woken from a nap, admits us into the hallway with a grunt. He hands me a pile of letters that have amassed for me, and eyes Nora with curiosity. We climb the stairs to my flat, feeling his eyes on us. Once inside, Nora bolts for the water closet, leaving me to look around at the dusty cluttered place I left behind a week ago, and wonder at Nora appearing like this, and alone (as if I had summoned her. In the end – did I? Did that prayer, that heartfelt wish made in the church at Smallhythe . . . A fear creeps along my spine. Who wants that power, really; it is unearthly and terrifying, surely . . .?). I am fiddling with the lamp as Nora comes back into the room, startling me with her voice, clear and ordinary, of course, not bewitched at all: 'I've left him. Alfred. I've been staying at my sister's.'

'How did you find me?'

'I went to your old place. Mrs Fortescue gave me your address.' She takes off her scarf, folding it, and springy curls tumble down in coils. She has a bag with her and shoves the scarf into it. 'I brought my toothbrush,' she says, grinning for the first time. It had never occurred to me that even Nora, cheeky, bold, mischievous Nora, could ever be nervous.

'What about Freddy?'

'He's with my sister tonight. You might have thought Alfred would make a fuss about me taking off with his son. But no. He has a – fancy-woman. It's for the best.'

'I'll make us some tea.'

I'm stalling, trying to make sense of what she's saying. So she left. But Alfred has someone else. Does that mean she'd still be with him, if it weren't for that? Is she just here for the night, is she looking for a job, or what? When I bring the cups and teapot back into the room, she has relaxed a little; she pushes a pile of books from the side table to allow me to put down the tray. 'I'm afraid there's no milk,' I say. 'I've been down in Kent, at Smallhythe with Edy and Christopher. I've been working on a rather big job . . .'

And I can't resist: no sooner am I home than I'm getting the sketches of the Tarot cards from my satchel and spreading them around the room to show her. I've missed them so much in the last few hours that I don't want to be apart from them. They leap and fly and ping from their folder and immediately seem to take over the room.

Nora is enthusiastic, picking up one then another and remarking on each detail, each figure excitedly. 'My – what a lot of work. Are they finished?'

'Oh no. Arthur is sending instructions all the time, and I thought I would come back here and consult a little with Florence. But – it's exciting. It's the most bully thing I've ever done. I can't stop thinking about them even in my sleep, and dreaming about them, and it's as if they parade in front of me and speak to me and oh, I feel I might *burst*, my head is bursting with them!'

'Look – you forgot to sign this one. Is that deliberate?'

'Oh, that's just one draft. I'll sign the next one. Each card needs around seven or eight revisions.'

The cards spill onto the table and in the lamplight I am reminded of the old French woman I met in Philadelphia and her predictions for me. A net of fish.

Nora is staring at one card in particular. 'I love this one,' she says, bringing it up close to her face to see it better. 'What does this one mean?'

I smile at the card she's chosen. I shake my head. 'Arthur will produce a little book for – divination. He says he's willing to share some of the secret knowledge, but not all of it. He calls himself Grand Orient. We haven't agreed what he will pay me, but he's thinking they might be pretty popular – you know, sell!'

'They could be. But maybe people will find them threatening, you know, work of the Devil, that kind of thing? Most people are so – boring! So many people don't want to know – anything. Anything mysterious, or surprising. Anything about themselves.'

'When I was in New York, Uncle Teddy told me that I was the child of an affair that Daddy had. Not my mother's daughter at all. I don't know what to believe. I have sort of – put it to one side.' I blurt this out. There. It is said. I have longed to tell someone, and now that I have I feel as if I've kicked a puffball in the grass, splintering it into a thousand tiny spores.

Nora's eyes widen and she shakes her head. 'But is your uncle correct? Maybe that's what he was *told*, but how can you be sure? I still believe what Spirit told us. Perhaps both are wrong. In the end, we can't know everything about the past, can we? Or the future. Some knowledge is *dangerous* . . .'

This sentence floats between us. *Dangerous*. I wonder if it is dangerous, to see your future? To get everything in the world you ever wanted? Is life perhaps over at the fulfilment of all desires? (*For behold I have been with you from the beginning and I am that which is attained at the end of desire.* Does a person actually *burst*? Because right now I feel like an overripe watermelon about to splat.)

'Nora. Have you come to – *be* with me?' I say this so softly, so that if she coughs, if she laughs, if she throws back her head and screams, I can take the words back. I'm trembling. I glance down at my cup and the tea is like a wild sea, thrashing and in danger of slopping right over the edge. 'I mean,' I add hastily, 'not just for this evening, but for . . . To live with me somewhere? I mean, it doesn't have to be *here*, we could go to – Cornwall, we could live – wherever, wherever is best . . . But do we have a life together? Could we live boldly, as Edy and Christopher do? You, me and Freddy?'

Nora places the card down, carefully gathering up the drawings and sketchbook to put them aside, piling them at the other end of the table so no tea spills on them. She stands up to do this. Her back is to me. I feel the world turn, and centuries pass. The weirdest picture comes to me, of Mama on her deathbed, with her mouth a surprised dark empty cavern, how I hated to see her mouth like that: a round O, a face of terrors, of a gargoyle. I feel I saw and understood everything that day when I looked at Mama's face. And then I promptly forgot it.

Nora turns towards me.

'If you'll have me,' she says.

The card she said she loved best is lying face up on the top of her pile, eyes on me. That choice, that one. Of course, of course. And maybe the cards *will* sell, and I will get the fame and glory I've longed for, the promise Mama made me on her deathbed, millions to know my gifts, and money, great piles of it would be pretty jam too. Oh yes, it would be ripping if this big job brought me some rewards in this life, or the next. But for now, there is this: Nora, removing the sloshing teacup from my hand, putting it on the table with a *tink* sound. A room near Battersea Park with a heron etching the sheet of sky. Nora, moving towards me: warm, hot, breathing. The feel of Nora's hands in my hair, all secrets contained in her like stars. Her mouth on mine.

★★★

There is knocking at the door. Someone – the porter – has let a gentleman in. Nora and I scramble to dress, giggling, to make ourselves presentable. She pins her hair up, but her face is flushed, cheeks pink. She perches at the end of our bed, putting her stockings on. 'You stay here,' I whisper.

It's Arthur. He strides in, takes off his hat, and hands me a couple of envelopes that the porter gave him.

'These are for you,' he says, without any other greeting. He looks expectantly around at my living room, as if to see the card drawings everywhere. He stares at my blank easel. My heart is beating awful fast and heat is radiating from me; he can surely feel it. A noise, and Nora comes out of our bedroom (but he doesn't know it's my bedroom, I tell myself), buttoning up her outdoor coat, saying, 'I'll just pop over to Mrs Brown's house now, Miss Smith . . . and see you tomorrow.' As if she is – as indeed he will assume – my housekeeper, having just finished a cleaning job. I am flustered but I walk her to the door and say firmly, in front of him, 'Yes, I will see you tomorrow, Nora . . .'

He is an ignorant man, and notes nothing of my courage.

'May I see them?' he says, flinging his hat down on a pile of my books. No niceties. Then, his tone changing, he asks, 'Do you know an artist called Austin Osman Spare? He is at the Royal College of Art.'

'No,' I say, opening my satchel to get the sketches from inside my leather folder.

'He was never a member of the Hermetic Order. The Golden Dawn. He knows nothing,' Arthur says, as if to himself.

I am still thinking of Nora. Of the conversations we had, long into the night. The practical decisions. How would we afford to live together? What earnings would we have? Her séances, perhaps, and my newly found success with paintings. What about Freddy: how did I feel about raising a child with her? The world would have plenty to say about two women doing that. And, just as I fell asleep, a strong vision came to me, of a fine, cream-coloured house that Nora and I would live in by the sea. I hear the voice of a little boy, I see a blond boy running in the garden, and a griffin carved onto a pillar somewhere, guarding the doorway, and, in the garden leading to the sea, purple buddleia and foxgloves and fleabane and birds – choughs chittering, so it must be Cornwall, yes, now beyond the green I see the sea, a long blue strip of blue cloth, and Nora and I making our way through the brambles towards it, and looking up to hear a meadow pipit –

Arthur is saying something, something about this artist fellow, this Austin Osman Spare fellow, he saw his work at the Royal Academy.

'Should I know his work?' I ask, trying to bring my mind back to the present. A certain softness and ache in the bowl of my body keeps reminding me of Nora. 'And why should we be worried about him?'

'One of your suffragist friends might know him. Isn't Sylvia Pankhurst at the Royal College of Art? He is working on a Tarot deck too. So we must hurry, to ensure ours is the one which comes out first.'

'Hmmph! I'm working as quickly as I can,' I say. I'm longing to open the envelopes he brought me, in case one contains payment, but his impatience is obvious. He is making a space – awkwardly – on one of my many crowded tables, moving aside a mermaid toy I'm sewing to sell at the pageant. I take her from him and throw her on the sofa, where she lies staring up at me, and I wonder if I might make some toys for Freddy too . . . What do little boys like? A monkey, perhaps?

I begin laying out my sketches of the cards.

'I'll make us some tea, while you go through them,' I say.

Arthur drops creakily to a chair and picks them up. 'So, see this, this is the High Priestess card, is it? But why the crystal ball on her head? That's not right. Yes, the pillars, guarding the temple, they're good – and her dress . . . But why have you added colours? That is not for you –'

'I looked at the colours on the stained-glass windows of the church at Smallhythe . . .'

'You need to add to the pillars the words "Boaz" and "Jachin". Not snakes: we need the letters from the Torah. Remember she is the signifier of the Greater Law, the Secret Law, the Shekinah –'

And then he is off, with all his Hebrew words and Kabbalism, and as he speaks Nora keeps coming back to me, Nora with her milky skin and that first time I saw her in her vivid blue dress, light radiating from her. Arthur notices my inattention and stops mid-sentence to say: 'Nora reminds me so much of my sister Frederica.'

His mentioning Nora startles me.

'We saw her interred without sacrament, my brother and I. At Kensal Green. It was a dark night indeed.'

'Who? Nora?' I squeak, terror striking at me.

'No. My sister, of course.'

He glares at me. The sense I always have of us being at cross-purposes, of not understanding at all what the cussed man is talking about, overtakes me.

He seems particularly angered by my many sketches of the High Priestess with my scribbles on them. I thought he wanted a popess – Pope Joan, perhaps – but he is shaking his head about that.

'It was Florence who suggested . . . Florence knows a great deal,' I say.

'This mythical female pope! Such ignorance! You might be picking up floating images from – anywhere – and we must be careful to honour the Greater Mysteries . . .'

'Picking up floating images! Either you believe I can do this work or you believe I'm an ignorant –'

This is the first time I've spoken so plainly to him. His shock is palpable. The kettle I placed on the fire chooses this moment to boil, screaming at us. As I go to attend to it, I notice him fold his arms across his chest protectively. It is a curious gesture, at once very male and stubborn and very childish, like a small boy sulking. The Emperor card, I think.

He unlocks himself cautiously to accept the cup of tea I'm offering.

'Miss Smith – Pamela, if I may. You are an abnormally psychic and imaginative draughtswoman. I have absolute confidence in your ability – with proper guidance and perhaps not a little spoon-feeding – to produce a Tarot deck that will appeal to the world of art. But you have no need to pretend to understand all the symbols, nor the Hidden Path along which I'm travelling . . .'

And so the afternoon continues. He did not appreciate my pagan Green Man notes for the Fool and that is why it was rejected. My Lady of the Lake is wrong for Temperance: she should be a winged angel, neither masculine nor feminine. There cannot be fish, and the cartomancy of Madame Balle or Madame Lenormand has no place in the Major Arcana. On some point I argue – to his surprise. Why *not* depict the Lovers card as having two women, as I have seen it before?'

'Where did you see that card?' he asks sharply.

'It was the Tarot de Marseilles. Florence says—'

'Florence! Haven't I told you that you must take instruction from Grand Orient and from him alone —'

To his surprise I leap up here, hands on hips, my face hot, and snap back: 'You have also said that the cards speak only in symbols, and — well, I have been paying attention and listening to them. I have been in Kent with friends who are rehearsing a pageant. And the cards do indeed speak to me, and I hear them, and I draw what I see and hear! And if you don't like it . . .' — and I begin gathering up the sketches, slipping them clumsily into my leather folder, some falling on the floor, some turning themselves the wrong way round.

He falls silent. His face is hard to read; his lips beneath that ridiculous moustache move in an expression that might be a smile, or might just be him chewing his lips. After a moment he gently puts out a hand over mine to stop me putting away all the cards.

'I have offended you. I apologise.'

'You will know that I have now had three exhibitions of my music pictures? That Ellen Terry considers me — a great success!'

'Yes, yes, Pamela. My admiration for you, I assure you . . .' His voice at last is kind, and human. My angry heart slows its beat.

'Well,' I say, sitting down. 'Seventy-eight cards is going to take me a while, at this rate, if I do eight versions for each card. I haven't even started on the court cards or the pips.'

'You may have a much freer rein with those,' Arthur says, mollifying. And then, his expression earnest, he says, in a voice humbler than I've ever heard him use: 'I do trust you. Of course. That's why I approached you. I see — I feel — all your gifts. And there is no canon of authority of Tarot symbolism. The adventure is entirely at our own risk.'

'A risk made an awful lot nicer if we could agree my fee!' I reply. There, it is out.

Arthur smiles, and this time there is no mistaking his expression. Amusement and admiration mingle there. 'Might we agree on sixteen pounds? I will bear the costs of printing the coloured cards with Rider, my publisher. I do believe – I sincerely believe, if I may say so – that your drawings are gates opening on realms of vision beyond the Golden Dawn and beyond occult dreams—'

'Eighteen pounds. Mr Stieglitz has just sold two more of my paintings for a good deal more than that.'

'Seventeen pounds and fourteen shillings . . .'

'And seven pence for a new sketchbook?'

'Done!'

He puts out his hand. Dead Waite. His hand is awful heavy, shaking mine.

Christopher's words come back to me: 'Are you famous now, then?'

Mr Waite might know all the Greater Mysteries, but he is not loved by one such as Nora and he can't so much as draw a stick man. Spoon-feeding me indeed! A picture of his malted-milk drink, its sugary sludge at the bottom of a glass of warm milk, appears in my mind, making me snigger. His look of shock when I stood up to him, answered him back! I am no longer the 'strange' creature so many of his type took me to be: I am a woman of the world, an artist. He needs me: he can't ditch me now. I show him to the door and return to my room with his various instructions ringing in my ears. I will go back to Smallhythe and finish this job.

★★★

Of course, afterwards, he sends me a letter to Smallhythe with further notes. More obscure Christian mysticism and Catholic things, Kabbalah references and other secret symbols. I gaze on them. I had forgotten he was a Catholic. He seems to think that the areas in which I've strayed most from his instruction are the High Priestess (he is very vexed by the various fruit symbols and troubled by any possible sexual meanings, unintended or otherwise), the Hanged Man and the Fool. Mostly the Fool.

I hear Ted laughing. He is outside the summerhouse, and I have a gramophone record playing. He is running, skipping – is he intoxicated? He has Nellie and Edward and Ben the dog chasing him, their screeches and barks distracting me. I get up to choose a different gramophone record to drown them out: something more liquid, less disturbing. Grieg.

I think of Nora and me and little Freddy, going to live somewhere else, and add some background to the drawing: the sea. A real cliff for my Fool to stand on. A precipice. Leaping off. I remember myself in Devon all those years ago, at the house of the Reverend Baring-Gould. False starts. Creativity. Trusting oneself. One's elf! The Pixie. I am the Pixie. The gift of my name from Ellen.

Then I draw Florence. Florence is the World card. How loving Florence is. How unique. And all her wisdom. Florence dancing, wearing a garland. Florence looking like Demeter. Florence with all the truths. Florence, priestess and Adept. The World is the last card of the Major Arcana. Arcana Secrets.

How lucky I am. I feel a swell of gratitude. It sweeps up from my toes; it envelops me. Instead of shrinking, I'm growing. How these women have loved me and loved me so well, starting with my dear cousin Mary. Ellen. Florence. Edy. Christopher. Nora. What does it matter who my true mother is? Mama loved me. Nurse Delphine did. And I have other mothers, the loving mothers: I am *loved*.

I draw a rose in the fool's hand. I colour it red. I scratch it out. I draw again, this time with a white rose. I tip the fool's chin higher towards the sun. (This is the expression Nora has, defiant, brave, is *she* foolish?) The divine trickster in my first book. Annancy. Nothing that a man can't do if he tries. The Jester, the Joker, the soul of beginnings and silliness and – Edward, little Ed, is now is rolling on the grass, shrieking hysterically, and the dog, Ben, is springing at Ted's feet as if to say *Catch me catch me* – and somehow everything in me is green, all green, flowing and flowing, and my heart is green and it is a seed coming into being, unfurling and staying alive *alive* for years, long after my death, long, long, I will exist in a room on a desk in the fingers in a field in the mind of a woman in a house in a field and here I am am I idiotic am I really or am I the world inside myself, am I rising rising like yeast like buildings like that little dog, leaping leaping flying here I am here I am in Smallhythe among friends and here I am everywhere, I'm alive, I can do this, I exist, you can see me, feel me, hold me in your hand.

I'm the rapture of the universe when it at last understands itself.

With my solid shanks my two wands my breasts

I'm no longer a fool but a woman of the world.

Pick me: my final message is unchanged.

Garland me in a green sheaf, you daughter to a witch, sister to a fairy.

Afterword

The Tarot deck described here was published in March 1910 by William Rider & Son Ltd, London. It was sold for five shillings and came with a book, *The Key to the Tarot* by Arthur Edward Waite, for an extra two schillings and six pence. The price was later raised to six shillings, with a new book by Waite, *The Pictorial Key to the Tarot*, for an extra five shillings.

On release, the deck and book were reviewed by Aleister Crowley: 'As to Mr Waite's constant pomposities, he seems to think that the obscurer his style, and the vaguer his phrases, the greater an initiate he will appear.' Pamela's contribution and artwork were sidelined by Crowley in favour of continuing his beef with his rival Waite, and he did not trouble to spell her name correctly, an error repeated often over the years. At first Crowley concedes that 'Pamela Coleman [sic] Smith has done some very beautiful and sympathetic designs . . .' But she has, he feels, 'evidently been hampered; I am infinitely sorry for any artist who tries to draw after dipping her hands in the gluey dogma of so insufferable a dolt and a prig.'

In 1911, Pamela converted to Catholicism and moved to Cornwall with Nora. Eight years later Uncle Teddy

AFTERWORD

died, leaving Pamela a bequest. She used this money to lease a house, Parc Garland, near the Lizard in Cornwall, where she lived until 1938. Then she and Nora moved to Bude, where Pamela died in 1951 at the age of seventy-three. It is believed she is buried at St Michael and All Angels Church in Bude in an unmarked grave.

Pamela's thoughts on the reception of the Tarot deck are not recorded. The deck did not make her rich or famous in her lifetime. Her comment in a letter to her friend and champion Stieglitz that 'I've just finished a big job for very little cash! A set of designs for a pack of Tarot cards 80 designs . . . some people may like them!' was at the forefront of my mind when writing this novel, because in every account of her much is made of her money troubles, and the fact that she died in penury, leaving everything in her will to Nora Lake but owing a great deal to the tax office.

Laurence Irving and Mabel Hackney died in the sinking of the *Empress of Ireland* in 1914.

The Rider–Waite–Smith deck became the most widely recognised set of Tarot images in the world, selling over 100 million copies to date and never going out of print. It has inspired writers, artists and musicians from T. S. Eliot, Sylvia Plath and Anne Sexton to Madonna, Pink Floyd and Gilbert & George. Stuart Kaplan of US Games probably did the most to popularise Pamela's version of the Tarot, producing versions of her deck from the 1960s onwards. However, all these sales came after Pamela's lifetime. Her reputation has been revived by the many artists and scholars now interested in her. I was introduced to her in Pam Grossman's book *Waking the Witch*. A 2018 exhibition of Pamela Colman Smith's work at the Pratt Institute, curated by Melissa Staiger and Colleen Lynch, had an unexpectedly large and devoted turnout.

I bought some original sketches by Pamela, but the process was convoluted and cloaked in mystery (my dealer at first named himself Dr Cornelius, later The Magician), so that I was never sure if they were genuine or not. The very last card of the very last batch arrived in the post just as I was finishing this novel. I turned it over and found scribbled on the back: *Seventeen pounds, fourteen shillings and seven pence.* The Justice card. I know she had a sense of humour. That card always falls out of the deck, whenever I ask it about Pixie.

Jill Dawson
Cambridgeshire, England, 2025

Acknowledgements

I am grateful to my agent, Caroline Dawnay, for many years of wise counsel. The enthusiasm which she and her colleague Sophie Scard showed for *Pixie* in its very early stages helped immensely to shape my novel and I am indebted to them both.

I feel lucky indeed to have found in Emma Herdman such a perceptive and astute editor, and delighted and grateful to the team at Bloomsbury for my new publishing home. Thanks too to Silvia Crompton for assiduous copy-editing, a sense of humour and many invaluable suggestions. Also to my sister, Dr Elizabeth Dawson-Goumy, for some lightning-fast translations when required.

Pam Grossman was the author who first introduced me to Pixie. I am so grateful to her and the staff at the Pratt Institute, particularly Holly Wilson and Melissa Staiger, for their help with the research for this novel. Also to Christina Oakley Harrington, whose wonderful bookshop Treadwell's is a treasure trove of courses and texts, and is now home to the mantelpiece that Pixie once owned in her house in Cornwall. Thanks also to Geraldine Beskin and her daughter Bali, of the fabulous Atlantis Bookshop in Bloomsbury, a shop with

ACKNOWLEDGEMENTS

such tremendous history and connection to Crowley and other major players in the Hermetic Order of the Golden Dawn and the world of magic. Both were both hugely knowledgeable and helpful.

My heartfelt thanks are also due to Susannah Mayor, the steward and archivist at Smallhythe, for sharing my delight in Pamela's work, as well as for her open and generous attitude and peerless insights into the life and character of Ellen Terry.

Frank Bowles, archivist at Cambridge University Library, offered me some terrific research in the form of letters about séances by W. B. Yeats and a wealth of knowledge and expertise. (Although he is my brother-in-law and I thank him in most of my books, I would like to take the opportunity here to express my gratitude again.)

My husband, Meredith Bowles, remains my first and best reader. I am lucky indeed that he is such an insightful one and his impact on my writing these last thirty years has been my great fortune. For that, and countless other things, I am forever grateful.

Foley O'Connor, E. (2021), *Pamela Colman Smith: Artist, Feminist, and Mystic.* Croydon: Clemson University Press

Greer, Mary K. (1995), *Women of the Golden Dawn: Rebels and Priestesses.* Vermont: Park Street Press

Holroyd, M. (2008), *A Strange Eventful History: The Dramatic Lives of Ellen Terry, Henry Irving and Their Remarkable Families.* London: Chatto & Windus

Isaac, V. (2018), *Ellen Terry at Smallhythe Place.* Swindon: Acorn Press, for National Trust

ACKNOWLEDGEMENTS

Johnston Graf, S. (2000), *W. B. Yeats: Twentieth-Century Magus: An In-depth Study of Yeats's Esoteric Practices & Beliefs, Including Excerpts from His Magical Diaries.* New York: Samuel Weiser Inc.

Kaplan, S. R. with Greer, M. K., Foley O'Connor, E. and Boyd Parsons, M. (2018), *Pamela Colman Smith: The Untold Story.* Stamford, CT: US Games Systems, Inc.

Katz, M. and Goodwin, T. (2015), *Secrets of the Waite–Smith Tarot: The True Story of the World's Most Popular Tarot.* Minnesota: Llewellyn Books

Maddox, B. (1999), *George's Ghosts: A New Life of W. B. Yeats.* London: Picador

Noble, V. (1971), *Motherpeace: A Way to the Goddess Through Myth, Art, and Tarot.* New York: HarperCollins

Pollack, R. (1997), *Seventy-Eight Degrees of Wisdom: A Book of Tarot.* London: HarperCollins

Rachlin, A. (2011), *Edy was a Lady: Featuring the 'lost' memories of Ellen Terry's daughter Edith Craig.* Leicester: Matador

Robinson, D. G. (2020), *Pamela Colman Smith, Tarot Artist – The Pious Pixie.* London: Fonthill Media

Terry, E. (1908), *The Story of My Life: Recollections and Reflections.* London: McClure

Vogel, K. (1996), *Motherpeace Tarot Guidebook.* Canada: US Games Systems, Inc.

Willett, C. (2023), *The Queen of Wands: The Story of Pamela Colman Smith, the Artist Behind the Rider–Waite Tarot Deck.* New York: Running Press

A Note on the Author

JILL DAWSON is the author of eleven novels and one poetry collection, and is the editor of six anthologies of poetry and stories. She is a Fellow of the Royal Society of Literature, has been a Costa Judge and has taught creative writing in many different settings. She lives in Cambridgeshire.

A Note on the Type

The text of this book is set in Bembo, which was first used in 1495 by the Venetian printer Aldus Manutius for Cardinal Bembo's *De Aetna*. The original types were cut for Manutius by Francesco Griffo. Bembo was one of the types used by Claude Garamond (1480–1561) as a model for his Romain de l'Université, and so it was a forerunner of what became the standard European type for the following two centuries. Its modern form follows the original types and was designed for Monotype in 1929.